"waiting for!"
—SOPHIE JORDAN

USA TODAY BESTSELLING AUTHOR

VIVIENNE LORRET

How to Forget a Duke

Misadventures in Matchmaking

U.S. $7.99
CAN. $9.99

DON'T MISS THESE OTHER IRRESISTIBLE NOVELS BY *USA TODAY* BESTSELLING AUTHOR

VIVIENNE LORRET

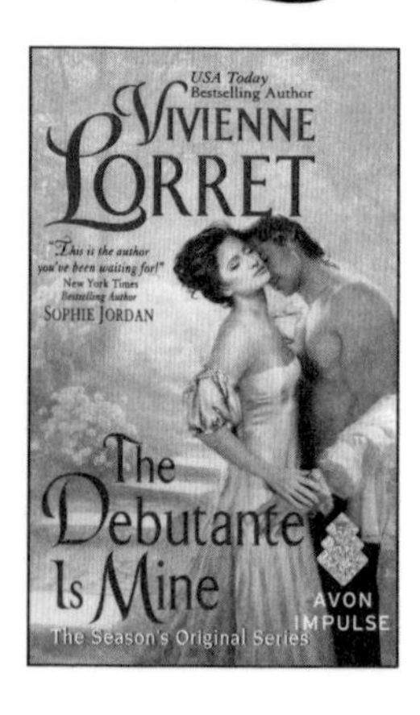

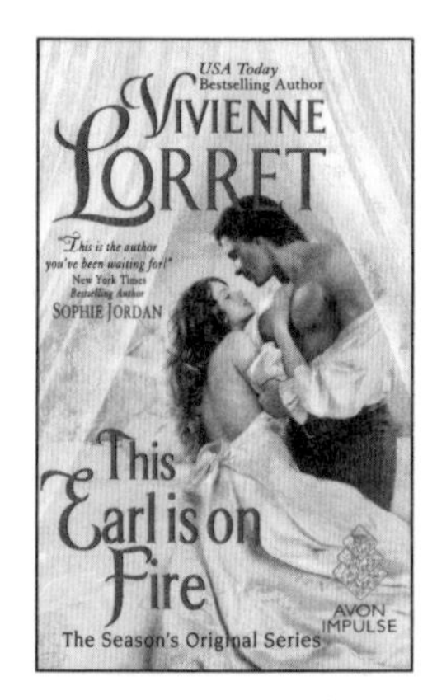

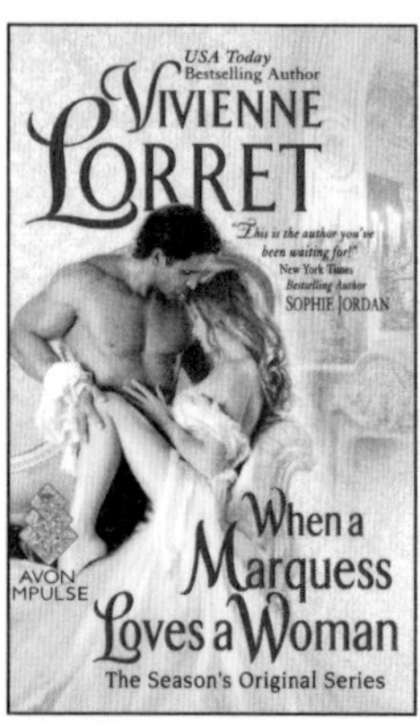

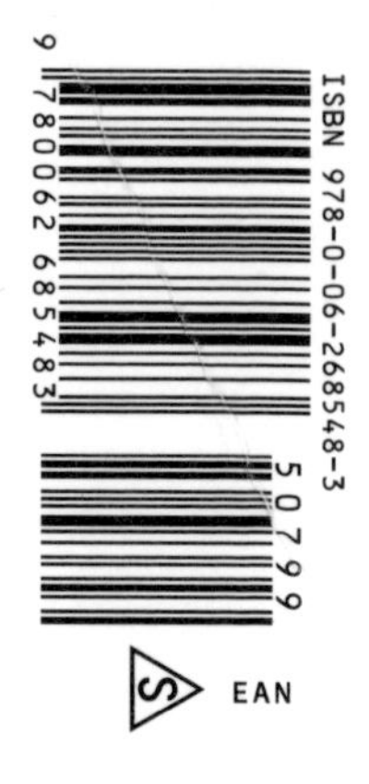
ISBN 978-0-06-268548-3

"I think you've kissed me."

"I'm quite perceptive, remember? And perhaps it was the way you looked at my mouth just now and earlier, too, like you'd . . . sampled it before." The temptress pressed her lips together. "*Hmm.* Is that the reason you glower at me? Because I've forgotten our kiss? Likely that is a deathblow to any man's ego."

And suddenly, there was a completely new type of mischief in her gaze. A feminine, sultry type that no conniving, spying debutante with amnesia ought to have.

Crispin was burning up, his cravat itchy. He fought like hell not to pull the linen away from his throat and give away his discomfort. Likely, she would make more of the gesture than it was—which was merely a reaction to starch. Yet even as the excuse formed in his mind, not even he believed it.

"You have not wounded my ego in any way because the event you mentioned never occurred."

Then the lips he'd never sampled spread in a guileless grin. "So you say, Rydstrom."

He gritted his teeth, letting her have the last word as she sauntered past him. It was the safer thing to do. But *damn it all* if he wasn't tempted to pull Miss Bourne against him and prove that there was no possible way she could ever forget his kiss.

By Vivienne Lorret

The Misadventures in Matchmaking Series
How to Forget a Duke

The Season's Original Series
"The Duke's Christmas Wish"
(in All I Want for Christmas Is a Duke and
A Christmas to Remember)
The Debutante Is Mine
This Earl is on Fire
When a Marquess Loves a Woman
Just Another Viscount in Love (novella)

The Rakes of Fallow Hall Series
The Elusive Lord Everhart
The Devilish Mr. Danvers
The Maddening Lord Montwood

The Wallflower Wedding Series
Tempting Mr. Weatherstone (novella)
Daring Miss Danvers
Winning Miss Wakefield
Finding Miss McFarland

How to Forget a Duke

Misadventures in Matchmaking

AVONBOOKS

An Imprint of HarperCollins*Publishers*

This is a work of fiction. Names, characters, places, and incidents are products of the author's imagination or are used fictitiously and are not to be construed as real. Any resemblance to actual events, locales, organizations, or persons, living or dead, is entirely coincidental.

First Avon Books mass market printing: June 2018

Print Edition ISBN: 978-0-06-268548-3
Digital Edition ISBN: 978-0-06-268549-0

Cover design by Amy Halperin
Cover illustration by Jon Paul Ferrara
Cover photograph by Media Photo LLC

FIRST EDITION

18 19 20 21 22 QGM 10 9 8 7 6 5 4 3 2 1

To my great-grandmother, Anna,
who told stories to my father,
who told stories to me.

Acknowledgments

Writing *How to Forget a Duke* has been a dream come true, which would not have been possible without a support team.

I want to thank my agent, Stefanie Lieberman, who agreed that maybe, just maybe, the concept of *Emma* meets *The Bourne Identity* wasn't as crazy as it sounded. And to my editor, Nicole Fischer, who gave the idea a chance.

I also want to thank the Avon Art Department, Amy Halperin, and the incomparable Jon Paul Ferrara for the stunning cover, as well as everyone who worked behind the scenes to make this book shine.

Thank you, Cindy Clough, my favorite librarian for your never-ending enthusiasm, and for using your interlibrary loan power to help feed my addiction to reserved books.

Many thanks to Kim and to Mary for your generosity and kindness from the very beginning.

And special thanks to JuLee, Tracy, and Lena for our Saturday mornings over tea, lattes, and black reginas. Our laughs and random conversations keep me on the sane side of the chicken coop. I couldn't have asked for better friends.

PART 1

Chapter 1

"Emma Woodhouse, handsome, clever, and rich, with a comfortable home and happy disposition, seemed to unite some of the best blessings of existence; and had lived nearly twenty-one years in the world with very little to distress or vex her."

JANE AUSTEN, *Emma*

Jacinda Bourne pressed her back against the study door, clutching a volume of *Emma* in one hand and a feather duster in the other. A breath of relief left her as the latch clicked softly into place.

No one had seen her.

Still, she knew she didn't have much time, not with the hazy light of dawn creeping into the Duke of Rydstrom's paneled study, spreading like accusatory fingers through the sunburst transom window above heavy pleats of midnight blue brocade. Soon, his servants would finish breakfasting below stairs. Then they would begin their daily tasks, which surely included lighting a fire in the cold-veined marble hearth along the far wall. Therefore, she needed to hurry her investigation and . . . *and* . . . *"Ah—choo!"*

Drat! Clearly, grabbing the feather duster had been a tactical error.

Her pulse hitched in a sudden nervous jolt. She went still, listening for any sound of movement beyond the door, but the riotous thrumming in her ears made it impossible to hear.

A warning voice in her head told her to slip away before she was caught. But Jacinda ignored it.

She had to. How could she leave before she found the evidence she was looking for?

The only problem was, she didn't know what the duke was hiding.

But he was hiding *something.* She'd been certain of that since he'd marched into her office at the Bourne Matrimonial Agency earlier this week.

Every inch of his tall frame had been stiff and guarded, his fists clenched, his expression hard and intractable. In response, a peculiar sense of expectation had filled her, a certain *knowing* that there was more behind the clipped, evasive answers he provided—secrets that she needed to uncover before she found him a bride.

After all, matchmaking was a serious endeavor. Jacinda and her sisters, along with Uncle Ernest, set out to forge lasting, happy unions for their clients. And finding a person's ideal counterpart wasn't easy. It took effort, careful consideration and, in Jacinda's opinion, tenacity. That was the reason she was currently disguised as a servant, complete with apron and a ruffled cap over her dark auburn hair.

It was all in the line of duty.

Early on, she'd learned that some of their clients neglected to reveal certain undesirable elements on their applications, like property entailments, inheritance disputes, madness, mistresses, gambling debts, and even illegitimate children. Because of that, each client of the Bourne Matrimonial Agency was obligated to undergo a cursory investigation.

Though, perhaps, sneaking into the duke's residence was a slight exaggeration of their contract.

Her sisters would be furious if they knew. Ainsley, the eldest, had already warned Jacinda that if her methods cost them clients, then her only contribution to the agency would be to serve tea in the parlor. Briar, the youngest, had skillfully plied Jacinda with guilt, reminding her that their business was created to honor their late mother, and to ensure that no one suffered her fate of marrying the *wrong sort.*

According to her sisters, doggedness only cast a favorable light on soldiers, not debutantes or matchmakers. But Jacinda didn't agree.

Proving a person was the *right* sort demanded equal parts determination and readiness, using any means to discover the information. Though, in the future, she would avoid using a feather duster to complete her disguise.

Pressing her ear to the door, all was quiet aside from the distant ticking of a pendulum clock. Relieved, her heartbeat gradually slowed, each thump reminding her that she was here for a purpose.

She was a *matchmaker.* Decidedly, the most important profession of all.

Her fingertips wrapped around her book, pulsing with this awareness. Shortly before their beloved mother had died, Heloise Bourne-Cartwright had gifted each of her daughters with a separate volume of *Emma*. To Jacinda, she'd given the first, in which Miss Woodhouse's character revealed her unabashed determination. To Briar, she'd given the second, in which Miss Woodhouse possessed the most hope. And to Ainsley, the third and final volume, in which Miss Woodhouse showed wisdom beyond her years.

Feeling the stamped leather press into the soft flesh of her palm, Jacinda's own determination was reborn. She drew in a deeper breath, her lungs expanding against the apron sash beneath her breasts.

For an instant, she'd nearly begun to doubt the plan she'd hatched at three o'clock this morning. But obviously, true genius could strike at any moment.

Besides, the duke had brought this upon himself. Not only had he refused to answer all her questions, he'd lied directly to her about his income.

Her recent visit to his solicitor revealed that Crispin Montague, the fifth Duke of Rydstrom, was nearly bankrupt, his estate in ruins.

His finances weren't the issue, however. After all, many in society would willingly accept the burden of rescuing his estate, if only to align their family with a duke. But why had he lied about it?

In Jacinda's opinion, a man who told one lie likely had dozens more stored away. She and her sisters had learned that from their philandering father. His betrayal had broken their poor mother's frail heart and ultimately led to her death.

How could Jacinda make a match for a man who spoke falsehoods and kept secrets? At the very least, marriage should provide each party with a sense of certainty that stemmed from honesty.

This was her moment of truth. It was time to discover what the duke might be hiding.

Wisping the feathered tips of the duster over his desk, she found it frustratingly tidy. There wasn't a single item of personal clutter to reveal more about him, not even an engraved carving knife or a pocket watch. No portraits or miniatures on the walls either, only a nondescript hunting scene above the mantel. Aside from a lamp, the inkstand and blotter, there was only a slender bronze calling card case and a short stack of brown leather ledgers.

It was very little to investigate . . . at least, without being overly intrusive.

After all, she drew the line at rummaging through his drawers. And besides that, upon initial examination, she found them all locked. Silently, she tsked him for having such an untrusting nature.

Reaching down to her hem, a frustrated growl escaped her. She'd forgotten to hide hatpins in the dress she'd borrowed from her maid. Sturdy pins were quite useful in circumstances such as this.

Drat. Without being able to find anything in the drawers, she settled for borrowing one of his calling cards—because one never knew when a duke's card might be of use—and tucked it inside her book before placing it next to the discarded duster.

Then she picked up the first ledger. Skimming the fastidious lettering, she noticed a peculiarity that repeated all the way through, from the front to the back. Each page was split into four quadrants, one solid, straight line down the center from top to bottom and another from the left margin to the right. A category heading ran across the top of each portion in bold, dark script. What an odd way to itemize expenditures.

She shrugged. And since the contents revealed more of what she knew about his meager accounts, she set it aside.

The second was an appointment calendar, also in quadrants, but with a surprising lack of scheduled dinners, balls, or parties of any sort. It was almost as if he was solely relying on the Bourne Matrimonial Agency to find him a bride, without the barest curiosity of the candidates who might be paired with him.

Strange, indeed. Most of their clients had already made unsuccessful attempts at finding a suitable spouse, and they sought a matchmaker because they longed for a close attachment that came from the commonalities in character and occupation. However, a gentleman who didn't attend any social events likely did not care about those things. By all appearances, his desire for a bride was nothing more than a business arrangement, or a trivial task he'd set before him.

The thought incensed her. It was the nineteenth century, not the dark ages when nobles married solely for money, property, and lineage. Many people were enlightened and had abandoned the old traditions, realizing that contentment in marriage, trust, and even love were inalienable rights.

Doubtless in the duke's case, once he received his list of potential candidates, he'd simply point his feudalistic finger at the name of the first heiress and say, "I'll have this one," and then expect the woman to be delivered to his doorstep.

Humph. Jacinda closed the ledger with a slap. When she did, however, a square of paper flew out from between the pages, flipped once in the air, and then drifted quietly to the floor.

Her secret-finding senses were instantly alert, sending a rush of prickles over her scalp and down her nape.

Taking a step away from the desk, she looked down and saw that it was a letter addressed to the duke. How could she have missed it?

Bending to retrieve the potential clue, she debated whether to open it or not. As it happened, however, her fingers accidentally slipped beneath the already broken seal and the page unfolded—with only the barest amount of encouragement—before she'd even lifted it off the carpet.

Still . . . reading another's letter was unpardonably rude. It seemed her only option was to skim the contents instead.

Disappointingly, the missive appeared to have come from a member of his staff. Signed *Mrs. Hemple*, Jacinda believed it was from his housekeeper, who wrote of the state of the linens and listed items in need of immediate repair, citing a recent storm and the subsequent leaks in the garret. There was, however, one odd paragraph that did not fit with the rest.

> *Sybil fares well but keeps a careful vigil at the windows that overlook the road. Even though I have explained to her that Your Grace will not return for weeks to come, she is determined to wait for you. I managed to lure her out of doors for a minute, but even in the north garden the sound of the sea crashing against the cliffs kept her from any enjoyment.*

Jacinda read it over again, committing it to memory. By all accounts, Sybil was not a servant. Perhaps Sybil was the duke's dog, who was waiting steadfastly for her master's return? And yet . . . the housekeeper would hardly write of *explaining* the duke's absence to a pet.

So then, who was Sybil? Other than the duke's aunt, Lady Hortense, he'd claimed to have no other family. Then again, perhaps he was hiding a mad relation or a mistress or—

"*Miss Bourne*, just what are you doing in my study?"

Jacinda jolted. The instant she heard that low, unforgiving voice—his tone as deep as a village well and frightfully calm—her head snapped up and the missive slipped from her fingers. Or rather, she dropped it like a burning coal.

He filled the doorway. Beneath a slight widow's peak of thick, backswept barley and wheat tendrils, his angular features were set in hard, irreproachable lines. He possessed high cheekbones and a wide jaw as if his ancestry had been forged during one of the battles between Viking marauders and the Roman knights who'd fought over this land ages ago. His skin was unblemished but slightly weathered in a way that indicated he enjoyed outdoor pursuits. And the shoulders inside his green coat were so broad that she wondered how often he injured himself passing through narrow doorways.

"Your Grace," she croaked. A combination of regret for having been caught, and a smidge of guilt for being here dried up all the moisture in her throat. What business did he have being awake at this hour? Swallowing, she attempted an innocent smile, but her lips felt somewhat like squirming caterpillars that were difficult to direct into the correct placement. "What a pleasant surprise. I was afraid I'd have to wait here for hours before you awakened."

With the toe of her shoe, she searched for the missive on the floor. Finding it, she stepped on it for good measure and hoped he hadn't seen her reading it.

His gaze flicked over her, from the top of her ruffled cap, down to the fingertips she pressed to the surface of his desk, and then rested on the discarded feather duster. He said nothing for a moment, but pulled the door closed behind him.

Chapter 2

> "It was foolish, it was wrong, to take so active a part in bringing any two people together. It was adventuring too far, assuming too much . . ."
>
> JANE AUSTEN, *Emma*

Click.

Had a latch falling into place ever sounded more ominous? The study seemed to shrink. Jacinda felt as if the entire room was the size of the paper beneath her foot, and her back was against a creased corner.

Dear heavens! What was he going to do? Call the guard? Or worse, cancel his subscription to the agency?

His hazel eyes were the color of a leaf beginning to turn, a fading green tinged with russet brown along the outer edge. And as he stared at her, silent and imposing, his mink brown lashes crowded together as his thick brows lowered. "It is pointless to pretend you are here for a social call."

"Of course not, sir. We are business acquaintances," she said lightly, attempting to add a measure of normality to her . . . visit. "As such, I would only call upon you in regard to your recent application with the Bourne Matrimonial Agency."

"After the report from my solicitor, I learned a great deal about your *supposed* business practices." He glowered, folding one arm across the other.

While the act of folding typically made things smaller, the opposite seemed true for him. With a glance at the swollen sleeves of his coat, she wasn't certain the seams would hold. He had the arms of a woodsman, the bulge of muscle clearly defined beneath the superfine wool, as if he spent his days chopping lumber with a very heavy axe instead of doing whatever it was that an antiquated-thinking duke was supposed to do.

Unable to help herself, she wondered what he might look like without his coat, and simultaneously a curious flutter burrowed into the pit of her stomach. "Your solicitor was quite helpful in providing the correct information, which you had neglected to supply on your application."

Honestly, Mr. Burke had been so easy to manipulate, she'd almost felt sorry for the older gentleman. A few flashes of the agency's contract—though without letting him read it verbatim—and a finger pointed to the duke's signature was all it had taken for him to speak to her. From that point, she'd carried on with her usual questions.

"I was under the impression that your uncle, Lord Eggleston, managed each account," the duke said, the cut of his jaw coming into sharp focus as he gritted his teeth.

She nearly laughed. Her mild-tempered and far too gullible uncle was no match for a deceptive duke.

"And he does," she said, resisting the urge to cross her fingers behind her back. Everyone knew that genteel women weren't supposed to have professions. They were only supposed to find husbands, or become poor spinsters who relied on the charity of family. Finding a position as a governess was also acceptable, but looked upon with great pity.

For the sake of their reputations, both personal and business, it was vital that the *ton* believed Uncle Ernest ran the agency. No one could discover that the romantic and gregarious viscount, whom haute society humored by welcoming his matrimonial agency, was actually just a figurehead.

While Uncle Ernest spent his days composing sonnets and wooing whatever lady had captured his fancy, his nieces ran the agency. Ainsley managed the office, kept the books, and compiled the lists of potential matches for each of their clients. Briar sorted the basic facts: age, class, physical description, income, property, beliefs, and interests. And Jacinda conducted interviews and performed the most essential task: the investigation. Though, preferably, without being caught.

Jacinda drew in a steady breath through her ever-tightening throat. "It was pure happenstance that I found myself in the vicinity of your solicitor's office. Since I was already there, it would have been silly to send my over-worked uncle on an errand that I could manage myself."

"Oh, you *managed* it, for certain. You badgered your way into Mr. Burke's office," the duke accused, unfolding his arms and pointing a long finger in her direction. "He told me how you twisted each of his answers in order to gain what you wanted. No doubt, you used the same methods to get past my housekeeper this morning as well."

Jacinda scoffed, indignant. "Frankly, sir, I am offended that you think I deliberately deceived your staff. I am a professional, after all."

And as such, she had come in through the garden gate, as anyone could have done. Then, keeping out of sight, she'd skirted the corner to the small terrace, up the stairs and to a deep-set lacquered door. As was the custom at her family's rented town house, the door had been propped open to let in the sweet, dew-scented morning air. It was almost as good as an invitation.

To her credit, she'd never trespassed in her life. Well . . . not unless she counted the time when she happened upon a Cyrano de Bergerac costume, complete with plumed hat and a mask with a bulbous nose, hidden in the back of Uncle Ernest's wardrobe. Or the time when she'd accidentally dislodged Ainsley's diary from a hidden desk drawer, letting loose a collection of pressed flowers that had littered the floor (and if it weren't for that errant bluebell sliver, she'd never have been caught). Then there was the time when—

Hmm . . . perhaps she had trespassed a bit.

"A professional busybody," the duke said with fractious scorn. "Have you no shame, no thought of conscience for your machinations?"

"Of course I have a conscience," she said with unflinching certainty, hiking up her chin. "When the circumstance warrants such feelings, it is the first to rear at me. This morning, however, you are the only one rearing, which tells me that you are prone to exaggerated emotions. This is something I must note for your file. If you'll excuse me."

Picking up her book from the desk, she held it against her like a shield. She had every intention of walking out the door. The only problem was, he was still blocking the way. Not only that, but she had his letter beneath her slipper. *Bother.*

"I will not excuse you, Miss Bourne. You are trespassing in my home, disguised as a servant, and—"

"Aren't we all servants to one another, sir, each in our own way?" She'd heard these very words from the reverend this past Sunday.

Fortunately, her impassioned piousness stopped whatever diatribe the duke had been proceeding to inflict upon her. However, *un*fortunately, it also made him take two hard steps toward her.

The carpeted floor bumped beneath her feet, resonating a warning up her body. *He is not one to trifle with*, her inner voice of reason whispered. Jacinda did not doubt the truth of it for an instant.

It was a shame that she had yet to heed the advice of that voice.

Standing at the corner of the desk, he loomed over her, the scent of cedar rising from his clothes, his eyes turning dark as a forest at midnight. Indeed, he was a lean-bodied tree of a man, all shoulders, and arms as thick as branches. A jagged vein streaked across his forehead, looking like a gnarled twig beneath the surface of his skin. His nostrils flared as his mouth compressed into a firm white-edged line. "They say even the devil can quote scripture, and I imagine that applies to Sunday sermons as well."

Devil, indeed.

The unfounded accusation caused his voice to drop lower, more vibration than words. Her skin reacted to it, drawing tight over her bones. The bare flesh below her sleeves felt like a freshly plucked goose as she rubbed her free hand over one arm. The heat he radiated did nothing to lessen this effect. In fact, the longer she stood in his proximity, the more she became aware of her skin and the fit of her clothes, especially how the fine cambric of her chemise seemed to have abraded her nipples until they were taut. She was even strangely conscious of her height and how—if she took a half step forward—her nose would touch the knot of his cravat. And if she were to tilt up, her lips would brush the shallow cleft in his chin.

She swallowed down the thought *and* the startling impulse to verify this suspicion. "But what would the devil be doing in church?"

This time, he was the one with a ready reply. "Sitting beside you."

He leaned toward her, and his hot breath drifted across her cheek, carrying the spiciness of a licorice lozenge as if he'd used aniseed tooth powder during his morning ablutions. The pleasing scent teased the glands at the back of her mouth where saliva pooled.

Beneath her cap, she felt the first prickle of perspiration and a hank of hair fell over her brow. She left it there, worried that if she moved at all she might brush against him. And she didn't know what would happen if they touched.

For some reason, the notion caused a quiver to climb up her back, plucking each vertebra to the base of her skull and making her scalp tingle.

Even though it was out of character for her to walk away without somehow gaining the upper hand, this time she felt it prudent to take a sideways step from him. Before she did, however, she slid the letter further beneath the desk, covering the scraping sound with a small cough. Then, sweeping that lock from her forehead, she looked from him to the door.

Escape was so close she could almost feel the damp morning air upon her skin. "Clearly you are too ill-tempered to discuss business this morning, and therefore I will leave you to brood over your morning tea."

"You have stolen into my house like a common thief and under a wholly false pretense." He laughed without humor, angling his body in a way that would allow him to reach out and take hold of her, if he so chose. "If I weren't a gentleman, I would put you over my knee and teach you the lesson that you obviously require."

"I am three and twenty, sir, hardly a child." He might have spared her the insult by threatening to call the guard, instead. *Not* that she wished for such. All the same, she stood her ground, straightening to her full—nose to his cravat—height.

His eyes darkened, his hand closing into a fist at his side. "Your behavior proves otherwise with the way you run around bullying elderly solicitors and getting into mischief when your uncle's back is turned."

"I'll have you know that my uncle has no—" She stopped her rant, closing her mouth with a clack of teeth. Then, clearing her throat, she took another tactic, using what her governesses had often called her *knack for dramatics*. Lifting a timorous gaze, she continued. "My uncle is in poor health at the moment, and I fear that if he learned of this episode, he might decline further. He's all the family my sisters and I have and we would be lost without him."

"Do not play the coquette with me. It is obvious that you are attempting to garner sympathy, casting a—likely false—woeful haze over your transgression. When, in fact, you are guilty of a crime."

Horrible man! Jacinda had never encountered someone so determined to point out this tiny, completely forgivable, act of trespassing. "How can you accuse me when I have not had the opportunity to state my business?"

He drew in a breath that expanded his chest and created horizontal furrows in his cashmere waistcoat. "I am a patient man by nature, but you've managed to whittle that down to a splinter. Give me one reason why I should not cancel my subscription this instant."

Without missing a beat, she boldly said, "I came here with a question regarding your application. The only family we have listed for you is your aunt, and my uncle was wondering if you had anyone else."

Perhaps someone named Sybil?

"I do not," he said quickly. "Nor do I see that information as having any significance."

Of course he didn't. All throughout the questions she'd posed upon their initial meeting, he'd made it patently clear that he saw little value in their process.

Name: Crispin Montague, the fifth Duke of Rydstrom
Age: 28
Property: an estate in Sussex
Income: £4,000 per annum *(a total fabrication)*
Beliefs: *refused to answer*
Interests: *refused to answer*

Hiding her irritation, she offered an inconsequential shrug. "Some debutantes find large families appealing and therefore are more interested in the match."

This earned a lift of his brow, his glower vanishing. "Have you a list for me, then?"

Oh, wasn't he the ever-eager bridegroom? She might have found it charming if he hadn't blatantly proven that he didn't care a whit for his bride—not her name, not her temperament, and certainly not her dreams. All he required was that a woman stood on the opposite side of the church aisle when he said his vows, effectively claiming her as his own.

A strange sort of ripple rushed through her at the thought. She shook her head, ridding herself of it. "None yet, but soon. At least, now that I have verified the *truth*."

A short silence hung between them, one deceiver sizing up the other. His broad mouth, no longer compressed with censure, revealed that it canted slightly to one side, as if he were deciding whether to smirk at her or not.

"The same truth that you have had all along," he said in apparent disregard of his solicitor's account and her knowledge of it. "That I require a wife and I employed your uncle's agency to find me one."

"Yes, but you conveniently did not reveal your *requirement* for one with a large dowry." Nothing vexed her more than a man who kept secrets, even small ones. "There was no reason to hide it. But by doing so, you might have cost my uncle a great deal of effort searching for a bride who complemented your character, and shared your interests and beliefs. It is better for him, at least, that I have discovered your deception."

The twig vein in his forehead reappeared. "I despise being called a liar. So be careful where you tread, Miss Bourne."

Unbelievable! "Are you still claiming to earn four thousand pounds per annum?" She knew it was rude to speak of money in the open, but the man incensed her.

"I never said *per annum*—that was your assumption," he said with a smug shake of his head. And before she could argue, he went on, looking down the straight ridge of his nose at her. "You asked how much I would earn this year. Since I plan to marry by year's end, and subsequently receive a promised wedding gift from my aunt, that sum is what I shall have."

She often used the truth as a tactic as well and suspected he had purposely deceived her. Being unable to prove it, however, irritated her to no end. "If all you need is a wife—

and likely a rich one at that—then why not simply take out an advertisement in the *Post*? Why bother with our agency at all?"

She noted his hesitation and discomfort as he shifted from one foot to the other. Clearly, he was not a man used to explaining himself, or being challenged to do so. She assumed they'd reached the end of their encounter, but he surprised her once again.

"Not that it is any of your concern," he began, "but there are stipulations to my aunt's gift. She requires approving of my bride. And with your reputation among the *ton*'s elite—in particular, with the Duchess of Holliford—my aunt hopes to eliminate any bride with ill-favored characteristics that could be passed on to my heirs."

"Yes. I've met your aunt," Jacinda said with genuine empathy in her tone. "Lady Hortense has rather exacting standards."

The instant his aunt had walked through the door of the agency, she'd demanded a list of all *first-class* debutantes so that she could peruse them beforehand. Thankfully, Ainsley's skillful ease with the clients had given the stern lady the comfort of knowing that all would be handled in due course.

Lady Hortense was also a wealthy widow, and Jacinda couldn't help but wonder why she hadn't simply offered the duke money without the necessity for a bride.

He acknowledged her statement with a stiff half nod. "Surely you can understand how a man of my rank in society would not wish to reveal *every* aspect of his personal affairs to a stranger."

Warmth rushed to her cheeks as a faint stirring of guilt returned. She was quick to tamp it down, however. After all, if she started to feel pangs of remorse for every person she investigated, the Bourne Matrimonial Agency would have no chance of survival. "If you had been forthcoming, I might never have been forced into action."

"Would that be the criminal action of trespassing or the elder-badgering of Mr. Burke?"

She wrinkled her nose at him without responding, prepared to walk past him and to the door. And she might have a chance because, it seemed, his demeanor had altered. The barely tethered fury he'd emanated at first was now more blustered irritation and a grudging acceptance of events, as if they'd both come to an understanding of each other's natures. He was faultily secretive, while she was plagued by righteous curiosity.

All the same, she hoped he wouldn't spot the letter beneath his desk until she was gone, and then think nothing of it.

She nearly had her hand on the ivy embossed brass knob when—

"What have you there?" He was behind her in an instant, an arm's distance from placing his hand against the door, should he choose.

Once more, her proximity to him was too close, her nerves running raw under the surface of her skin. She'd never suffered this sensation before. But standing near him, for reasons beyond her understanding, flustered her.

Anxious, she wet her dry lips before lifting her head to meet his gaze. "My own book. I am not a thief."

With a frown, he glanced to her mouth as if expecting to find a lie lounging there, mocking him. "Then let me see it."

She didn't want to. His borrowed card was tucked within the first pages. She knew, however, that refusing would only make her appear all the more culpable. Reluctantly, she handed it to him, hoping he would be satisfied with a look at the title.

There was no reason for their fingers to touch. Her hand was much smaller and she purposely kept her grip to the bottom of the book, offering him the top. Instead, he took the volume from the middle, his long, tanned fingers splaying just enough to brush against the tips of hers.

A jolt slid over her sensitized nerves, causing an unbidden shiver. He seemed to hesitate before withdrawing, as if the current passed between them, and they were both like helpless frogs pinned to a surgeon's table for reanimation. Yet, his inscrutable expression revealed nothing, leaving her to wonder if he had, indeed, felt anything at all.

She had the sense that he'd wanted to make a point—that he was in control. He was the man and she the woman. He was the master of the house, and she the trespasser. And if she wanted to leave, then he would be the one to allow it. Or not.

Whatever his intention, she did not particularly like the way it kept those currents arcing through her, helpless to the effect he had on her.

Taking the book in hand, he rubbed the broad pad of his thumb over the worn, gold embossed title. "Why did you carry this with you today?"

"As I said, I came here on business and that book is something of our hallmark. If you'd read Miss Austen's magnificent story about Miss Emma Woodhouse and her calling to become a matchmaker, you would understand."

"I have read it," he said, amazing her. But when he continued, her shock quickly transformed to exasperation. "Though, I cannot say that it gives me any more faith in the Bourne Agency's abilities than I would give Miss Woodhouse. She was a complete failure in her attempts."

Of course he would feel that way—he was a man, and men typically did not appreciate the nuances of a well-written, clever heroine. "My sisters carry their own volumes as well."

"Are they as meddlesome as you are?" The cant of his mouth—that almost smirk—returned, becoming more pronounced as he handed the book to her. This time, he left her room to grasp the book without a collision of fingers.

She tugged it to her breast. "We each have individual accomplishments to best serve our agency. Of course, for a man who has no care for the type of bride he will wed, but only that marriage to her brings forth an income, I'm certain you would not understand."

"I did not realize matchmaking was a philanthropic endeavor for your family. I was under the assumption that it was a business, and therefore required paying clients. Now that I know differently, I shall rescind my subscription. I should rather hire an agency that is motivated by something other than foolish inclination." He glanced down to her book.

"We are the *only* agency in London," she corrected on a breath, feeling the weight of *Emma* upon her. "The matches we make are essential, offering the happiness that may have been otherwise unattainable for our clients."

"No. You help those who are willing to settle for anything and anyone," he said with such conviction that it left no doubt he was including himself. "Does the Duchess of Holliford know that you scurry around, sneaking into homes under the guise of aiding your uncle?"

For the first time, Jacinda felt true fear in a swift deluge of icy blood in her veins. The Duchess of Holliford was their benefactress, and the weight of her good name offered the Bourne sisters a degree of leniency when they *assisted* their uncle. Not only that, but Her Grace's generosity was the only way they could afford to live in London at all. Uncle Ernest, though a kind and wonderful man, was a terrible money manager and had been forced to let his small estate in Hampshire. To lose the duchess's support would make them homeless. "We are ever grateful for her patronage."

He took no apparent pleasure in the thready sound of her voice, but seemed to crowd closer to her without moving an inch. "You are fortunate that I have more of an immediate desire for a wife than I do to inform my aunt's friend of your less than scrupulous practices."

"I'm afraid it is not that simple," Jacinda croaked, that doggedness in her character unwilling to keep quiet. "It is a matter of personal pride that we only pair our clients with those best suited to them."

"Then find me a woman who only wants to be a duchess, and nothing more." He offered half of a wry smile and the barest glimpse of straight white teeth.

The sight of the tantalizing tilt of his full, flesh-toned lips caused her skin to heat and tingle as if she were slowly breaking out in hives. The sensation covered her from head to toe, tightening her flesh, prickling her scalp, much like the time she'd foraged for garland greenery, not realizing it was poison ivy.

At the time, she'd been so agonizingly itchy that one might imagine her only memory of the event had left her with a supreme fear of feeling that way ever again. And yet, she couldn't help but remember how intensely good it had felt to give in to one long, blissful scratching session.

Perhaps that was all she needed right now. If the duke would hold still, then she could rub up against—

Jacinda stopped instantly, appalled by her own thoughts. *What* had come over her? She honestly had no idea.

Gathering a semblance of composure, she tore her gaze away from his near-smirking mouth. "What of your aunt's stipulations?"

"If you procure a bride quiet enough, then my aunt may never know a whit about her character to find unappealing. And I need never reveal your actions today."

Was he blackmailing her, then? Find him a bride, no matter how incompatible they might be, in order to save the family business?

There had to be another way. She refused to pair a person with the wrong sort and force them into a life of misery and heartache. Before she agreed to forge any match between the duke and his potential bride, she would have to know more about him. "If you would only answer a few more questions, then I'm certain we could—"

"Enough, Miss Bourne," he snapped, every ounce of humor dissolving.

In the next moment, he angled toward her to grip the doorknob, creating a blockade around her. When she looked up, he hesitated before moving, his gaze dipping to her mouth once more. His early-autumn eyes darkened, the green eclipsed by pupils that expanded like spills of ink, leaving only a penumbra of russet brown. His scent filled her nostrils. She didn't intend to inhale the warm cedar essence so deeply, but his intrusion into her breathable space made it impossible not to. And now she feared she would never be rid of it.

Then suddenly, he pushed open the door and took a step back in a clear invitation for her to leave. "I have stated all that is essential. If you wish to keep my coin in your uncle's account, then I suggest you pry no further into my affairs."

This was likely one of the instances where she ought to let sleeping dogs lie. Yet, something in her nature demanded to have the answers to the mystery he posed. And his attempt at blackmail only heightened her suspicions.

She truly wished he would have cooperated. That way, she wouldn't have to resort to drastic measures. But now there was only one way to find out all she needed to know.

Jacinda inclined her head. "Very well, sir. I shall see that you have a list of names to consider by week's end."

He frowned. "Why not by the end of the day?"

"I'm afraid I will be leaving town shortly on an urgent matter," she said without elaborating. Then, because her ruse was over, she left the study and walked to the foyer instead of toward the servant's entrance. She could feel his watchful eyes following her all the way to the wide oaken door at the front of the town house. And with a glance over her shoulder, she confirmed it. "Good day, Your Grace."

He said nothing more, but merely glowered at her as she plucked the cap from her head and then disappeared into the chilly morning air.

Chapter 3

"Matrimony, as the origin of change, was always disagreeable . . ."

JANE AUSTEN, *Emma*

Crispin stared down at the polished surface of his desk and tried to regain a sense of composure.

Drawing in a deep breath, he focused on the quadrants. Top right—inkstand. Bottom right—bronze calling card case. Bottom left—stack of ledgers. Top left—he exhaled slowly—an errant feather duster in the place where he would have his tea tray.

It didn't matter that it was there, he told himself. A servant would tidy up in no time at all, removing every trace of Miss Jacinda Bourne. Then he could forget that she'd been here, standing in this exact spot, and ignore that she'd left a sweet, utterly feminine fragrance lingering in the air. And he also told himself that the only reason his pulse was ticking like a pocket watch wound too tightly was because he'd caught her trespassing. Surely that circumstance allowed a man the right to an erratic heartbeat.

Yet when he'd first entered the room and saw her, those robin's-egg blue eyes widening, her pink lips parting on a soundless gasp, his first impulse hadn't been to call the guard. Instead, he'd had the urge to cross the room, take her by the shoulders, haul her up to her toes and . . . and . . .

He shook his head, raking a hand through his hair. *No.* He absolutely had not had the impulse to kiss her. It had only been a wayward thought, a momentary lapse in judgment.

In these past four years, he'd learned to control all of his base, undisciplined hungers. He certainly wasn't the least bit tempted by a young woman with criminal tendencies, one who'd disguised herself as a servant in order to rifle through his things.

The only thing that had saved her from a more severe punishment was that he knew she couldn't have been in the room for any length of time. It was still just past dawn, and she'd had no candle to light her way. So she couldn't have found anything incriminating.

Besides, he was far too careful. He had to be.

Just then, the narrow servant's door on the opposite wall opened and the cinder maid slipped into the room. Used to finding him here at this early hour, she did not startle but briefly curtsied, her pail and broom rattling with the motion, before she proceeded to make quick work of sweeping out the ash from the hearth and lighting a fire.

Crispin sat at his desk, positioning his chair directly in the center. Unconsciously, he adjusted the angle of his calling card case and then reached forward to uncap the inkwell. He decided to forget about Miss Bourne's visit and focus on more important matters . . . like anything other than Miss Bourne.

Yet, as he scrutinized his accounting ledger, subtracting from an already paltry, abysmal figure, her voice entered his mind. *Yes, but you conveniently did not reveal your* requirement *for one with a large dowry.*

An *immense* dowry was closer to the truth. Though, frankly, he was still stunned that the question had arisen at all. The need to state the obvious had never occurred to him. He was a duke. *Of course* he would marry to increase his wealth and landholdings. Had there ever been a duke who had not?

And with an heiress, he presumed, there would be other

benefits as well. A woman reared in the lap of luxury would possess an endless desire for travel, ample friends to keep her company and, most importantly, absolutely no desire to live with him at Rydstrom Hall.

If his bride-to-be turned into someone who wanted to spend every waking moment with him, then once he explained about his crumbling estate, the matter should sort itself out. At least, that was his hope.

He would prefer it if he didn't have to marry at all and could keep his life just the way he had arranged it. Unfortunately, because of the ever-deteriorating walls of his home and his lack of any constant, reliable income, he—like every duke in his family before him—had to marry for money in order to keep it standing.

"Your Grace," the maid said, her voice cutting through his thoughts. "I found this on the floor."

He paused in checking over his figures in the ledger and looked up. The instant he saw the letter in her hand, a chill of icy dread sprinted through him.

"Thank you." He reached for it with a surprisingly steady hand, pretending to be unaffected. The maid bobbed once more and quietly left the room.

As soon as the door closed, he leapt to his feet and began to pace the room, poring over the contents of the letter, all the while wondering if that meddlesome intruder had read it.

But of course she had.

Only now did he remember that he hadn't burned it the way he typically did with the other correspondences from his housekeeper, Mrs. Hemple. Instead, he'd hastily tucked it inside a ledger yesterday when Aunt Hortense had entered this room. He hadn't wanted her to read it either. And he'd left it in the ledger. Of that, he was certain.

There was no way it could have fallen to the floor on its own.

Too late, Crispin crumpled the missive in his fist, the remnants of the wax seal pattering down to the hardwood floor at his feet. Then he tossed it into the flames. The curling paper glowed bright orange at the edges for an instant, then turned to mat black before finally disintegrating into ash.

Gone.

He only wished it was that simple, wished that his efforts to protect Sybil were as easily remedied. Yet he worried that Miss Bourne's doggedness would prove all his efforts futile.

The woman was worse than a hunting hound, attempting to sniff out every secret he held. The thought made his head ring. He pressed his fingertips to his temples—something he'd been doing frequently since he met Miss Bourne, three days ago.

Usually he stayed away from curious people who asked too many questions. Circumstance, however, had forced him into her company.

When he'd first gone to the Bourne Matrimonial Agency, he'd expected to speak solely with the proprietor, Lord Eggleston. The viscount was an amiable fellow, but one who valued charm above intellect. Still, Crispin had felt a sense of reassurance dealing with him, knowing that he would never question why a duke would need to hire an agency to find him a bride.

Regrettably, at the time, Eggleston had claimed to have another appointment and directed Crispin to a small parlor. And that was where he'd first encountered Miss Jacinda Bourne.

He'd known it was a mistake in an instant. Even before they were introduced, a sense of warning clambered through him, settling into a tense knot at the base of his skull.

Unlike her uncle, Miss Bourne did not smile at him excessively in an effort to put him at ease or welcome him. Instead, she'd narrowed her eyes, studying him from the crown of his head to the soles of his well-worn Hessians with the shrewdness of a geologist identifying the layers of rock cut away from a cliff side. Without a word, she'd scratched a few notes onto a slip of paper, which she'd somehow found amidst the plethora of clutter on the small desk.

Then, the moment Eggleston had left the room, her questions began.

"Why has Your Grace engaged the services of the Bourne Matrimonial Agency?"

Bristling, Crispin hadn't cared for the impertinence in her honeyed tone. "I should think the answer obvious."

She'd written another hasty note, a lock of auburn hair falling carelessly over the left side of her forehead, giving her the same disheveled appearance as her desk. As one who preferred order, he'd itched to tuck that lock back in place, but he'd forced himself to look away instead.

From that point, her questions had only become more intrusive. "Are you seeking a love match, or is this visit a means to an end?"

"Surely this is not the method in which you conduct business." He'd clenched his teeth, his gaze darting back to her. That lock had taunted him, the burnished dark red appearing almost hot to the touch, as if it were leaving a mark on her forehead. He hadn't understood why she didn't brush it back. The pull to cross the room and do it for her had grown even stronger, the compulsion making his fingertips tingle.

When she'd leaned forward to dip her pen into the inkwell, a pleat of lavender muslin brushed against a haphazard stack of papers. The top slip had teetered on the edge of her desk. It hung there, suspended, the corner drooping from the weight of gravity pulling it downward. Its hold on the desk had been tenuous at best, much like his patience. And when she'd scribbled on that page again, murmuring something under her breath about *uncooperative clients*, the paper slid to the floor, drifting on a current of air to land at his feet.

Irritated, he'd swiped the page off the floor and laid it on the small rosewood table nearest him. It was the only surface in the room that was bare and therefore out of place in this chaotic excuse for an office. "Just what could you possibly be writing?"

"I am getting a sense of your character. Now, if you please . . ."

With every one of his clipped evasions, she'd kept digging further, trying different versions of the same questions, and apparently taking him for a half-wit who was blind to her manipulations.

His tolerance exhausted, and a near obsession building because of that errant lock, he'd issued a somewhat forceful request to have a list supplied to him within the week. Then, before he'd turned to leave, Miss Bourne offered her acquiescence, but with a decidedly mischievous curl to the corners of her plump mouth.

He'd seen that same look this morning.

That smirk, along with the challenging glint in her eyes and another stray, fiery lock over her brow, had made him half wild with the need to have her gone from him. He couldn't account for it.

In truth, that had been the only reason he'd let her leave his study at all. With her, his sole aim was to be rid of her, and the sooner the better.

If he'd been thinking clearly, he would have caught the hint of suspicion in her probing question. *"The only family we have listed for you is your aunt, and my uncle was wondering if you had anyone else?"*

A chill slithered down his spine as he realized what a mistake he'd made. She had read the letter, for certain. He never should have let her leave without setting matters aright by making up a lie to appease her rapacious curiosity.

Now there was no telling what she might do to find the answer. And he needed to stop her before it was too late.

Chapter 4

"The real evils indeed of Emma's situation were the power of having rather too much of her own way, and a disposition to think a little too well of herself."

JANE AUSTEN, *Emma*

"You did *what*?"

Jacinda flinched at the harsh volume of Ainsley's voice, rising to the ceiling, where the delicate plaster moldings likely quivered to the point of cracking. And when her sister shot up from the rose-tufted chair behind the slender writing table as well, it seemed the castigations had only just begun.

Not wanting Uncle Ernest to overhear, Jacinda shut the white glazed door to the hallway. However, just as she closed one door at the back of the Pomona green room, another opened.

From the adjacent sitting room, used as another office, their youngest sister burst into the room in a flurry of buttercup skirts, looking first to Ainsley. "What has happened?"

In response, Ainsley pressed a hand to her forehead and carefully smoothed back the fine chestnut brown tendrils that slipped free an instant ago. "Ask *your* sister."

"What did you do this time?" Briar did her very best to look intimidating by setting her hands on her slender hips and casting a blue-eyed glare toward Jacinda. At twenty years old, it wasn't Briar's fault that she was the least formidable of them, possessing Mother's perfect doll-like face and pale, wispy blond hair.

In truth, they each had variations of Mother's shape and delicate features. Though, Ainsley had a bit more of Father, with his coloring, sealskin brown eyes, and the tendency for her cheeks to turn ruddy whenever she drank wine that wasn't watered down properly. Jacinda's auburn hair and the turquoise blue of her eyes, she was told, had come from their grandmother. But Briar was Mother's perfect copy, all the way down to her fanciful nature and gentle demeanor.

Because of that, Jacinda preferred to shield Briar from many of her less scrupulous activities. "Nothing at all, pet. Ainsley and I had a simple misunderstanding. Say, is that the aroma of tea and Mrs. Darden's lemon-anise scones in the air? Dear me, but I'm famished. Would you mind terribly . . ."

"I'm not leaving the room this time," Briar said, her meringue-soft voice cracking from the rare use of force. Jacinda might have been alarmed by this alteration in her sister if Briar wasn't so adorable.

It gave Ainsley another reason to frown, however. For a woman of six and twenty, and too pretty to be a curmudgeonly spinster, she certainly didn't hesitate to act like one. "Since the news affects all of us, I see no reason why Briar shouldn't hear how *her* sister stole into the Duke of Rydstrom's town house at dawn—"

"The door was open," Jacinda added to no avail.

"—crept into his study, and rifled through his things."

"*Rifled* is rather harsh, even for you. I merely happened upon a letter."

Briar gasped, her hand covering her mouth as her eyes grew larger. "You read his correspondence?"

"Of course not." Jacinda tsked, stepping past a pair of gilded armchairs on her way to the mantel where Mother's music box waited. It was a puzzle box as well, and you had to know the trick of it to hear the music. "I merely *skimmed* it for pertinent information."

"And then," Ainsley continued, her chastising tone adding a touch of unneeded drama, "he caught her in the act."

Briar sank onto a golden tasseled hassock, her lamenting sigh accompanied by the muffled crunch of horsehair stuffing beneath her. "We'll be ruined."

"Nonsense," Jacinda said with a flit of her fingers, brushing a tiny speck of dust from the center of the glossy rosewood lid where an inlay of gold leaf formed a starburst. "It isn't as bad as all that. He let me leave, after all."

Ainsley crossed her arms over her sensible aubergine frock. "Only because he underestimated you. Had he an inkling of your espionage abilities, you would be wearing leg shackles this instant."

Jacinda grinned, pleased to have her talents appreciated for once.

"Shouldn't we be referring to the duke as *His Grace* instead of *he*?" Briar asked in a whisper as if she feared he was outside this very room, listening. "It seems almost sacrilegious to refer to him—or *His Grace*, rather—as if he were a mere man."

"For it to be sacrilege, he would have to be a religious figure. Besides, he is most definitely a man, and a dishonest one at that." Another one of those currents arced through Jacinda as if she were now a conduit that reacted at the sheer mention of him. And worse, she could still smell him, that warm cedar essence seemed to have permeated her clothes.

Just to be certain, she turned her head and lifted her shoulder for a sniff. And there it was—the scent of Crispin Montague, Duke of Rydstrom, Roman conqueror, Viking, woodsman, and avaricious bridegroom. She closed her eyes and inhaled one more time, but only for utter certainty.

But when she opened them again, she found Ainsley squinting at her. "Why do you say that?"

"Because he purposely omitted the whole truth about his income."

"No." Ainsley shook her head. "I meant how you referred to him as 'most definitely a man.'"

"A passing observation. Nothing more." Feeling her cheeks grow hot, Jacinda returned her attention to the music box on the mantel, withdrawing the square near the corner and pushing up the hidden peg at the bottom. The brass cylinder turned inside, the metal tines pinging with the soft melody that Mother used to hum from the window seat of their snug cottage in Hampshire.

She would gaze out that window for hours waiting for Father to return. It wasn't until she'd learned about the other family he'd been keeping on the side that she'd finally given up waiting for him. Her broken, frail heart had forced her to give up on other things, too, like singing and laughing as well as eating and getting out of bed. Ultimately, Heloise Bourne-Cartwright had died of a broken heart. And all because she'd married a man who kept secrets. A man who had no sense of duty to his first family nor a single shred of honor.

"No matter what we call His Grace," Briar said, cutting into her thoughts, "we are still at risk of losing our business."

"Not if we find a match for him." Jacinda turned away from the music box, filled with a renewed sense of determination. She would save every person she could from making the mistake of marrying the wrong sort. But in order to do that, the Bourne Matrimonial Agency needed to stay in business.

And as much as her presence had angered him, there was still an underlying desperation for him to find a bride. Likely, he would marry anyone in order to gain the monetary gift his aunt promised him.

Then, once they found the duke a match, the Bourne Matrimonial Agency would become the premier establishment for *all* society matches. Currently, and aside from a scant few viscounts, three heiresses, and one French count, their client list consisted of members from the lower rungs. Barons, baronettes, landed gentry, and those who could not afford a Season in London, were quite eager to fill out their applications. And while the agency could secure matches for those outside of their client base—for a fee, of course—that would hardly promote the longevity of their business. So, they primarily relied upon subscriptions.

Sadly, even with the Duchess of Holliford's patronage, many of the upper echelon were hesitant to engage their services.

Yet, that could all change if they made a match for the Duke of Rydstrom. Not only would it secure their reputations among the *ton*, but it would also guarantee paying clients for years to come, *and* shoo the moths away from the barren family coffers.

She'd already seen evidence this week. When rumors of the duke's name on the agency's client list reached a few well-connected ears—thanks to the Duchess of Holliford—a half dozen title-hungry society mamas spent their pin money on subscriptions for their daughters, two of them with embarrassingly large dowries. It was only a matter of time before more would follow.

Ainsley released an exasperated sigh. "But you said he's the 'wrong sort.' That was the reason behind your reckless behavior this morning."

Jacinda's conscience—which had been drowsing for much of this morning—was now rearing at her. Was she actually considering making a match for him just to save their business?

Behind her, the music box wound down, issuing three final, and painfully slow, pings before falling silent.

Jacinda swallowed. No. She couldn't find him a bride without knowing more about him first. And just who was this Sybil person? A mistress, perhaps? A mad relation?

All questions that must have answers, she thought. "I

said that I *believe* he's the wrong sort, I just haven't proven it. But I have a plan."

Briar slumped forward and buried her face in her hands. "Not *another* one. I don't think I want to hear any more."

"You always confuse foolish impulses with forethought."

Jacinda ignored the histrionics from one sister and the incorrect—and frankly offensive—assumption of the other. "I'll take the mail coach into Sussex and apply to his housekeeper for a tour of the grounds, pretending to be on holiday. Once I'm inside, I'll learn everything there is to know about the duke, including whether or not he deserves a perfect match."

"Absolutely not," Ainsley said firmly. "Think of the rumors you would incite, traveling all the way to Sussex without a chaperone. Even though we are poor, as daughters of a baron we are still among the elite in society."

"I hardly think Father, or his title, has any bearing on my decision, considering he abandoned us more than ten years ago." As far as Jacinda was concerned, she owed Michael Cartwright, Lord Frawley, nothing. In fact, so great was her and her sisters' desire to right the immeasurable wrong he'd done to Mother, that they'd even taken their mother's maiden name as their own when they'd gone to live with Uncle Ernest.

"We are also nieces of a kind and considerate viscount who took us in after Mother died. We owe Uncle Ernest our best behavior in London society, not more of your supposedly *accidental* explorations." Ainsley glanced purposely at an oval frame, which held a single bluebell blossom pressed between glass, hanging by a silver ribbon on the wall near the door.

Would Ainsley ever forget about that dratted bluebell sliver? It wasn't as if Jacinda had made a habit of reading her sister's diary. At least, as far as Ainsley knew, there had only been that one instance.

"Yes, but if it wasn't for Jacinda's unconventional deeds,

then we never would have found the perfect match for the Duchess of Holliford's nephew, and there never would have been a Bourne Matrimonial Agency at all," Briar said somewhat distractedly as she rose from the hassock and smoothed her skirts.

"Thank you, Briar," Jacinda said with a smug grin. "You are now my favorite sister."

Briar inclined her head regally as if fully aware of her tendency to say the perfect thing at the most opportune time.

Their first client—before there even was a family business—had been the Duchess of Holliford. It all came about when Her Grace revealed that she'd given up hope that her awkward, solitary nephew would ever marry. At the age of six and twenty, it seemed that he was more interested in his insect collection than in women.

However, during a visit to Her Grace's country estate for afternoon tea, Jacinda—left to her own devices for a few minutes—had happened upon a collection of letters, yellowed and long forgotten. They'd been tucked inside a camouflaged pigeonhole at the top of an escritoire, practically falling into her lap, really. Well, *after* she'd encouraged the compartment to open by way of a letter knife and while balancing on the arm of a chair.

Nevertheless, the letters revealed that the duchess's nephew, Clyde Ableforth, had once been deeply in love with a budding lepidopterist named Nelly. And when Jacinda revealed her discovery to a stunned Duchess of Holliford and her owl-eyed nephew, the truth had come out. Mr. Ableforth had loved Nelly, and no one else since her. Yet, when that long-ago summer romance had ended and Nelly had returned to the strict bosom of her family, they'd lost touch.

Overwhelmed by curiosity, Jacinda hadn't been able to let the matter rest. So, after bribing a few tight-lipped servants with ginger comfits—courtesy of Briar's supposedly secret hiding place—and a bit of digging, Jacinda had discovered all she'd needed to know.

Mr. Ableforth and Nelly—or rather, Miss Cordelia Smith of Northumberland, bluestocking and spinster—were married last June.

In the end, the appreciative Duchess of Holliford had become their patroness, allowing them the use of a fine town house in St. James's. Her Grace would have lived here herself if not for the occasionally rowdy clientele at Sterling's, the gaming hell across the street. Though, since the location gave the agency good exposure, the Bourne family didn't mind. Well, except for Ainsley, who loathed the club and its owner, Reed Sterling, citing that it was a den of iniquity and he the devil incarnate.

"Those intrusions might have been overlooked in the country because of our results, but they won't be here." Ainsley tsked, wearing her stick-in-the-mud expression. Or rather, in her case, it was more like an Excalibur-in-the-stone expression. She would not be moved from her argument. "Sometimes I wonder if you are incapable of behaving yourself and following the rules that the rest of us live by."

"As far as I know, the Bourne Matrimonial Agency's *only* rule is never to fall in love with the client," Jacinda added. This had been set in place, primarily, because Uncle Ernest fell in love so easily and had spent too much time charming their first patrons. "I guarantee, *that* is one rule I will not break, especially in this circumstance."

Who would ever fall in love with a man as intractable and secretive as the Duke of Rydstrom? Not any woman with sense, she was sure. Clearly, she would have to find an immensely wealthy idiot for him to marry.

"For you to make such a declarative statement all but guarantees our ruin," Ainsley muttered through clenched teeth. "I wish you would stop for a moment and think about how your actions could affect your sisters' reputations as well as Uncle Ernest's."

"Did I hear my name?" The door to the hallway opened and their uncle entered, an ever-present smile on his lips that made him look years younger than six and fifty. He was of average height and slender build, with a pale, aristocratic complexion. Yet matrons and widows remarked endlessly on the handsomeness of his thick, silvery hair and blushed whenever their gazes met the glint in his lapis blue eyes.

Jacinda made her way to him, slipping her arm through his. "You did, indeed. We were just speaking of how fond we are of you."

Even though Uncle Ernest had a kind, gentle nature and tended toward the romantic, he was no fool. He arched a silver-threaded brow. "It sounded rather like a heated discussion."

"Not at all," she said with a pat to his sleeve. "You know how we tend to increase our volume whenever we discuss our purpose, and how we are ever so grateful that you opened this agency."

"There isn't anything I wouldn't do for the three of you. I only wish I'd done more for your mother." Uncle Ernest sighed, his gaze alighting on a demilune table near the door, where Ainsley kept volume three of *Emma*, resting in the curved arms of a small, bronze easel. "But at least we are helping others avoid her fate, in our way."

Abruptly, Jacinda's mood turned wistful. There were moments when she missed Mother so desperately that she felt the ache of it in the between-beats of her heart where there would always be emptiness.

"You've said, many times, that our collective determination will make us successful." Briar's uncannily providential words drew Jacinda out of her doldrums and back to her current purpose.

Uncle Ernest nodded. "I firmly believe it, too. The Bourne Matrimonial Agency should stop at nothing in order to guarantee our clients' happiness."

"Within limits," Ainsley added.

Jacinda wrinkled her nose at her sister before turning

back to their uncle. It was a commonly held belief that half of Uncle Ernest's heart was comprised of romantic poetry, love letters, and the need to fall irrevocably in love at least twice a week. And Jacinda may or may not have used this knowledge to further her own pursuits, a time or two.

Releasing his arm, she placed a hand over her heart and offered the sigh of hopeful yearning she reserved for moments of desperation. "But are there limitations to love? I think not."

Uncle Ernest nodded thoughtfully, drawing in a deep breath. "So true, Jacinda. We should go to the ends of the earth for the sake of that most precious of all feelings."

Ainsley coughed. "But what about all the way to Sussex *and* without a chaperone?"

"Is someone going to Sussex?" Uncle Ernest asked, looking from Jacinda to Briar, and finally back to Ainsley.

She pressed her fingertips to her temple, likely trying to claim a headache and earn his sympathy. "Jacinda has this notion to travel to the Duke of Rydstrom's estate in order to—"

"To ensure the happiness of our most prestigious client," Jacinda cut in, speaking over her sister.

"Yes, indeed. This *is* important. His Grace must be matched with someone quite special," he said thoughtfully, tapping a finger to his chin. "You would require a chaperone. However, if I were to accompany you, during any of the three days we are open for clients, then the agency would have to close until my return. I don't think that it would be fair to those who are depending on us to introduce them to their true loves."

Having foreseen this argument, Jacinda readily supplied a solution. "Then I will take Ginny with me."

"And what are we to do while our maid is with you? Curl each other's hair?" Ainsley asked with a pointed look to Briar, reminding them all of the last time any of them attempted to wield the curling tongs.

Briar inhaled sharply, covering one hand over the tip of her ear, where there was likely still a dark spot from the last burn. "No, no, no. We cannot do without Ginny. As capable as we are, there are certain things that require more skill than any of us possess."

Sadly, it was true. After Father had left, they'd only been able to afford one servant, and Mrs. Darden acted as both housekeeper and cook. Therefore, Jacinda and her sisters helped with the washing and cleaning, and did the mending and gardening on their own.

Even when they'd gone to live with Uncle Ernest, their financial circumstances were not much altered. So, as they grew into womanhood, Ainsley, Jacinda, and Briar had attempted to help each other become presentable in society. But their curling tong skills were sorely lacking. In fact, before the Duchess of Holliford sent Ginny to them, they'd typically earned sideways glances for their *interesting coiffures.*

"Very well," Jacinda said, undeterred. "I have a few coins tucked away. I shall hire a maid to accompany me." Of course, this meant she would have to borrow from her own dowry. The funds had been entrusted to each of them by their uncle during a brief but solvent episode.

Nonetheless, it wasn't as if she would have need of the money anytime soon. After all, what gentleman would marry her for a mere two hundred pounds? He would have to be wealthy to the degree of not requiring a wife with any dowry at all. Unlike the duke.

The instant she thought of him—*drat it all*—yet another current buzzed through her, settling into the pit of her stomach. She pressed a hand there to quell the unwanted sensation.

Across the room, Ainsley gave a huff of indignation as if she knew precisely how Jacinda would pay for this venture.

This seemed to give Uncle Ernest pause. "But how long should you be away? I do hate to worry."

"I shouldn't think I'd be gone more than four or five days. I'll return before you miss me." She pressed a kiss to his cheek and glanced at Ainsley with a tiny speck of gloating. "There is absolutely no need to worry. I have the perfect plan and nothing can possibly go wrong."

FORTUNATELY FOR Crispin, the Bourne Matrimonial Agency was a quick jaunt through King Street, away from his aunt's town house in the square.

After repeated raps of the bronze wreath doorknocker, Mrs. Darden, a somewhat frazzled, corpulent woman, answered the door. She was balancing a teapot in one hand and a salver brimming with correspondences in the other. How she'd managed to open the door at all was something of a mystery, but one that he had no time to solve.

Promptly, she led him up the marble stairs, past several arched niches filled with the needless clutter of Cupid statues in various poses, a wide corridor dotted with an uneven number of straight-backed chairs, mismatched demilune tables positioned beside every doorway, and into Lord Eggleston's parlor.

"Your Grace, what a pleasant surprise," the viscount said, rushing past the plume-filled urns on either side of his desk to greet him. Dressed neatly in a Corinthian blue coat and striped cravat, his polished appearance provided a sense of professionalism to the agency.

Crispin could not imagine this gentleman ever disguising himself as a servant and trespassing into a client's home.

"Would you care for a cup of tea, a scone, biscuit . . ." Eggleston asked before Mrs. Darden was too far beyond the door.

Crispin shook his head, appreciating the viscount's artless air and amiable demeanor that, under different circumstances, might have helped ease his anxiety if the situation wasn't so dire. "Thank you, no."

"Well, then, I hope your journey here was pleasant. I must say, the weather is rather fine. Not a cloud in sight. Would you care to have a seat?"

"Thank you, no," Crispin said, feeling as if he might crack his teeth on another polite refusal. The urgent desire to settle this matter burned through him like lemon juice on an open wound. "I came here on a brief errand to amend my application. Your niece, Miss Jacinda, recently inquired after my pursuits. At the time, I could think of none"—certainly nothing he considered anyone's concern aside from his own—"but something just came to me this morning."

If Miss Bourne wanted answers, then he was fully prepared to lie through his teeth. It had to be done. For Sybil.

Lord Eggleston's smile broadened, crinkling the corners of his eyes. "Ah, yes. Having a spouse who shares our pursuits makes for a happy union. I'm glad Your Grace has come. Now, let me see . . ." He began opening the drawers of his desk, one after another as if he had no idea what each might contain, and eventually came up with a sheet of foolscap.

Realizing the purpose, Crispin quickly interrupted the viscount's search for a sharpened pen. "I thought I might tell Miss Bourne directly. She seemed rather . . . adamant that I complete the application."

Lord Eggleston laughed fondly, lifting a blunt-tipped quill from the inkstand and waving it like a wizard's wand as he spoke. "She's always had a streak of determination, that one. Her mother—bless her soul—wanted each of those girls to have a firm sense of their own individual demeanors. I cannot imagine any greater blessing than to have three such singular girls under my roof."

Crispin smiled patiently. "You are a fortunate man. Now if I may . . . where would I find Miss Jacinda this morning?"

While he would have liked nothing more than to report her actions to her uncle, he didn't know her well enough to be certain she wouldn't reveal what she'd read in the letter.

"Oh, not here." The viscount shook his head as if the fact were obvious. "She left about"—he mused over the clock on the mantel—"an hour ago. Gone on an important quest. She possesses no lack of gumption. Yes, indeed."

Crispin withdrew his brass pocket watch and noted that the mantel clock was twenty-three minutes slow. "When do you expect her return?"

"Not for days, to be sure. 'Tis a long way to Sussex."

Crispin closed the watch with a startled snap. He was certain he hadn't heard correctly. "Sussex?"

"Yes, sir. In fact, that niece of mine was in such a rush to depart that she didn't want to wait for the mail coach leaving Piccadilly this evening. Instead, she and a maid hired a stagecoach. I imagine they'll make good time—no more than a day."

No. It had to be a coincidence.

His pulse ran riot, drumming hard against the side of his throat as he tried to think of another reason for her sudden journey toward the county where his own estate resided. "Have you family there?"

The viscount shook his head. "All we have is each other. And we each do what we can to honor their mother's memory. You see . . ."

The ringing in his ears returned and Crispin was no longer able to hear Eggleston as he continued. Besides, he already knew the reason she'd gone.

Because of the letter.

"Oddly enough," Crispin said remotely as he walked to the office door, "I, too, am off to Sussex."

"Capital!" Eggleston clapped his hands together, the paper and pen forgotten. "Perhaps Your Grace will even cross paths with my niece. After all, she is on an important matter of . . . Well, I shouldn't say until she returns. But

I've no doubt she'll come back, brimming with the best of news."

"If I do happen to encounter your niece, I will be certain to pass along your wishes for her hasty return." And Crispin intended to send her back to London as quickly as possible, even if he had to stuff her inside a trunk and drive her back himself.

PART 2

Chapter 5

"Surprizes are foolish things. The pleasure is not enhanced and the inconvenience is often considerable."

JANE AUSTEN, *Emma*

"Beg pardon, Yer Grace."

Crispin jolted upright on the carriage bench, then instantly regretted the sudden movement as a sharp pain pierced the side of his neck. Cringing, he asked, "Have we arrived at another inn, Jones?"

Still half-asleep, he hunched forward on the crushed burgundy velvet seat and scrubbed a hand over his face, feeling a full day's growth of whiskers scrape his palm. They'd been driving hard, checking every inn along the way for most of yesterday and all night, in search of Jacinda Bourne's coach. He wondered what village they were in this time.

"Din't warnt to wake you, sir," his driver said, his gravelly West Sussex burr thicker than usual. "So I asked the keeper meself."

"Good man," Crispin said with a wealth of gratitude. Squinting against the orange light of early morning, he focused on the travel-worn man standing on the road outside the carriage.

Jones's dark button eyes were puffy around the edges and the lower portion of his face was enshrouded in stubble as black as chimney soot. Beneath a dusty garrick, his lean frame teetered with drunken exhaustion, causing an errant leaf to fall from the brim of his battered hat. "En says there hasn't been no customers fer a week, and no women a 'tall fer mar than a momf."

Crispin frowned at that. *Damn.* He'd had a feeling from the start that he'd left London too late. Unfortunately, Aunt Hortense had stopped him before he could depart.

"As I have already stated, my wedding gift to you comes with conditions. One of which is that you reside here until we have found an appropriate bride for you," she'd said, her voice hitching higher along with her stubborn Montague chin.

The sight of those cold steel-gray eyes had him gritting his teeth. "Understood. I have every intention of honoring our bargain, just as soon as I return from a brief errand."

For four years, he'd received hardly a word from his aunt and then suddenly, two months ago, a letter had arrived. Without preamble, salutation, or inquiry into his health, she'd stated that a man of his age should marry. And then, she'd dangled a shiny, £4,000 lure in front of him.

He could not afford to resist it.

"Make certain of it, then. You spent too many years as a reckless ne'er-do-well, cutting a swathe of wickedness through the streets of London, and you cannot amend that reputation by becoming a recluse. It is your duty to marry and uphold the integrity of the dukedom, just as my brother did before his untimely death."

Crispin had bit down on his unpleasant retort, not requiring the reminder—either of his obligation to marry or his own culpability in his father's death. Yet the latter would always be a black stain between them.

So without another word, he'd turned to leave.

"Perhaps I should come with you," she'd said, halting him in his tracks.

The last thing he needed was to worry about the possibility of having two uninvited women at Rydstrom Hall. His response had been a firm, unequivocal, and even ducal "*No,*" and he'd left without further argument.

Now, withdrawing his pocket watch, Crispin discovered that it was even later than he thought—nearly eight o'clock in the morning. Yesterday's efforts at dissuading his aunt had used up valuable time. Miss Bourne had already left a few hours ahead of him, and they still hadn't caught up with her. "How many more inns are there to go?"

"Narn, sir. We be in Whitcrest now, an' Rydstrom Hall be just up the hill."

With a start, Crispin lurched forward, peering in the direction of Jones's pointed finger, to the salt-bleached gray stone monstrosity near the cliff's edge. He closed his eyes, half in homecoming and half in despair.

This was the only home he'd ever known, but also the residence of his living nightmares.

Breathing in, he knew he should have recognized the familiar sharp, briny scent in the air sooner. He remembered hating the odor of the sea, ranting at his father that he wanted no part of living here in a crumbling heap.

When he'd entered university, he'd wanted to live like his friends whom he stayed with during holidays, traveling to exotic places, living in the finest houses, and enjoying the affections of soft, perfumed women swathed in silks who'd treated him like a king.

Father had accused him of turning into a stranger before his very eyes and allowing enticements of hedonism too great of an influence over him. And of course, Crispin had denied it to the very core of his being, prepared to continue on his path.

Then in one fell swoop that all changed. He went from being a wild, recalcitrant young man determined to slough off the responsibilities expected of a duke's heir to a man whose sole identity revolved around the duties demanded of the title. And there were times when he felt as if he'd aged four lifetimes in the past four years.

Yet, thinking of the letter he'd neglected to burn, he admitted that he was no better at shouldering responsibility than he'd been in the past. He still had to worry about Miss Bourne and to stop her from finding Sybil before it was too late.

"Did we miss an inn along the way?" he asked Jones and received a weary headshake.

Curious. Crispin was nearly convinced that Miss Bourne would have been on this direct path to his estate. Unless . . . she'd already managed to squirrel her way into his home before he had the chance to warn Mr. Fellows and Mrs. Hemple not to allow her admittance.

A shudder rolled through him.

"You're a fine, solid man," he said to Jones, grateful for the driver's unswerving loyalty and hoping that his efforts weren't all for naught. "It's time to drive home so you can rest a long while. I'll ask Fellows to send a few pails of hot water to the stables, and you can have a nice long soak."

Jones's grin looked tipsy, his shoulders slumping as if he were already imagining the soaking tub. "Aye, sir."

And in a moment they were off, the team digging in for the final climb, the carriage jerking with each rut, rock, and sharp turn along the narrow, winding path.

Crispin was still shocked that he hadn't found Miss Bourne and was beginning to have a small kernel of doubt on the purpose of her visit to Sussex. Could it be that he'd made more of the letter than need be and there was an innocent explanation?

Innocent? He nearly laughed aloud at the thought. She would be the last person he'd ever suspect of possessing a pair of angel's wings. Well . . . unless she'd stolen into heaven and plucked them from an unsuspecting angel all by herself.

Hadn't he already underestimated her once? Only a fool would do so again.

Now only one question remained—where was Miss Bourne?

A SHRIEK awoke her. The piercing sound burrowed through her temple and directly into the pulsing center mass of her brain.

Do be quiet, would you? she thought, too tired to form the words.

All she wanted to do was sleep. Unfortunately, she was lying prone on the worst bed imaginable. Hard and lumpy, it dug into her rib cage and pressed painfully against her cheek and temple. Clearly, she needed to turn over.

Yet when she shifted, her entire body seized, stiffening as if she'd been stitched together with frozen limbs that had yet to thaw. A sudden shiver wracked her body, her teeth chattering. She tasted salt and something coppery. The harsh flavor coated her tongue, making her gag and cough. She winced at the rawness of her throat, feeling as if tiny pebbles lined the tender flesh all the way to her lungs.

Ugh. She was definitely going back to sleep until she felt better.

Then another shriek closed in, followed in quick succession by a high chirruping voice. "Thank the two magpies, she's alive!"

The exclamation barely rose above the heavy *whooshing* sound of the wind, the low growl echoing inside her ears. Yet, it made resting impossible, all the same.

Curiosity overtook her, sweeping through in a fierce rush of prickles down her spine, too urgent to be ignored. The phrase *She's alive* aroused a plethora of questions. Who was the supposedly near-dead-but-not-quite woman? And why was that person so near to this uncomfortable bed in this loud chamber?

Even without having the answers, she was far too alert to consider dozing off again.

When she opened her eyes to investigate, however, something dark and wet blocked her vision. Blinking several times did not help. And lifting a hand to her face to clear the impediment away took a great deal more effort than it should have. Her shoulder, arm, and elbow seemed weighed down by some unseen force.

Struggling, she managed to take hold of the dark mass. Yet after a painful tug, a wince, and a startled groan, she discovered that it was her own hair.

A frown puckered the flesh of her brow, and she stared at the deep reddish-brown strands. Strangely, they seemed foreign to her. New. And she watched in perplexed fascination as a thick hank curled over her gloved fingers.

Gloves? Now that was another oddity. Why was she wearing leather gloves in bed? More important, why were they wet?

She couldn't think of an answer.

Though, perhaps she needed more sleep, after all. Even now, her heavy lids were drifting closed . . .

"Mr. Lemon, we must fetch the parson, or mayhap the doctor," the chirruping voice interrupted, sounding closer now. "Mr. Craig may do as well. He's just over the rise, unloading his fishing smack. Ack, but he is such a curmudgeon. True. True. Mrs. Lassater has seen her fair share of injuries, but do we wish to bother her when she is up to her elbows in the village laundry? Though you are likely correct, my good sir. Yes, indeed. We should be happy if any of them were here with us and this *purr* creature."

The woman's words tumbled out with such rapidity, and edged with such an indistinct drawl, that it was difficult to keep track of them all. Still, it seemed clear that there was a *purr*—or rather *poor—creature* somewhere.

So why was she, herself, lying in bed with all this excitement around her?

That stabbing pain at her temple made it impossible to concentrate on the answer. And attempting to sit up, brought more difficulties. Not only was her body stiff and sore, but she quickly realized that her gloves weren't the only things wet. In fact, she was drenched from head to toe, her garments clinging to her limbs and hindering her movements. She shuddered again, biting her lip. This time she tasted more of that coppery flavor and realized that it was blood.

"No, no, my dear bedraggled mermaid. I'm sure you shouldn't move. By the look of you, I'd say you took quite a spill, and believe you me . . ."

All concentration halted on the word *mermaid*. Everything was frightfully puzzling. To whom was this woman speaking?

Yet before she could ask, she felt a slight pressure on her arm.

She turned her head slowly, mindful of the sharp pain in the side of her neck, and watched as an ungloved hand curled over her sleeve, warmth penetrating the thick burgundy wool. The fingers were spindly, with discolored, uneven nails and a dark mole near the base of the thumb.

Then, lifting her gaze, she saw that the mole had a large twin or perhaps a parent, given its circumference. It rested on the cheek of the narrow face peering back at her from beneath a tattered black bonnet.

It was an unfamiliar face. The woman's skin was like vellum, pale and faintly creased, clinging to high cheekbones and a thin blade of a nose. Wind buffeted the fraying ends of the black ribbon tied in a knot beneath the blur of her rapidly moving lips and a shapely chin. And if it wasn't for the mole, it was easy to imagine that she might have been quite pretty in her bloom.

". . . Mr. Lemon and I have seen our share of curiosities wash up," the woman continued, only now with a face to go with the voice. "We come here a-mornings anywhen the tide is low. Why, you should see my collection of green and brown bottle glass. Smooth as river rocks, they are . . ."

Tide?

Glancing away from the woman, she stared down at

the uncomfortable surface beneath her and discovered it was not a bed at all, but a huge gray rock. It was hard but smooth, the bumps and pits worn down to silken, rounded edges. Still, it made a terrible mattress.

Forcing herself to sit upright, she clenched her teeth through the pain and took note of her surroundings by degree. Patches of wet, gray sand. A mixture of glossy stones in various earthy shades. A narrow strip of beach. A streak of bubbly white foam inching into her line of sight. Then her focus expanded to the roar of white-capped waves, rolling closer in long barrel-sized loops. They crashed over other large rocks like hers that resided further out into the endless expanse of water that could only have been . . . the sea.

What was she doing here, sleeping on a rock?

That headache stabbed harder this time, making her eyes sting and turn bleary. Unable to concentrate, she knew that the only person who might be able to answer this question was the woman with the mole.

"Are we ac—" Her raspy words stopped as she clutched her throat, the lining feeling shredded.

"Acquainted?" mole-woman helpfully supplied.

Nodding in response seemed safer than trying to speak again.

In answer, mole-woman shook her head. "I shouldn't ought to think so, unless you are the sister of Mrs. Matthews. She is expected anywhen now. But by the look of you, I shouldn't suppose so. I met her once, a Miss Anson from Shropshire. But she was fair-haired. And I'm sure any kin of the Matthews' shouldn't ought to have clothes as fine as yours."

Halting the endless blur of words, mole-woman straightened, pressing vellum-skinned hands down the front of her high-necked black dress as if she were trying to look her best. Yet the ruffled collar and cuffs were frayed beyond mending.

Glancing down at her own soggy clothes, she compared the style and stitching, quickly concluding that she was not dressed like mole-woman. Her heavy burgundy redingote was more elaborate, with a double row of fawn-colored cloth buttons, embroidered cuffs and layered embellishments along the hem, above the tips of her black ankle boots. While she didn't know what it meant, she knew her garment was different.

"Indeed," mole-woman said in awe, her admiring gaze tracing the scalloped design on the cuff of the redingote's sleeve. "Yours is some of the finest embroidery I've seen since Whitcrest had a duchess in Rydstrom Hall. You must be an important lady. In fact, I'd hazard a guess that you must be a guest of . . ."

An important lady, hmm? On her rock, she sat up straighter and made every attempt to conceal her discomfort. Her efforts were for naught, however. Pain tunneled through her, beginning at her head and stiffly tumbling down each vertebra. Light-headed, she leaned forward, her hands securely on the rock for support.

". . . Everyone in the village is talking about the rumors that His Grace plans to marry." Mole-woman stopped on a gasp. "And here I am, yammering on while we have a veritable duchess in our midst. Isn't that right, Mr. Lemon?"

As mole-woman spoke, a small white dog appeared from behind her skirts. He was shorthaired, wide-legged, and sported black markings around his nose and mouth that made it appear as if he were smiling in greeting. He offered a gruff *woof* and something of a nod before he lifted a foreleg and pawed a bit of sand from his snout.

"I hope you will forgive us. We usually have far better manners. In fact, my very own father was a schoolmaster for a time. He even tutored the late duke and—Oh dear, I'm doing it again, aren't I? Well, I'll just say that I am Miss Elmira Beels, your ladyship," she said with an awkward curtsy, accompanied by the slurping sound of her shoes sinking into the sand. "And what am I to call you?"

"Pleased to make your acquaintance, Miss Beels," she

rasped, the rawness of her throat receding marginally. "I am . . ."

It wasn't until that very moment, sitting on the rock with her mouth open and nothing coming out, that she realized she couldn't remember her own name.

BY THE time the carriage reached the flat slope in front of the weathered oaken doors of Rydstrom Hall, Crispin was nearly ill with fatigue.

Mr. Fellows was already standing outside on the old flagstone path. Age had rounded the shoulders inside of his blue livery coat, and as he moved toward the carriage, the wind caught the silvery tufts of hair that formed a horseshoe shape over his gleaming pate. "Good morning, Your Grace. A pleasant journey, I"—his cloudy gray eyes widened as Crispin emerged from the carriage—"I trust."

Admittedly, Crispin was a little worse for wear. Under normal circumstances, he held himself to a high standard of personal grooming. But since he met Jacinda Bourne, he'd found his entire world in disorder.

"The devil's own, but that matters not," Crispin said, reassembling his limbs one by one as he stepped down. It felt freeing to move about, but he was stiff from head to toe. Reaching back into the carriage, he grabbed his greatcoat and shrugged into it. The heavy garment draped over his shoulders in clean, symmetrical lines that offered a semblance of respectability to his appearance. "Tell me, have there been any visitors while I was away? Or a traveler who might have applied for a tour of the house?"

All the way up the hill, Crispin had imagined a dozen ways that Jacinda Bourne might have schemed her way into his home, each one more disturbing than the next.

"None, sir." Fellows shuffled past him to retrieve the satchel from the carriage floor. "Should I have a chamber prepared for your bride?"

"My *bride*?" Crispin parroted. Still thinking of Miss Bourne, he was caught off guard when an image of her flashed across his mind's eye—her face lit by altar candles, her eyes glowing that bright, robin's-egg blue, and a fiery lock of hair carelessly draped over the left side of her forehead. He violently shook his head to ward off the unwelcome vision. The woman had clearly become a plague on his senses. And the sooner he rid himself of her, and her uncle's agency, the better. "I was only gone for a week. And besides that, I do not plan to bring my bride anywhere near Rydstrom Hall."

Fellows looked at him with confusion corrugating his brow as his hair swirled like morning mist in the wind. "Not at all, sir?"

"Of course not," he said with a growl of impatience. He'd already explained the reason, and he'd assumed Fellows had understood that bringing a bride home to Rydstrom Hall would be detrimental to Sybil. She was fragile and needed to be protected from the cruelties of the outside world.

Ignoring the frown he received from Fellows, Crispin sent Jones on to the stables. Once the carriage trundled out of the way, he shielded his eyes and gazed down the hill, briefly scanning the crescent-shaped village that hugged the rocky, cliff-lined coast for a sign of a coach that might have followed.

The absence of any carriages on the narrow lane between the tight clusters of thatched-roofed, chalk white cottages provided a modicum of relief. There were only a few horse carts and villagers on foot, tending to their routine tasks. And at the cliff's edge, fishermen were hauling up their boats—or *smacks*, as they called them—by rope and pulley to secure them from the swells of churning water below.

By all appearances, it was a typical day in Whitcrest.

Even so, he still could not shake a lingering sense of doom that the thought of Miss Jacinda Bourne stirred within him, warning him to be on his guard. Absently, he squeezed the back of his neck to ease the knot residing there.

"How long do you plan to stay, sir?"

"Not long. I only returned to sort out a . . . business matter." *And to ensure that my own carelessness hasn't put Sybil in danger of being exposed.*

As if in concurrence with his turbulent thoughts, from the corner of his eye, he caught sight of a frothy swell of waves, crashing against the jagged white cliffs. Even from a distance, the icy spindrifts reached him. The bellowing wind blew in like kite strings attached to the scarlet-hued clouds on the horizon.

"A red sky, sir," Fellows said from beside him. "We'll have company by nightfall, I imagine."

A shiver stole over Crispin. The villagers believed that fast, vicious squalls brought unexpected visitors.

"A mere superstition. That color of sky foretells a coming storm. Nothing more," Crispin said, his pragmatic mind rejecting the nonsense. Even so, he recalled witnessing a sky like this four years ago—the same day that Sybil had arrived.

But that was just a coincidence.

He knew there was a wholly different reason to feel a bone-deep coldness when looking at a sky like that—because violent storms often brought violent deaths. And he should know. His own parents had died in such a storm and on the very spot where the sea was rising to shake its fist at the sky.

It had been four years since Crispin had ventured to the cliff's edge. Four years since he'd seen his parents' broken bodies upon the rocks below. The memory still haunted him, and left him with a sense of guilt for which there was no remedy.

"If you say so, sir."

Crispin nodded, more to himself than to Fellows and turned toward the open doorway. He was here to guarantee there would be no irksome, interfering meddler poking around where she wasn't wanted. There was no remote possibility that he would ever allow Miss Jacinda Bourne admittance into Rydstrom H—

"Your Grace! Your Grace!"

Before Crispin could even finish his thought, a frantic voice hailed him in the distance. He turned to see Henry, Dr. Graham's errand boy, bounding up the path and waving his arms above his dark head as if he were directing a frigate through the reef.

"A woman, sir," Henry shouted, his voice breaking. "She washed up on the beach. Dr. Graham sent me here straightaway after he caught sight of your carriage."

A jolt tore through Crispin, his gaze automatically veering toward the cliff, where a band of violet-edged clouds now lined the red horizon. The last thing he wanted was to witness another broken body upon the rocks, but it was his responsibility to take care of matters in Whitcrest.

Not wasting time, Crispin met the boy on the path and started walking down the hill at a fine clip. "Is this woman alive?"

"Yes, sir. But Miss Beels wasn't sure at first. When she saw the body, there weren't no signs of life. She reckoned the woman was covered in blood, oozing out of her everywhere," Henry panted, his declaration carrying the excitement of one who was too young to have seen many catastrophes. When he continued, however, his tone listed downward in disappointment. "But then Miss Beels realized that the dark red was only the particular shade of the woman's hair."

Crispin missed a step, pebbles skittering down the hill from the toe of his boot. His entire body stiffened as that peculiar knot of tension returned to the base of his skull. "Did you say, dark *red* hair?"

"Yes, sir."

And suddenly, Crispin knew that Jacinda Bourne had found him after all.

Chapter 6

"... and with all her advantages, natural and domestic, she was now in great danger of suffering from intellectual solitude."

JANE AUSTEN, *Emma*

"Why can I not recall my own name?" she asked to no one in particular. At the moment, her only companion was the rock beneath her and the brackish blue sea rushing into the cove. Worse, because of the throbbing in her head, she didn't know how long she'd been here, or even how long she'd been wondering who she was.

She was certain—well, moderately certain—that she'd spoken to a woman moments ago. Unfortunately, amidst a confusing jumble of words swimming around in her head, the woman's name escaped her. Though she did remember a rather distinct mole on the woman's face. Surely that wasn't something one randomly conjured from imagination. Was it?

Growling in frustration, she closed her hands into fists hard enough to squeeze water from her gloves. Since they were doing nothing to warm her, she peeled off the garments, one after the other, and dropped them with soggy *splats* onto the rock.

The sight of her hands distracted her. The tops were pale and smooth with faint pathways of blue veins beneath the surface, her fingers long and slender, and her nails neatly rounded but bloated around the edges. Turning her hands over, her fingertips were puffy with white-edged whorled furrows, like shriveled, colorless currants. And all through her examination, she had the strangest sense that she'd never seen them before.

But that was ludicrous. They were her hands, after all. She couldn't have suddenly sprouted from this rock, drenched and nameless.

She must have a name, surely.

Yet her thoughts were in a frightful muddle. She couldn't seem to grasp hold of one for any length of time. Even now, she caught herself staring blankly at the lavender-gray clouds lumbering in the distance, their bodies so plump and swollen they nearly touched the waves, and looking as if they required a long rest upon the shore. Once they reached her, she sensed that they would flood the cove in a less than pleasant rain shower. And she did not particularly wish to be here when they arrived.

But where would she go?

Again, she had no answer. All she knew was that she should seek shelter, wherever she could.

Gradually, she slid her feet down to the sand, her boots sinking through the top soupy layer to the packed granules beneath. Legs wobbling, she splayed both hands on the rock to steady herself.

Just then, something shifted beneath her coat, slipping down her middle.

Clumsily, she tried to clutch the thing before it could fall. Though, for all she knew, it was a large, scaly sea creature with snapping claws and venomous tentacles—if such a monster existed—and yet she was more curious than alarmed by it.

The thing eluded her. Dropping too quickly, it landed, a sharp edge striking the top of her boot. She winced from the unexpected sting and glared down at the object.

Rectangular, damp and glossy, it was folded in layers of some type of cloth. *Not a sea creature, then.* Bending slowly, mindful of the fragile hold she had on her equilibrium, she picked up the object and placed it on the rock. The wrapping was smooth, the fabric oil slicked, and inside she discovered a book—a beautiful red leather volume, darkened around the corners.

Overwhelmed by a nameless urge, she flattened her palm over the cover, still slightly warm from the meager heat of her body.

Her heart tripped beneath her breast as if a sea bubble was trapped inside, and an inexplicable sense of certainty filled her. *This is my book.* Why else would she have kept it so secure?

Now, if only she could remember why.

But the effort caused renewed pain to explode at her temples and behind her eyes. She squeezed them shut. For the next few moments, even the dim, stormy light was too bright, the sound of the surf too loud.

Still, she refused to let go of the question. The answer was just out of reach, she was sure, and if she could keep her head from pounding, she might figure out everything. Concentrating, she tried harder. Then a wave of nausea gripped her as well, churning like the roaring waves behind her.

She swallowed and blinked several times to clear her vision until, gradually, the sensation ebbed. *Well, that didn't work*, she thought, annoyed by her own limitations.

She studied the book. If she couldn't find the answers inside her own head, then perhaps she could find them here.

Like her fingers, the edges of the paper were slightly bloated and rippled, creating a gradual rise from the spine to the block of cream-colored pages. Then, opening the book, she searched for clues.

As luck would have it, she found one. There was a name printed along the upper edge near the spine, in a row of neat block letters: JACINDA BOURNE.

Was that *her* name? Odd, but she did not possess the same sense of ownership over the name as she did the book. Then, turning a page, the title greeted her. *Emma.*

This time, a spark of recognition buzzed through her on pins and needles.

"Miss Emma Woodhouse," she whispered, the words caught by the wind. In that instant, she felt rooted to these pages and knew the story and each character by heart—better even than her own name. The title was like a friend offering a smile of comfort.

Closing the cover, she expelled a sigh of gratitude for this one familiarity, drew the book to her breast, and embraced it. Hope was not lost, after all.

Still, larger questions plagued her. Who gave it to her? Why were her own hands, hair, and clothes unfamiliar? Why was she here? And where exactly was . . . *here*?

She thoroughly despised the mystery of it all and needed to uncover it as soon as possible.

As she was fretting over this, a pair of voices drifted to her. With a glance over her shoulder, she saw two people descending a narrow winding footpath through the tufts of grasses and scattered rocks over the rise, beside the chalk white cliffs. Walking toward her were one pale-haired man, one black-shrouded woman, and one small white dog.

The mole-woman! What a relief that she hadn't imagined her. This was cause for celebration. Though it was short-lived because, in the very next instant, she realized she still couldn't dredge the mole-woman's actual name out from the seawater in her own head.

It appeared that this leather tome was the only thing she knew at all.

But not for long, she thought, determined to start remembering everything from this point forward. Then, as if to mock her, another stabbing pain sliced through her brain at the temples.

Frustrated, she gripped the book harder. Not wanting to shut her eyes—for fear of the man and mole-woman disappearing—she bit down on her lip to fight the pain and focused on their approach.

Mole-woman's mouth was a blur of movement, the constant sound of her high-pitched drawl mingling indiscernibly with the gathering wind. Beside her, the gentleman nodded occasionally in response.

Leaning heavily upon a cane, he was dressed in nutshell brown from his coat to his trousers. While his clothes were plain, they were not bedraggled like the mole-woman's were. His coat fitted him squarely, clearly tailored, but with a mismatched button that told her it was not new, but well-tended.

His blondish white hair and mustachios were speckled like seafoam with shades of sandy brown and boulder black. And behind a pair of half-moon spectacles his eyes were small circles of dark, inquisitive blue, the corners marked by a spray of deep wrinkles. He was no more than forty-five or even fifty, she thought, noting that his overall frame was still straight. There was no paunch about his middle either, which indicated that he moved around quite a bit. Though, with that leg of his, he surely wasn't a laborer but had another profession . . .

She stopped, wondering why her thoughts had brought her to such a conclusion. Strange. It was almost as if she were cataloguing him. But for what purpose?

Yet before she could summon a reason, she caught sight of two others joining their party, coming into view just over the rise.

One was only a boy with a mop of tousled dark hair. The other was an imposing man, looking positively thunderous in a slate gray coat with a caped edge that accentuated the impossible breadth of his shoulders. His stride was crisp and exact, his hands fisted at his sides. Waves of thick brown and golden hair whipped in the wind as if he were the creator of it. Accentuated by a growth of whiskers, the set of his jaw seemed comprised of the same rock that littered the beach. And while she couldn't see the color of his eyes, she noticed that they flashed and crackled in time with the approaching storm.

More than that, she saw that they were focused solely on her.

She felt a peculiar static charge rise within her, taking the air from her lungs.

He stopped a few paces from her, never looking away even as the pale-haired man approached him. The two men exchanged a few words, and then, with a nod between them, the older man turned to her, advancing slowly, the tip of his cane sinking into the sand.

"My name is Dr. Graham," he said, offering a kind smile.

A weighted pause followed his declaration. If he was introducing himself, she quickly concluded that he did not know her. Yet as she opened her mouth to reply with her own name, the one she'd found just moments ago, she'd already forgotten it.

A cold wash of worry made her shiver. "I'm pleased to make your acquaintance. My name is"—slyly, she peeked inside the cover—"Jacinda Bourne."

The doctor glanced down at the book, too, his mustachios pulling down as he pursed his lips. "Were you unsure of it, just now?"

Though she wasn't certain why, her first inclination was complete denial.

"Of course I would know my own name." Her gaze flitted to the tall, forbidding gentleman. Instinctively, she felt as if admitting to any shortcoming in front of him would put her at a disadvantage. "It only slipped away for a moment because of this headache, you see."

"Mmm . . . yes," he mused. "It appears as though you've taken a spill, Miss Bourne. May I?"

Then, without introducing her to the tall gentleman or even the boy, the doctor laid his cane against the rock with care. It did not escape her notice that no one came forth with a ready embrace, a smile in greeting, or even a question regarding how her clothes came to be wet. Clearly, no one knew her.

Her identity and the reason she awoke here were still just as much a mystery as before.

Chilled by a keen sense of isolation and loneliness, her gaze strayed to the tall gentleman and found him staring at her expectantly. She wished she knew the reason.

The doctor stepped in front of her, regaining her attention when he pointed to the side of her head that was in pain as if he meant to touch it. She eyed him with speculation, not knowing if whatever he planned to do would hurt. Yet, after a moment of consideration, she nodded, allowing him to lift her hair out of the way.

During his brief examination, she focused on the tall gentleman. He watched the doctor turn her head this way and that, while probing the area surrounding her temple. She noted the alterations in his expression and kept searching his face for something familiar. And there was *something*, she thought, but couldn't quite place it.

"Now, if it wouldn't be too much trouble," the doctor continued, "could you tell me how many fingers I'm holding up?"

She glanced at the hand he held in front of his chest and wished he would have asked a more difficult question. Perhaps if he asked her the things she couldn't readily put to mind, it would serve as a prompt, calling forth her immediate, unthinking response. "Three."

"Very good. And how many am I holding up now?"

Disappointed, she bit back a sigh. He was asking her simple questions as if she were a child, and she could clearly see from the shape of her own figure that she was not. "Four, and if you add them together that makes seven. But I'm afraid mathematics is not my current concern."

"And what would you say is?"

She hugged her book to her breast, closed her eyes in humiliation, and lowered her voice. "My thoughts are in something of a muddle. You see, I seem to be having a bit of trouble with . . ."

"Your memory?"

Her eyes snapped open and she looked at the wisdom etched in the knowing lift of his white brows, as if he'd suspected the answer all along. "Yes," she breathed.

He offered a sage nod. "Do you remember who I am?"

"Well, of course, it was only a moment ago that we met, after all. You're the doctor," she said with utmost confidence.

"And my name?"

She opened her mouth and—*drat*! It had slipped away already, falling into one of the sneaky spaces between her brain and her tongue. Likely, the same place her own name had gone. It was as if everyone were wearing a blank schoolroom slate board around their necks and it was up to her to mark them correctly. Though, even if she had a piece of chalk, she doubted she'd have been successful.

"Dr. Graham," he supplied with a placating pat to her shoulder.

"My apologies, Dr. Graham. I'm certain it would have come to me . . . eventually." But she wasn't certain at all, and felt the prickle of frustrated tears at the corners of her eyes. Panic was beginning to set in as well. What if she never remembered?

Curling her fingers around the book, she repeated her own name silently. *Jacinda Bourne. I am Jacinda Bourne.* She glanced down to her left hand and—finding it without a ring—surmised that she was in fact, *Miss* Jacinda Bourne. Thankfully, she hadn't forgotten a husband as well. At least, she didn't think she had.

"Here, my dear." The doctor handed her a folded white handkerchief with a letter *G* embroidered on the corner. G *for Graham*, she thought, feeling a trifle steadier.

"Thank you," she said, hastily ducking her head and dabbing away the moisture. Which was silly, she supposed, when her entire person was wet, her hair plastered to her cheeks in soggy strips.

"I know you are frightened, Miss Bourne," the doctor said, soothingly. "But if there is anything you might remember—even something seemingly small and insignificant—we might discover more about how you came to be here."

She wanted the answer more than she could imagine wanting anything else. "All I know is that I awoke here upon this rock, at which point I met . . ." Jacinda hesitated with a glance toward mole-woman who smiled at her with encouragement. Inwardly she cringed, feeling dreadful for having assigned such an ugly moniker to one of her only acquaintances.

"Miss Beels, dear," the woman supplied, pressing a hand over her black-shrouded bosom. A low *woof!* came from the bowlegged white dog. "And don't forget Mr. Lemon."

Jacinda nodded with gratitude, the pair of them grinning in return. "Yes, of course. Then I met you, Dr."—again, her mouth opened and nothing came out for a second or two, until she remembered the *G* on the handkerchief, and then his name came out in a triumphant breath—"Dr. Graham. However, I'm afraid I do not know the other two gentlemen."

"That is my fault. I withheld an introduction in an effort to avoid any potential . . . confusion."

The boy quickly stepped forward, offering a regal bow with a wide sweep of his arm. "Henry Valentine, your humble servant, my lady."

She felt her mouth quirk into a grin, thoroughly charmed. "Pleased to make your acquaintance, Mr. Valentine."

"Not yet, Henry," the doctor chided, before he returned his attention to her. "And where did you find your book, Miss Bourne?"

She pressed a hand to her midriff, but quickly withdrew it when she saw the tall gentleman's gaze follow her gesture. And with that one glance, her stomach turned several disconcerting Catherine wheels.

Feeling somewhat shy, she averted her gaze and focused solely on the doctor. "Apparently, it was on my person. The moment I stood, it slipped out from beneath my redingote, wrapped in that." She pointed to the oil-slicked fabric lying beside her gloves. "I must have been worried that it would become wet."

The doctor pursed his lips. "Clearly, you care for it a great deal to want it with you in your travels, and to protect it so securely."

"I had come to that conclusion as well." Obviously, the book was important to her. But why?

"Then perhaps there is another clue we might discover within its pages."

His logic made perfect sense. Quickly, she held the book before her and opened the cover once more. Kindled with a fresh sense of hope and determination, she traced the title with her ruched fingertips. Then carefully, she turned one page and then another, until she spotted a card.

Even though the bone white rectangle appeared blank from its current position tucked into the stitching margin, she had no doubt that the other side would reveal a name. From what little she knew of herself, she already believed she did things with intent and purpose.

"May I?" Dr. Graham asked.

Breath caught in her throat, she nodded, her hands and arms trembling with excitement. And, perhaps, a bit of trepidation as well.

Behind her, the storm was brewing ever closer. The chill wind at her back suddenly turned fiercer, whipping her skirts hard against her legs like a sail against the mast of a ship. She stiffened to brace herself against it, ignoring the keen aches along her spine, hips, and torso.

He picked up the card and turned it over. "This is very interesting, indeed."

"What is?"

Instead of answering directly, the doctor handed her the card.

Somewhat confused by the keen glint above the rim of

his half-moon spectacles, she read it aloud. *"Crispin Montague, fifth Duke of Rydstrom."*

Her voice must have carried because, just beyond the doctor's shoulder, she saw the tall gentleman stiffen, his shoulders arrow straight. His thick brows lost their subtle arch and flattened into an intractable ridge. Then after a moment, twin furrows lined the bridge of his nose in apparent irritation, and all of it seemingly directed at her.

"That's you, isn't it?" Jacinda asked, seeing the accusation hit the mark in the way he flinched. Which meant they must be acquainted. After all, why else would she have his card? And why would she be in a place where no one knew her?

She heard Miss Beels gasp and Jacinda's gaze flitted to her long enough to take note of the dreamy smile that lifted the mole on her cheek, her hand splayed over her heart.

Quite unexpectedly, as if some of the seawater between her ears had drained away, she recalled the things Miss Beels had mentioned earlier. The words became so clear, they might have been having the conversation this instant.

Yours is some of the finest embroidery I've seen since Whitcrest had a duchess in Rydstrom Hall. You must be an important lady.

. . . Everyone in the village is talking about the rumors that His Grace plans to marry.

Suddenly everything made perfect sense. "Am I to be your wife?"

Chapter 7

> "Men of sense, whatever you may chuse to say, do not want silly wives."
>
> Jane Austen, *Emma*

Wife?

Jacinda Bourne's question stunned Crispin into speechlessness.

All of his fears were coming true. His most recent nightmare had arrived in Whitcrest, just steps away from Rydstrom Hall.

Though she looked less like a bogeyman and more like a wounded sea nymph washed up on the beach, her hair spilling down her shoulders in dark red ropes, and an angry red wound near her temple. The sight of it caused a surprising jolt of tenderness to rush through him.

Clearly, he was reeling from finding her here and wasn't thinking straight.

"No, Miss Bourne. We are not betrothed." The notion was absurd. Would he marry the one woman who'd single-handedly set out to annihilate any semblance of peace that he might have possessed a mere week ago? Never.

She frowned, the corners of her mouth canting downward and drawing attention to the unnatural paleness of her lips. "But we are acquainted, are we not? There could be no other reason that I would have your card."

Oh, he could think of one: thievery. She must have stolen

it from him when she'd trespassed in his study. *Meddlesome bit of baggage.*

"The reason is simple," he answered succinctly. "I've had dealings with your uncle."

Her brow knitted together as she silently mouthed the word *uncle*. "So you and I have met."

"Briefly, yes."

"And you know a few things about me, like where I live and the fact that I have an uncle."

Those light turquoise eyes fixed on him with such beseeching hope that he had the urge to tell her all he knew. It was as if she cast a spell on him, one meant to unlock every secret he kept.

Unsettling, to say the least.

Dr. Graham cleared his throat. "Forgive me, Rydstrom, but I do not believe this conversation will benefit Miss Bourne. By telling her too much at this point, she may develop false memories."

"I do not see the harm in that," Miss Bourne said with near-breathless eagerness. "Once my true memories return, everything will sort itself out."

"In my experience, it isn't that simple." Graham's frown softened with empathy, and yet concern was still etched in his features. "You see, I've spent years working with soldiers who developed amnesia after a battle. The worst thing that could happen is to offer up information too readily, as it prohibits the patient from finding their own answers and thereby healing the wounded portion of the brain."

Contemplating this, Crispin nodded. It made sense that she would require time to recuperate. And once she returned to the bosom of her family, they would tend to her needs. Perhaps, by the time she reached London, she wouldn't remember ever being in Whitcrest at all.

Instantly, he saw this working to his advantage. "Then I will simply order a carriage to send her back to—"

"I'm afraid I cannot recommend travel of any extent,"

Graham said, interrupting once more, his statement punctuated by a crack of thunder as the storm began to close in on a sudden blast of cold wind.

They all glanced out to sea. Dark clouds now eclipsed the horizon, and a thick gray curtain of rain approached, undulating in the direction of the wind. Typically, storms did not earn a great measure of surprise among the residents. Inclement weather was factored into the hardships of living on such a brutal stretch of sea where the waves often crashed together from opposite directions. One had to be prepared for disaster in order to survive here. Yet this storm was blowing in fast, leaving little time to prepare for the worst.

Dr. Graham turned to face Crispin, his intentions marked clearly in the lines of his countenance. "There's only time enough to make Rydstrom Hall, *if* we make haste."

An icy shiver sliced through the marrow of Crispin's bones. He didn't want anyone to enter Rydstrom Hall, least of all Miss Bourne. Surely, there had to be another way.

His gaze quickly surveyed the footpath to the village. Clusters of winter brown grasses bowed, nearly lying flat against the ground. Waves rose, pummeling the rocks and sweeping over their upper edges. That way was too treacherous, and he couldn't, in good conscience, force them to travel it. But there was no other way out of this cove. The doctor was right; the sensible route was up the hill, heading away from the storm.

Left with no other choice, Crispin offered a curt nod. "Very well."

He would simply confine his guests to the entry hall and main parlor, and send word to Mrs. Hemple to keep Sybil on the upper floors. This group would wait out the storm while he decided where to put Miss Bourne. "Henry, run up ahead and warn Fellows to make ready . . ."

While he continued his instructions, he caught sight of Miss Bourne bending toward the rock, hurriedly wrapping the cloth around her book, and then gathering the wet gloves that had blown onto the sand. Yet when she righted herself, she swayed on her feet.

Reflexively, Crispin took a step toward her, his orders cutting off midsentence. But Dr. Graham was beside her first. He took hold of his cane with one hand, and offered her his free arm. Though, clearly, there was no way that Graham and Miss Bourne would be able to assist each other. Distracted, he sent Henry on his way, certain Fellows would see to the matter.

Prepared to do what had to be done, Crispin moved toward Graham and Miss Bourne, only to have Miss Beels step in front of him, hold up a finger, and give him a wink before turning to face the others.

Confused, it took a second before he understood the reason. And by then it was too late.

"Dr. Graham," Miss Beels shouted over the roar of the wind, her dog huddled near her skirts. "I wonder if I could bend your ear a bit longer. You see, Mr. Lemon had a terrible cough this morning and I'm almost certain that he's been nibbling on Mr. Craig's fish net again. If he has a bone lodged in his throat, I don't know what I would do."

Miss Bourne, who had just laid her hand upon the doctor's arm, abruptly withdrew it. "I'm certain I can manage. I'm feeling much steadier now."

Before the doctor could argue, Miss Beels hooked her arm through his and walked toward the path, chattering away and pausing only to cast another wink in Crispin's direction, as if she'd arranged for him to walk alone with Miss Bourne.

Bollocks. The last thing he needed was to have the village featherbrain telling presumptuous stories to his servants or the villagers and believing herself to be a matchmaker. He already knew one too many of those.

Exhaling his frustration, Crispin strode through the sand to Miss Bourne's side and offered his arm. "If I may."

"You needn't trouble yourself," she said with a lift of her

pert chin, her eyes reflecting a flash of lightning. A warning growl of thunder followed, foretelling the near arrival of the storm. "Contrary to what you might believe of my injuries, my vision is healthy, and I can see your reluctance quite clearly."

Not having time or patience to deal with a feminine snit, Crispin clenched his teeth. "My only concern at present is to leave this beach and seek shelter before either one of us is struck by lightning. And since I am the taller of us, no doubt the bolt would find me. Now, if you would give me your arm."

"I don't think I shall. I'm perfectly capable of walking unassisted."

She busied herself with tucking the cloth wrapping around her book, the tip of her ear peeking out from beneath a curtain of wavy burnished hair. His fingers twitched with the unmistakable desire to tuck those loose locks out of the way so that he could see the delicate half-heart shape of it.

He grew irritated, betrayed by the unwelcome urges of his mind and body. "And I am perfectly capable of tossing you over my shoulder like a coil of fisherman's rope."

Her gaze whipped up to meet his. "What a brutish thing to say, especially to one you found in such a helpless state."

"Miss Bourne," he began, his voice low and deceptively calm. "I believe I can say this with utmost confidence—there isn't an ounce of helplessness in you. Certain types of people are determined to survive no matter what odds they face. In fact, I suspect that the sea was tired of fighting against you and simply tossed you onto the shore as a means of self-preservation."

The hard patter of rain upon the water and the bellow of the wind through the crags muted her responding huff of indignation. He knew from experience that storms like this could bring slabs of the cliff face down upon their heads and send rocks tumbling toward them.

Crispin didn't want to take that chance.

There was no more time to argue. Therefore, without

making another request, he simply bent down, swept Miss Bourne into his arms, and made his way toward the hill.

JACINDA GASPED as her feet left the ground, the wet sand nearly claiming her boots. Her head spun from the suddenness of his movements. "Put me down at once!"

"Be thankful that I did not toss you over my shoulder."

Frankly, she wasn't sure if this was better . . . or worse. He was holding her with one arm beneath her knees and the other at the middle of her back, his hand curled over her rib cage, a scant few inches from the bottom curve of her breast. She became increasingly aware of the heat of his hand, and the way it sifted through the heavy layers of her clothes.

In contrast, her own flesh felt much cooler, drawing uncomfortably tight. Even her heart reacted strangely, beating out a hard, erratic rhythm, as if she were the one carrying him. It made her breathless and so exhausted that part of her wanted to relax into his warmth, permitting him this small victory.

Yet if she gave in to that urge, she sensed that she would lose a bigger battle in the end. She had no choice but to fight it.

He cast a quick glower down at her. "Stop squirming and have a care for your injuries. I can see how much you are pained each time you wince. It's likely that you wouldn't have made the first rise without fainting and would have required my assistance regardless."

"You know nothing of the sort." Book in hand, she pushed against his hard chest, and instantly felt a corresponding twinge in her side. She fought to keep her features neutral, but by his growl and headshake, she must have given something away. "Your quick strides are hardly helping the situation."

Being carried in such a manner felt awkward. The tangle of her sodden redingote around her legs made them of little use, and she didn't know what to do with her arms and elbows. At least, not until he turned swiftly past an outcropping of rocks.

A rush of dizziness swept over her, forcing her to hold on to him. The thick muscles beneath her hand felt as solid and unforgiving as stone. Had she first thought that the layered cape offered the mere *illusion* of broad shoulders? Oh, how very wrong she was.

Then again, perhaps this was merely clever padding and she should investigate further . . .

"Please, Miss Bourne," he said, making her jolt with guilt and a bit of embarrassment. Yet, when he continued, she realized he wasn't chiding her for having inquisitive fingers, but for something else. "You must not tax yourself by fumbling over endless words of gratitude for my assistance. I'm sure you would have been content to linger upon that rock for days on end."

Jacinda bristled at his mocking tone. Once again, she stiffened in his arms to gain some sort of barrier between them. "Appreciation to a man who has made it abundantly clear that every one of his actions is done under extreme duress? Ha. I suspect that you would have liked nothing more than to leave me on the beach and forget you ever saw me."

He grunted in response but did not deny the claim. Then he pulled her closer as he leaned into a steep portion of the hill, rendering all of her efforts of separation ineffective.

Impossibly, he showed no signs of strain, as if he were carrying nothing more than an empty basket in front of him as he climbed. Since there was certainly no padding to his shoulders, there likely wasn't any in the firmness of his torso either. Fortunately, this time, she managed to resist squeezing him to be certain. She would give him the benefit of the doubt. Which was far more than he had given her during this brief exchange.

Scrutinizing his features from this intimate distance, she

looked for clues, hoping to spark a memory of how they came to be acquainted. Right off, she noticed that the flesh around his eyes appeared dark, shadowed, and tinged purple as if he had not slept. There was also a substantial growth of cinnamon-colored whiskers along his cheeks and jaw, just above the rumpled edge of his cravat.

"Wouldn't a gentleman shave *before* donning a cravat?" she asked, wondering if perhaps she might recall seeing his face once she could, in fact, see it.

He slid her a wary glance. "Usually, I am not called to the beach to rescue an injured woman at such an early hour."

Would he have her believe that he took time to tie a cravat as he rushed out the door? It seemed unlikely, for the garment was decidedly flat and wrinkled. To her, it was more plausible that he'd only just arrived home—and possibly from a night of carousing—when he'd learned the news of her. "Were you traveling last night?"

He glanced down at her, his furrowed brow revealing a jagged vein on his forehead. "Surely you have other thoughts to occupy your mind at present."

Hmm . . . She must have touched on a nerve.

Curiosity rose within her in a storm of tingles. They felt like small, prickling alarms of awareness that told her, *There is a mystery here that needs to be uncovered.*

"A goodly many, indeed," she said, watching him closely, her fingertips burrowing beneath the flaps of his cape to the edge of his shoulder. But only for a surer grip, of course. "Yet since I only have memories enough to fill the past half hour of my life, I am trying to stitch them all together to form a more cohesive pattern. But there are pieces that do not fit.

"For example," she continued, "you were all politeness to the doctor and Miss Beels, and yet quick-tempered with me. I find that quite suspicious, especially when—as you say—we have no long-standing acquaintance."

It was only after she spoke that she realized the remark

did her no favors. Nevertheless, the man clearly detested her, *and* had from the very first moment he'd seen her upon the beach.

He kept his gaze straight ahead, but the muscle along his jaw twitched. "We have not met above two times."

"Only twice? Come now." She tsked. He must take her for a fool. "How am I to believe that I have earned your ire in so few encounters?"

"Perhaps you have an innate talent for it. Or perhaps my terseness has caused you to form an incorrect assumption. Needless to say, these are not the best of circumstances for either of us."

An evasive answer, if ever there was one. "If what you say is true, then I am not to blame for your irritability, and yet you offer no concrete explanation or even a gentlemanly apology for your rudeness toward me."

"I never apologize, Miss Bourne," he said, his eyes a cold pine-bough-in-winter hazel. "And I suspect that is the one thing we have in common."

His expression closed off once more as he focused on the path, leaving her to mull over his statement. What could she have done—and in only *two* instances—to necessitate her apology to him?

She wasn't surprised when a ready answer did not come forth. Though, it was rather arrogant of him to speak with such certainty of her character if they were hardly acquainted.

Just when Jacinda managed to keep her thoughts together, the pain in her head suddenly returned, full force. Briefly, she closed her eyes and gave in to the comfort his steady cadence provided.

"It isn't far now," he said, his gruff tone edged with a trace of gentleness.

She didn't know what to make of him. Irritability and petulance notwithstanding, he had something of a sympathetic heart. After all, he could have left her on the beach, or even waited until she fainted *before* assisting her up the winding path. Therefore, it seemed a reasonable assumption that he was compassionate to anyone who showed signs of frailty.

Hmm . . . Perhaps even enough to take pity on her and divulge more information?

Jacinda wondered if she should feel guilty for the quick turn of her thoughts to manipulation. She didn't, of course. Not even a little bit. In fact, she felt compelled to stop at nothing to satisfy her curiosity.

Musing over this, she glanced forward. A dozen paces ahead of them, the doctor leaned heavily on his cane while Miss Beels bobbed her head in apparent conversation. And further, beyond a copse of spindly, battered yews, she caught a glimpse of a pair of white stone towers topped with toothlike crenellations that all but disappeared into a thick shroud of gray clouds.

Rydstrom Hall, she presumed before another turn made it impossible to see more. Though surely such a forbidding and romantic set of towers would have been permanently stamped upon her memory, had she ever seen it. And yet, none of it was familiar to her.

Jacinda was already fed up with not knowing who she was, why the duke despised her, or why she was here. If she could just uncover the answer to one of those, she was certain the rest would fall into place.

Feeling that it was her only course of action, she tucked her chin slightly toward her chest and lifted her eyes in an effort to appear shaken and defenseless, instead of single-mindedly plotting to suit her own purpose. Then, as if she might have scripted it herself, a blast of cold wind blew, causing a perfectly natural shiver to bore through her—though she might have dramatized the sensation with a quivering chin for effect. "I don't know what I would have done without your assistance. My only wish is that I'd made a better impression on you when we met previously."

A crack of thunder accompanied the dark, skeptical look he gave her. Another gust of wind lifted the flaps from his shoulders to press against the back of his head as the first icy sprinkles of rain fell upon them. "You would do well to give up your coquettish manipulations. They'll only serve to prolong my ill temper."

Humph. She narrowed her eyes and wrinkled her nose at him, her hand tightening around the spine of her book. Drat that man! Sympathetic heart? Apparently not where she was concerned.

"For all I know this foul mood is your permanent state." Then, because she felt like it, she used the front of his coat to wipe away the droplets from her face.

In the same instant, she caught a fragrance that seemed to spark a memory . . . perhaps. She wasn't certain. All she knew was that a warm tremor raced through her, tunneling deep in her midriff.

The aroma was pleasantly disarming—sweet, earthy, and with a subtle base of something darker, bolder—like a blend of cedar and cloves. She gasped in wonder that she even knew what those things were. And even though she couldn't see this *memory*, she felt as if it were just out of reach.

She tried to angle closer to capture it. Then, as luck would have it, the storm broke over them in a hard clash of rain, thunder, and wind. The duke expelled an oath, hitched her higher in his arms, and started to run.

She was forced to hold on tighter, too, but this time she did not mind. With the book secure between them, she unabashedly slid both arms around his shoulders, and curled into him. And with his head bent to shield them, her face naturally nestled into his cravat.

This close, she could hear him breathe, hard and swift, the air rushing in and out, matching the rhythm of his hurried steps. The firm press of his chest, rising and falling, made her aware of how her own flesh yielded to his, rocking against him, her breasts pliant and yet taut. Tantalizing waves of heat rose from him, practically inviting her to burrow closer.

And she did, settling deeper into the crook of his neck. With her eyes closed, she drew in another breath, no longer feeling the cold around her.

"Miss Bourne." His voice was a hoarse, brusque growl, his shoulders stiffening beneath her hands.

Jacinda was so completely focused on seizing the elusive memory—or whatever it was—that she didn't realize he'd stopped. Her brain gave every indication that they were still moving together. She could feel her stomach sway with it, pulsing.

Somewhat dazed, she lifted her head from his neck, her face near enough to see the rim of russet striations surrounding his enlarged black pupils. She could even feel the heat of his breath against her lips.

Her lids grew unexpectedly heavy and her gaze dropped to his mouth. "Yes?"

His own gaze dipped lower and he swallowed. "Are you able to stand?"

Able to, yes. Wanting to? Not entirely.

She licked her lips. "Of course. I told you all along that I was capable of"—she stopped short when he quickly lowered her feet to the floor—"fending for myself."

A door closed behind her with a heavy *thunk*. The corresponding, booming echo startled her and she was thankful to still be pressed against his side, his warm, solid body providing a measure of comfort.

It was only now that she realized they were indoors, the deafening patter of rain muffled. Glancing behind him, she saw a wide, recessed stone archway filled with an immense oak door, complete with iron braces. Together they stood in a snug, unadorned entry hall made of smooth blocks of white stone, but void of rugs or windows.

Directly ahead, a brace of flaming torches hung on either

side of another thick door. The opening revealed a larger, longer hall with high stone walls lined with shuttered window casings and arched alcoves that gave a sense of having been part of this land since the day the earth was formed.

Further into the room, there were ancient rugs and tapestries aplenty, and a fire burning in a great hearth. A genuine medieval castle, by the look of it. Jacinda nearly laughed because, for some strange reason, it suited the duke perfectly.

Then, an amusing notion crossed her mind that the irritable duke planned to keep her in a dungeon.

She was about to make a jest and ask him that very thing when an older man in a blue coat with brass buttons emerged from the shadowed vestibule. The soles of his shoes clapped smartly on the flagstone as he stepped around them to address the duke. When he bowed, the flickering light from a nearby wall sconce illuminated a ring of wispy gray hair that surrounded his baldpate.

"Your Grace, the guests are in the juniper parlor." Though he did not smile, he gave a sense of contentment in the way he drew in a deep breath that puffed out his chest.

Abruptly, the duke removed his arm from Jacinda's side, then frowned at the way her hand lingered on his shoulder. "Miss Bourne, if you have recovered . . ."

She should probably feel guilty for clinging to him. Even with a misplaced memory, she realized that it likely wasn't appropriate. Reluctantly, she lowered her arm. He took an immediate step apart from her, leaving her cold and half tempted to pretend to swoon just to have his arms around her again. But then she thought better of it. Best to save a fainting spell for when she needed it most.

"Now then, Fellows," the duke began. Walking through the broad doorway, he shrugged out of his coat and handed it to the butler. "Where is Mrs. Hemple? Still breakfasting?"

Jacinda followed him and, seeing his actions, decided to remove her wet redingote as well. Though, needing both her hands, she handed over the wrapped book to the duke, muttering, "Hold this, please. Thank you."

"No, sir. Mrs. Hemple is"—the butler paused, surprise in the lift of his wiry brows as his gaze darted between Jacinda and the duke, before clearing his throat—"seeing to matters within the keep. Consequently, after young Henry's announcement, I've taken the liberty of securing a guest chamber for Miss Bourne."

The duke frowned down at the book in his hand as if he didn't know why he was holding it, and then gave it to Fellows. But, of course, this left him with the only free hands to assist her out of her coat.

She presented her back to him. "If you would be so kind . . ."

A low growl rumbled out of the duke, but he set his warm hands on her shoulders, nonetheless. At least, briefly. Then, in a single, fluid movement, he peeled off the wet outer garment, turning the sleeves inside out along the way. Then he handed it to Fellows, who in turn handed Jacinda her book, humor glinting in his cloudy gray eyes.

Clutching *Emma*, she grinned even as a shiver passed through her, nearly making her teeth chatter. "We're quite good at this roundabout, aren't we, Mr. Fellows?"

"Indeed, miss."

Then, abruptly, the duke muttered an indecipherable oath beneath his breath, snatched his own coat away from the butler's arm, and settled it over her shoulders.

The heavy weight of it was startling as much as the warmth was soothing. She wanted to be aggravated at the duke, but she couldn't, not when the fragrance of sweet, warm cedar enveloped her, eliciting that same flutter of familiarity that burrowed deep into the pit of her stomach. Now she wanted to curl inside his coat and live there.

It wasn't until she glanced down to ensure her book was safely out of the way when she saw the likely reason for his actions. Even through the barrier of her burgundy wool dress, the hard, pebbled state of her nipples was blatantly evident. And at last, she felt a heat of her own making spread through her.

Though, in her own defense, the cut of the gown revealed nothing else scandalous. To her, it appeared modestly cut, skimming down her slender waist and the slight curve of her hips. All the same, she tugged the lapels of his greatcoat closer, the bottom of the garment dragging on the floor.

She lifted her gaze to thank him, but only saw his profile and the muscle ticking in the hard line of his jaw.

"Miss Bourne will only be staying until the storm passes," he said to Fellows. The clipped precision of the words left no doubt that she was unwelcome.

Truth be told, she already knew this. Yet that didn't stop the unexpected wave of loneliness that washed over her. She had no friends here in Rydstrom Hall, and no memory of others anywhere else.

Not exactly a warm and comforting realization.

"Yes, of course, sir," Fellows replied, disapproval marked in the hard line of his thin, colorless lips. He cast a kindly glance toward Jacinda. "Given the circumstances of her injuries, Dr. Graham suggested a quiet room for the duration. I thought the tower would be best."

The notion of a dungeon returned to her. Only this time it wasn't amusing.

She offered a patently false grin to the duke's inscrutable profile. "If it would make you feel better, I'll take a room that comes complete with iron bars on the window and a wooden beam across the outer door."

"You have just described the gull chamber in the lower tower. But we only use that for prisoners," the duke said, turning to her briefly, his expression impassive. Then he directed his attention to the butler. "Fellows, what room have you prepared?"

Fellows expelled an audible exhale. "The gull chamber, sir."

The duke slid her a glance, offering a highly unsympathetic shrug and a subtle lift of his brows. Then he gestured forward with a casual sweep of his hand. "Right this way, Miss Bourne, *if* you are able."

"Of course I am." Her first few steps down the hall were a trifle unsteady, however. Part of the reason was due to her exhaustion. The rest stemmed from the weight of his coat and her garments, and the squish of her boots. Something slithered down her calf as well. She was fairly certain that it was not a wayward sea creature, but she surreptitiously shook her leg just in case. This caused her echoed steps to falter out of rhythm and slow.

The duke didn't seem to notice. He simply forged ahead like a man on a mission to be rid of her as soon as possible.

Fueled by irritation, she quickened her pace on the flagstones, passing another arched alcove, and pressing her free hand to the hitch in her side. Then, finally, she caught up with him, reaching a narrow corridor.

Entering this dimly lit nook, she saw a set of curved stairs, illuminated by a meager light from some mysterious place above. However, when he walked ahead of her, his shoulders blocked out nearly all of it. And with no handrail to aid her, she did her best to keep her wrapped book and a gather of wet garments in one hand, while the other pressed against the inner curve of the cold, pitted wall.

She was out of breath after a dozen steps. "How kind of you . . . to trust my . . . motility when it is most convenient . . . for you."

He did not spare her a backward glance, and his footfalls never halted. "Now that we are no longer at risk of being struck by lightning, I merely imagine you are eager to prove yourself. You seemed quite determined to do so earlier."

"No more determined than you were . . . to find a reason to keep all of us from Rydstrom Hall. I saw the . . . calculated look you gave to the path leading to, I presume, the village."

He did not answer. In fact, he gave no indication that he was listening to her.

Since the timetable of her entire life was so small, she couldn't help but focus on every bit of it, weighing each word, smile and rebuff with the same gravity. "Then again . . . I also recall how your countenance darkened when I asked if I was to be . . . your wife. So, perhaps that is at the crux of your irritability."

Still he said nothing, but his measured footfall faltered slightly, skidding on one of the stairs.

Hmm.

"If you are so worried that I have marital designs on you, then I am surprised you are escorting me yourself, instead of asking a servant," she said, sarcasm dripping from every panted syllable. "After all, who knows what types of ideas I'm likely to entertain when I'm alone with you."

After climbing another dozen steps, or more, he finally stopped. "A gentleman need only be concerned if he is either tempted or caught in a compromising position. Rest assured, in this circumstance, neither is the case."

Jacinda winced. The feminine ego, which she didn't even know she possessed until this instant, took a direct blow. Not only did he find her character repellant, but he clearly found her unattractive as well.

It was silly to feel hurt by this, especially since she knew she was a frightful mess with wet clothes, soggy boots, tangled red hair, and a wound on her head. In fact, she didn't even know what she looked like. For all she knew she had crossed eyes, a hooked nose, and . . . *Dear heavens!* She didn't have an unsightly mole, too, did she?

She felt her shoulders slump forward as she trudged up the last few steps to where he waited on a small landing. Now she didn't even want to look in his direction. But with the torch burning brightly beside him, she couldn't help stealing a glance. Thankfully, he wasn't paying attention to her—and why should he if she was a troll—but was unlocking a slender wooden door with a large iron key. Then he slipped the key into the pocket of his green coat.

Alarm quickly overrode concern for her vanity. "Are you truly putting me in a dungeon?"

His pitiless gaze fell on her, the corner of his mouth twitched ever so slightly. Was he going to smirk at her? But no, he did not. Instead, there was just the ghost of one lingering. "As much as I would like to, no. The iron bars on the window and the beam across the door were removed decades ago."

Annoyed, her spine went rigid. "Were you teasing me earlier or trying to frighten me?"

His only answer was the subtle lift of his brow, as if stating he would leave that for her to decide.

She turned her head with a snap, ready to rail at him for putting her in a cell. Though, much to her surprise, a snug rounded room greeted her.

There was little space for any furniture aside from a spindled washstand and a narrow bed swathed in a ringed canopy of tea-stained lace, but a welcoming fire crackled in the small fieldstone hearth. It was nestled into the wall with a base wide enough to serve as a bench. The recessed window slit revealed little other than a darkened sky. Torchlight illuminated the sprite-like dust motes sifting through the air. And while she doubted that this was where the welcome and important guests slept, the chamber was quite cozy.

"This room is only temporary. Once the storm recedes, Fellows will find you a place at the inn where you will be more comfortable. In the meantime, I'll send a maid to assist you," he said, keeping to his side of the door.

Assuming they were both eager to be out of each other's company, she faced away from him. "Then take your coat, if you please."

She waited for one moment—*two*—until she heard the soles of his boots shifting over the brown-and-gold woven rug. Another hesitation followed, a stillness that almost compelled her to look over her shoulder to ensure he was still there.

But she didn't need to turn around to be aware of where he stood. She could feel him there. His tall frame blocked the heat from escaping the room, incinerating the air around her, blanketing her.

He let out a staggered breath, his lungs like a blast furnace. The hot rush of air warmed her in places that a single breath shouldn't have been able to penetrate. And when another brushed the side of her neck, she closed her eyes on a head-to-toe waterfall of fiery tingles.

Was this type of response common between enemies? She knew too little about herself to surmise the truth. All she could do was study the nuances of his responses to her, primarily in the alterations in his breathing. When he'd first spotted her on the beach, he'd held his breath. When he scowled and clenched his teeth, it came out through flared nostrils. And whenever they were close, it came out in a warm, heady rush.

Perhaps he didn't find her repellent after all. At least, not entirely.

Now, when his hands curled over her shoulders, his breath fractured. Hot and firm, his long fingers stretched out over the flaps.

He was inches above the high swells of her breasts, but somehow her flesh felt heavier, ripe, drawing tighter, as if his hands cupped her.

She was warm all over now, restless and tingly with a strange sort of electricity arcing through the deepest parts of her body. Her blood lumbered through her veins as if unsure of where to find her heart, and then gave up the search, settling with a heavy, unsatisfied throb in the pit of her stomach instead.

An impatient, strangled mewl rose in her throat. She wished he would hurry. "Please take the coat."

Take . . . whatever you want. Surely, she wouldn't have such a reaction to a mere stranger. There had to be something more between them.

The duke seemed to be struggling with the simple request, emitting waves of heat and restraint as if halted by some unseen barrier.

Gradually, his hands curled into fists, his fingertips dragging the heavy gray coat, parting it open like a curtain, exposing her clinging dress to the flicker of firelight.

Then suddenly and without a word, he left, taking the coat with him.

Jacinda turned in time to see him duck his head and angle his shoulders through the doorway. He left the scent of cedar in his wake and she drew in a deep breath as she moved to the door.

"There is something familiar about you, Rydstrom," she said, stopping him on the landing. When he glanced over his shoulder, she caught sight of a brief flash of unease. "I'm not going to rest until I discover what it is."

Chapter 8

"Better be without sense, than misapply it as you do."

Jane Austen, *Emma*

Crispin left the gull chamber and strode through the dark, narrow passages leading to the keep, his fist tight around the iron key. He'd been tempted, beyond all reason, to lock Jacinda Bourne inside that room.

The terrifying part was, he wasn't sure which side of the door he would have been on. Outside, and secure in knowing exactly where she was? Or inside, and succumbing to a desire that surprised him with its potency?

If he'd have known a greatcoat could cause so much trouble, he never would have lent it to her.

Then again, he'd had to. The instant she'd removed her redingote in the gatehouse, he'd known she was cold—a fact evident by the perfect delineation of her taut nipples. In his own defense, he hadn't meant for his gaze to rake over her, or to linger on the supple curves displayed beneath wet, clinging wool. Hadn't wanted to notice that her breasts would fit nicely into the cups of his palms, and that their centers were the size and shape of tart sea buckthorn berries, small and ever so slightly oval.

It was more of an accidental awareness.

So when Crispin had first draped his coat over her, he'd thought covering her would help him forget. Or, in the very least, *not* imagine peeling off every damp layer. And until a moment ago, he thought he'd succeeded.

Then she'd asked him to remove the coat.

Instinctively, he'd known this was perilous territory. Because, *hell*, he'd practically lost his mind from having her body wrapped around him, her face nuzzling his neck, her hair meshing with his whiskers. Until today, he never thought that last bit was an eroticism. But the fact that he wanted to feel the tug and tangle of her thick, damp strands again gave him cause for warning.

That was the reason he'd hesitated to remove the coat. He'd needed to make certain that when he touched her, he would be able to stop.

Yet when she'd repeated her request, her voice a breathless, sultry rasp, arousal had waylaid him. It had coursed through him in a swift, inescapable, and painful surge, the heated length of his flesh pressing hard against the confines of his trousers.

He'd done his best to assuage his lust by focusing on other things. First, he'd separated the room into quadrants—door, hearth, washstand, *bed*. But that hadn't worked as planned, because then he calculated the steps to the too-tiny bed—one and a half—counted the buttons on the back of her dress—four—imagined kissing her everywhere, laying her on the bed, covering her wanton naked body with his, but absently realized that the frame would have collapsed beneath their combined weight.

And it was this bit of rational thinking that saved him from losing control. In the end, he'd managed to walk away.

Even so, resisting the impulse to touch and caress her was akin to offering a leg of lamb, roasted to perfection and dripping with juices, to a man who'd vowed to exist on nothing more than bread and water. Pure torture.

But he *had* resisted, and that was all that mattered. Besides, she was injured, weak, in need of protection, even if only from her own foolhardy escapades. And this, for reasons he could not surmise, made it all the harder to walk away.

Striding through the Great Hall at a fine clip, temptation hot on his heels, he tried to understand his reaction to Jacinda Bourne. What had begun in London as nothing more than an irritating impulse to kiss her—an errant ember, easily dowsed—had ignited into something far more dangerous.

It made no sense. His rational mind had no place, no compartment for this unforeseen occurrence. Jacinda Bourne did not even belong here. How dare she bring her chaos into his life of order!

Clutching the key tighter, he needed to put the volatile urge where it belonged—*far away from him.* With each step through the vast, towering hall, he told himself that he was not attracted to her. He couldn't be. His unsolicited response stemmed from something else, surely. His accelerated pulse, for example, was likely the result of having carried her up the hill. The same could be said for the tightening of his muscles and tendons. And naturally, his blood would have run hotter through his veins afterward.

Yes, he thought. That made perfect sense.

And yet, when he looked down at his other hand—the one that gripped his greatcoat in a stranglehold—he knew he was only fooling himself.

For in that same instant, he recalled with perfect clarity precisely how Jacinda Bourne had looked in that delectably wet dress. Then without warning, his mouth watered and he became unaccountably and unbearably aroused again. There was no mistaking the thickening of his pulse. No other reason for his blood to pool in a hot frenzy at the base of his cock, imploring him to pivot on his heel and do something about that key in his hand. Like lock them both inside the tower room, for hours, days . . .

Damn.

Furious at himself, and her—for so many reasons he

could never list them all—he growled and continued storming through the vast room.

The rich gold-and-burgundy tapestries lining the walls rustled in his wake, woven battle scenes undulating to life. And when he passed the ancient pair of long, black dining tables that flanked either side of the hearth, he tossed the coat onto the scarred and rutted surface and kept walking. He wanted to be rid of the reminder for good.

Unfortunately, it wasn't that simple. Because now he knew how it felt to have her in his arms, to have her scent fill his nostrils. She even made the odor of the sea appealing. Soaking wet, she was covered in that sharp brininess, but underneath was her own essence, a warm, sweet fragrance that reminded him of a dish of vanilla custard.

Stepping through the adjacent door to the buttery, he relished the cooler temperature of this small anteroom. He paused long enough to draw in a deep breath, filling his lungs with the bold essence of fermented hops and barley rising up the narrow spiral staircase from the ale barrels in the cellars below. All the better to rid himself of her scent.

Yet with every footfall up the pitted mortar and stone stairs, it clung to him. And *damn it all*, he despised her for it.

Winding his way through castle corridors and up a series of staircases, his temper smoldered like embers beneath a curfew, ready to ignite. And he was glad of it because he would rather be angry at her than feel any other way. It was an easy task, too. Her presence put everyone he'd sought to protect at risk.

She was too meddling, too inquisitive, and far too reckless. A woman like her did not think of the consequences of her actions beforehand. Hell, she'd even put her own life in jeopardy for a foolish scheme. And seeing that raw gash on her head, her pale skin, and the way she winced when she moved had made him angriest of all. Even now, the urge to shake her, to rail at her for nearly drowning was equally as strong as his other wayward impulses.

Did she not realize that there were seamen—good village men—who'd navigated those waters their whole lives, and yet, some of them never returned home? No! Likely Jacinda Bourne only thought about her ridiculous investigation and not what it would have done to him to find her lifeless body on the rocks instead.

A fierce shudder washed through him as if a deluge of ice water sluiced over his skin and inside his veins. It set him off balance. Pausing on the stair, he propped a hand against the wall as a wave of strength-sapping nausea rolled through him.

"Your Grace, I didn't think to find you back so soon."

At the sudden appearance of his housekeeper at the top of the stairwell leading to the donjon, he lowered his arm and continued with measured steps up the final treads as if nothing were amiss. "Good day, Mrs. Hemple."

She backed away from the door, beaming at him, her broad smile lifting her plump, ruddy cheeks. As was her habit, she absently wiped her hands in thc center of her apron, where a perpetual yellowing stain was embedded in the pale cotton. "Mightily glad, we are, to have you return and already with your bride. I just knew that London would be brimming with heiresses."

Crispin gritted his teeth. "I have not found an heiress, Mrs. Hemple."

She clasped her hands to her bosom, and emitted an elated sigh. "Bless us, it's as I hoped! You've made a love match. And quick work on your part I must say, sir. It must have been the pin I found the day you left. I knew it would bring about luck."

He ignored the way her graying, mouse brown eyebrows waggled beneath a serviceable, ruffled cap. As he'd explained before, many times, dukes did not marry for love but for money and property. Neither his butler nor his housekeeper seemed to have heard him. Though, since the pair had been with him since infancy, he allowed for some leniency. *Some.* "The situation is not what you think. That woman will not be staying for long. As soon as the storm subsides, I'll send her to the inn."

"No reason to be shy, sir. Rydstrom Hall is surely large enough for a pair of lovebirds. Oh, and look"—she pointed to his chest and sighed again—"she's already made you lose a button and wrinkled your cravat."

Distracted, he looked down at his waistcoat and noticed a pair of dark, frayed threads where there should have been a button. It seemed everything in his life was starting to unravel.

"You have a very tousled look about you," the housekeeper continued, crooning, "and I think it makes you all the handsomer. I say, a man ought to have a few well-placed wrinkles in his clothing. I always wanted you to find a duchess with a contented and *affectionate*"—another eyebrow waggle—"nature. For then there will surely be lots of children scampering about."

"Mrs. Hemple," he said sharply. "I came up here to speak to you about Sybil."

"*Pah.* No need to worry about her, sir. Sybil will be thrilled by the match."

"Actually, I would prefer it if Sybil knew nothing of—" He broke off as the unmistakable clatter of stiff-soled shoes on the wood floor made it evident that the object of their discussion was upon them.

"I'm afraid, it's too late for that, sir." Mrs. Hemple laughed as a slim form in a white pinafore skipped into view.

Sybil was a gangly colt, all knobby elbows and knees, along with a mop of blond curls that likely resembled her late mother's. In addition, she had a perfect cherub's face that was grinning at him from ear to ear . . . Until a crack of thunder suddenly rent the air.

She paled instantly, her gray eyes shuttering closed, vague and distant. For a girl of ten, she'd seen far too many terrors.

"I've heard reports of a certain young miss who keeps a

vigil by the window," Crispin said in a tone of mock disapproval. "And yet you cannot even spare me a smile? Come now, where is my welcome?"

Locking eyes with him, Sybil slowly stepped forward and slipped her small, cold hand into his. She cast a brief, fearful glance to the roiling sky beyond the oriel window behind her.

They shared an inherent dislike of storms. It began on the auspicious day they'd met four years ago—the same day his own mother, and *their* father argued by the bluff.

Before then, Crispin had not known he had a half sister. Father had been good about keeping his affair a secret. No one knew about his mistress, the house he'd kept for her, and especially not the child they'd had together. But all of it was discovered the day Sybil arrived, mourning the death of her mother from fever.

Then on the same day, she lost her father as well. And Crispin refused to allow Sybil to suffer any more than she already had.

He patted her reedy shoulders, the blades sticking out like wings of a bird when she wrapped her arms about his waist and squeezed him, her head resting just at his sternum. "Ah, so you did miss me. And I was only gone for a week."

She lifted her face and shook her head. Releasing her hold, she held up eight fingers to correct him.

This was one of her ways of communicating. He'd only actually heard her speak once, four years ago, when she'd first introduced herself in a shy whisper. "My name is Sybil Montague and I should like to see my father, if you please."

Then, the next time he heard her voice had been the last.

The memory of that day would always haunt him. He'd been striding out of the Great Hall, furious and planning to leave Rydstrom Hall *and* his father's hypocrisy for good. But all of a sudden he'd felt a quake beneath his feet as a terrible, ominous growl and reverberating *crack* split the air.

Then he'd heard Sybil's scream—a raw, endless shriek

that shook the windows in the morning room. And that was where he'd found her, trembling and stark white, standing at the bank of windows that overlooked the cliffs.

The very place where his parents had been standing a moment before.

He learned then that the quake he'd felt beneath his feet had been the rock face sheering away from the cliffs and crashing to the sea.

Witness to the horror, Sybil had been mute ever since. Somehow, the scream had been so powerful that her vocal folds had torn. The London surgeon that Dr. Graham had summoned said that her throat appeared shredded to the point where he could not imagine it ever healing properly. At best, she would be able to whisper.

Yet in these past four years, Crispin could not persuade her to try. And when he was met with the utter desolation and fear in her eyes, he never pushed her. She had her own method of communicating and he was fine with that.

"Have it your way, then. Eight days, it is." He ruffled her downy head. "What have you been doing during this *endless* stretch of time? Practicing your letters, I trust. As I recall, your *A*s have forelocks and your *B*s have tails. And you add so much flourish to your *Q*s that they nearly require a page to themselves. Before long, you'll use up an entire inkpot for one word."

Sybil rolled her eyes at him before rushing over to the small mahogany table in front of the window. Grabbing a sheet of paper, she skipped back to him, and handed it over, shoulders straight, chin high, and beaming.

He glanced down at the drawing, used to having Sybil converse in this manner. Even though she knew how to read and write, sometimes she preferred to show him how she saw the world around her. In the past, she'd drawn countless nightmarish images of the cliffs, in an effort to explain her outright terror of them, conveying the message that a ten-year-old vocabulary could not.

The sketch in his hand was far different, however. There were no hard slashes of charcoal on the paper, but soft, delicate sweeps showing a likeness of him . . . *and* Miss Bourne.

Drawn from the perspective of this window, and looking out over the old bailey, he was clearly carrying her as he had been. Yet in this rendering, it appeared as if he were resting his cheek upon her head. It looked like a page from a fairy-tale storybook. Apparently, his sister saw the episode as something wholly romantic and not what it had actually been. A gut churning, irritating, and worrisome agony.

Having Jacinda Bourne under this roof put the safeguards he'd set in place for Sybil in jeopardy. No one aside from Mrs. Hemple, Fellows, and Graham could know about her real identity.

Here in Whitcrest, the villagers believed the story he'd concocted—that Sybil was the child of Mrs. Hemple's late cousin, who'd had no other family to raise her. They even credited him for making her his ward and permitting her to live at Rydstrom Hall as if it were her own.

He couldn't risk the truth reaching London. He'd purposely stayed away these past four years, had cut off ties with his former friends, in order to avoid any repercussions for her.

He'd kept Sybil's true identity a secret, wanting to spare her from tainted labels given to the illegitimate daughters of nobles. Society would spurn her, make a parody of her existence. Gentlemen, like the ones he'd admired in his youth, would only deem her worthy of becoming a mistress. And Crispin could not let such a tawdry life befall her.

Crispin hadn't even told Aunt Hortense about Sybil. Because, more than any other person he knew, his forthright aunt believed that every disgrace brought upon a family must be punished. He knew from experience that, for her, there were no exceptions to this rule. And he had no doubt that his aunt would know the truth at first glance. After all, paintings of her younger self—near perfect copies of Sybil—filled her apartments.

He'd managed to hide the portrait above the mantel as well as the miniatures, but there was nothing he could do about the mural on the wall, aside from cover it with a dust sheet and ask that only Mrs. Hemple clean the room. And while he felt confident that his servants would not be tempted to steal into those locked rooms out of curiosity, the same could not be said of Miss Bourne.

Now, and before he knew what he was doing, he crumpled the paper in his hand.

Sybil reached out to rescue the sketch and sent him a chastising glower as she smoothed out the page over the flat front of her simple blue dress. When finished, she inspected it, her frown turning into a wistful smile as she returned to the small writing desk at the window and propped it up between the inkstand and the bronze lamp, displaying it as if it were a treasure.

"Sir, Sybil wants to know when you're going to marry her," Mrs. Hemple offered.

Crispin suppressed a growl. Had everyone gone mad? In the past hour, he'd been inundated with assumptions that he planned to marry the most meddlesome creature he'd ever encountered. It was starting to grate on his last nerve. "There is no cause to compile any foolish notions. Miss Bourne was injured and I merely carried her to get us both out of the storm. And as soon as the rain stops, she will be gone from Rydstrom Hall."

Then, once he sent her back to London, he would dissolve his membership with the Bourne Matrimonial Agency and seek other, more manageable, options.

Sybil scribbled on a scrap of paper and handed it to him. *"You said you were bringing home a wife."*

"I said I was *searching* for a bride, not that I ever planned on bringing her here. Besides, whomever I marry will stay in London and keep a house there." Or some other part of the world, so long as it was far away from here.

While he spoke, a mixture of confusion and sadness

flashed over her features as she pointed a finger to herself. He realized he'd said the wrong thing.

"No, dearest, it isn't because of you. Of course she would care for you, as anyone would. It's only that . . ." He tried to think of a way to explain that would make sense to a girl of ten. When she was older, she would understand that he was only trying to protect her. "A woman of society would not want to live here while Rydstrom Hall is under repair. She would prefer to see it in all the glory one might expect of a duke's castle."

Thankfully, Mrs. Hemple—who'd lived here long enough to know that this house would never be completely finished—kept quiet and didn't even send him a look of reproach for his lie. They all wanted to protect Sybil from the outside world.

Sybil took the scrap from him and, at her desk, wrote a line below the first before returning it. *"Where would you live?"*

"I explained this already. I would spend part of the time in London, and part here." He handed the page back to her, hoping this would satisfy her.

But again, Sybil returned to her desk, dipped the quill into the inkpot, and wrote in her impeccable, flowing script. *"But isn't she pretty?"*

He read the question aloud without thinking, his throat closing over the last syllable. His mouth suddenly dry, he asked, "Who, Miss Bourne?"

Sybil offered an expectant nod. He looked to Mrs. Hemple for a redirect of the conversation topic only to find that she was looking at him with eagerness as well.

Bloody romantic fools, the lot of them.

"To a gentleman, physical beauty matters little," he hemmed, shifting from one foot to the other and trying not to think about snarls of red hair, uncanny blue eyes, a plump red mouth, and . . . sea buckthorn berries. He swallowed and cleared his throat before continuing. "A gentleman looks for someone who has an upstanding character and a clever wit." And, in his case, a great deal of money as well.

Miss Bourne had none of the most necessary qualities.

Crispin didn't know the reason, but a slow smile bloomed over Sybil's face. She snatched the paper from his grasp, rushed back to her desk, and then handed it back to him with a new line written in large, taunting letters. *"You do think she's pretty!"*

He read the accusation with a start, a ready denial on his lips. But as he looked at his smugly grinning sister, standing with her hands clasped before her, her pale golden brows lifted, he reminded himself that she was merely ten. For the past year, she'd become obsessively romantic, marrying two of any creature she encountered, from the cats in the keep to the frogs in the north garden, and even drawing wedding pictures of the fish served at dinner. There was no reasoning with her at this age.

Fighting the urge to roll *his* eyes, he bent forward and pressed a kiss to her forehead. "Your time would be better served on your lessons, especially your handwriting." Then addressing the housekeeper, he said, "Mrs. Hemple, perhaps you can keep her occupied for the next few hours with repetitive sentences."

As he expected, Sybil did not appreciate his advice and scrutinized the script on the page. When she shot him a hard look of disbelief, everything in her countenance and posture proclaimed that her letters were perfect. And, in truth, they were. Nevertheless, it was his turn to smirk at her.

Then with a nod, he left her in Mrs. Hemple's care and went into the main house to check on his *guests*. He needed to make travel arrangements for them as soon as possible.

By the time the storm ended, Jacinda Bourne would be settled at the inn, and he could breathe easier.

Chapter 9

"*She* certainly had not been in the wrong, and *he* would never own that he had."

JANE AUSTEN, *Emma*

"Thank you for the dress," Jacinda said to the brown-haired maid, while slipping into the borrowed dark blue frock.

"No trouble at all, miss." And as Martha buttoned up the back, Jacinda took note of the neat rows of simple stitches at the cuffs of the short, banded sleeves. They reminded her of how Miss Beels had decided that Jacinda was of a different class, simply by the cut of her clothes.

Distractedly, the kernel of an idea sprouted.

If one wished to explore a castle without anyone the wiser, likely it would be best to blend in with one's surroundings. Wouldn't it? And surely in a castle this size, no one would notice an extra maid walking the corridors.

Her pulse skittered with excitement at the thought, beating so quickly that it whirred beneath her skin and in her ears. And her lungs felt like knotted balloons with all the air trapped inside, her breaths short and fast.

Splaying her hand over her clambering heart, she wondered if she'd ever felt this way before. It was quite thrilling—the notion of disguising herself as a servant. Though, if that was all it took to excite her, then clearly, she'd led a dull life and wasn't used to mischief of any kind.

Perhaps she was a quiet, unassuming girl who dutifully

waited on her ailing uncle. She might be sweet and . . . *ugh* . . . an awful bore.

Yet that would hardly explain why the duke despised her. If they'd only met twice, a quiet mouse would hardly have made a lasting impression.

"'Tisn't anything near as fine as your clothes, miss. 'Tis only homespun, but it's me Sunday best. I made it meself." The maid smiled proudly, displaying a pair of deep dimples on either side of her round cheeks. She had a wholesome, scrubbed-clean look about her and an innocent vibrancy that made it easy to like her.

Jacinda hoped she wouldn't get her into any trouble. But if the duke planned to send Jacinda away as soon as the storm broke, then she had to explore Rydstrom Hall as quickly as possible. After all, there was a reason she was here, where no one, save him, seemed to know her. And she was determined to find anything that would lead her to the answer.

"It's lovely. Truly," Jacinda said, smoothing her hands down the dress, unadorned aside from a bit of white piping along the modest neckline. The fabric was somewhat itchy on her bare skin, but she willed herself not to think about it.

"I'm sorry for not bringing a shift, but I only have the one." Martha plucked at the front of her gray maid's dress, her cheeks coloring. Then lowering her eyes, she crossed the room to busy herself at the hearth where rain steadily dripped down the chimney, splattering on the logs with sibilant hisses and tiny curls of smoke. "I'll make sure to launder your fine cambric first so that you can have it back by the time you finish your bath. It'll only be a short while till the water's ready. And after, I have a special recipe for a nice posset to help you sleep."

Sleep sounded divine. Jacinda would love to curl up beneath a warm coverlet and sleep for days. After Dr. Graham's examination and endless series of questions, he'd offered her laudanum. But her insatiable curiosity didn't want sleep. It wanted answers.

After she'd declined, the doctor had warned that all the aches from the bumps and bruises from her tumble in the sea would soon catch up with her, and to rest as much as possible. But to her mind, that was all the more reason to make haste.

"You've been splendid, Martha. I think I'll lie down for a while," she said, holding open the door.

Arms laden with wet garments, Martha bobbed a curtsy and shuffled out the door. Then she hesitated, casting a fretful glance toward a tray of tea, broth, and bread resting on the hearth's ledge. "Mayhap I should ought to stay. His Grace left strict instructions for you to eat every morsel."

"Never fear," Jacinda added quickly, turning Martha toward the stairs with a friendly pat on her shoulder, stopping just shy of pushing her out the door. "I'll gobble it up straightaway."

Martha nodded uncertainly. "If you say so, Miss Bourne. But if you need anything in the meantime, the bellpull's by the window. Pay no mind to the water dripping through the casing. It always does that when it rains."

"I'm sure I'll only sleep after I eat." For good measure, Jacinda feigned a yawn behind the cup of her hand. Then, as an afterthought, she pointed to the top of Martha's head. "Would you mind if I borrowed your cap? It might help to keep my head warm."

Martha, ever generous, readily agreed, not knowing how she'd just completed the perfect disguise.

Jacinda closed the door, waited a minute, then opened it again. Leaning out, she perked her ears to the sound of nearby footsteps. When nothing but silence greeted her, her lips tilted up at each corner.

It was time.

Making her way down the narrow stairs, she tucked a few stray auburn curls into the borrowed ruffled cap. Yet, when she accidentally scraped the red lump at her temple, she winced, the wound throbbing with renewed vigor. Her vision went blurry.

"Don't you dare, Jacinda," she scolded, bracing her hands against the millstone grit wall for balance. "On top of everything else, you will not add falling down the stairs to your ever-growing list of catastrophes."

So, after a deep breath and a little mental pinch of determination, she set off again.

Beyond the base of the tower, Jacinda found narrow corridors encased in thick stone walls with fat rough-hewn beams overhead. She passed several doors that intrigued her, but they were locked tight. Since she didn't have much time—or a key for that matter—she continued onward, rounding corners and ducking out of sight whenever she heard footfalls nearby.

Fatigue began to take its toll when she found herself in a particularly lengthy corridor that seemed to go on forever. She paused briefly in an alcove to gather her breath, the damp air musty and sweet. Standing there, the hushed patter of the rain and the murmured rumbles of the storm tempted her to give in to exhaustion, to curl up in this space and close her eyes.

But she couldn't do that. She hadn't discovered anything yet.

Fighting a yawn, she chafed her hands over her arms and set off again. Then, at the end of the corridor, she found herself in a wide hall. Flickering sconces bathed the clay-colored walls in burnished gold. And with a quick look from left to right, she saw that no one was about.

Like in the gatehouse, storm shutters covered the recessed windows. And above her was an open minstrel's gallery with mischievous faces carved into the corbels beneath the wooden parapet. They seemed to look down at her as if they knew what she was up to, and so she smirked back at them and continued her sly exploration.

Unfortunately, her wet ankle boots were starting to make slurping sounds with every step. Trying to walk on tiptoe didn't work to silence them. It made them squeak instead. *Drat.* If she couldn't silence them, she would be discovered.

Just as the thought entered her mind, a narrow slit of a door opened, not two steps ahead of her.

Jacinda darted to the shadowy corner in a hasty *splunch, splunch, splunch* of steps and pressed her back against the cool wall.

A heaping bale of linens gradually emerged, followed by the maid carrying it, the pile so high it went to her eyebrows. Using her hip to prop open the door, the maid squeezed into the hall, but then her apron caught on the latch, jerking her to a halt and sending a few items to the flagstone floor.

She muttered an oath under her breath, followed by a drawling singsong of words as if she were mimicking someone. "'We must ready the duke's and the duchess's chamber with haste,' Hemple says. 'Are you able to carry all these linens at once?' Oh, of course I am, ma'am. I'm part octopus, after all. And never mind the fact that you took Martha away to play lady's maid, leavin' me with all her duties, and"—she stopped her tirade the instant she stepped on one of the fallen—*"Blasted, cursin', rot!"*

Before Jacinda knew what she was doing, she stepped forward and bent down for the fallen pillow slip. "Here you are," she said, tucking it between the maid's elbow and the huge bundle.

"Betsy, is that you?"

Jacinda hesitated, frozen. Fortunately for her, the maid's view was obscured by the mountain of laundry. Though, just in case, she tugged on her borrowed cap to look more like a fellow servant. Then, as if she belonged there, she helped to free the maid's apron from the door latch. "Yes, of course it is."

The maid laughed. "Oh, listen to you Miss Hoity-Toity. If you're tryin' to be chosen for lady's maid, you're too late. I tried it, too, even scrubbed my cheeks pink, but Fellows isn't having it. He chose *Martha*, even though I've been here longer. And I know what you're goin' to say, so don't even bother. He chose her because she wasn't the one caught kissin' Rodney by the stables."

In the stairwell above them, a door closed and they both startled.

"Quick. Check the steps to be sure I didn't drop somethin' along the way. Hemple's in a dither, to be sure. Even though none of us expected His Grace's return from London so soon, she'll still have my head if one thin' is out of place. Say, aren't *you* supposed to be fetchin' rain pails for the guest chambers?"

Distracted by the news that Rydstrom had just returned from London, Jacinda didn't respond at first. It was a clue, to be sure. Only she didn't know what it meant. However, she did know that they both seemed to find themselves in Whitcrest at the same time. And now, she wondered if she had come from London as well.

"Betsy?"

"Oh yes." Jacinda snapped her fingers and pushed against the pile of laundry as if she were tucking something inside. "There now, nothing left behind, and I'd better get those pails before Hemple has *my* head."

With a rueful laugh, the maid walked away, and Jacinda made her way up the constricted staircase.

At the first landing, she paused to catch her breath, pressing a hand to the sharp pain in her side, the scratch of simple fabric abrading her tender fingertips.

The chambermaid had left the door open to this floor, providing a view of two-toned walls, painted a watery blue and trimmed in eggshell white. Sounds of quick, muffled footsteps and a hollow, echoing rattle drifted to her. With a peek into the hall, she spied a blond-headed maid carrying pails. *Betsy, most likely.*

Jacinda wondered what information she might learn from her. More about the duke's return from London? Or perhaps, the reason why everyone—aside from the duke himself—assumed that she was here to marry him. *Hmm.*

Yet, before she could follow Betsy, another door opened across the hall, and Jacinda hesitated in the shadow of the stairwell.

A sturdy, matronly woman appeared, her hands worrying the center of an apron, her short legs moving with crisp efficiency down the hall. "Betsy, have you finished with the pails? We must have them in place before His Grace ventures to this floor, which might be as soon as he finishes speaking to Dr. Graham."

"This is the last one, ma'am. But I still don't understand why we're putting pails in the rooms that don't have leaks."

"Tush, now. That isn't your concern and you would do better to keep quiet about it all the same. Even Mr. Fellows agrees that this is necessary."

"Necessary for what?"

"Never mind that. Fetch some water and spill a little into each pail, and quickly."

Jacinda frowned, unable to find a clue in that odd exchange. However, she believed she'd just met—in a roundabout way—Mrs. Hemple, the apparent housekeeper of Rydstrom Hall.

Then eyeing the door she'd seen Mrs. Hemple step through, a fresh tingle of curiosity swept through Jacinda. The housekeeper's sole focus seemed to be on ensuring the bedchambers were made ready. Was it possible that she had just come from the duke's?

Believing that she might find more clues there, Jacinda slipped across the hall.

But behind that door, another staircase greeted her. *Ugh.* The rush of excitement that had filled her with enough energy to leave the tower chamber was waning with great haste.

Trudging up this next flight, she wondered if a person could die from climbing stairs. Then, at last—with lungs burning on every wheezing breath and pain stabbing her side as if she'd swallowed a knife—she reached the door at the top. A single sconce burned at the end of a dark paneled corridor. Beside it stood a door, left ajar.

No matter where or how delicately she walked, the wooden floors creaked beneath her squeaking shoes. Regardless, with a *splunch*, *splunch*, *splunch*, she made her way to the end of the hall, but found, yet another stairway.

Having come too far to turn back now, Jacinda made the climb.

Yet she should have been more careful because when she reached the top, someone was waiting for her.

THE CONSTANT ping of water dripping into pails accompanied Crispin's heavy footfalls out of the keep and through the wide, domed corridor toward the gatehouse. The storm made him all too aware of the repairs Rydstrom Hall needed.

Up ahead, Fellows directed two of the footmen to capture the most recent leaks. This ritual was such a commonality that there was a closet solely dedicated to pails. Among the groomsmen he employed, one of them was a cooper's apprentice, who not only made ale barrels but kept them in a good supply of rain pails as well.

Still, it never stopped bothering Crispin. The irritation he felt over the gradual—and often times not so gradual—decline of Rydstrom Hall crawled beneath his skin like a thistle barb that sent an angry jolt to his nerves whenever he brushed against it. He wished that his predecessors had thought more of securing the future of their legacy instead of spending all their days, and fortunes, on adding more rooms that required upkeep.

Consequently, over the years, Crispin had learned a thing or two about repairing roofs, plasterwork, and loose stones from the outside walls. Especially the ones to the south that bore the brunt of the sea's attacks, the outer curtain having all but fallen ages ago. Chimneys were rather difficult with his broad build, however. So he closed off the rooms where the damage was too severe and his funds too limited.

Living in a crumbling castle was a costly endeavor. What had once been a small estate with tenants and farmers enough to turn a profit on the land, had grown far beyond the means of its income. In truth, he could only afford to employ thirty servants and keep them well fed. But because of the size of Rydstrom Hall, they were spread thin to perform their duties.

Though once he continued the family tradition and married his own heiress, his first order of business would be to hire more—not only servants but stonemasons and carpenters—in order to ensure that Rydstrom Hall would be safe for Sybil.

Crispin expelled a weary breath. He should be in London finding a wealthy bride, not here, beleaguered by an unwelcome guest and wondering what disaster might befall him next.

Frowning, he stood in one of the alcoves and stared out the window. Sheets of rain obscured his view, turning the sea and cliffs into a child's watercolor landscape. It would be easier to live somewhere else, in a place that wasn't so full of his own regrets. But this was his home.

Beside him, he heard the unmistakable step-shuffle of Dr. Graham coming closer. Continuing to stare out the window, he said, "If the rain doesn't let up soon, the roads will be impassable."

"I'm afraid it's too late for that." Graham stopped near him, propping his cane against the wall. Then he proceeded to remove his spectacles for cleaning as if he hadn't delivered the worst news imaginable. "Even if it were to stop this instant, the flooding would take time to recede. At least overnight. And there's the mud to consider, stodgy enough to rob a man of his boots and trousers."

Crispin already knew this, but he'd foolishly been holding on to one last hope.

Rubbing circles over the lenses with a yellowed handkerchief, Graham slid him a sideways glance. "However, I don't believe your concern is for the state of the roads, but rather for having unexpected guests."

"Henry is a good lad, and Miss Beels knows her place well enough." They wouldn't think of trespassing in his aunt's apartments. Only one person beneath this roof would dare such an intrusion, if given the chance.

"Ah, then it is only the presence of one that bothers you."

"You know the reason."

"I'm not certain that I do," Graham said. "If your concern is that rumors regarding Sybil's true identity would make their way to London, I'd say that the chances of that happening rely upon you. Miss Bourne would only learn of this if you chose to tell her."

Crispin scrubbed a hand over his unshaven jaw. He was still in complete disorder, missing button and all. "If we were speaking of any other person in England, I would agree with you. However, Miss Bourne likes to live by her own rules. She has this impossible tenacity etched into her character such that—if she senses a secret, no matter how trivial—she won't stop until she discovers what it is. Why else do you think she's here?"

"Apparently, you know."

Crispin gritted his teeth and proceeded to explain the nature of their acquaintance, beginning with his aunt's stipulations and ending with finding Miss Bourne in his study.

Graham's mustachio twitched at the corners as if he were holding back a grin. "Then it is fortunate for you that she has amnesia."

"Indeed, but for how long? An hour? Two? Even you said her memory could return at any time." He glanced toward the corridor that led to the tower. Thinking of her there and wondering if, even now, she was remembering everything, helped him dismiss how tempted he'd been by her. It was simply a reaction to physical exertion, he told himself. Nothing more.

"And then you'll explain that she traveled all this way, only to discover what everyone else believes—that you have taken your housekeeper's young relative under your care."

"To which she would reply with a request to see the graves herself in order to confirm the story," Crispin said ruefully.

Graham chuckled. He didn't understand that, since Crispin had first met Jacinda, he hadn't had a single moment's peace. It was as if he'd sensed, all along, what havoc she would wreak in his life.

And here she was, having traipsed all the way to Whitcrest, recklessly putting her own life in danger, simply because she was curious about a name she'd read in a damn letter! A woman like that wasn't apt to believe the story that the villagers had accepted so readily. Not without proof.

He expelled a hard breath and scrubbed a hand over the back of his neck where the past two days had tied every nerve ending into a tight knot. Perhaps he was being paranoid. It wasn't as if she possessed a preternatural power for seeing through him and reading his secrets. Even though he feared that was true.

Then, caught by something he detected in Graham's last words, Crispin felt the flesh between his eyebrows pucker as he turned his head. "What did you mean when you just said 'and then you'll explain'? Is Miss Bourne already asking questions? Or do you have news for me regarding your examination?"

"Actually," Graham began, but paused to replace his spectacles with care. He took a moment to smooth down the bristly hairs on either side of his mouth before he continued, the hesitations marked by the drips falling into the nearby pails. "I wanted to speak to you about that. And believe me when I say that I understand you are a man who prefers order. So it is with a certain degree of wariness that I must ask you if she could remain—"

"No. Absolutely not," Crispin interrupted. "Miss Bourne

is *not* staying beneath this roof until she regains her memory."

Graham held up his hands and wore an expression of patient trepidation as if he were trying to calm a wild horse, his tone low and soothing. "You are her only link to herself. If we put her in an unfamiliar environment, it's entirely possible that she will never regain her memory."

"Rydstrom Hall is not a familiar environment."

"Perhaps not, but *you* are familiar to her."

Even worse. Crispin took a step back, gesturing with a sweep of his arm toward the door. "She has a family. As soon as I send word, they will come for her."

"Days from now, perhaps. You will get no messenger to them today, nor tomorrow with the roads as they are," Graham reminded needlessly. "And more to the point, Miss Bourne is in no condition to travel."

He suspected that, of course, but hearing it didn't make it any easier to accept. "When will she be?"

"I do not know, and quite frankly I worry about overtaxing her. If she were to return to her family too quickly, I fear that their affection for her might hinder her recovery." Graham tapped his head to make it clear they were speaking of her memory.

Crispin leveled the doctor with a dubious glare. "Come now, this excuse sounds far *too* convenient. A family hindering her recovery? I've never heard of such a thing."

"Perhaps think of it this way," Graham began with his usual patience. "Families see their loved one struggle to remember and, with the very best of intentions, begin to regale them with memories of childhood antics, former pets and playmates, of deceased relatives and all manner of recollections that you and I take for granted. Yet without the link to the memory, the only emotion gained from these picture-less stories is not love or fondness, but irritation and frustration. And I believe that those who are not allowed to heal on their own become nothing more than mimics leading hollow lives and forming no attachments. It is a terrible way to live."

Crispin felt contrite for his assumption. A fresh wave of worry rolled over him, churning in his stomach. The thought of Miss Bourne experiencing such a dire fate bothered him, and more than he expected. Of course, he would feel the same stirring of sympathy for anyone in this circumstance, he told himself. And yet he was suddenly at war with his duty to protect Sybil and an unexpected compulsion to do the same for Miss Bourne.

Disgruntled by this undesirable emotion, he rubbed his palm against the building pressure at his nape. "You speak as though you have experience with this."

"My own brother," Graham answered quietly. "We fought together on the *Royal Sovereign* at Trafalgar. While he was healing from the cannon blast, I was the one who made the mistake of feeding him his past, which ultimately confused and overwhelmed him. He was sent home and lived another year with our parents before he put an end to his own torment."

Crispin briefly reached out and clutched the doctor's shoulder. He knew all too well what it was like to blame oneself for a loved one's death. "I understand what you are saying, and no matter what my feelings toward Miss Bourne might be, I would not wish such a fate on her. Nevertheless, I cannot keep an unmarried debutante beneath my roof without a chaperone."

Then he reminded himself that it wasn't his ultimate decision to make. Her uncle was her guardian. Eggleston would have to make the choice.

"For tonight, she has the local doctor to keep her reputation intact. Tomorrow or the day after, you could ask Miss Beels to stay on—"

"The town's feather-wit is hardly a suitable chaperone. I could seduce Miss Bourne while in the same room with Miss Beels and likely receive applause instead of condemnation."

The doctor lifted his wiry brows. "Are you afraid that you'll be unable to resist Miss Bourne's charms?"

"I would sooner have my way with Miss Beels," he said with a convincing amount of effrontery. At least, he hoped it was. "If she stays here long, her reputation will likely be in ruins—unless *you* are her chaperone. I can see no other way."

The doctor turned, accepting this with a nod, and then stared out to sea for a moment. "I cannot help but think that Miss Bourne would have had a maid with her."

Crispin's gaze drifted to the water as well. "I had thought of that when I saw the flotsam rising and falling with the swells. It looked to be the remains of a small skiff. I didn't want to bring it up in front of Miss Bourne in case . . ."

He didn't finish. Both of them knew that the body of a maidservant might very well wash up on shore in the coming days.

"Yes. Silence is best, until we know for certain."

"When the weather clears, I'll send footmen out to the bordering villages to ask for any information, including the name of the boat's owner." Perhaps then he'd discover why she hadn't taken a coach directly to Whitcrest. Then again, she may have altered her route by design, negating the chance that their paths would cross. She was too clever by half.

"Then you'll keep her?"

After all was said and done, Crispin didn't see that he had another choice. Yet, more than anything, he wanted to confine her to the tower, keeping her far away from Sybil. He nodded with reluctance.

"Her injuries, are they"—he broke off as another disconcerting clench of worry gripped his stomach—"more severe than you first thought?"

Graham pulled thoughtfully on his beard. "She has many contusions, though not as many as I have seen from other near drowning victims. As you know, our coastline is not the most forgiving. And then there's the reef . . ." He shook his head. "I cannot imagine how she navigated it all."

Now that clenching sensation began to burn with anger because of the danger she'd put herself in. "Miss Bourne's resiliency and resourcefulness does not surprise me. As we already have proof, she was determined to sail, swim, and likely even crawl her way to Rydstrom Hall."

"Then she has earned the rest she was so eager to have before I left her."

Crispin went still. "What do you mean . . . *eager*?"

Just then, he heard the rush of footsteps and turned to see the chambermaid Fellows had assigned to Miss Bourne's room.

Clutching her side, Martha panted, her round face chalk white. "Forgive me, Your Grace. I went to Miss Bourne's room just now and she's gone. I dunno where she could have gotten to in such a state."

Damn. It was already beginning.

Chapter 10

> "But I," he soon added, "who have had no such charm thrown over my senses, must still see, hear, and remember."
>
> Jane Austen, *Emma*

A slender girl in a white pin-tucked pinafore stared at Jacinda through the open archway of a cozy sitting room. Behind her, a brace of candles on a desk sent a spill of golden light through her pale hair, making her look like an angel.

The candlelight also illuminated an oriel window, turning the surface into something of a mirror. Seeing herself in a borrowed dress and cap, Jacinda said the first thing that came to mind. "I've come to remove the linens."

Of course, that declaration might have worked better if there were actual linens in the room.

A slow, impish smile spread over the girl's face and she shook her head. Living here, the girl likely knew all the servants. Perhaps she was a servant as well, or the child of one.

Jacinda tried again, continuing with another lie because she didn't know what else to do. She hadn't thought this far ahead, and her head was throbbing again, making it difficult to think at all. "I could go to the kitchen to organize a tray of tarts and biscuits, if you like."

The girl's smile broadened. She stepped forward and took Jacinda by the hand, quickly drawing her into the room.

Jacinda went along, watchful, but letting the child guide

her. When the girl closed the door behind them, a draft of wind caused a paper on the desk to flutter to the floor.

Jacinda bent down automatically, but wished she hadn't. A wave of dizziness swam through her head, nearly toppling her over, though she managed to right herself with a hand flat to the desk. And the girl was beside her in an instant, laying a small, cool hand over Jacinda's, a pout of concern on her face.

"There were a lot of stairs," Jacinda said by way of explanation.

The girl nodded, a commiserating puff of air accompanying it.

"I believe this is yours." Jacinda handed her the paper that had fallen.

But the girl did not take it. Instead, she clasped her hands and rolled her lips between her teeth, her cheeks lifting in a barely contained, expectant grin as her bright gaze darted from Jacinda to the paper.

Jacinda looked down at the page, too, and what she saw surprised her. It was a drawing, and a rather good one at that, depicting a likeness of the duke. There was no mistaking those broad shoulders and that granite jaw, after all. And in the picture, he was holding something. Or someone, rather. *Her.*

The sketch showed Jacinda clinging to the duke. Curled in his arms, she did not appear to be the struggling, unwieldy baggage that she had tried to be. And he did not look like the glowering, intractable duke that he actually was. The slanted lines illustrating his face portrayed nothing of the animosity she'd experienced from him. In fact, from this perspective, he looked somewhat . . . protective.

A rush of heat swamped her cheeks. Though she'd never admit it aloud, she had felt safe in his arms. His strength and willingness to step forward—even when it was clear he did not want to—had helped to douse her climbing fears in a way that the doctor's reassurances had not. How strange that it was the bristly duke's sense of duty that had ultimately soothed her.

"Did you draw this?"

The girl nodded, her expression animated with eagerness. Then, unlacing her fingers, she pointed from the figure of the woman in the duke's arms and then to Jacinda.

"Ah." Jacinda's ruse as a household servant was at an end. She returned the paper with a wry smile. "I'm afraid I've come out a little worse for sea bathing."

The girl grinned. Taking Jacinda's hand, she drew her toward a small milieu table situated near a crackling fire in the aged limestone hearth. There, she sat in one of the two straight-backed chairs and gestured to the other.

Jacinda obliged her, only now realizing that she had yet to hear the girl speak. Though perhaps, like Jacinda, the girl wasn't supposed to be here either and preferred to keep quiet in order to avoid discovery.

The girl didn't appear to be wearing servant's clothes. Her garments were simple without any embroidery along the hem of her blue dress, but the fabric was of a fine muslin and not a coarse homespun. Of course, there were a few charcoal smudges on her white pinafore and, correspondingly, on her fingers. However, her curls were tidy, her face clean, which seemed to indicate that she had no other occupation than drawing. And scattered among the papers on the table were what appeared to be school lessons.

A torn page lay on top of the others with one line written neatly over and over again until it filled every blank space.

Crispin thinks she's pretty!

Curious, Jacinda wondered what that could be about but was distracted by other drawings—a pair of birds on a windowsill, a pair of cats by a hearth, among others—each one equally remarkable. "You're very talented. If I may . . . how old are you?"

The girl flashed both hands, fingers spread.

Apparently, their quiet game was continuing. "Ten years

old? That's a lovely age. At least, I think it is. To tell you the truth, I don't actually remember being ten, or any other age for that matter. At the moment, I don't even know how old I am." She quirked her lips and pointed to the raw lump near the edge of her borrowed cap, trying to keep her tone light to stave off her own worries. "I could very well be four and eighty. What do you think? Do I look like an octogenarian?"

Another huff of air escaped the girl, her cheeks lifting as she shook her head in obvious amusement.

Of course, Jacinda knew she wasn't that old because she'd seen her own reflection in the mottled oval looking glass above the washstand in the tower room. Unfortunately, nothing of her appearance had been familiar. It was like peering through a window and seeing a stranger staring back from the other side.

Quite honestly, she was tired of meeting strangers. The sooner she regained her memory, the better. And she felt, without a doubt, that the answer was here, somewhere in Rydstrom Hall.

"No? Then perhaps . . ." She couldn't finish. Just as her lips parted to say something comical, to coax a true laugh out of the girl, a wave of light-headed exhaustion crashed through her, leaching out every last ounce of strength she possessed. It seemed she'd reached the pinnacle of her endurance.

A chill stole over her, sudden and bone deep. The shiver was unlike what she'd experienced earlier. This one emanated from her marrow, radiating outward. She wondered if the fire had gone out. But no, when her gaze alighted on the hearth, it was aglow with flickering orange flames. Yet she could not feel any warmth from the inviting blaze.

Standing up from the chair to get closer to the hearth, a dizzy spell blurred her vision and she braced her hand on the table's edge. After blinking a few times, her focus returned, if not a bit cloudy around the edges. Beside her, the girl's mouth tipped downward and Jacinda pretended that her intention was to lean over the table in order to get a better look at the sketches.

"My, my, you already possess a remarkable talent," she said, out of breath as she examined a pair of figures standing beneath a leafy archway. Their faces were indistinct, but it was clear by their forms that one was a man and the other a woman. Evidently, this girl was a romantic at heart and, for some mysterious reason, the notion comforted Jacinda. "Though most artists, I imagine, sign their works. How else will people trace your illustrious career?"

The quiet girl beamed. Then, quick as a wink, she shot up from the table, grabbed a haphazard handful of drawings and crossed the room to the desk. Taking a mottled quill in hand, she dipped it into the inkpot.

While she was busy signing her name, and each time with more flourish than the last, Jacinda made her way to the hearth.

The few short steps were more difficult than they ought to have been. Her limbs were both frozen stiff and boneless at the same time, and she had to keep her hand to the back of the chair to keep from listing forward. The floor beneath her squishy boots seemed to slant in a different direction with each step. But, at last, she triumphed and curled her hand over the smooth lip of the mantel for support.

Her new friend came up to her side and presented the faintly wrinkled sketch of the duke carrying Jacinda. Only now, a name was written in grand, sweeping letters across the bottom.

"Sybil," Jacinda read aloud. The light of the fire flickered, mesmerizing her, as she mused over the name. There was a sudden ripple disturbing the wading pool near the center of her brain where all of her memories floated without care. The name was like a pebble that fell into the water with a tiny splash of familiarity. "Hmm . . . Sybil is a lovely name. I feel as if I've heard it before."

Across the room, the door burst open with such force that it smacked the wall behind it.

Startled out of her trance, Jacinda turned to see the duke barging in, that angry vein rising beneath the flesh of his forehead.

"Miss Bourne, what do you think you are doing in here?"

Another shiver wracked her, her teeth chattering. "Clearly, I'm s-standing by this f-fire, admiring a w-work of art."

Beside her, Sybil grinned sheepishly, but after a warning glance from Rydstrom, she pressed her lips together. Still, by the evidence of a lingering cherubic dimple, it was apparent that she wasn't at all threatened by the duke's presence.

This realization was a tremendous relief because Jacinda didn't think she had the energy to battle the duke into showing fairness to the girl—who may or may not be trespassing in this part of the castle. In fact, she didn't think she could summon the strength to cast him a single verbal parry on her own behalf either.

"I cannot leave you unguarded for one moment. You were supposed to remain in the tower," he muttered through gritted teeth. Raking his gaze over Jacinda, a dark scowl furrowed his brow. Then he jerked off his green coat and strode toward her. "You're pale and shaking. I don't suppose you bothered to eat anything. I gave specific orders for you to eat everything on that tray."

Order? Furious castigations lined up on her tongue, but they were sluggish and cold, too, refusing to leave her mouth to rail at him. Before she could utter a single one, he wrapped his coat around her shoulders.

Pleasurable, cedar-scented heat enveloped her and she nearly moaned. She couldn't stop herself from swaying toward him. Worse, the room seemed to be growing darker, making her want to close her eyes and rest.

"Not your prisoner . . . Never order me . . ." *There*, she'd told him.

"Sybil, run along and have Mrs. Hemple bring Miss Bourne a cup of tea with a great deal of sugar stirred in. And make haste because she will likely faint unless—*Damn it all.* Miss Bourne"—he tapped her cheek with his fingertips, tilting her head up to his—"you must rally."

"Cannot." The volume of her voice eroded like sand beneath crushing waves. She was no longer even trying to stand on her own, but shamelessly sagging against him for support. It was his own fault for being so strong, capable, and wonderfully, decadently warm. With her head resting against his shoulder, she had the opportunity to study his cinnamon-colored whiskers closer and wished she had the strength to lift her hand to see if they would dissolve into powder like the spice. "Too tired."

And then she fell into a weightless dream, where she was no longer touching the floor, but cradled in his arms again with him muttering oaths beneath his breath.

DAMN IT all to hell.

For the second time that day, Crispin lifted Jacinda Bourne into his arms. Not having her wiggling around to injure herself further should have been a relief, but it wasn't. Not when she was so pale even her lips were drained of color, and a chill colder than a February gale emanated from her entire body.

Standing near the hearth, he held her as close as he could without injuring her. For all her fire and pluck, she felt entirely too soft and fragile.

When another shiver wracked her, his arms tightened instinctively, yet he'd never felt more powerless.

Ever since he'd met her, she'd begun stripping control away from him. Just now he'd walked into his worst nightmare—Jacinda in the same room with Sybil—and he wasn't even given the opportunity to rail at her. Instead, he was overcome by an urge to heal her, to do whatever he could to turn her back into the most bothersome meddler that'd ever walked the earth.

The very thought shook him.

Insanity! Here she was, in his arms, and dressed as a servant . . . again. Either she'd regained her memory, or the need to create havoc had been ingrained in her character since birth. Though, after his conversation with Dr. Graham a moment ago, Crispin was more inclined to believe the latter.

If Graham thought she must stay here, then Crispin had to put her someplace where he could keep an eye on her. The only solution was one of the guest rooms on the same floor as the master chamber. And, if he had to, he would hang a bell above her door.

Or around her lovely little neck.

He eyed her now, taking note of the ruffled cap, the delicate design of her half-heart–shaped ears, and the one fiery lock of hair that rested over her brow. He itched to put it back in place, and if he had a free hand he just might take the opportunity to do so. But that was an impulse better left alone. Because, if he decided to give in to *one* impulse, then he might give in to another and another, and each more dangerous than the next.

With that thought in mind, he carried her out of the donjon.

Forced to adjust his hold in order to traverse the narrow staircase, he angled her, cradling her head into the curve of his throat, shielding her from the wall. With her body curled closer, it was impossible for him to be unaware of the fact that she wore no corset and no stockings. In fact, it was entirely likely that she had on nothing more than this dress.

Given the circumstances, a swell of lust was *bloody* inappropriate, not to mention unacceptable. He swallowed, steeling himself against the way his blood quickened.

At the bottom of the stairs, Mrs. Hemple rushed up to him, Sybil close behind and worrying her bottom lip as she stared at Jacinda.

"I summoned Dr. Graham, Your Grace," the housekeeper said. "And I have a chamber all prepared for your guest. My, but she is lovely, isn't she?"

In front of Sybil, Crispin refrained from reminding Mrs. Hemple that Miss Bourne was not a guest, but an intruder. His housekeeper hurried down the hall, her steps efficient enough that he never had to slow his stride. Yet as they passed door after door of the guest chambers, turning down corridors that he would normally take to his own suite of rooms, he was suddenly wary.

"Mrs. Hemple, where precisely is this guest chamber you've prepared?"

"You see, sir, the storm has become a problem. There are now leaks in every chamber save for the one Dr. Graham will occupy. In addition, the rose room has a loose stone in the fireplace, and the jonquil room has a cracked windowpane. And even when the storm recedes," she went on quickly, "we'll have the drafts to contend with—hardly the environment for an ill woman just washed up from the sea."

Ahead, the corridor ended, but first widened to accommodate a broad, wooden staircase, leading to a private solar. Across the expanse of polished flooring, strewn with blue and gold runners, were two doors, standing on opposite sides. His own chamber was to the right, and to the left . . .

"This is the duchess's bedchamber," he said to Mrs. Hemple as she disappeared into that very room. A glance over his shoulder proved that Sybil was still with them. Her pale gray gaze darted from him to Jacinda, a dreamy, hopeful expression lifting her cheeks.

No. No. No. This would not do.

Without a word to his sister, he lingered just outside the door. "Mrs. Hemple, this is highly inappropriate. I have already explained that I am not going to marry Miss Bourne."

At his declaration, the woman in question stirred in his arms—the barest tremble—before she burrowed closer. Instinct taking over, he stepped beyond the threshold and crossed the room. Laying her on the bed, where the thick coverlet had already been turned down, he rested her head on the pillow.

When he tried to slip his arms free, Jacinda frowned and gave a soft mewl of distress, her body twisting to get near him. His hold tightened and a soothing *shh . . . shh* left him. He wasn't sure which disturbed him more—his automatic desire to comfort her, or the fact that the gesture mollified him as well.

"She requires another coverlet," he said briskly, needing to release her. "Sybil, fetch the one from my chamber."

Later, he would explain to her that Miss Bourne was only going to remain here long enough to recuperate. He did not want his sister to form any attachment to his unwanted trespasser or to seek her out during the interim.

"And I'll ready a warming pan," Mrs. Hemple said, already sifting through the fire bed for the heated stones kept there for such a purpose.

Looking down, he saw that Jacinda was wearing her wet boots. The leather was starting to dry and crack around the ankles, but the toes were still a glossy black. He reached out and adroitly worked the stiff lacings free, tugged gently, and let them fall to the floor. Her feet were pale and well formed, but the tips of her toes were waterlogged and bloated. Covering them in heavy silk, he curled his hand around one, and then the other, massaging blood and warmth into them.

Mrs. Hemple rushed over with the warming pan. And as he slid free, settling Jacinda into a downy, silken nest, he made one egregious error.

He tucked that auburn lock beneath her cap.

Chapter 11

". . . and when they did meet, his grave looks shewed that she was not forgiven."

JANE AUSTEN, *Emma*

Jacinda blinked open her eyes and tried to focus, though she wasn't entirely sure if she was awake or dreaming.

She could hear the crackling of a fireplace and see the faint flicker of shadows over heavy pleats of azure velvet, gathered by a burnished silver medallion in the center of the canopy.

As far as she knew, she'd never seen this bed before. Then again, as far as she knew, she'd sprung from the sea all too recently as a fully grown woman with no past that she could remember.

Still, on an oddly bright note, she did remember waking up on a rock, meeting Miss Beels and her dog, along with Dr. Graham, young Henry, and the intractable, mysterious, cinnamon-whiskered Duke of Rydstrom. At least she hadn't forgotten anything new.

Well, other than how she managed to fall asleep here—wherever *here* was.

Confused, she sat up on a cushiony mattress, a gray coverlet soft as ermine falling to her lap. Looking down at herself, she noticed that she was dressed differently—not in the burgundy wool she'd worn when she'd first come into awareness on the beach, nor in the borrowed servant's dress—but in a frothy white nightgown.

She plucked at the ruffled cuffs. Why was she not wearing the dark blue homespun?

From her recollection, she'd walked through the castle disguised as a servant in order to find answers. A completely sensible thing to do. After that, however, everything became a dreamlike blur.

She wasn't entirely sure if the golden-haired little girl she'd met was real. And surely, she *must* have imagined the duke lifting her in his arms, that flash of concern in his features, and his gruff voice ordering her to rally. Hmm . . .

Yet without having full access to her faculties, the only true possession she had that linked her to her actual life was a volume of *Emma*.

With a start, she realized that if she didn't know where she was, then she didn't know where her book was either. "My book!"

In heart-thudding panic, she flung off the coverlet—or coverlets, rather, since there were two piled on her—threw her legs over the side of the bed, and pushed frantically against the velvet drapes to find the opening.

That book was all she had. All she knew of herself.

"There, there, fear not, miss. You're not in a coffin. I just closed the bed curtains so that you could rest in peace. Dear me! I didn't mean to say *that*. You're not to *rest in peace* like the dead but peacefully like a mouse in a wardrobe." The curtains slid apart in a clatter of colliding rings on the upper rail. In the pale golden light slanting in through the recessed, diamond-paned windows, a young woman with sprite-like features, mud brown hair and eyes, and a spattering of freckles on her cheeks stood grinning at her. "I'm ever so happy to clap eyes on you again, Miss Bourne. I don't think I need to tell you, but when you left in that boat, I feared the worst."

The boat? All the urgency writhing inside of Jacinda stilled. "You know me?"

"To be sure. I'd not likely forget the young woman who

rescued me," she said with a smile, splaying a hand to her heart. "Though I wish I could have done the same for you. But since I have a dreadful fear of the water, I couldn't climb into that tiny boat with you. I did, however, keep your satchel in perfect condition even if I did weep over it for a time when I thought you were never to return to the inn."

"The inn . . ." Jacinda parroted, trying to put the pieces together, to visualize this inn, and get a sense of how she got here. But no images sprang forth from the sludge in her brain. Her recollections went no further back than the beach.

"The Dappled Cod, miss." The maid blinked. "Oh, but what am I saying? Mrs. Hemple explained to me that you'd taken a bump to the noggin and lost your—"

"It isn't *lost*," Jacinda said quickly. Standing up, she smoothed down the layers of white ruffles, but then a rush of dizziness hit her. She sank back down, gripping the side of the mattress to make sure she didn't tip forward and wind up on the floor. "My memory is fully intact. It's just . . . temporarily misplaced. And speaking of . . . I need to find my book. Am I still inside Rydstrom Hall?"

Quite honestly, she wasn't certain. Other than the smooth, pale ashlar stones along the outer wall, this vast room looked very little like the chamber in the tower. Shimmering blue silk wallpaper lined the inner walls. A broad, elegantly carved wardrobe stood in the corner with ovals of mirror glass set into the doors. A sumptuous gray fur lay beneath her feet, while the rest of the floor was swathed in intricately woven sapphire, ruby, and emerald threaded carpets. The bedposts were tall spirals of an exotic gray-grained wood, polished to a silver tone finish. And the bedside tables, vanity, and hearth were adorned in opulent, blue-veined marble. She couldn't help but wonder at the sudden change in her accommodations.

"Indeed, we are," the young woman said with an elfin grin. "*And* we're in the duchess's chamber."

Jacinda watched, speechless as the maid crossed the

room and picked up the familiar red leather volume from a table near the door. It took a moment for the words to sink in, but she immediately decided she couldn't have heard correctly. "The *what*?"

The maid repeated herself, her grin expanding as she handed Jacinda the book.

No. This did not make sense. The duke had not even wanted her in Rydstrom Hall in the first place. He certainly would never have permitted her in this chamber. Oh dear.

Numb, she reached for her book and wrapped her arms around it. Then slowly, she sank back onto the mattress and stared up at the silver oval in the center of the canopy. "Did I creep in here sometime during the night and fall asleep?"

For some reason, this did not seem implausible.

The maid issued a small, lilting laugh. "From what I heard, His Grace put you here himself. Carried you down from the donjon."

"He had me in the *dungeon*?" Jacinda bolted upright. But when another wave of dizziness assailed her, she sank back down again. She could still be angry at that beast of a man from this position.

"Not dungeon, but *donjon*," she said, articulating carefully. "From what I heard, it's the highest room in a castle. And with the size of Rydstrom Hall, I'd say he carried you a long way. The chambermaids are all talking about how they'd never seen a more romantic sight."

Drawing in a breath, Jacinda carefully sat up and took in her sumptuous surroundings again, wondering if this were a dream. Thinking back to the way all the color had drained from the duke's countenance when she'd first asked if she was to be his wife, she realized that yes, this was a dream. And a silly one at that. "Impossible. I can say with almost certainty that this is the last room the duke would permit me. The man despises me."

"Perhaps His Grace had a change of heart, miss." The maid lifted her slim shoulders in a shrug before bending toward the steaming kettle hanging from an iron bar in the hearth. Removing it from the hook, she carried it to a blue-and-white teapot waiting on a nearby table. "I don't rightly know the particulars as I only arrived this morning—a full day since we last parted."

"Did I sleep through most of yesterday?"

"To be sure. Though I would have been here sooner if not for the storm and the thick mud it left behind. By then, news of the *mermaid lady*—you—reached me in the next village. When they spoke of your auburn hair, I knew it had to be you." Then she lowered her voice to a whisper. "But don't worry, I didn't say a word about the boat you . . . um . . . *borrowed.* I know you had every intention of bringing it back. Though, I don't imagine it's in any shape to return to the owner now."

In a slow trickle, Jacinda absorbed this information. Absently, she watched the maid return the kettle to the fire as the earthy fragrance of steeping tea filled the chamber. She'd slept for a day and, before that, had borrowed a boat? Hmm . . . she wondered what happened to it, not recalling a boat on the beach with her. Yet there were these bits and pieces of . . . "Wait. Was there anyone else with me?"

She squeezed her eyes shut. *Oh, please tell me that I was alone.*

"You were quite determined to make it on your own."

Jacinda's shoulders sagged as a breath whooshed out of her. Thank heavens.

Pouring tea into a waiting cup, the maid shook her head, oblivious to the overwhelming relief she gave. "And if I may say, I never took you for someone who would be so handy with the oars, but off you went by yourself, cutting through the water like a spoon through cream. It helped me to fret less once you rowed out of sight and around the bend."

Jacinda was glad to know that her character, while reckless, was not wholly irredeemable. It was a start, at least.

"Then perhaps I grew up in a fishing village," she mused,

trying to conjure a memory of rowing a boat, the water lapping against the hull, her hands gripping the oars, the sun shining down on her face. Hmm . . . still nothing.

Then that pesky, throbbing headache returned, proving her efforts futile.

"Perhaps, miss, though I couldn't rightly say," the maid said, handing her a cup and saucer.

Jacinda opened her mouth to thank the maid, but realized with a stab of irritation that she couldn't remember her name. *What an immense surprise*, she thought wryly. "There is one additional result of my boating adventure, and that is the fact that I cannot recall your name."

"Understandable, considering the circumstances, miss. I'm Lucinda Stowe, but everyone calls me Lucy."

"I'm very pleased to meet you, once again, Lucy," Jacinda said and received a lighthearted curtsy. "You said I rescued you?"

Jacinda lifted the cup to take a sip and instantly cringed at the unexpected, overly sweet, milk-laden brew. She could scarcely taste the essence of the leaves, and it became instantly apparent that her palate was not accustomed to such a concoction. Experimentally, she tried another sip and shuddered. One benefit to the disaster in her cup, however, was that she learned something about herself: Jacinda Bourne despised sweet, milky tea.

Still feeling a trifle dizzy, she set the cup and saucer down on the bedside table and settled back against the bolster pillow.

"Oh yes, miss." Lucy, in the process of tying the bed curtains to the posts, dropped the braided silver rope and placed both hands over her heart. "I was in a heap of tears, despairing for my life. I was sure I'd never find another position, not after leaving Lord Comstock without notice. But I had to, even you said so. When a gentleman makes improper advances toward his servants, then there are only two alternatives—to stay and endure or to leave and face the consequences."

"That despicable cad!" Jacinda railed, furious. "How dare he take advantage of his position!"

Lucy went still and stared at her, agape. "Uncanny, Miss Bourne. That's precisely what you said outside the servant registry in London. Then on that very spot, you offered me a position as your maid and chaperone. Have you now located your misplaced memories?"

"Unfortunately not," Jacinda grumbled. Though it was a relief that she seemed to exhibit the same character traits as before. At least she was still herself. Whoever that was. "Though, now that I have you here with me, I should have an accounting of who I am in short order. Tell me, how many years have we been together?"

"Well, miss," Lucy began. "You see, we met not three days past."

"Three days . . ." The words left Jacinda on a deflated rush of air. Drat. This was as disconcerting as it was confusing. And apparently, she was a young woman of society who wore fine clothes, rowed boats, and did not have her own maid. She tried to wrap her mind around it, but was distracted by something Lucy said before. "Hold on a moment. Did you say London?"

"Indeed, miss. Not far from St. James's Street if that helps."

A rush of prickles skittered up Jacinda's spine and tightened her scalp, as if they were setting off nerve endings that only sparked at suspicious happenings—her very own curiosity sensors.

Both Jacinda and Rydstrom arrived in Whitcrest on the same day?

Quite the coincidence. Only she didn't believe it was a coincidence at all. It couldn't have been.

"Did I happen to mention why I required a companion on such short notice?"

Lucy shook her head. "You may have done, but I was in such a state that I was quite overcome with . . . illness."

She looked down to the hem of her simple brown dress and sniffed. "There's no easy way to say this, so I'll just have out with it and tell you that I either retched or slept for the entire journey. My poor satchel bore the horror of the episode for as long as it could." She gulped, even now looking a little green around the edges. "I see how helpful it would have been if we'd engaged in conversation, and I hope you forgive me for saying so, but I'm ever so thankful that you have no memory of those topsy-turvy hours."

Drat.

"Think nothing of it," Jacinda said, holding in a sigh of disappointment. She was surrounded by strangers. All but one.

There had to have been a reason she traveled here with the duke's card tucked in her book. Finding the answer was the key to regaining her memory. So, whether Rydstrom wanted to or not, he was going to help her.

"WHY DID you put me in the duchess's chamber?"

At his desk, Crispin jerked his head up in time to see Jacinda sweep into his study as if she had every right. "Miss Bourne, what do you mean by this, barging into a room without bidding admittance or even announcing yourself?"

"The door was open." Unaffected by the bluster in his tone, she continued toward him, her lavender skirts shushing against the woven rug. Her hair was pinned back into a braided coil at her crown, the wound at her temple glistening with the honey salve from the kitchens. And at her hairline, one auburn lock threatened to droop over her forehead. Mocking him.

Color had returned to her skin, her cheeks now tinged with the pink of health. Far different from the alarming ashen white of yesterday morning, or the sallow tone he'd witnessed in the afternoon. Graham had assured him that she'd simply required a recuperative rest and showed no signs of fever. In response to the doctor's placating tone, Crispin explained that the sole reason for checking on her repeatedly had been to gather information for the letter he would send to her family. Nothing more.

And this morning, he'd finished that letter with the news that Miss Bourne's strength had much improved.

In fact, a few moments ago, Mrs. Hemple had informed him that his *guest*—she seemed to make a point of stressing that word whenever she could—had eaten a goodly portion of coddled eggs on her breakfast tray and then enjoyed a lengthy soak in the bath. The reason his housekeeper had added the last bit, he did not know, but he advised her that in the future he did not require such a full report.

Ever since, he'd been plagued with the image of Jacinda Bourne lounging in the slipper tub, her hair cascading down in fiery wet tendrils, the length of her bare arms along the rim with steam rising from her skin, and cresting just above the surface of the water, her breasts, glistening with fragrant oils . . .

"Nevertheless"—he cleared his throat—"a gentleman's study is a place where he has the freedom to do as he wishes, to conduct business, to speak frankly, smoke, or drink if he is so inclined, and without fear of offending any delicate sensibilities."

"I don't believe you're worried about offending anyone, least of all me. After all, you told me you never apologize, *and* that it was the one thing we have in common," she said, her ire up for reasons he could not fathom.

He was about to say as much until, with a glance down, he noticed that he'd spilled two red drops of sealing wax on his desk. *Bollocks.* Now he would have to let it dry before having his desk tidy once more.

Crispin preferred to keep this room in segmented order. It was a practice he'd had since childhood. Having things in their proper place gave him a sense of peace.

At least, usually. Any sense of calm he'd once possessed had left him in recent days.

Still, he welcomed the familiarity around him. In the upper left quadrant of his study was the door with a burgundy and gold rug resting over the hardwood floor, where Miss Bourne was currently tapping her foot at him, the toe of her cream-colored slipper peeking out from beneath her hem. To the right of that was the second quadrant, where the broad hearth took up much of the far paneled wall, along with a comfortable chintz sofa, flanked by a pair of tables and upholstered bronze armchairs. Beside Crispin, bookshelves lined the third quadrant, the outer wall adorned with heavy brocade curtains over a recessed window seat. And his own quadrant—opposite of Miss Bourne and her glare in his direction—hosted a large burled wood desk, which faced the room, and a towering escritoire behind him.

"Therefore," she continued, "I find it quite strange that you should have placed me in the duchess's chamber. And not at all against your will, for I heard you carried me there yourself."

He gave Jacinda a warning glare before returning his attention to the letter. "Refrain from any romantic notions. I put you there out of necessity. The other chambers are in need of repairs."

"*All* of them in this entire castle?"

Rankled by her dubious tone, he accidentally pressed his signet ring into the pool of wax off center. He cursed under his breath before his gaze snapped back to her. "I'll have you know that the original keep is more than six hundred years old. With the additions over the life spans of my ancestors, there are ninety-seven rooms in all. It takes a great deal to maintain an estate this vast. Between the onslaught of time, the weather, and the pounding of the wind and sea, there is a constant list of repairs to be done."

"Ah. Now I understand." She crossed her arms beneath her breasts, causing the ribbon border to pull taut.

Crispin did his best not to notice the soft delineation of plump, creamy flesh rising above the edge of lavender muslin, or that he was suddenly craving sea buckthorn berries again. "What precisely?"

"The reason you are searching for a wife. Miss Beels mentioned it on the beach."

Alarmed, he stared at her, counting the beats of the pulse beneath his cinched cravat, and wondering how to word his response. He didn't want to trigger her memory. "The matter does not concern you."

Her turquoise eyes sharpened, a gleam lit from within as if he'd confessed all she needed to know. "If that is the case, then I must not possess the wealth you require."

She was like a never-ending storm that just kept battering against the rocks. If he wasn't so worried about the damage such a person could bring to Sybil, he might actually be impressed by her acuity and sheer determination.

At the inane thought, a hollow, circumspect laugh escaped him. "There are many other reasons we are not suited."

"Having only met you yesterday, I already agree with you on that account. Wholeheartedly," she replied, her crisp enunciation cutting through the air like that first crack of thunder before a spring storm. "But what I do not understand is why both of us left London on the same day, only to end up in Whitcrest. More puzzling is that if you are searching for a wealthy bride, then surely London would be the best place to find one."

He kept his expression bland as if her statement garnered nothing more than idle curiosity. "Do you remember London?"

"Nothing more than a basic knowledge that it is a large city, an epicenter of culture and society, and up until very recently, my home. Though, at the moment, I only have an academic understanding of these things, as if I've read the information in a traveler's guide. I can conjure no images, sounds, or fragrances from thinking of it." She flitted her fingers in an unsettled, absent gesture, unaware of the relief she gave him. "And now are you going to acknowledge my question?"

She did not give him a chance to answer before she moved forward, stepping out of her quadrant and into his.

The scents of lavender, bergamot, rose water, and a hint of vanilla crowded closer. That faint, intoxicatingly feminine breeze threatened to smother him. Then a pair of perturbed blue irises raked over him—seemingly in a gesture to put him in his place and dismiss him—but it had the opposite effect.

It was her fault, entirely, for her gaze hesitated—not once, not twice, but *thrice*—on his jaw, his shoulders, and his hands. Then she committed the worst sin of all. She wet her lips.

His nostrils flared as he inhaled, his blood heating. Even after a day had passed, he could still feel her body against him so distinctly that he imagined, if he looked down, he would see the outline of her head, her arms, and her breasts pressed into his clothes.

His errant gaze skimmed over her before settling on her hands where the tip of her finger was near the edge of the wax droplet.

On an otherwise tidy surface, the red droplet and her pale, elegant hands were glaringly out of place. Especially when he could think of a dozen ways to keep the latter better occupied.

The carnal images that flashed through his head surprised him, and he was ashamed at the lack of control he had of his own thoughts. "Mind your hands, Miss Bourne. You are perilously close to smearing spilled wax."

Narrowing her eyes, she purposely pushed her fingertip into the wax. It wasn't entirely soft at this point, but the pressure caused a divot, and likely discolored the wood beneath it. Then she lifted her chin and crossed her arms once more, framing her plump breasts.

He gripped the edge of his desk and rose, more in an effort to keep his gaze level with hers. "I will not keep you here against your will, Miss Bourne. You may ignore the doctor's recommendations, if you so desire."

He prayed she would take him up on the offer, if only for a respite on his overrun senses.

"Though, according to the doctor, to my own detriment."

"Possibly," he answered, saying nothing else. Her color was high now, her cheeks suffused in crimson smudges—far different from yesterday's startling pallor. Comparing the two, he preferred her irritated rather than frail.

No, he reminded himself, he preferred her *gone* instead. He'd just gotten rid of Miss Beels and her dog a short time ago. Henry had left at first light, wanting to brave as much mud as possible. And now Crispin was all too aware that he was virtually alone with Jacinda Bourne, her chaperone nowhere in sight.

She exhaled a puff of air, dislodging that fat red tendril. It fell in a soft burnished swish, curling against the arch of her left brow. His fingers twitched, eliciting a series of pulses up the length of his arm. Clenching his jaw, he fought an unhealthy urge to reach out, haul her across the desk, pull her onto his lap, and—

"Ah. There you are Miss Bourne and Rydstrom," Dr. Graham said, stepping into the study. "I'm glad to find you both here where I can speak to you about my plans for Miss Bourne's recuperation."

"Perhaps it would serve me better to return to London for answers," Jacinda replied, narrowing her eyes at Crispin. "Besides, I might have people depending on me."

Crispin subdued a snort. *Oh yes, for who else would be willing to pilfer gentlemen's town houses for the sake of matchmaking?*

As if reading his thoughts, her agitated gaze flashed bright blue before she turned to Dr. Graham.

"As I explained, Miss Bourne," Graham said with his usual manner of patience, "such an act could be harmful to your recovery. In your current state, you can hardly be of service to anyone. Therefore, it is in your best interest to remain here for a time."

She huffed. "How much time?"

Graham came closer, peering through his spectacles at the wound on the side of her head. The swelling of it had gone down a great deal, but it was still raw. "Since many of your injuries are not too severe, I imagine we will see much improvement within a fortnight. From what I learned from Miss Stowe a moment ago, you discovered your preference for strong black tea. Why, by tomorrow you may have true memories."

This statement did not sit well with Crispin, and the warmth in his veins abruptly cooled. He did not want her memory to return until she was far away from here and less likely to wreak any more havoc than she already had.

"And to hasten the process for one as determined as you are, I've planned an afternoon of memory exercises. We could begin with the commonplace tasks that occupy most debutantes each day, like sewing and playing the pianoforte. If you feel up to it, that is."

Crispin didn't want to puncture Graham's hope-filled bubble by pointing out that his plan would work better if he chose a *commonplace* debutante. Miss Bourne was far from that. In fact, Crispin doubted she did anything that a typical debutante would. He could no more picture her sitting demurely in a parlor and sipping tea than he could imagine her taking flight.

"And each evening," the doctor continued, "we will gather here in this study and recount your recollections of the day."

Crispin frowned, not appreciating an open invitation into his sanctuary.

Jacinda pointed an accusatory finger at Crispin. "There are already true memories here in this room, if Rydstrom would supply what he knows of me."

"But those would be his accounts, not yours," Graham said.

"If both he and I share them, I see no difference." Miss Bourne tucked her finger away as Graham led her toward the upper right quadrant of the room.

Crispin resumed his seat and drew in a breath to steady himself. Yet the enticing permeation of her fragrance still filled the air, and he wondered, abjectly, if he would ever be free of it.

"Yes, however, each person has individual experiences," Graham said. "Even the simplest things can illicit different reactions, colors, fragrances, and the like. Take the hearth for example. What do you see when you look at it?"

"What anyone would," she grumbled, but studied at it all the same, turning in such a way that the firelight bathed her cheek and the column of her throat in a golden glow. "A warm fire burning over the logs on the grate."

"And, Your Grace"—Graham turned to look over his shoulder—"if I may pose the same question?"

Inwardly, Crispin jolted, feeling like a boy being caught with his hand in the biscuit tin. He chastised himself for his wayward gaze, and gave the hearth a cursory glance. "I see that there are only two logs on the grate, an empty wood-box, and a pile of ash that needs to be collected."

Miss Bourne huffed, holding her arms stiffly at her sides. "But do you concede that there is, in fact, a warm fire?"

He shrugged, taking perverse pleasure in goading her, in having those charged irises alight on him. "It could be warmer. This is a large room, after all, and this half hosts a drafty window."

"No doubt the primary drop in temperature originates from your corner."

"And thus, you understand that my interpretation was the

correct one," he said with a scholarly nod, pretending he did not catch her insult.

She moved closer again, her steps taking her to the invisible border that divided the room. And when she drew in a purposeful breath, he felt a crushing sensation in his own lungs as if she'd taken it directly from him. "The air is quite *stuffy* over there as well."

He jerked his chin in the direction of the fireplace. "Then by all means, return to where you are most comfortable."

"I would," she said, taking not one but two steps toward him before propping her hands on his desk as she leaned in, "*if* you would direct me home to my uncle."

"If that is your wish, I'll ring for a carriage this instant."

"I realize this is asking quite a bit under the circumstances," Dr. Graham interjected from the sofa. "However, I have great hopes that in a short amount of time your memory will be restored."

She wrinkled her nose at Crispin, while she replied to Graham. "A fortnight seems like a great deal of time, if you ask me."

"Perhaps it will be less," Graham mused. "We could start our exercises now, if you like. Tell me what you recall from yesterday."

Crispin eased back in his chair and lifted his brows, gesturing with a casual wave of his hand for her to proceed. In return, Jacinda issued a frustrated growl and turned her back on him.

"What purpose would it serve, since we all experienced the same events?" she asked.

"Here again would be an example of how our perspectives alter memory," Graham said. "I am only interested in what you remember and how you are shaping new memories. Perhaps with that knowledge it will help to unlock the ones that are trapped inside your head."

"Very well." She drew in a breath of obvious impatience. "Sometime yesterday, I awoke on a rock and greeted Miss

Beels and her dog, Mr. Lemon. Then you came along, and were kind enough to offer your handkerchief, embroidered with a *G* for Graham to help me remember. And then came Henry in his new boots and—"

"Why would you say that his boots were new?"

She lifted her shoulders in an indolent shrug. "Because the leather wasn't creased and he had the legs of his trousers tucked inside as if to show them off."

"Remarkable." Graham tilted his head slightly, studying her. "You have quite the gift for noticing details. Pray, what did you notice about our host?"

Crispin went still while the hidden pulse beneath his cravat hammered as her attention returned to him.

She set her hands on her hips, her chin tilting up at an angle that unsettled the lock over her forehead. "Rydstrom seemed in a great hurry, and yet stopped cold when he saw me, almost as if I were Medusa rising out of the sea, ready to turn him to stone."

A chuckle escaped Graham, but he was quick to cough in order to conceal it. "Ah, very good. You know your myths. This is one thing we may look into further tomorrow." His mustachios twitched as he slid a wry glance to Crispin. "Is that all you noticed?"

"He glowers at me, and far more than he ought toward someone he scarcely knows."

"Not this again," Crispin muttered under his breath.

"In addition, he looked as if he'd slept in his clothes, he was unshaven but smelled like cedar, and up close his whiskers resembled—" She broke off unexpectedly. Then a slow saturation of watercolor red spread across her cheeks.

This sudden alteration caught Crispin's interest. Was she blushing? He never would have guessed that the unapologetic, scheming, audacious Miss Bourne had a bashful bone in her delightful body.

"Anything you notice is important, Miss Bourne," Graham said, his tone uncharacteristically bright and helpful. "There is no judgment here. What did Rydstrom's whiskers resemble?"

"Yes. I should like to know as well," Crispin added, his voice low as if the matter was just between the two of them.

Ever brave under scrutiny, she straightened her shoulders and locked eyes with him, never backing down. "Though it matters little in regaining my memory, your whiskers resembled dusted cinnamon. Now, Dr. Graham, perhaps we can start immediately on those exercises."

And then, without another word—head high and cheeks awash in color—she strode out of the room.

But before she could get away, Crispin called out, "One more thing, Miss Bourne."

She stopped at the threshold, half in the study, half in the corridor. Her hand gripped the edge of the doorframe, the tips of her fingers white with strain, very like the tight, impatient smile on her lips. "Yes, *Your Grace*?"

"As I mentioned before, many places in Rydstrom Hall are in disrepair. Therefore, for your own safety, you should never venture anywhere without either Dr. Graham's escort or mine."

She hissed in a breath, eyes narrowed, lips parted, her countenance captivating in its fury. "So, in a manner of speaking, I am to be locked in the dungeon, after all."

"For your own safety," he said without arguing the points on limited freedom versus none at all. He glanced briefly to Graham and received a half nod that was more token of acceptance than support of his decision.

Clearly, Graham still couldn't fathom the full scope of Jacinda's ability to steal her way into forbidden places. Crispin wouldn't be surprised if, without a constant guard, she found her way to the locked door of his aunt's apartments by the end of the hour. Though, out of precaution, he kept the key on his person.

"Or perhaps you could arrange a tour and simply indicate the dangers," she replied a bit too sweetly.

"Certainly. As soon as your health improves and faculties return—assuming my schedule allows for the distraction—I should be *delighted* to be your guide."

Both disbelief and challenge met him in the upward arc of her brows. "No doubt, with all that is demanded of you, your schedule will be quite full."

"Quite." Again, he had the ludicrous urge to grin as if they were engaging in some sort of flirtation. But this was far from it, he reminded himself. This was a matter of dire importance. His expression remained severe. "Nevertheless, the main purpose for your stay here is to recuperate, not to traipse around crumbling corridors, putting yourself in danger. Now, if we have concluded our impromptu meeting, I should like to return to the lengthy list of tasks required of me."

"And I should not wish to keep you. Dr. Graham, if I may have an escort far away from His Grace's domain?" She stormed out without another backward glance.

Graham chuckled, rising from the sofa. "I suppose I've been summoned, haven't I? A shame, really. The exchange was . . . enlightening."

Crispin frowned, not liking the knowing gleam behind Graham's spectacles as he crossed the room and disappeared through the doorway.

"What you witnessed was nothing more than a clash of wills," he said, but his declaration fell flat, without anyone other than himself to hear it.

Distractedly, he scratched his freshly shaven jaw, caught by a fleeting curiosity about the admission that had colored Jacinda's cheeks. He wondered what else she had noticed about him. But that would be like opening Pandora's box. He'd do well to tamp down this urge and tuck it away like he had all the others.

He certainly didn't want to repeat yesterday's lapse with *the errant lock.*

Chapter 12

"... till she saw her in the way of cure, there could be no true peace for herself."

JANE AUSTEN, *Emma*

Yesterday's exercises left Jacinda weary. She was no closer to remembering who she was, or why she was here, than she had been that first day on the rock.

Aside from her table manners and handwriting, she appeared to have no true accomplishments as a debutante. Her clumsy work on the pianoforte proved that, while she understood how to read music, she had no skill in placing her fingers on the correct keys. Her attempts at the harp and viola were painful to anyone with ears as well as to her own fingertips.

"Music is not necessarily for everyone," Dr. Graham had said with a patient smile, and only a hint of cringing.

After a few hours of failure, Jacinda had retired to the duchess's chamber and spent the remainder of the day reading *Emma*.

Ingrained in her, she knew each scene and each character as if she'd once lived inside the book. Yet there was an unsurpassable wall between herself and the memory of reading it before, or how it came to be so familiar to her.

She was eager to read on to the second volume in the hopes of finding the link. Yet while browsing the otherwise impressive collection in Rydstrom's library this morning, she could not find it.

She'd been in this room for the past three hours with Dr. Graham, furthering her exercises. They'd pored over mythology books, one after another, hoping to spark her memory.

Jacinda was familiar with most of the stories, but it was as if the knowledge came to her by rote instead of by memory. A completely different part of her brain understood what she liked to eat and drink, how to read and write, how to scrub her face and brush her hair. And all the basic essentials. But her memories were still swimming in a pool of seawater, too far beneath the surface to call them forth.

It still seemed that her only hope to uncovering the mystery of her own identity resided with Rydstrom. And yet, by all accounts, he made it a priority to encounter her as little as possible. A fact quite evident given that she'd only seen his countenance twice yesterday—his morning glower in his study and his evening scowl at dinner. Did he even know how to grin?

She doubted it. Nevertheless, his absence left her with no other choice than to look for answers on her own.

"I'm quite impressed with your education, Miss Bourne. I daresay, not many men are as learned in Greek and Roman mythology," Graham said, closing another book as she accepted this compliment with a gracious nod.

He laid the book on the ever-growing pile atop one of a pair of mahogany tables, its twin standing empty on the opposite end of the long narrow room. If not for that incongruity, she might have thought a grand mirror bisected the library, because both halves of the room were nearly identical.

Every object was positioned with great precision, from the pair of azure blue and silver-hued rugs that flanked either side of the tables, to the two wingback chairs in dark, faded leather, facing each other at a standoff. Even the floor to ceiling bookshelves, lining the inner wall and separated by the doorway, seemed arranged with similarly sized books. It was as if the room was built on a great scale that demanded equal weight on each side. Though, to be fair, there were different tapestries hanging at either end.

Despite all of the fastidiousness, she liked this room. The musty sweet aroma of the books soothed a forgotten part of her.

She wondered if Rydstrom came in here to survey his lands, admiring the view of the picturesque, tumbled hillside and forest glade to the north. If he ever lingered inside the pages of a book until the tapers burned down to the quick. If he ever put his feet up and warmed them in front of the broad fireplace . . .

"Perhaps we will alter our course to philosophy next," Graham said, interrupting her peculiar domestic musings. Which was for the best. She had plenty of other things on her mind, and didn't need the distraction.

What she needed was answers.

As luck would have it, in that same moment, Mr. Fellows appeared in the open doorway and cleared his throat.

When the doctor joined him in the corridor, she tried to position herself to capture an errant word or two. Pretending to scan the shelves, her fingertips inattentively glided over the book spines, her ear tilted toward the doorway.

The conversation was too muffled to overhear every word, but she caught the essentials—*farrier*, *shoe*, and *temperamental stallion*. Hmm . . . she wondered if her watchguard might be called away.

Only a simpleton would not see this as an opportunity.

When the conversation came to an end, she quickly plucked a book from the shelf and made it appear as if she were engrossed in the contents by bending her head and then turning it right side up.

"I'm being summoned on an important matter in the stables, Miss Bourne," Dr. Graham said, moving to her side. "Would you mind perusing the shelves without me for a short duration?"

She placed her finger on a line of text as if to mark her

place and pursed her lips in a mask of disappointment before offering a reluctant nod. "I'll wait here until your return."

Dr. Graham left the room and disappeared down the hall with Mr. Fellows.

In the very next instant, and with no one else about, Jacinda slipped out of the library and up the nearest staircase.

After traversing a confusing array of corridors, she found herself in the hall beneath a minstrel's gallery. *Wait a minute* . . . she'd been here before, on the first day after she'd slipped out of the tower room. Hadn't she?

Her mind flashed with glimpses of an angelic, golden-haired girl, a table full of sketches, and a neatly scrawled name of *Sybil*. Then Jacinda recalled Rydstrom himself, furious and holding her tightly against him, his gruff voice oddly soothing.

It was this last part that made her wonder if she was imagining things. Of course, she could simply ask Dr. Graham or Rydstrom if there was a girl named Sybil beneath this roof. But what if there wasn't?

If there was a possibility that Jacinda had lost a bit of sense as well as her memory when she'd hit her head, she didn't want anyone else to know.

There were certain things a woman kept to herself, after all, like uncomfortable stomach ailments, for example, and . . . a moderate case of lunacy.

Therefore, she decided to proceed on her own.

Spotting the narrow servants' stairs, she climbed up one floor and then another, pausing to catch her breath along the way before traversing the winding corridor and then . . .

She expelled a breath of relief. Through the doorway, she saw the girl sitting at the desk in front of the window.

CRISPIN GRIPPED the ebony hilt of the broadsword, the weight natural in his hand as if the weapon were an extension of his arm. He slashed through the air in a fluid arc, mindful of the rectangular table in the center of the armory, and lunged forward toward an unseen opponent. But in his mind's eye, he was battling himself.

If anyone deserved to be thoroughly slaughtered, it was him. Because he was the fool who'd put Jacinda Bourne in the bedchamber across from his own.

Had he truly imagined her presence would have no effect on him, other than giving him the ability to keep a closer watch on her?

"Idiot." Growling, he made another series of revolutions, relishing the bite in his shoulders, the strain in his arms, and the first prickles of sweat.

He should have foreseen the distraction she would pose. He'd understood it all too well last night when he'd escorted her to the room. She'd been tired and hiding her yawns behind a napkin all through dinner, so much so that she hadn't needled him with questions. And more than that, he'd noticed a faint, purplish hue beneath her eyes, marking her exhaustion.

She'd done too much. And Crispin had found himself quietly brooding, angry at Graham for having overtaxed her with memory exercises. It was only for that reason that Crispin offered to escort her from the dining room to her chamber. And every step of the way, he'd fought the urge to press his hand to the small of her back and offer his shoulder for her to lean against.

Thankfully, he hadn't succumbed, but the temptation irritated him, nonetheless.

That mood had stayed with him, starting this morning when he dressed. With his valet still in London, there was no idle chatter to distract him from the fact that Jacinda was across the hall. Facing the door while he buttoned his clothes and tied his cravat, it was if he stared through a window instead.

He'd imagined seeing her a dozen steps away—sleepy, warm and rumpled, her hair a mass of auburn tangles, her cheeks flushed—and a keen, nearly painful arousal had built within him.

"Only a . . . masochist . . . fantasizes about . . . his living nightmare. Take . . . hold of . . . yourself," he huffed, slaying hundreds of invisible marauders, leaving their carcasses in heaps at his feet.

Out of breath, he set the point of the blade on the stone floor and rested his hands over the pommel. Looking around the room to the four walls covered in weapons and shields—each side proportionate to the other, of course—he felt centered once again, more like himself.

This was his home, his domain, ergo he was in control. He wasn't about to let some misguided, inexcusable temptation get the better of him. *No, indeed!*

Moving toward the high table, he set the broadsword down, intending to polish the steel before replacing it to the stand. Before he'd begun his exercises, he'd removed his coat, waistcoat, and cravat. But after mopping his brow and the back of his neck with a handkerchief, he set about dressing again. He just finished tucking the edge of his cravat into his waistcoat when Fellows appeared at the door.

"Ah, Your Grace. I thought I would find you in here," Fellows said, lifting a polished silver salver where a single square missive lay. "You asked that I bring any correspondence from Miss Bourne's family whenever it arrived."

Crispin stared at it, his stomach twisting unpleasantly. He'd sent a rider and a pair of his fastest horses, but he never expected to have a response so quickly. And now, for some unknown reason, he was reluctant to remove it from the salver.

So instead, he reached for his coat, shrugging into the garment that was a little snug after his exertions. "Just set it down on the edge of the table, if you will."

Fellows inclined his head, wearing a pleasant grin that had become a recent addition to his countenance, the worried lines from the past four years altering their direction in more of an upward tilt. "Miss Bourne will be happy to hear from her family, I should imagine."

"It would not be prudent to tell her of it at this time," Crispin said with a note of warning.

"Yes, of course, sir. Now that you mention it, Dr. Graham did say something along those lines when I escorted him to the stables a short while ago."

Adjusting his cuffs, Crispin went still. "But if Graham is in the stables, then who is with Miss Bourne?"

Chapter 13

"The visit afforded her many pleasant recollections the next day . . ."

JANE AUSTEN, *Emma*

The floor creaked beneath Jacinda's feet, and the girl looked over her shoulder.

An instant smile bloomed on Sybil's face, her cheeks lifted, her gray eyes twinkling. Hopping up from her chair, she rushed out into the corridor.

"Good day, Sybil."

The girl tilted her head to the side and then wiggled her fingers in a wave.

"Ah. We must be playing the silent game again today," Jacinda said, stepping through the doorway.

"She does not speak, Miss Bourne."

Jacinda startled, turning guiltily. "Oh, Mrs. Hemple . . . I did not think I would find anyone here. I was just looking for . . . my room, you see, and I must have gotten turned around."

The housekeeper, whom she'd met yesterday morning, was sitting in the chair nearest the fire, holding a length of fabric, an open sewing box on the milieu table in front of her. But at Jacinda's statement, a knowing gleam lit her brown gaze as her lips curled slightly. "You are welcome to stay. I see no harm in it."

In response, Sybil skipped around the table and wrapped her slender arms around Mrs. Hemple's shoulders.

"Thank you. After the morning I've had, I could use a diversion." Still weak from her boat-borrowing ordeal—not to mention climbing *five thousand* flights of stairs—she crossed the room toward the chair she'd occupied the first time she was here. What a relief that Mrs. Hemple was not as strict and forbidding as the duke. "Is Sybil your daughter, then?"

The housekeeper hesitated, glancing briefly to Sybil and then back to Jacinda. "She is in my charge and has been since she came to Rydstrom Hall four years ago."

A series of prickles tripped the nerves along Jacinda's spine in what she'd begun to think of as her curiosity sensors, but she couldn't quite understand the reason for them in this circumstance. There was nothing suspicious in the statement. Likely, this time, the reaction was nothing more than a lingering chill.

Smiling, the mute girl blinked coyly at Mrs. Hemple and pressed a kiss to her cheek.

The housekeeper clucked her tongue as she tenderly brushed back the gold fringe of curls from Sybil's forehead. "Ack, go on with you, now. Back to your studies. His Grace expects a neat column of figures."

Sybil rolled her eyes and trudged back to the desk, but brought her pages and chair to the table, sitting beside Jacinda.

"Rydstrom marks her schoolwork?" Jacinda asked, somewhat stunned. This didn't seem like a typical task for a duke. Then again, Rydstrom was the only one she knew.

Still, something about it seemed strange, only she didn't know what.

Mrs. Hemple began plying her needle once more. "Without a tutor in the keep, I can think of no keener mind. Though, I gather you are sharp-witted as well."

Distracted by her thoughts, she absently asked, "What makes you say that?"

"Perhaps because you are always carrying a book with you."

Forgetting that she had it, Jacinda looked down at the blue leather tome and placed it on the table. "Oh yes, I haven't read this one yet. Fascinating subject."

Mrs. Hemple lifted her gaze from the sewing to study the book more closely, her brow wrinkled.

More interested in learning about her new acquaintances, Jacinda turned her attention to Sybil. "Do you know that for a while, I thought I'd imagined you? That, perhaps, you were part of a dream I had, nothing more than a pretty fairy spending her time drawing, while waiting for her wings to grow."

The girl made a singular sound—a laughing wheeze through her nose. As if to play along, she craned her neck to peer over her shoulder and down her back. Then she shrugged.

"No wings today, hmm? Well, we'll check again tomorrow." Jacinda glanced over at Mrs. Hemple to ensure that was acceptable and received a nod and a pleased grin. "Now what have you been drawing since we last met?"

Sybil scrambled to put together a pile of her most recent pages and rushed over to Jacinda, standing tall as she handed them over.

Looking through the stack, Jacinda admired the girl's talent, remarking on the beauty of each drawing. Again, she noticed that every object in the pictures was displayed in a romantic pair—two fleas, two mice, two flowers—as if everything in her world belonged joined with something else. A veritable matchmaker in the making.

"Have you ever read the story of *Emma* by the incomparable Miss Jane Austen?" When Sybil shook her head, Jacinda pursed her lips thoughtfully. "Well then, we shall have to remedy that. If Mrs. Hemple approves, of course."

Sybil unleashed a look of so much eager yearning that Jacinda wasn't surprised by the housekeeper's instant consent.

"As long as you don't neglect your studies." Mrs. Hemple gave a pointed look down to the untended page.

Grinning broadly, dimples on full display, Sybil returned to her column of figures, scribbling out her sums furiously.

"Miss Bourne, you are welcome anytime you like."

"That would be lovely." But at the mention of *time*, Jacinda noticed a rosewood clock on the mantel and realized she'd been away far too long. "Oh dear. I imagine Dr. Graham has returned to the library by now. I do not wish to be absent so long that he sounds the alarm, affording Rydstrom another reason to glower at me."

She lifted her eyes and sighed comically, earning a broad grin from Sybil. "It seems we both have studies to attend, and I fear that I have only been a good example of truancy."

A stuttered puff of air accompanied Sybil's *laugh* in something of a snort, and the effect of the charming, unabashed sound lifted Jacinda's own cheeks. "I'll see you tomorrow, then."

Leaving the room, she felt as if she'd made two new friends. And while she wasn't any closer to remembering why she'd traveled from London to Whitcrest, she had managed to navigate the castle by memory.

". . . many places in Rydstrom Hall are in disrepair. Therefore, for your own safety, you should never venture anywhere without either Dr. Graham's escort or mine," the duke had said. But the more she made her way through the halls, the more she was convinced he'd only wanted to know her whereabouts. And likely to avoid her so that she wouldn't find out whatever information he was keeping from her. *Ha!*

A rebellious grin curled her lips and stayed in place as she traversed down two sets of stairs, and around three—*or was that four?*—corridors.

Yet, when she did not find herself in the minstrel's gallery as she expected to, she stopped congratulating herself.

Her surroundings were completely foreign. This corridor was much narrower than the others and not adorned with a single table or bench. The ceiling hung low overhead, the plaster seeming to droop in between wooden supports. The planks beneath her feet tended to rise in the center, nearly buckling.

And suddenly, it was all too clear that she'd found her way into the part of Rydstrom Hall that the duke had warned her about. *Drat.*

She had to leave before he found out and had something to lord over her.

Thankfully, the door was just behind her. Though, when she tried it, she found it wedged in place. Tucking her borrowed book to her breast, she leaned her shoulder into the thick panel, but still her efforts failed to yield a result.

It made no sense. She'd just come through this way, hadn't she? Yet, as she looked down the corridor, she saw that she'd passed a good number of doors.

A tiny frisson of worry skated over her. She was no longer certain which door she'd come through.

Retracing her steps, she tried each one in turn, but found them all stuck. Frustrated and a little more than worried, she stormed down the canting corridor, hoping that the pretense of confidence would somehow seep inside her. By the time she reached the end, she was prepared to use whatever force she had to in order to escape this portion of the castle.

Lifting the latch, she pushed with all her might.

The door scraped away from the casing inch by inch, push by push. Then with an abrupt resounding squawk it swung open, leaving her floundering, arms waving, and staring down at a room with . . . *no floor*!

Jacinda didn't even have time to scream. Momentum propelled her forward before she could grab the casing. She was falling headlong into the abyss.

Then something hard wrapped around her waist and snatched her back.

In the next instant, she found herself turned and crushed against a solid wall of chest and arms. A pair of large hands covered her back, holding her in place as if to keep her from bolting. But that was the last thing on her mind.

Jacinda knew it was the duke without even looking up. No one else smelled like him, that heady combination of cedar, cloves, and sweet earth. No one else warmed her all the way to her bones with a single touch, or felt as solid and safe.

"Damn it, Miss Bourne. What in the hell were you thinking?" With every harsh word, his hold on her tightened, her dress pulling taut as if he were fisting the muslin in his hands. His lungs worked like a bellows, fanning heated breaths over the whorls of her ear.

Reflexively, her fingers splayed over his waistcoat and over the broad expanse of muscle beneath. Struggling to catch her breath, she was pressed against the entire length of him, from her cheek to her ankles. Even his firm thighs anchored hers in place, chasing away any errant shivers of fear.

"I did not expect to find you here, Rydstrom," she said, her voice raspy, her heart beating in a peculiar, fluttering rhythm beneath her breast.

"That doesn't answer the question."

"Well, it was a rather rudely worded question, wasn't it?" And yet she wasn't offended in the least. A peculiar thrill trampled through her from those passionate expletives, the gruffness in his voice. Or perhaps it stemmed from the way he held her so tightly, as if he would never let her go. And, considering the turbulent state of their acquaintanceship thus far, that notion was as confusing as it was appealing. "Besides, shouldn't you be occupied with duke business or something?"

"'Duke business'?"

At her temple, she felt the shift of his cheek as if it were lifted in a grin. But was that even possible?

Part of her wanted to draw back just to see if her speculation was correct. However, the rest of her—the parts that were pressed wantonly against him—wanted to know what he might feel like without this waistcoat.

Absently, her fingertip brushed the crisp border, where the superfine wool met with his linen shirt beneath. "Oh, you know, ordering people about, locking visitors in your tower room . . . finding an heiress to marry. That sort of thing."

Apparently, that was the wrong thing to say. She could tell he was glowering now—not simply with his brow, but with his entire person.

His hands slid down her back, tightened at her waist briefly, and then released her. Taking a step away, he moved to the yawning archway and jerked the door closed with such force that the crackle of splintering wood tore through the stilted air. "You were supposed to be in the library."

"I *was* in the library," she said, looking around for the book she must have dropped during the ordeal. She found it, half hidden beneath her skirts and bent to pick it up. "See?"

He said nothing in response. Instead, his gaze drifted over her face, darkening with irritation and . . . something she hadn't seen before and, therefore, could not catalogue it with the various forms of his glowers.

Needing to know what it was, she asked, "Why are you staring at me that way?"

A muscle ticked in his jaw. "There was no particular way. I was merely noticing your ears."

He'd noticed her mouth, too. Her lips felt plumper now because of it.

"What about my ears?" At the moment, she couldn't remember what they looked like. She couldn't remember much of anything, not with the way his strangely intense gaze roamed from one ear to the next, pausing briefly to study her mouth as she spoke. Self-conscious, she wet her lips.

He expelled a breath that flared his nostrils. "I have never before seen a pair that were solely designed to be ornamental. Just a pretty shell on either side of your head."

Under his scrutiny, she felt them grow hot, burning beneath a thin layer of flesh.

"In the future, Miss Bourne," he continued, his voice deep with warning, "I would prefer if you would use them to listen to me. I will not always be nearby to save you from your own foolish mistakes."

"Perhaps if you would say something of interest, then I might listen. But all you seem to do is rail at me and bark orders. Surely, my uncle expected us to be better friends than this, or else he wouldn't have introduced us."

She waited for a beat to see if he would confirm this with a word, a twitch, something. Yet the moment he lifted his brows in clear exasperation, she knew he hadn't taken the bait.

"Come, Miss Bourne," he said, striding past her and around a hidden corner.

Without further conversation, he guided her through a maze of corridors and down the stairs. Though, to his credit, he stayed close to her side, his watchful presence returning a sense of security that—she didn't realize until now—had left her while she'd been wandering the castle alone.

By the time they reached the familiar mischievous faces carved into the corbels of the minstrel's gallery, she was feeling more like herself. Or at least, what she knew of herself.

"I like it here." She slowed her steps, lifting her gaze to the vaulted ceiling where various shades of green and blue paint created the illusion of a leafy canopy and a clear sky overhead. Over time, it had faded and bits of plaster must have fallen away, for there were a number of sections of newer, white plaster that overlapped the design. "There's a sense of joy here, as if the walls remember the sound of laughter and music."

Her escort grumbled with impatience. "Enjoy it while you can, because you'll likely not return."

"Back to the tower for me, is it?"

That unidentified glower returned as he looked at her, his expression and stance both hardened with coiled tension. Then he turned away and strode toward an open door just beyond this hall. Beneath his breath, he muttered, "I should be so fortunate."

She hastened her step to follow, only to have him stop at the threshold, turn to her and say, "Wait here."

Well, of course she didn't listen. Frankly, it surprised her that he would speak the two words designed to incite her curiosity. Foolish man.

Strolling in behind him, she quickly found herself in a room covered in weapons. Rows of swords and shields hung on the walls, along with a pair of suits of armor standing sentinel on opposite sides of the door. A pleasant, earthy fragrance lingered in the air, inviting her to draw a deeper breath that hinted at cedar. Her gaze shifted to Rydstrom automatically, to the broad shoulders straining against the seams of his coat as he reached for a sword on the table and carefully set it on the hooks extending from the wall.

Aside from the scrape of his footfalls against the stone floor, the stillness here evoked a sense of reverence. Not a single dust mote floated in the air, and every blade was polished to a mirror gleam. Even these strange, spiked iron balls attached to chains held a certain luster.

Not knowing what they were or how they were used, she studied them, her fingertips gliding along the grooved wooden handles. "What are these called?"

Yet before the question went past her lips, she accidentally dislodged the handle from its mounting. Unthinkingly, she gripped it hard to keep it from falling. But she was too late.

Rydstrom was at her side in an instant. His hand enveloped hers as the spiked iron ball fell, the weight of it jerking her wrist as it swung like a pendulum in a grim reaper's clock. Yet she felt no pain from the sudden movement because he was there to guide her in a slow downward arc, giving way to the impetus of the iron ball. Together, they became part of the weapon's swing, watching as those filed points coasted over the layers of muslin near her leg. But she had no fear that it was going to touch her. She knew that Rydstrom would never allow it.

All the same, Rydstrom let out a heavy breath, and growled, "Must you interfere with everything, Miss Bourne?"

Intuitively, she knew his statement encompassed more than their brief acquaintance here. Rankled by the fact that she couldn't remember what had happened between them before, she lashed back with equal vehemence. "As a matter of fact, yes. Curiosity fills me like a swarm of bees that never rests. At the very least, you could tell me the name of the object in my grasp so that I can quiet the hive for a single minute."

"It is a flail," he answered, his voice deeper as he leaned closer to dislodge the thick handle from her grasp. At the touch of his long, adroit fingers and the rasp of his warm, callused palm over her bare knuckles, a pleasant shiver stole over her.

Then, too soon, he took the weapon and moved away to put it back in place. "And what is its purpose?"

"That wasn't even a minute. Your curiosity seems more like a swarm of wasps, stinging repeatedly, without tiring." His eyes narrowed in speculation, his mink brown lashes crowding. And yet, one corner of his mouth twitched in the faintest specter of a smirk. "In the right hands, a flail is designed to reach out past an opponent's shield and disarm him."

Jacinda imagined that it could do a great deal more than disarm a man, but Rydstrom wasn't the kind of gentleman to speak of such things in front of a woman. Already, she understood that he not only guarded himself, but those around him as well.

While she may have found it frustrating, it certainly wasn't a terrible attribute for a man to have.

"Has every weapon in this room seen battle, then?"

"Yes. They are kept here because it is important to honor those who have gone before me." He scrubbed an absent hand along his jaw before he briefly pointed to the wall of shields. "See that one at the top, the one that's rent in two and looks like a pair of splinters held together by a peg?"

"Mmm-hm," she murmured with a nod, but if she were honest, all of her attention was on Rydstrom. The easy richness in his voice and bright gleam in his hazel eyes made it clear that he took great pride in the memory of his ancestors, and in the history of this keep.

Yet it was more than that. There was something different about him. In here, surrounded by his own history, he seemed more in his element, freer.

"The first of the Montagues to take up arms against invaders. He'd been little more than a farmer, but that hadn't stopped him from doing everything he could to protect his wife, his children, and his home. And that grit in his blood, was also in his son's, and his son's and . . ." Rydstrom stopped on an indrawn breath and cleared his throat in apparent discomfiture.

Thoroughly enthralled, her heart pulsed a half beat faster, warming the blood within her, warming toward him.

"You shouldn't be in here," he said, his brusque tone breaking the spell she was under. "You don't belong in this part of the castle. Come, I'll take you back to the library."

"I hope you realize that I am a person and not a misplaced object."

"If only you were the latter, Miss Bourne, for then I could lock you away in a cupboard. For now, however, I shall escort you to the north wing so that you can return that book."

"I don't want to return it." She stiffened. "I want to read it."

He glanced down at the tome. "It is in French."

"And?" Jacinda peeked at the book, too, only now realizing why Mrs. Hemple had wrinkled her brow in confusion earlier. It hadn't even occurred to Jacinda that it was written in another language because she could decipher it so easily. This was certainly an unexpected development.

Those mocking brows lifted. "Are you fluent in French?"

"Apparently so."

He took a step closer and placed his hand on it, tilting it away from her bodice to see the cover. His fingertips grazed hers and suddenly she went still.

This was . . . familiar.

"I feel as if I've been here before. Not this room, but another one somewhere, with paneled walls and . . . and . . ." Jacinda held her breath as tingles and tingles—*so many tingles!*—coursed through her body.

The memory was flashing too fast behind her eyes for her to see it clearly. She closed them to better concentrate.

But she might as well have tried to grasp a breeze and tuck it in her pocket. It was useless. The image was gone.

Subtle traces lingered, however. She was almost certain she had felt this way before, rapid breaths, heart rising to greet the pulse fluttering at her throat. Inhaling, she focused on the sweet, not-quite-musty fragrance of the book mingling with the permeation of cedar and the faint hint of aniseed. "Your hand and mine on a book. Our close proximity. The scent of your breath . . . tastes like . . . a licorice lozenge on my tongue." Her mouth watered, lips pulsing as if they remembered being pressed to his. "You and I have stood like this before."

Crispin went stock-still, trapped by the keen light in her bright turquoise eyes. They seemed to close in on him.

He took a step back. "No such familiarity was part of our brief acquaintance. I can assure you—"

She took a step forward. Studying him, her eyelids lifted slowly in a fan of dark, burnished brown lashes that tilted at each corner. "I think you've kissed me."

An instant hot flame burst low in his gut, flowing in thick

pulses through his veins like molten iron. On a single indrawn breath, her sweet essence filled his nostrils, and his mouth watered. Even now he couldn't stop wondering what she might taste like.

Reckless, his gaze dropped to her lips. Something shifted inside him—the sudden weight of a terrible notion, overloading the scales where his sanity usually rested.

He swallowed. "Whatever would inspire you to conjure such an outlandish notion?"

"I'm quite perceptive, remember? And perhaps it was the way you looked at my mouth just now and earlier, too, like you'd . . . sampled it before." The temptress pressed her lips together. "*Hmm.* Is that the reason you glower at me? Because I've forgotten our kiss? Likely that is a deathblow to any man's ego."

And suddenly, there was a completely new type of mischief in her gaze. A feminine, sultry type that no conniving, spying debutante with amnesia ought to have.

He was burning up, his cravat itchy. He fought like hell not to pull the linen away from his throat and give away his discomfort. Likely, she would make more of the gesture than it was—which was merely a reaction to starch. Yet even as the excuse formed in his mind, not even he believed it.

"You have not wounded my ego in any way because the event you mentioned never occurred."

Then the lips he'd never sampled spread in a guileless grin. "So you say, Rydstrom."

He gritted his teeth, letting her have the last word as she sauntered past him. It was the safer thing to do. But *damn it all* if he wasn't tempted to pull her against him and prove that there was no possible way she could ever forget his kiss.

Chapter 14

> "And you have forgotten one matter of joy to me," said Emma, "and a very considerable one—that I made the match myself. I made the match . . ."
>
> Jane Austen, *Emma*

When a brooding Rydstrom escorted her to the library, and summarily left her there, Jacinda surprised herself by waiting dutifully for Dr. Graham's return. Not only that but, she even began reading the book like she'd promised.

Well, *after* she rearranged the chairs, angling them toward the window. It was much cozier this way. And once Rydstrom saw this arrangement, she was sure he would appreciate her assistance.

A soft wry laugh escaped her at the idea. If she knew one thing for certain, it was that Rydstrom wanted all the objects *and* the people inside this castle to remain precisely where he thought they should be.

Though, considering the events of earlier, she decided to heed his warning.

At least for now.

Thinking back to those moments in the abandoned corridor and then in the armory, she found that she was even more curious than she'd been in the beginning. If the condition of the castle was any indication, financial strains had plagued Rydstrom for some time.

So, why had he waited until now to look for a wife with a large dowry?

Book quickly forgotten, she curled her feet beneath her on the comfortable chair, let her head fall back against the worn leather, and thought of Rydstrom. To her, it seemed strange that he didn't have a bride waiting at the altar right this instant. There must be scores of women eager to marry him. He was a duke, after all, quite strong and smelled nice, too. And handsome, even when he glowered—not that she would ever admit such a thing to him.

But, more than those outward characteristics, he possessed a deeply ingrained sense of duty that made him an appealing marital prospect . . . for an heiress, of course.

A woman without a fortune, or even without a maid of her own, needn't concern herself with his attributes. Whomever he did marry would have to contend with his overbearing demeanor. Or at least stand up to him when he went too far. His bride would need a strength of her own.

Musing over this, she caught herself absently brushing her fingertips over her lips. *Had* he kissed her? She wasn't certain. However, his reaction to her accusation had been rather strong, either from shock at her audacity or guilt because she'd hit the mark.

But if he had . . . Well, she wished she had that memory most of all.

Then again, if he had, she should be furious at him. After all, what business did he have kissing a woman he wasn't intending to marry?

But, perhaps for a single moment, the temptation of her lips had been too great for him to resist. She smiled at that, letting the notion bloom.

They might have been at a ball, both of them finding themselves in the paneled room that had flashed through her mind earlier, and . . .

The sound of laughter interrupted the passionate scenario before it even began. She expelled a disappointed sigh. But it was for the best, she supposed. It was futile to spend the day speculating about the nature of her acquaintance with Rydstrom, when she should be searching for proof instead.

Closing the untended book on her lap, she looked over her shoulder and spotted a pair of chambermaids, chatting while they moved feather dusters efficiently over every picture, statue, and table in the wide hall outside the library. She recognized them—Martha, her onetime lady's maid, and Betsy with the rain pails.

"There's a new man in Whitcrest. Young and handsome," Betsy said, her tone full of intrigue. "Word around the village is that he's looking for a wife."

"Aye, a Mr. Alcott," Martha said with a giggle, stretching to reach the top of the doorframe. "I heard 'bout him from Mrs. Lassater when she came nosing around here for news on His Grace's special lady guest."

"Always looking for gossip, that one."

"Along with all the rest of them. *And* us."

"I s'pose," Betsy admitted. "But she shares her gossip a bit too freely, if you ask me."

Jacinda perked up at this information. Mind already turning, she wondered if Mrs. Lassater would know anything of use to her. Jacinda wouldn't need much, just a few clues here and there.

"All the better for me," Martha continued, "for I learned that Mr. Alcott was once part of a fleet, but hated the weeks at sea, wanted to spend more time ashore. So he bought the old Burkett place."

"Then he'll need a wife to keep his house and mend his nets, and I've a knack for sewing."

"I can mend a net as well as anyone. Besides, I thought you were sweet on Rodney."

Betsy whacked her duster along the legs of a demilune table, her topknot of blond curls swishing angrily. "I was, until he kissed Clara by the stables. Turns out, he made a fool out of me, Clara, *and* Mary from the kitchens."

"No!" Martha turned to face her friend. "What sort of

fellow courts three women, in the same house, and thinks he can get away with it?"

"The wrong sort," Jacinda heard herself say, every syllable uttered with conviction as she stood and walked toward them. She didn't know why, but suddenly she felt different. Air seemed to fill her lungs without her taking a single breath, expanding on a rush of exhilaration. Of *purpose*.

"Oh, Miss Bourne!" Martha dropped her duster, the sunlight from a nearby window illuminating a small windstorm of glittering particles.

Betsy shifted, hiding her duster behind her back. "How good to see you looking so well."

"You're too kind. I look a fright with this red scrape, and the purple bruises around it." Jacinda hesitated, not wanting to admit she'd been eavesdropping, but wanting to return to the topic, all the same. "I wish to thank you for helping Lucy, too, and welcoming her as you have done. Although . . . I supposed someone should warn her about Rodney, hmm?"

"You heard that?" Betsy's cheeks turned the color of pomegranate seeds.

Jacinda nodded, and feeling an overwhelming urge to speak her mind on this topic, said, "It was a dreadful thing to do to you. And to Clara and Mary, too."

"I was ready to swear off men altogether," Betsy admitted.

Martha nudged her. "Until Mr. Alcott came to town."

"Well, is it wrong to admire a man who wants to be his own master? I wouldn't mind having my own home and a husband. But there are very few prospects for a girl in service. Most men want a girl with a bit more than the clothes on her back."

"A sound argument," Jacinda said, easily commiserating. Other than an apparent education and different wardrobe, it appeared as though she was in the same situation as the maids were, with nothing but herself to offer a gentleman.

A rather distressing thought considering she didn't even know who she was.

"Even so," Jacinda continued, "you wouldn't want to settle for the first available man. What do you know of Mr. Alcott? Does he have family here? Or perhaps his own family somewhere else? I should hate for you to find out that he's the wrong sort after your heart is already engaged."

Betsy considered this with a frown. "I don't want to waste my half days on a man who isn't the *right* sort. I've already done that."

"With the Spring Festival coming, only four days hence, we should ought to know these things," Martha said, inciting Jacinda's rapacious curiosity.

"A Spring Festival?"

"It's more of a winter-be-gone celebration," Betsy explained. "Each year, Whitcrest gathers at sunrise to welcome spring with a day of festival games, a bit of drink, and most important, a full day off for the servants."

"And there's the seed-planting ceremony, too, for new life, good fortune, and—if you're lucky—*love*," Martha added.

"Then you'll need to find all you can about this man before the festival," Jacinda said, already forming a quick, but no doubt brilliant, plan. "Therefore, I'll go into the village and see what I can discover."

"If there's anything to know about anyone, then Mrs. Lassater is the one to speak to. She even knows things people wished she didn't," Martha offered helpfully.

Betsy turned a worried look from Martha to Jacinda. "Oh, but His Grace would never let you go, Miss Bourne. Not until you're well. He's terribly protective of you."

Something warm and fluttery quivered inside Jacinda at the thought. She could still feel his arms cinched tightly around her, smell the heady scent of him lingering on her clothes, hear his gruff warnings *and* his muttered wish to lock her in a cupboard. *Hmm . . .* Betsy was likely right.

Yet that didn't deter Jacinda. In a peculiar, unexplainable way, she felt as if it was her duty to investigate Mr. Alcott to make certain he wasn't the wrong sort.

And if she happened to learn a thing or two about Rydstrom from the gossiping Mrs. Lassater, then all the better.

"I'll simply ask Dr. Graham to escort me. Surely Rydstrom couldn't object."

"I SEE no true harm in permitting Miss Bourne to visit the village," Graham said that evening, returning to the Great Hall after escorting Miss Bourne to her chamber.

Crispin shook his head. "That is akin to saying a hurricane poses no threat to the shore."

The instant she'd uttered her foolish request, he'd done the sensible thing and refused. Hadn't she had enough adventure for one day?

Graham smiled, clearly believing the statement a mere jest as he lowered into his chair at the long, scarred table. "And is she the hurricane or the shore?"

"She is both. For if she does not conjure disaster, it will find her, nonetheless." Crispin took a hearty gulp of wine, recalling the events in the abandoned corridor earlier. He'd aged forty years in the seconds it had taken him to reach her. "Likely, she even attempted to enlist your aid to persuade me to her cause."

Graham shook his head. "I received no such request. We merely spoke of the events she recalled from the day."

Crispin watched the footman clear her place from the table, annoyed that she'd claimed a headache and retired early, instead of keeping with the agreement they'd decided upon. She was supposed to complete this memory exercise in his study at the end of each day. But as of yet, she had not honored her part of the bargain.

Of course, this wouldn't have bothered him if not for the fact that he'd written it in his schedule ledger. He'd made generous allowances for the intrusion—two entire hours for their usual banter, heated discussions, and, of course, her exercises.

Since he accounted for his daily tasks in quarter-hour segments, this would leave a gaping hole. Now what was he going to do with the remainder of his evening?

Distracted, he stared at the vacant arch leading to the corridor. A queer, lopsided sensation passed through him as if the Great Hall was somehow out of balance without her counterweight on the opposite side of the table from Graham.

"I see no purpose in her going," he said with a fractious growl. "Whitcrest holds but one shop that might interest her, if her fancy runs to hair ribbons. She would hardly have need for a blacksmith, trawling nets, or a desire to see the fish barrels filled for market."

"All the same, I would encourage it if only to provide her the opportunity to encounter something familiar, a sound or a scent—"

"Of rotting fish entrails?" Crispin scoffed, sinking deeper into his ill-tempered mood. He drained his glass.

"Well, yes. I've found that fragrances often evoke the most potent memories. A whiff of gunpowder can take me directly to the memory of when that musket ball pierced my leg." Absently, he ran a fisted hand over the outside of his thigh.

"I still don't like it. You don't know what she's capable of," he said, peering down the empty corridor again, and thinking of her quick acceptance of his refusal. An uneasy shiver rifled through him. "Why, the moment I acquiesced, I'd surely see the village burst into flames because she was curious to see how hot the blacksmith's furnace could become."

Or she could find herself in a dangerous place and opening the wrong door, or even commandeering another skiff and sailing into rough seas. It was a miracle she'd survived to the age of three and twenty.

The doctor chuckled and removed his half-moon spectacles to polish them with a corner of his handkerchief. "It is true that she has an extraordinary gift of curiosity. But you needn't worry for Miss Bourne's safety."

"I'm not *worried*," he interjected quickly. "I am . . . honor bound to protect all who reside beneath this roof. Temporarily that includes Miss Bourne. When I wrote her uncle, I vowed to ensure she returned to London in good health, and in turn he has put his faith in me."

"Your sense of duty does you credit," the doctor said carefully. "But if the day is fine without the threat of another squall, I'm certain I can keep her from danger."

"I would not wish someone so crafty upon you."

"Surely you don't mean to keep her inside until she leaves for London, as if she were fulfilling a prison sentence." When Graham received a deflected grumble in response, his wiry brows crowded closer in disappointment. "But that's it, isn't it? You're punishing her for washing up on your beach, for invading your haven."

"Of course not. Keeping her inside, and myself trapped along with her, would be more of a sentence to me, don't you think?" He meant it as a jest, but it rang too true. He'd been crawling out of his skin since Miss Bourne's accusation in the armory.

I think you've kissed me.

Her words had been taunting him all day. His appetite had become unpredictable—ravenous one minute and then dissatisfied with whatever was on his plate the next. At any given moment, no matter where he stood in the keep, he would catch a faint whiff of her bath oil as if she were always nearby. And worse, he found himself thinking about her accusation and imagined doing wholly inappropriate, passionate things to her. Plundering her lips. Raking his teeth over the shell of her delicate little ears. Dragging down her dress, inch by inch, until her breasts were bared to him, her nipples ripe and ready for his tongue.

Twice he'd wound up in a state not fit for a man of his

position, with his flesh engorged and straining against the fall of his trousers at midday.

"Pardon me for saying this, but we both know that you are rather deliberate in most things." The doctor glanced down to the arrangement on the table where Crispin's empty wine goblet and full water goblet were at precise distances from the edge of the table. "Additionally, I am one of the few who know that you have denied yourself many of life's pleasures, including female companionship, these past four years because you seek to punish yourself for the deaths of your parents."

Clearly, Crispin had made a mistake in confiding in Graham during a rather low point, telling him about the life of debauchery he'd lived in London and believing that those choices had contributed to the reason his parents were arguing by the cliffs. A vow of celibacy seemed an appropriate penance.

He gave Graham a dark scowl. "Abstinence is a matter of maturity. Nothing more. As a younger man, I behaved with little regard for others and now I am more disciplined."

"You have a will of granite, that much is true." The doctor paused with significance. "And you are a good man."

Hearing those words from one who knew all of his sins and still thought him redeemable, touched Crispin, though he refrained from showing it. Instead, he dropped his napkin onto the table and stood, giving his lapels a firm tug to bring his coat to order.

"I think I'll follow Miss Bourne's example and retire as well." Graham rose, too. "There is one thought I should like to leave you with, however. No man should be so strict with himself, *all* the time. Every now and then, he needs to give in to something small—oh, like a glass of brandy on a cool night, for instance. That way, he won't be so tempted to make a bigger mistake. After all, even granite breaks occasionally."

Crispin offered an absent nod as if he didn't know what the doctor was saying. And yet, his thoughts veered unerringly back to Jacinda.

She was the tempest he'd allowed inside Rydstrom Hall, battering relentlessly against his own resolve. Which, in the end, made her absence from his study for the next two hours necessary.

Chapter 15

"I would rather not be tempted."

Jane Austen, *Emma*

The moment Crispin entered his study, he noticed the iron horse bookend sitting on the mantel. *Not* where it was supposed to be at all.

The bookend was one of a pair—the other still on the shelf in the far corner where it belonged. Since he'd been in this room before dinner, and everything had been in its place, he knew it hadn't been accidentally left there by one of his servants. There was only one person beneath this roof who would have moved an object for the sole purpose of annoying him.

Jacinda Bourne.

"Ah. I see you found my present," the culprit said with honeyed mischief in her tone. She sauntered into the room, her hips swaying beneath a length of cream-colored muslin, her slender arms bare, her hands nonchalantly grasping a pair of gloves as if she'd decided to start undressing. Here. In his study.

He gripped the horse by the neck and glared at her. "You were supposed to retire to your chamber, Miss Bourne. That was the purpose of bidding you a good night earlier."

"Mmm . . ." she murmured, stepping into his quadrant and bringing a rush of heat with her. She propped her hip against the side of the sofa and absently plucked at the fringe from a silken silver pillow. "Then I realized I was still famished. It's your fault, after all. You declined pudding altogether, and Dr. Graham and I could hardly ask Fellows to bring syllabub just for us."

Crispin turned and strode to the shelves. He situated the books that had fallen over and placed the horse down with a heavy *thunk*. The only reason he'd declined pudding was because he thought she didn't care for sweets. She never took sugar in her tea, and she'd only picked at the tarts. "I made it perfectly clear that you could have what you wanted."

"You did no such thing. You used your imperious tone, which everyone in Rydstrom Hall knows is your way of expressing your displeasure. Even the footmen stood straighter, glancing at the sideboard to ensure that the pair of candelabras were spaced evenly apart."

"You're being ludicrous again."

With a smirk, she purposely laid that pillow next to the other, instead of in the correct placement at the opposite end.

He clenched his teeth. "You may seek to goad me, but it won't work. Having a sense of order, knowing where you belong *and* where objects belong is part of being a mature adult."

While he might like to keep things in certain order, he'd never once commanded his servants to do so or chastised them when something was out of place.

Though, until Miss Bourne's arrival, nothing had ever been out of place.

From as far back as Crispin could remember, Fellows had always inspected each room with a ruler in hand before he checked it off his list. And there was nothing wrong with the fact that Crispin ensured that his desk and papers, his bookshelves, and his person were in order. He found the employment of such behavior gained him a sense of peace, a semblance of control.

"Only a child flings their possessions about the room without care." He gestured with a sweep of his hand toward the sofa, and then to her person. "Only a child keeps a disheveled appearance."

The upward tilt of her lips abruptly flattened, and her eyes narrowed. She tossed her gloves over the arm of the sofa. "There is nothing out of place in my appearance."

"Then explain the curl that always falls over your left eyebrow." He arched his own in question, waiting.

She pushed the lock back with a careless sweep of her fingers and settled her hands on her hips. "There. Am I an adult now, according to your confounded standards?"

Then, as if to mock her, the curl fell again. The corner of his mouth twitched.

She wrinkled her nose at him. "What I would like to know is why it matters to you if the pillows are together, or if one bookend is on the mantel? And why you separate your food into sections on your plate. Then if a pea strays into the barren paths, you are quick to herd it back into the fold. And also why you take one bite from each section in turn, and never out of sequence."

"My only answer is that you should pay more attention to your own plate."

"Many of the rooms I've seen are like that as well," she continued. "A prime example is the library. Have you ever thought about rearranging the—"

"Do not touch the library."

A slow, cagy smile lit her features. "It's bound to happen eventually, soon after you find your heiress. Have you ever thought of that?"

"Not once," he answered succinctly, putting an end to her conversation. He knew very well that his future bride would not alter a rug, curtain, or a single piece of furniture in Rydstrom Hall because she would never live here.

Jacinda Bourne certainly had a great deal of cheek, always ready with an intrusive question or comment, always overstepping her bounds. The only time he'd managed to stop her was when he'd taken her off guard with that comment about her ears. She hadn't responded for a full minute or more, and in the silence, that watercolor red suffused her cheeks and spread all the way to the tips of those delicate shells, making them look like frosted confections.

So now, when she opened her mouth to issue another, likely out-of-bounds, comment, he simply slid his gaze to her ears.

She blushed instantly.

Congratulating himself, he returned the pillow back to its correct placement. Ignoring her gloves for the moment, he straightened to his full height and walked toward the door, gesturing for her to leave.

"Things should be kept where they belong." Like matchmakers who lived in London and dukes who did not.

If things began to stray, there was chaos.

"At opposite ends? Yet, by your own words, these pillows"—she reached down and snatched it again—"and the iron horses are mated. Why not allow them to be side by side like your peas?"

"An object's design is not to be consumed but admired. Those are book*ends*, one at either end. You would not have your ears on one side of your head, crowded together, would you?" He added this, hoping to quiet her.

This time it did not work.

"You are rather obsessed with my ears." From her quadrant, she tilted her head to study him. "See? I do use them to listen. On occasion. You even said they were pretty. Do you really think so, or were you trying to unsettle me?"

Suddenly his mind was back in the corridor again, hands gripping, bodies flush, sheer panic transforming into a reckless desire.

He glanced down at the silver pillow. Only now he realized that it matched the hue of the counterpane on his bed. Then, he was helpless to notice the way she gripped it, the tips of her modestly manicured fingernails pressing into the silk.

An unrepentant surge of arousal tore through him. "Miss Bourne, would you return the pillow to its proper place, take your gloves, and then leave my study?"

In response, those lips curled again.

His palms began to itch, craving the delicate abrasion of cream-colored muslin, and the softness of the flesh beneath.

"You just looked down at my lips again." She tsked. "A clear indication that you have, in fact, kissed me."

"We've already discussed this."

"And you didn't deny it."

"I am now."

She shook her head, adamant. "It's too late. Your denial is invalid."

"Well, I *am* denying it because that, Miss Bourne, is the truth."

She would not let it rest. He had not even concluded a week of his fortnight prison sentence with her and he was ankle deep in a swirling chasm of madness.

"So you say now . . ." She shrugged. "I do have one more question, however. Do you—"

"By all that's holy! I can take no more. You refuse to give me a moment's peace until your curiosity is satisfied. Then so be it."

He crossed the empty path between the rugs—the first step on the hardwood echoing like the twelfth strike of a clock tower, the second muffled by the woven wool.

"Rydstrom, I—"

Crispin took her by the shoulders and lowered his mouth.

But she lifted her face to his at the same time. So, instead of capturing her lips, he met with her impertinent chin.

He was undeterred. He'd come this far, he'd be damned if he would stop now.

Determined to prove his point, he stayed with her, gliding his fingers over her shoulders, touching the warm silk of her throat. He took her face in his hands and rasped his mouth across the valley between her pert chin and plump lips as if this slow slide had been his intention all along. And he felt her tremble.

Her unbidden response unleashed the long-denied hedonist within him. Greedy for every tremor, every taste, he crowded closer, his mouth coasting upward to settle against hers.

Then, all at once, he was lost in a pliant, pillowy caress. He wasn't prepared for how right—how utterly *sublime*—her mouth would feel giving way beneath his, parting on the barest of gasps, shyly welcoming the brush of his tongue into her dewy warmth.

His hand slid to her nape, the other skimming down to the slope of her waist, gripping the rise of her hip. Soft, lithe, and fragrant, she fit against him in a way that made him forget all the reasons he shouldn't be doing this. What he did remember was that even the doctor said Crispin should allow himself one taste. A man cannot deny every urge, after all.

With the barest nudge of his mouth against hers, she arched her neck, allowing him to sink deeper. And he was glad to have abstained from pudding this evening because he wanted to gorge himself on her sweet flavor, to savor each decadent sip. So he kissed her in slow, deep strokes that earned him soft, needy whimpers, her hands rising between them, gripping his lapels.

Desire and warning tunneled through him in lush, heavy pulses, engorging his flesh. She was eradicating his control, but he couldn't tear himself away. She tasted too good, the inexpert slide of her tongue only enhancing his hunger. And he realized that, if he didn't gain some distance, this sampling might consume them both.

By rote, he began by cataloging her lips, focusing on their irregularities. The bottom one was full and soft, the upper a degree smaller, velvety and firmer. He nipped them both for full assurance of his findings. In turn, Jacinda did the same to him, driving him to the brink of madness and making him start all over.

He separated every part of this kiss into quadrants—first, skimming his tongue along the seam of the upper left portion, the right, and then the lower until he'd sampled every delectable morsel. Fitting his own lips against hers, he discovered that they were not perfectly matched, neither corner to corner, nor top to bottom.

Even so, this off center, imperfect kiss was now branded into his being. He might never think of his own lips without thinking of hers.

The unexpected awareness set a hot brand of terror against his soul, and it was the jolt he needed to break free.

He took one step back, but no more for fear of staggering, and cleared his throat.

Jacinda still had her head tilted back slightly, her eyes hooded with desire, and her plump bottom lip still glistening from their kiss.

A wealth of male pride filled him at the sight. Fundamentals be damned, clearly, he was a kissing genius.

"There. That clumsy effort should be enough to satisfy all your doubts," he said modestly, his voice hoarse. "There will be no more questions regarding whether or not I kissed you."

She pressed her lips together, blotting the dampness and slowly smiled. "Of course not, because now you *have* kissed me. Though it would be a shame if I forgot this one, too."

He wanted to return to her, to make certain she would remember this kiss for all the days of her life. No other would compare.

Yet he could not afford to give in to the craving again. Proof of that was the need—a ragged sort of lunacy—filling him, challenging him to find a way to continue what he'd foolishly started.

"No. The point of this demonstration was to prove that there was not one before," he growled. "This was a necessary evil to put an end to your impertinent questions. Nothing more."

She laughed quietly, her eyes impishly bright. "Then I

should hate to tell you that, before you set out to prove your point, I was only going to ask if you have reconsidered my trip to the village."

He pointed to the door. "Leave me now, Miss Bourne. I can take no more. I'm half tempted to—"

"To kiss me again?"

"To ship you off to London, regardless of Dr. Graham's warnings."

"So you say, Rydstrom," she said on a breath, her gaze slipping to his mouth one last time before she disappeared through the doorway.

He let her go without an escort, knowing it was better this way. Far less dangerous.

And it wasn't until he scrubbed a hand over his jaw, that he realized he was grinning.

Chapter 16

"Sorrow came—a gentle sorrow—but not at all in the shape of any disagreeable consciousness."

JANE AUSTEN, *Emma*

In the early morning fog, Jacinda took the winding path down to the village. It was refreshing to stretch her legs. After kissing Rydstrom last night, she felt the need to expel a wealth of energy.

She hadn't wanted him to stop. And he, if the way he'd returned to her lips again and again was any indication, hadn't wanted to either. And during that moment—with her mouth against his, their bodies flush, not even a breath apart—she'd felt as if she'd belonged there and nowhere else.

It was the closest thing imaginable to what returning home might feel like.

But Rydstrom had been right all along. Amnesia or not, there wasn't any way she could have forgotten kissing him. Now she felt rearranged like a thoroughly shuffled deck of cards. Whatever she'd begun to understand about herself was foreign to her once more. And she could not seem to think any thought that did not link directly to him.

Which was silly, of course. They'd only shared a single kiss, and she wasn't even entirely certain she liked him. He was arrogant, glowered excessively and, honestly, what gentleman needed shoulders that broad? His wife would surely be called upon to apply a balm to his flesh whenever he bruised them in narrow doorways.

Such an endless chore, she thought, a sigh slipping past her lips as she imagined helping Rydstrom remove his shirt, rubbing salve over those hard muscles and bare flesh—*Drat!*

Looking down, Jacinda saw that she'd just meandered off the path and directly into a cluster of thistles covered in barbs and dew.

Irritated, she began the prickly process of removing the thistles scattered along her hem. She'd snagged a fawn-colored thread as well. Frankly, she was fortunate she hadn't been walking near the cliff. Clearly, daydreaming about Rydstrom was far too dangerous an occupation.

At least, when one was out of doors. Though, perhaps, when she found herself sitting in the library later, amidst a pile of new assignments, she would have to remember to pick up this salacious thought where she'd left off. As a lark, she wound the thread around her finger so that she wouldn't forget.

By the time she reached Whitcrest, it was already teeming with activity. Chalk white shop fronts crowded together in a row, decorated with empty green flower boxes beneath white-trimmed windows.

Doors were left ajar as the village women walked to and fro, carrying their baskets laden with sundries. The mouth-watering fragrance of freshly baked bread wafted from the baker's, along with the scent of something savory that roused a needy mewl from her stomach.

She figured out what it was the instant a trio of children skipped out of a shop marked only by a wooden fish swinging over the door. In their hands, they each held a roasted fish on a skewer, their laughter rising above the chatter, the rushing din of the wind and sea, and the rhythmic *clink-clink-clink* coming from the blacksmith's hut.

Recalling what Lucy had said about Jacinda sailing the small skiff, she wondered if she had ever lived in a place like this.

"Look at you, Miss Bourne," Miss Beels said from one of

the shop fronts along the narrow cobblestone lane. "Up and about and with a fresh rosy glow about your cheeks. We've all been wondering—*Mrs. Lassater, Mrs. Parish, and I*—how you're faring at Rydstrom Hall under His Grace's care. Has your memory returned?"

While speaking, Miss Beels gestured first to a dark-haired woman walking out of Mrs. Lassater's Laundry & Mending, her hands stained indigo, and then to another woman peering out of the adjacent shop window of Mrs. Parish's Drapers & Finery, who used her apron to scrub a clean circle on the cloudy glass. The women nodded to her in greeting.

Jacinda didn't fault them their bold curiosity. In their shoes, she would have done the same, but without being so obvious about it. She had standards, after all.

In answer to Miss Beels, Jacinda shook her head. "Alas, there has been no change. But Dr. Graham is doing all he can."

"We'd heard you share an acquaintance with His Grace," Mrs. Lassater said, crossing her arms and scrutinizing Jacinda as if ready to begin bartering over a parcel of goods. And they were. After all, the maids had said that Mrs. Lassater held a treasure trove of rumors.

"So I am told," Jacinda answered frugally, unwilling to give up her secrets first.

"You're the only visitor to Rydstrom Hall in four years," Mrs. Parish said as she bustled out of the shop, smoothing hands over her frilled apron.

Jacinda frowned, skeptical that she was getting solid, genuine information. Curiosity sensors sparking, she looked from Mrs. Parish to Mrs. Lassater and then to Miss Beels. "Not a single guest for four years?"

"Not a one until you." Miss Beels smiled fondly. "I dread to tell you that we'd all worried for a time that His Grace would marry some hoity-toity miss with more money than sense."

As she spoke, women and children alike began spilling out of shops and merging into a crowd around Jacinda. There was even an older man, bald-headed, wearing a black eye patch and carrying a tray of buns. And each expression was bright and eager with expectation. Because, apparently, they assumed she was going to marry the duke.

"Actually," she began, knowing that now was the ideal time to tell them all that Rydstrom had every intention of marrying an heiress—intellect to be determined—but Mrs. Parish spoke over her.

"But be warned, His Grace was a wild one, to be sure."

"Hush now, Polly," Mrs. Lassater said. "Miss Bourne was about to say something before you interrupted."

The village seemed to go quiet all at once as they looked at Jacinda, waiting. She weighed her options with swift, thoughtful precision—speak the truth or hear more about the wild Rydstrom?

Jacinda waved her hand in a flippant gesture. "Never mind all that. What was it you were saying, Mrs. Parish?"

"His Grace was quite the rascal for a time." Her answer was met with nods of agreement.

"But who doesn't like that in a man?" the woman beside the eye patch-baker said, tossing her long blond plait over her shoulder. He gave her a grin in return.

Distracted, Jacinda found herself replaying Rydstrom's perfectly sublime, not at all *clumsy*, kiss. "I wouldn't rightly know . . ."

"You must forgive Mr. and Mrs. Stokes," Miss Beels whispered. "I'm sure they didn't mean to make you blush so, but newlyweds often forget themselves, or so I am told."

Wanting to distance herself from talk of newlyweds and heiresses, Jacinda quickly altered the topic. "Did I hear mention of a festival?"

"A grand time, to be sure," Miss Beels said excitedly. "The children have races. Some of the women have tables of preserves and puddings. And the men do their best to show off in tests of strength."

"Years ago, the late duke and duchess used to host the festival on the top of the hill in the lower bailey." Mrs. Lassater gave Jacinda a cool, appraising stare that seemed like a challenge. "We would all love to see it return to Rydstrom Hall."

"Oh, indeed we would," Mrs. Parish said directly.

Jacinda suddenly realized that they were looking at her for a reason. Little did they know that if she asked Rydstrom to host the Spring Festival, he would likely do the opposite and cancel the event altogether. Especially if he discovered that she'd sneaked out of Rydstrom Hall this morning after he'd specifically—though not entirely convincingly, in her opinion—told her not to go.

Hmm . . . but since they didn't know, she wondered if she might gain more information if she let them believe what they wanted. "I could mention the festival to Rydstrom, if you like."

"GOOD MORNING, Your Grace," Fellows said from the open front door of Rydstrom Hall. Bright sunlight glinted off his pate, turning the wispy tufts of white hair into dandelion fluff as he stopped sweeping and hastened to tuck the broom out of sight.

After all these years, the butler still believed that the sight of cleaning implements was an egregious offense. Never mind the innumerable tasks to repair the keep that Crispin performed himself.

Even so, Crispin felt a grin tug at his lips as he checked the time on his pocket watch. "And to you, Fellows. Any news to report?"

Each morning, before he breakfasted with Sybil upstairs, the butler gave him a list of the state of things in the castle.

He included a variety of issues, from the latest cracks in the castle's foundation to the health of the servants.

In these past days, he also informed Crispin of Miss Bourne's activities, beginning with her time of waking and whether or not she'd ordered a breakfast tray from the kitchens. Therefore, it was somewhat puzzling that he failed to do so this time.

"And our guests?" Crispin prodded, closing the polished brass with a snap.

"I believe Dr. Graham is still abed, sir. I imagine he is not used to walking so many halls." Fellows stood up a bit straighter at this. He was Graham's senior by a dozen years but clearly saw himself as more fit. "Though, I must say, you are looking quite hale of late, as any man in his prime ought."

"Thank you, Fellows, as are you," Crispin answered with a nod. He hadn't been sleeping these past nights, due to his idiotic decision to keep temptation across the hall. Yet this morning, he felt rather invigorated. Strong and healthy, too. More so than he remembered feeling in a long while.

His thoughts returned to Jacinda and to the information that Fellows had not supplied. Apparently, he would have to ask directly. "And has Miss Bourne ordered her breakfast tray?"

"No, sir. She came down a short while ago and permitted me to give her a small tour of the gatehouse, and was thoroughly fascinated by the old murder holes we've long since bricked up . . ."

Crispin frowned as Fellows continued. Was Jacinda hoping to break her fast with him? Considering how she had never done so in the previous days, he wondered if—after last night—she might have gotten the wrong idea, her head now filled with romantic notions.

Hmm . . . He feared this would happen. Walking to the window, he absently looked over the village and practiced exactly what he would tell her.

Yes, the kiss was exceptional. Here, he would pause for her to release a sigh in remembrance. Then continuing, he would state that it had been a mistake, and that she was a temporary guest beneath his roof. Nothing more.

With that settled in his mind, Crispin began to turn away from the window, fully intending to head toward the breakfast room. But suddenly, he spotted a flash of auburn in the distance and went still. *No.*

"Then Miss Bourne decided to stroll into the village this morning," Fellows concluded. Needlessly, as it turned out.

Jacinda Bourne had gone into the village, and *after* he'd denied her request. Had yesterday's mishap in the corridor taught her nothing?

His blood burned hot and cold in equal measures, brewing the perfect storm within him. "Have Jones ready a gig. I'm going after Miss Bourne."

Chapter 17

> "Mr. Knightley, in fact, was one of the few people who could see faults in Emma Woodhouse, and the only one who ever told her of them. . . ."
>
> Jane Austen, *Emma*

Jacinda's head spun as the villagers shared endless accounts of their past memories of the Spring Festival—the games for the children, contests for the men and women, and every morsel of food that had passed their lips.

Each tale sounded more wonderful and delicious than the last. And when her stomach issued an embarrassingly ravenous growl, Mr. Stokes immediately offered to bake her something special to break her fast. He wasn't to be outdone by the owner of the Swinging Fish, however, for Mr. Trumbledown vowed to roast her a fish so tender and flaky that she would hear angels.

Well, then. It would have been rude to resist.

"Ack, but here we are talking about the festival, and His Grace hasn't even attended for these past four years," the widow Olson said, keeping a trained eye on her three rambunctious boys.

There it was again, the mention of the four years. Jacinda's curiosity sensors sparked again and she looked to Miss Beels.

"Since the deaths of his parents," she said solemnly. "But His Grace took to his duties right off, if not stoically."

Mrs. Parish pressed her hands to her heart. "His Grace

never once turned his back on us. Even took in that poor relation of Mrs. Hemple's, giving her a better life than she'd likely have had otherwise."

They admired Rydstrom greatly, and rightly so, for he was humble and hadn't even mentioned Sybil to Jacinda or boasted about the way he'd assisted the orphaned girl.

Beneath her hand, Jacinda felt a warm fluttering sensation. Rydstrom was a good man. And she could almost forget about all the things he did that bothered her.

Unfortunately, she couldn't forget that he was going to marry an heiress.

At the thought, that pleasant quiver in her stomach abruptly twisted into something hot and bitter.

"His Grace even helped our newcomer, Mr. Alcott," Miss Beels interrupted. "Gave him the wood he needed to shore up old Burkett's cottage and enough to fix the hole in the abandoned smack."

The widow Olson sighed, her gaze drifting to the last shop on the row. "He'd make a right fine husband."

They all turned in unison toward the simply monikered, Net Shoppe.

The chalk white exterior was marred by long, uneven orange stripes of rust, spilling down from iron hooks that hosted a messy conglomeration of wide trawling nets. Anchored by knots along the bottom row, the nets shifted in the cool, briny breeze, one of them falling in a tangled heap to the ground. And there, rounding the corner, was the man in question. *Mr. Alcott.*

Jacinda barely had time to notice the dark hair and square jaw before she heard the rapid pounding of horse's hooves in the distance. Curious, she looked over her shoulder, but instead of seeing the source of the thundering sound, she saw Mr. Stokes rush out of the bakery, hoisting a flaming baguette and cursing at the white dog that scurried beneath his feet.

The culprit, Mr. Lemon with the black markings around

his mouth to form a grin, darted off toward the Swinging Fish just as Mr. Trumbledown emerged. The former fisherman teetered on his wooden leg, barely missed squashing Mr. Lemon, and then . . . dropped her skewered fish.

Her breakfast.

Suddenly, the dog snatched the skewer and sprinted down the lane, through the rolling hoop, past the net shop, and toward the cliffs.

And before Jacinda knew what came over her, she rushed off to save Mr. Lemon.

CRISPIN SET the brake on the gig, and watched in horror as his prediction came to fruition—Jacinda at the center of fire and chaos in Whitcrest.

He leapt down, prepared to haul her back to Rydstrom Hall by any means necessary, and before any new disasters occurred.

But it was already too late.

Striding past the baker, who was busy cursing and stamping out the flames of a torched baguette, Crispin saw catastrophe looming even before Jacinda did.

He broke into a run an instant after Jacinda began to chase that fool dog. She was headed straight toward the net shop, where there were always heaps of rope on the ground, camouflaged by stones and tall grasses.

Didn't she realize how close she was to the cliff's edge?

Crispin sprinted faster, plowing past the villagers, icy panic clawing through his veins. He was four strides away when he saw her falter. Foot snagged, she lurched to a halt, her arms shooting forward to brace herself for the fall. Only two strides now. He was determined to catch her. And then, just before he reached her, a fisherman caught her by the shoulders, pulling her upright once again.

Relief rushed out of him on a series of hard, panting breaths as he came upon the scene. Recognizing the man as Mr. Alcott, a newcomer to Whitcrest, Crispin opened his mouth to thank him for his assistance.

But when he saw Alcott's hands still clasping Jacinda's upper arms, different words came out instead. "Mr. Alcott, I do believe Miss Bourne is no longer in danger of falling."

Alcott swung his gaze in Crispin's direction, his broad grin slanting into a confused frown. "Pardon, Your Grace?"

Closing the distance, Crispin discovered that he was seething more than respiring, every sound coming forth in a low, foreign growl. He didn't know what was wrong with him. He wasn't normally this quick to temper but he couldn't seem to help himself. Seeing the pair of them, nearly twined together in front of the entire village, set his teeth on edge. "Your hands, Mr. Alcott."

"Forgive me, sir," Alcott said, lifting his hands away carefully as if Jacinda were a powder keg and Crispin was holding a torch. "I meant no disrespect. I merely wanted to keep her from falling. These nets can be tricky."

Jacinda sent a venomous glare to Crispin before she turned to smile to Alcott. "Your concern does you credit. I would have tumbled head over heels if not for your assistance. I am in your debt."

Coming to her side, Crispin set his hands on her waist and lifted her from the tangled coils, ignoring her outraged gasp. "Are you able to stand?"

"Only if you put me down," she snapped, and her voice lowered further as she clenched her teeth. "You are causing quite the spectacle."

He disagreed and focused on the more important matter at hand—freeing her so that he could take her back to Rydstrom Hall and rail at her for the remainder of the day.

Moving her away from the netting, he noticed that she'd lost one slipper. Before she had the chance to balk, he fished through the ropes and retrieved it. When he bent down to slip it over her stocking foot, his sudden shift in position left her no choice but to grip his shoulder for support, and that was fine with him. At least she was no longer holding on to Alcott.

Then standing before her, he kept her secure with a hand at her waist for one more instant. "Is your ankle twisted?"

The daggers she'd been throwing with her glare abruptly transformed. Those uncanny, bright eyes widened, blinking up at him. "It is not."

Regardless, to be safe, he placed her arm into the crook of his before addressing Alcott. "Since Miss Bourne is a guest in my home, then by all rights the debt for seeing her uninjured is mine to repay. Whenever you require an equal favor, do not hesitate to ask me."

Then, without another word, he set off with Jacinda, only to slow his steps when he noticed a small crowd of two dozen or so eager-eyed village women, their children, and a few men who'd formed to watch the exchange. Even Miss Beels with her unruly dog.

Walking toward the gig, he received bows and well wishes for his health. He inclined his head and returned the gestures with a short, "And to you as well."

Crispin admired these people. They were a hard-working lot, who'd experienced their share of tragedies, losing loved ones to the rough seas as well as to the cliffs. They always came together in support of one another, lending charity where it was needed. Good, solid people. And yet, at times, they were somewhat interfering.

Proof of that was in the whispers he overheard as he passed by.

"Oh, how dashing His Grace looked as he hastened through the village."

"There'll be a wedding soon, mark my words."

"And a babe in Rydstrom Hall by Christmastide."

For a flash of an instant, he caught a glimpse of that picture. A tiny, pink-cheeked infant, drowsing in the cradle of his arms, and there by his side, his wife, leaning in to kiss their child as a lock of auburn hair fell over her forehead—

His steps faltered, the toe of his boot catching on one of the stones, breaking the rhythm of his even strides. Jacinda clutched his forearm as if to save him from falling.

"She'll make a fine duchess. Ever so kind and amiable."

Too late, Crispin realized his mistake. By coming down to fetch her instead of sending one of the footmen, he'd given the wrong impression and plenty of fodder for the village gossipmongers. If word reached London . . .

He cursed beneath his breath.

Now that his momentary panic receded, he realized how easy it might have been for them to misconstrue this episode, making it more than what it was—a duke doing his duty, by ensuring that someone under his care came to no harm. That was all.

Reaching the two-wheeled gig, he lifted Jacinda without a word, his thoughts preoccupied. No matter what the villagers might believe at this moment, he was not going to marry her. He needed an heiress. And in little more than a week, Miss Bourne would be headed back to London, never to return.

Before he climbed up, he experienced a queer sensation right then, a sort of off balance, sinking that made him feel like a net set adrift without a tether to haul it back.

"Rydstrom, are you unwell?" Jacinda asked, apparently having noticed the alteration in him.

Without knowing the cause, he shrugged it off and stepped up, fitting beside her in the snug seat. He was keenly aware of how close she was, with the crush of her skirts between the meeting of his firm hip and the gentle curve of hers.

Reaching forward, he wound the leather reins twice around the hand that was closest to hers. "Never venture near the cliffs again, Miss Bourne."

"I'm not that foolish, Rydstrom. I would have stop—"

"But you *are* that foolish," he interrupted, his tone low with warning as he set off. "You've just proven it by traipsing into the village without my permission, without a chaperone, and without any common sense whatsoever. I should have taken you across my knee like I threatened to do in London and maybe then I wouldn't be ready to lock you up for the remainder of your stay here."

The fact that she continuously put herself in dangerous situations had to stop, if only for his own peace of mind.

"What a boorish thing to say!" She twisted in the seat, her knee colliding with his, crowding him until his clothes were suddenly too tight. "If we'd only met twice before, how could I have possibly earned such a threat?"

Damn. He'd said too much again. "It's best that I not answer that question."

She huffed. "Then explain to me why you behaved like a barbarian just now, threatening the man who gallantly saved me from falling. Did it ever occur to you that I might have wanted to stay in the village? The people there are quite nice, far more than some others of my limited acquaintance. And Whitcrest is a lovely, quaint village. I'm certain your *heiress* will enjoy it."

Crispin shot a look to Jacinda. "What did you mean by that?"

"I meant nothing other than your *very rich wife* will find some redeemable companionship here." She reached out and grasped his arm. "Mind the path, Rydstrom, or you'll put us in the thistles."

Bothersome baggage. She never left him with a moment's peace.

"Apparently you are under the misconception that you have liberty to speak to me with more censure than I've heard in years. You are not." Looking ahead, he clenched his jaw and pulled back with his right hand to turn the horse around the curve. "Obviously, my actions late last night left you confused. I never intended to offer you any indication that I have, or ever will have, designs on you. I can assure you, that is the furthest thing from the truth. I made a point and that was all there was to it."

"Fear not, after one clumsy kiss, you are safe from my devious clutches." She issued a harsh, hollow laugh. "And what a blessing for Mr. Alcott that you saved him from *me*. After all, the moment I uttered a startled cry, I was certain he would propose marriage. Of course, then I would have had to explain about how I might very well have a husband in London that I've completely forgotten. So it would have ended rather awkwardly."

"You do not have a husband."

"Oh? No doubt you are thinking that with all my failings, no one would have me," she said, the volume in her argument diminishing on an indrawn breath.

Glancing over, he saw sadness creep across her countenance. Perhaps, with all that had gone on this morning, and in such a short time, he had overstepped a few boundaries as well. "You are rather tenacious when you want to be, but I wouldn't consider it an entirely flawed characteristic."

"Do be careful, Rydstrom. That sentence fairly reeks with the beginnings of a compliment. You wouldn't want me to form any romantic notions about you." She looked toward the sea, as they rounded one of many corners, averting her face. "But rest assured, I will never lose my head over you because of that sloppy kiss or anything else I learned about your character this morning."

Sloppy? He tried not to take offense, but each time she brought up their kiss, his part was sounding worse and worse.

"What did you learn?" he asked, foolishly offering her another opportunity to wound his ego.

She took a moment to torment him with silence before she answered. "In the village, before you arrived and saved me from a libertine net"—she slid him a wry glance—"I heard all the villagers speaking very highly of you."

Well, that was not the response he expected. Somewhat uncomfortable by the accolade, he shifted in the seat, but only managed to rub up against her.

He snapped the reins to speed up the horses. "Their fondness for me is a recent occurrence. As a young man, I was a veritable terror, racing this very conveyance along every stretch of road, and angry at everyone who chose to live in Whitcrest. For me, this village had once felt like a prison. At the time, I believed that everyone else was living the life that I deserved."

"And your opinion altered when your parents died?"

He nodded, and decided that there was no harm in answering, in sharing one small aspect of his life. "The villagers offered their support in dozens of small ways, not the least of which was walking the funeral procession with me. It was in those first days following the tragedy that I'd realized they gathered together for everyone. The reason wasn't because I was their duke—at least not all of it—but that I was one of them. They helped me remember who I was."

She was quiet for a moment, her gaze searching his, her expression full of tenderness. "While I am sad for the event that led up to it, I am glad you found something of a family to be with you during that time."

He didn't know why this exchange made the stiffness in his shoulders wane, or why he eased back into the seat beside her and no longer cared that their limbs were crowded together. He actually welcomed the close comfort.

Perhaps this wasn't such a small thing he'd shared with her, after all.

"Ever since you mentioned that I live with my uncle, I've presumed that my parents have died as well. Do we have that in common?" she asked, then shook her head. "But no, I suppose you will not answer that."

"Would you want me to, though? I think it would only bring more questions and not ease your mind."

She seemed to consider this and gradually shook her head. "Perhaps, but it bothers me that I do not remember my mother, in particular, or even know if I resemble her. Did I inherit my curiosity from her? Was she stern and always scolding me for my tenacity? Or was she affectionate and patient?"

Even though Jacinda lifted her shoulder in a hapless shrug, Crispin heard the slight break in her voice.

"I sincerely wish I knew the answer, for your sake." And it was true. He saw the toll that her amnesia was taking and, consequently, he was struck by an inexplicable need to cheer her, to release the reins and wrap his arm around her.

"*Ugh*, do not listen to me. I'm just . . . hungry and frustrated, I suppose. And I cannot stand to have this mystery locked inside my own head."

"If it's any consolation, given the fact that you are still quite tenacious and curious, your mother likely indulged you. I imagine that the best of mothers love their children for precisely who they are."

He must have startled her because she turned her head toward his, so suddenly that he caught the sheen of tears in her eyes before she blinked them away, her lashes clumping into glistening spikes. "That was surprisingly kind of you."

Her complete astonishment was somewhat insulting.

"I have my moments."

"Mmm . . ." she murmured, tilting her head to study him, clearly doubtful. "And did you have the best of mothers as well?"

"Aye." He nodded immediately, and even felt a slight tug on his lips as a memory caught him off guard. "Often, she would play a game with me called the four battlements of the Great Hall, where enemy invaders were poised at either ends of the two tables. Then we would race together through the halls to find Father, and coax him into playing a game, too."

He slowed the horse as they crested the hill and looked at the façade of Rydstrom Hall. In the past four years, he'd only been able to recall the times when Mother had been sad, Father absent. This was the first time, in a long while, that he recalled how happy his childhood had been here.

He glanced down at Jacinda and saw her smiling up at him, her eyes bright, her cheeks glowing from the wind and from her reckless morning jaunt. Several locks of her hair had come undone from her coiffure, and he wasn't sure that he'd ever seen a more beautiful woman in his life.

Startled by his own thoughts, he cleared his throat quickly and cemented a frown to his brow. He couldn't for one moment allow himself to forget the risks of having her here. Because then he might become careless, even more so than he already had been. "In the future, you will not venture into the village."

"I have no intention to . . . other than to attend the Spring Festival," she said with an absent flick of her wrist that drew his attention to the pale flaxen thread wrapped around her slender index finger.

"No. I forbid it. As I've said before, I promised to deliver you back to your uncle in one piece. And I cannot always be there to rescue you from a foolish inclination."

"Then host it here. The villagers said it used to be a grand occasion at Rydstrom Hall."

He shook his head. "That was long ago. And the answer, in case you are unclear, is still no."

"Then you'll have to lock me in my chamber because I will attend," she challenged, her brows lifted, an unrepentant smirk on her plump lips.

His blood heated, though not entirely in irritation. The desire to kiss her, *hard*, to prove that he was her protector and that he would decide what she did or did not do nearly overwhelmed him.

"Miss Bourne, do not tempt me." Jaw clenched he glared down at her, watching as she swiftly, angrily, began to unwind the thread. "What *is* that on your finger?"

"Nothing but a string," she said crisply.

He shifted the reins into one hand and reached for hers to still her motions, but he was the one who went still instead. The simple touch—his hand engulfing hers, his thumb skating over the loosened thread—seemed to anchor him and banish that drifting sensation that had come over him a short while ago.

Abruptly, he released her and gripped the lead once more, his knuckles white with strain. "Were you injured by the nets?"

"No. It is a remembrance string," she said casting it over the side. Turning away, she watched as it drifted sinuously on a breeze. And then a long, arduous sigh escaped her. "Why do you do that—act with almost tender concern for me one moment and then keep me at arm's length the next?"

Because he kept forgetting how foolish it would be to care for her. Apparently, they were both suffering from a form of amnesia. Though, he would make sure his was temporary.

Instead of telling her this unwelcome truth, he offered a more ambiguous answer. "You know the reason."

From the corner of his eye, he saw her nod.

"Because of your heiress," she said, startling him. Because it was only then that he realized he'd completely forgotten about his necessary bride. Absently, Jacinda rubbed the mark the string left behind. "I wish you would start remembering her sooner."

So do I, Crispin thought and wondered if he should tie a string around his finger, too.

Chapter 18

"These days of confinement would have been, but for her private perplexities, remarkably comfortable . . ."

Jane Austen, *Emma*

After this morning, Crispin could not fathom anything more complicated than having Jacinda Bourne beneath his roof. But then her sister came to call and he was proven wrong.

Fellows paced the floor, peering worriedly at the doorway to the juniper parlor, where Miss Ainsley Bourne was with Dr. Graham, discussing the possibility of removing Jacinda from Rydstrom Hall. "Miss Bourne cannot be taken from us yet, Your Grace. She and I have yet to finish her tour of the castle, and she was ever so eager to hear the history of the minstrel's gallery."

"And the cook is preparing a special recipe for turtle soup for our Miss Bourne," Mrs. Hemple added, worrying her hands in the center of her apron again.

He realized now that it had been a mistake to send out his daily letters to Eggleston, explaining the injuries to Jacinda and her progress. He'd only hoped to ease the worry that her family would likely endure by not hearing from her, while also assuring them that she was under the care of a competent doctor.

Unfortunately, Miss Ainsley Bourne must have confused his letters with an open invitation. She'd arrived in the same coach as his valet, Bartram, whom Crispin had finally sent for after realizing his stay would be extended.

He'd also written to Aunt Hortense so that she did not hear the news from the Bourne family patroness, the Duchess of Holliford. It was a relief that his aunt didn't arrive unexpectedly as well. Because then she would want her apartments aired and left open so that anyone might stroll within the rooms and see what he'd kept hidden for years.

But he wouldn't need to worry about Jacinda making the discovery, if Ainsley Bourne took her sister away.

Thinking of that possibility, a peculiar knot of tension gathered at the base of his skull. Though why the notion would give him anything other than elation, he did not know. He wanted to be rid of her, he reminded himself.

"She is not *our* Miss Bourne," Crispin said, rolling his shoulders to dispel the confounding, tight sensation. He glanced over to Mrs. Hemple. "Is she still in her chamber, resting?"

"Yes, Your Grace," she said quickly, but swallowed and glanced down at her fingernails.

His eyes narrowed with suspicion. With Jacinda left very much alone, she could be up to anything. "Are you certain?"

Perhaps he should check on her, ensure she wasn't up to mischief. Even the thought of seeing her with his own eyes caused his pulse to accelerate, his blood warming in his veins.

"Quite, sir," Mrs. Hemple said with a quick nod. "She had an eventful morning, and then ate no more than a bird's share. She should be quite tired and likely not even able to travel . . ."

Crispin expelled a breath. "We will wait to hear what her family has to say before we send for her."

Yet, even as the words left him, he found that he could not stand still, his boots shifting on one of the four rectangular rugs on the floor. He was impatient for Ainsley Bourne to leave the parlor and tell him her decision.

Then suddenly the door opened. Both Dr. Graham and Miss Bourne walked out, but when Crispin took a step forward, so did Fellows and Mrs. Hemple.

He paused long enough to address them. "Forgive me for pointing out that there may be work to be done in Rydstrom Hall."

Fellows put a hand over his heart, his brow wrinkled. "But, sir, how can you expect us to—"

Crispin held up a hand. "Whatever decision has been made then I—the master of this castle, in case you have forgotten—will hear it first."

He strode away from them, wondering how Jacinda's amnesia could have infected everyone in Rydstrom Hall. No one even knew their places anymore. And he looked forward to returning to a semblance of order, with everything back to the way it ought to have been.

So then why did each heavy footfall that brought him closer to Ainsley Bourne only make Crispin feel muddled inside?

It was not a question he wanted to answer.

Directly ahead, Graham bowed to Miss Bourne and took his leave, offering a nod to Crispin as he passed by, and revealing nothing definitive in his countenance. Ainsley Bourne, on the other hand, appeared quite troubled.

In such a circumstance—if this might have been Sybil instead—Crispin didn't know what he would do either. He felt a sense of empathy for her, even as his unease grew.

"I should not wish to intrude or tarry any longer, Your Grace," she said the instant he neared, her tone matter-of-fact.

"Of course. I'll send for your sister." He nodded, his lungs tight.

"I'm afraid I'll be leaving without her."

Turning on his heel, Crispin stopped. "Pardon me?"

"As much as I had every intention of taking Jacinda home with me, Dr. Graham has warned me of the irreversible damage that action could inflict. He also mentioned that there were no guarantees she will recover fully, either way." She paused, a breath stuttering out of her lungs. "Yet, how could I rightly put my own needs ahead of hers? After all, it is my duty to watch over my family and to protect them to the best of my ability."

Her last statement made him feel as if she were a kindred spirit. He knew this decision could not have been easy, and because of that he admired the sensible, stalwart Miss Ainsley Bourne.

She was pretty, too, in a reserved, quiet way. And he didn't feel that terrible knotted sensation with her, or any stirring of attraction that would ultimately lead to a distraction he could not afford. Precisely what he was hoping for in a bride. It was a pity she was not an heiress, otherwise he might think of marrying her and save himself all sorts of trouble.

Not that he intended to fall into trouble with her sister . . . it was just that he didn't like where his mind and body were always taking him when Jacinda was near. He didn't like that she'd awakened part of him that he'd had under firm control for years.

"I understand," he said, offering his handkerchief when her eyes misted over. "As I said before, she is welcome here—you both are."

Again, she shook her head. "When I asked to see her, Dr. Graham warned me of confusing her. There is, of course, the chance that she might remember me. But then, there is also the chance that someone would have to introduce us, and from there the complications would begin. It is a risk I am not willing to take."

"I will make sure that everything is done to aid her." The two sisters could not be more different—one was all about risk and the other all about protection. If only the eldest had first handled his application, then none of them would have been in this situation.

"Thank you," she said, her lips curving in a soft smile

that was wholly absent of impishness. "You are kinder than we deserve, I'm sure. After all, you must know that she is not here by accident. While I do not know her reason, I do know she traveled this way to finish her investigation before assigning your list of potential matrimonial candidates." She blushed, embarrassed. "My sister tends to have a streak of tenacity that borders on excess."

Borders on? He stifled a wry laugh. Jacinda Bourne was completely irredeemable.

"Our agency strives to ensure proper matches. Though, given the circumstances, our methods may be somewhat flawed," Ainsley continued, humbly. "It is clear to me that you are a fine and noble gentleman and I apologize for all the inconveniences you have suffered. If you will permit me, I will see that you have a list of viable candidates sent to you shortly after I return."

"I should like that very much." Once more, he marveled at how different the two sisters were. "Please know that my carriage is at your disposal, and should you require lodgings, I will send my driver with coin. It is the very least I can do."

She hesitated, but then accepted with a nod. Then at the door, she paused and looked up at him. "May I ask a question, Your Grace?"

"Of course."

"Did my sister have a book with her?"

He nodded. "A volume of *Emma*, I believe. She kept it wrapped in cerecloth to keep it dry."

She sighed with relief. "Good. I know that when—*if*—she regains her memory, she never would have forgiven herself if anything happened to it."

He wondered how the entire family seemed so attached to these books.

"And might you do me one more favor?" She lifted the worn satchel she'd been carrying all this time. "I've packed a few of her things, along with our mother's music box in the hopes of sparking . . . something. Would you give this to her and ensure it is kept safe?"

As much as he did not want to *spark* Jacinda's memory, he agreed. Then, bidding Ainsley Bourne adieu, he left her to the care of Fellows and the driver who would take her to the inn.

But when he turned back, he looked down the length of the gatehouse and saw Jacinda.

She was standing at the far end near an archway, her brow knitted, her mouth tilted down in a frown, and she looked almost pained.

He couldn't help but wonder if she'd seen her sister, recognized her, and now recalled everything.

Chapter 19

"And I am not only, not going to be married, at present, but have very little intention of ever marrying at all."

JANE AUSTEN, *Emma*

Forgoing a much-needed rest, Jacinda spent the remainder of her morning with Sybil. They were having a picnic on the floor of the duchess's chamber, with little sandwiches filled with thinly sliced salmon, buttery scones, and rich dark tea—though Sybil preferred hers with sugar and milk.

Reclining on the pillows strewn about, Jacinda read from *Emma*, requiring a bit of comfort after the way her outing had concluded with Rydstrom. She didn't want to think about him or his heiress any longer. So she dove headlong into the story once again, pausing every now and then to brush a few crumbs from her skirts.

While listening, Sybil lay on her stomach with her knees bent and her stocking feet stirring the air as she sketched pictures of what she thought the characters would look like.

At first, Jacinda only remarked on the effortless quality of each drawing. Then all at once she saw something quite familiar. "This looks just like Mr. Fellows, and you have him dressed like Emma's father in a robe, slippers, and stocking cap."

Sybil grinned, scrambling up to her knees to sort through her stack and handed her another.

"Why, that's Miss Beels and with Mr. Lemon by her feet.

And this looks very much like Mr. Trumbledown. Then again, I don't know another man with a wooden leg. And there is Mrs. Lassater, and the Olson boys . . ." She shuffled through them all, amazed again by this girl. "Oh, and here is one of Mr. Alcott, and a handsome likeness, too. It's a pity my visit to the village was cut so short. I never had the chance to find out more about him."

Sybil snatched the picture away and turned it facedown on the floor. Then, frowning, she whipped through the other drawings until she handed one, in particular, to Jacinda.

It was Rydstrom, the sketch complete with chiseled jaw, broad shoulders, and something Jacinda had never seen on his countenance—a smile.

Unable to stop the urge, she traced those lines with her fingertip, wondering if this was what he would look like if he ever smiled at her. But she tucked that thought away for now and focused instead on the reason Sybil had put this in her hand.

Jacinda believed she knew. The girl was a romantic, after all. Likely, she had decided from the first moment she'd drawn the image of Rydstrom carrying Jacinda toward the castle that there was something between them.

And there was, of course—amnesia, discord, secrets, and an heiress, just to name a few.

"This sketch is a handsome likeness, too. However, I believe that Betsy and Martha would prefer the other one. You see, they have heard about the newcomer to Whitcrest and are curious about him. I volunteered to speak to Mr. Alcott in order to find out if he was a worthy prospect."

A bright grin replaced the disgruntled pucker and Sybil lifted the sketch of Mr. Alcott off the floor, returning it to the stack. Apparently, he was no longer in danger of being cast out of the paper village.

"I wish I'd been at liberty to exchange more than a few words with him. I don't know how many more opportunities I shall have before I . . ."

Her words trailed off as she saw a ghost of worry cross Sybil's face, dimming the light in her perceptive gray eyes to the color of smoke. Jacinda shifted uncomfortably, knowing that she needed to make it clear that she would be leaving Rydstrom Hall.

But when her hand brushed the edge of the open book, she thought of something else instead. "Then again, Miss Emma Woodhouse would not be deterred by a minor setback, not when a potential match was at stake. Perhaps, while I am here, you and I could work together. As an artist, you have an amazing eye for detail, and that is precisely what any good matchmaker requires."

Jacinda felt her pulse race suddenly. Her heart squeezed tightly against her lungs and rose up along her rib cage like bubbles inside an untended glass of water. That peculiar sense of rightness, *of purpose*, that she'd first experienced in the library yesterday, filled her again. Only stronger this time.

Sybil leaned forward and laid her hand over Jacinda's on the book and nodded eagerly, her curls bouncing. Then, as if she, too, had been similarly struck with an exhilarating sensation, she bounded to her feet. She didn't even give Jacinda the chance to question her before Sybil took her by the hand and pulled her toward the door.

Caught up in the girl's excitement, Jacinda went along and soon found herself skirting around corridors and up stairwells until they were, at last, in the cozy room at the top of the castle.

As soon as they entered, Sybil went to her desk in front of the oriel window, picked up a brass cylinder and gave it a twist until it extended.

"A telescope? But what does this have to do with matchmaking?"

Sybil gestured to the window, a mischievous grin on her lips.

Still a trifle puzzled, Jacinda put the glass to her eye and peered through the window. And that's when she saw a clear bird's-eye view of the village. "I can see everything from here. What a clever girl, you are." Then, because it needed to be said, she added a halfhearted, "But we both know that spying is wrong, of course."

Sybil pressed her lips together, lowered her chin, and offered the barest of nods, but there was no disguising the twinkle in those rounded eyes.

Jacinda bit back a grin. "Unless . . . it is done for a very good reason. And I believe that matchmaking would be at the top of that list, don't you?"

Beaming brightly, Sybil nodded. Then, in a flurry, she snatched a page of her school lessons, turned it over and wrote, *"The Matchmakers of Rydstrom Hall."*

"A list—what a splendid idea! Though, with a title like that, it nearly sounds like a book, wouldn't you agree?"

Sybil's lips parted on a soundless gasp and instantly took up a fresh sheet of paper, scrawling *Once upon a time* with great flourish.

"I should love to read such a book." But when the words left her lips, a cold, wistful sensation crossed over her like a cloud passing in front of the sun. Her time at Rydstrom Hall would surely not last long enough to fill the pages of a book. Soon, she would be leaving the only home she knew and venturing back to the one she couldn't remember. "Will you promise to write it?"

Sybil, already scribbling on a second sheet of paper, nodded absently. Which was lucky for Jacinda because she didn't have to worry about hiding the moisture collecting in her eyes.

Thoughts adrift, she stared out the window and leaned closer to cement this view in her mind, of the chalk white cottages in the distance, the winding path up the hill toward the castle, the slate roof over the gatehouse, and . . . Wait a moment. Was that a carriage waiting just outside Rydstrom Hall?

Leaving Sybil to her story, Jacinda rushed back through

corridors and downstairs, curious to see who had come to visit Rydstrom. Yet as she left the first corridor, it occurred to her that the carriage may not have been waiting for someone who had arrived, but for one who was leaving, instead. Consequently, her steps slowed as she considered the consequences of her actions early this morning.

Had she gone too far and Rydstrom was now sending her away? Or had her uncle written, demanding her return? Or perhaps her uncle was inside the carriage.

Then again, it might very well be a visitor for Rydstrom. A friend from London, perhaps. Or even—she swallowed—an heiress.

Gripping the newel post at the bottom of the stairs, she stared into the yawning mouth of the arched corridor that led to the gatehouse. A peculiar and seemingly foreign wave of trepidation dampened her ever-present curiosity. Did she truly wish to know what lay ahead of her?

Regrettably, the answer was still yes. In fact, the more she thought about it, the more she had to find out, even at the risk of her own heart.

Heart?

She balked at her own wayward thoughts. Her heart was not involved in this matter, or any other matters beneath the roofs of Rydstrom Hall. And whenever her memory returned, she would do well to remember that.

One at a time, her fingertips released the carved finial as her feet moved forward, taking her down the corridor. But when she reached the threshold to the gatehouse, she stopped cold.

Her inquisitiveness had led her astray.

At the far end, Jacinda saw the duke standing with a woman, her head tilted back to gaze up at him, and likely adoringly. Though, from Jacinda's vantage point, she could not see the woman's face, only the top of a straw bonnet, tied with a brown ribbon beneath her chin. What she did see, however, was Rydstrom.

Jacinda marveled at the tender concern softening the hard lines of his features. Gone was the fierce glower. There was no arrogant ghostly smirk on his lips either. No jagged vein rising from beneath his forehead. No clenched jaw. In fact, his countenance expressed wholehearted *welcome* to this woman.

Clearly, there was an attachment between them. Perhaps, an understanding as well. The thought made her stomach crumple like paper, twisting and tightening into a hard ball.

She pressed a hand to her middle, not knowing why she had this strange reaction. What did it matter to her if he'd found a bride—*an heiress*? Nothing at all. In fact, she might even pen a condolence card to the woman, if they ever met.

And yet, Jacinda did not want to meet her. Not one bit.

Curiosity did not propel her forward this time. She wanted to know as little about this woman as possible.

It made no sense. After all, since Jacinda's entire world consisted of very few acquaintances, she should want to make as many new ones as she could.

She frowned, puzzled by this melancholic sensation. Then turning around, she began to step away but hesitated for an instant, wanting one last look at the pair.

Yet that was another mistake.

The woman disappeared into the sunlight streaming in through the open door, and when it closed with a heavy *thunk* behind her, the duke was left alone beneath the arch.

Then he turned and looked directly at Jacinda.

Their startled gazes collided. Even in partial shadow, she saw the way his brow instantly knitted above the bridge of his nose. His glower was back.

Disheartened and irritated, she pivoted on her heel and strode briskly down the corridor.

"Miss Bourne," he called out, his gruff voice echoing around her, his purposeful hard steps not far behind.

Her pace quickened to the speed of a skater over ice, too fast for the heels of her slippers to touch the stone floor. Just ahead, the open doorway of the library cast a haven of rectangular light into the corridor.

Rushing inside, she snatched a book from the shelf and he charged in right behind her. She averted her face, lips parted, panting, and acted as though she were gathering a collection to peruse at her leisure. Never mind the fact that her heart was hammering so hard beneath her breast that it just might crack through the cage of her ribs.

"You heard me call your name just now."

Jacinda glanced over and saw that crooked vein on his forehead. "Did you? Hmm . . . I must have been preoccupied."

Pivoting slightly, she added another book to the ever-increasing stack in her arms. She knew it was silly to pretend that they hadn't just played a game of cat and mouse down the corridor, but complete denial was the only thing she could think to do.

"You know very well I saw you in the hall," he growled, taking three hard-footed strides to her side. "We looked directly at one another before you scampered off in a great rush."

"Surely it is not a crime to be in a hurry. Then again, perhaps you are more of a dawdler. I myself find that, if I have someplace to be, I should like to get there with haste."

"Must every conversation with you become an inquisition and evasion?"

When he expelled a patently frustrated breath, the corner of her mouth twitched, tugging her flesh into a smirk. She took odd pleasure in his exasperation. "If you would stop the inquisition, then I would certainly stop the evasion."

"No. No. I am not at fault. You were born with a forked tongue and an inability to utter a syllable of truth." Reaching out, he took her by the shoulders and turned her to face him, his glower fiercer than ever. "The reason for my pursuit in the corridor was because I noticed an alteration in your features. You appeared to be confused or perhaps troubled. Tell me, have you regained your memory?"

Was that why he'd chased her—to find out if she was well enough to be rid of her for good?

Jacinda held tight to her pile of books. "What a fanciful imagination you have. I might have been distracted because I was looking for Dr. Graham, but hardly *troubled.* And I left because, when I saw you involved in a romantic interlude with that woman, it would have been rude to interrupt."

"That woman?"

"Surely you still remember her," she said with a hollow laugh, ignoring the fact that he was still grasping her shoulders, his touch giving more warmth than his stern expression. "After all, you were standing close enough to catalogue every single one of her eyelashes."

When the furrows disappeared from his brow and the corners of his eyes crinkled ever so slightly, she regretted the waspishness in her tone. Now he had reason to laugh at her.

The corner of his mouth twitched. "You saw me at the door with another woman—with Fellows standing not two feet away, mind you—and assumed I was engaged in a . . . *romantic interlude.* And *that* was why you ran away?"

She shrugged out of his hold and began cramming the books back on the shelves. When she thought it would have been nice to receive a different expression from him, she had not wanted mockery.

Correction—she did not want anything from him other than information that would help her retrieve her memories. Not a single thing.

"Whatever you do in full view of your servants is none of my concern. Furthermore, I did not run. I merely decided to look for Dr. Graham elsewhere and *walked* down the corridor at my usual pace." She shoved the last book onto the shelf, fully intending to storm out of the room. Yet just when she thought that was all she had to say, apparently, she wasn't finished. "And how dare you kiss me—even if it was only to prove a point—when your lips belong to another. I thought you were looking for a bride, not that you'd found her."

He studied her for a moment, his expression no longer amused at her expense, but thoughtful. "For your information, my valet has arrived from London. As for *that woman*—as you refer to her—she shared the coach with him."

She expelled a breath. "Oh."

Surely an heiress would never share a coach with a valet. She would have her own conveyance, and likely another for her servants.

Rydstrom stepped closer, the timbre of his voice lower and hushed, a far too perceptive intensity darkening his eyes. She wished she hadn't put down the book because she felt bare, exposed without it.

"Though, even if I were going to marry her, or anyone else, you have no grounds for being jealous. There is nothing between you and me, but this mutual"—lifting a hand, he brushed a lock of hair away from her forehead—"animosity."

A current of warmth showered through her, bathing her in tingles from head to toe. And it took all her strength not to close her eyes from the pleasure of his brief touch.

"I was not jealous." She kept her gaze steady, locked with his, hoping that he couldn't hear the wild pounding of her heart that would reveal this lie. "And you are absolutely correct—there is nothing between us, Rydstrom."

Chapter 20

"This is an attachment which a woman may well feel pride in creating."

Jane Austen, *Emma*

"I have not seen that dress before," Jacinda said about the pale celadon frock draped over the foot of the bed, before realizing how silly that sounded under the circumstances. The number of things she did not recall seeing was as numerous as the grains of sand upon the beach below the cliffs. "What I mean is that I wasn't aware I'd packed another in the satchel you brought."

"I'm told it is one of yours, miss," Lucy said. "Though, according to Mrs. Hemple, His Grace's valet brought it all the way from London. The maids are all talking about how romantic it is."

"Pray tell, *how* is this romantic?"

Lucy blinked, pursing her lips as if Jacinda were a simpleton who could not understand that one plus one equaled two. "If His Grace's valet brought it, then it's the same as if His Grace hand delivered it himself. Your families must be well acquainted."

"Perhaps . . ." Jacinda said for lack of a better response. She still did not see the logic in her maid's argument.

This morning, her mood was very like the tea in her cup, cold and bitter. The few sips she'd swallowed churned restlessly in her stomach, reminding her that she hadn't eaten much at dinner last evening. But that was Rydstrom's fault.

Throughout the entire meal, he'd worn that impossible glower. He'd set that hard look on everything he gazed upon, from his plate to his silverware, and to the torches and tapestries on the wall.

In fact, the only object or person who'd escaped his disapproval was Jacinda. And that was because he'd never once looked at her. Not even when Dr. Graham had reported that—along with the discovery that Jacinda could speak and read French—she also knew Latin, Greek, and German.

While she'd been rather impressed with herself, Rydstrom's response was quite the opposite.

"I'm not the least bit surprised," he'd said, his focus on the far wall, his hand gripping the stem of his goblet. "Such a talent would be an asset to one with Miss Bourne's particular . . . skills. In fact, I shouldn't wonder if she'd have deciphered the Rosetta stone before Champollion could, if given the chance."

Gruffly spoken, it had not sounded like a compliment.

And in the light of day, Jacinda still didn't know why he'd become so surly since their last encounter in the library. If anyone deserved to be cross, it was she.

She'd reached her limit of questions inside her head—who she was, why she was here, why Rydstrom was so changeable around her—and one more would surely make her gray matter explode.

Even now, her headache reared. Pressing her fingertips to her temple, she felt the tender scrapes covered with fine striations of healing skin beneath the light application of salve. Soon there would be nothing left of her injury. At least, on the outside. She still did not know how long it would be until—*or if*—the one inside healed.

"Your family sent this dress, a fresh petticoat, chemise, stockings, and a pair of slippers," Lucy stated as she laid the items out across the coverlet.

Grateful for the interruption, Jacinda set her musings aside to mull over at another time.

She focused on the garments spread out over the counterpane. Obviously, her uncle was a kind man, and quite thoughtful, too. A fresh addition to her wardrobe, giving her a three-day rotation in dress instead of two, was most welcome.

"They sent this as well," Lucy said, placing a scarf bundle on the coverlet. "Forgive me, miss, but earlier I noticed that there is a box inside."

Curious, Jacinda unwrapped the cream-colored scarf embroidered with little sheaves of wheat that matched the russet trim on the dress. Within the folds, she found an ornate wood box with an inlay of gold in a starburst pattern. The small irregular impressions on the surface indicated that it was not new, but still lovely and she surmised that it was sent for a sentimental purpose.

Perhaps her uncle wanted to aid her in recalling a memory of it.

Picking the box up in her hands, her fingertips skimmed over the silkiness of the finish as if it had been held often. Inhaling, she caught the sweet scent of liniment polish, reminiscent of beeswax and turpentine. But she remembered nothing. Tiny brass hinges on one side told her that it was meant to open in some way, yet there didn't seem to be a latch, or a key for that matter.

A puzzle box, then. *Splendid.* She did not have nearly enough to decipher already.

Grumbling, she decided that she needed a pleasant distraction this morning. Perhaps she would breakfast with Sybil and see how her book was coming along.

After donning the new-to-her dress, Jacinda wended her way up the stairs. Though, distracted by her thoughts, she forgot to be stealthy. She was creaking along the corridor without a care when suddenly she caught sight of Rydstrom.

Jacinda sucked in a quick breath and pressed her back against the wall. But in such a narrow corridor he would surely see her. Fortunately, he was turned away, the broad expanse of his shoulders taking up much of the doorway, leading into the donjon.

She was just about to sneak off when she witnessed something that startled her into stillness—Rydstrom ruffling a hand through Sybil's curls, the huffed, wheezing sound of her laugh, and her willowy arms slipping around his waist.

"Absolutely pitiful excuse for a paper boat. Why this looks more like an elephant," he said with a laugh, a deep throaty sound.

Here again was another example of how different he was with everyone other than Jacinda. What would it be like if he were equally at ease with her, not tense and glowering?

A foolish wish, she thought, feeling a telltale sting along the lower rims of her eyes. If she had not known before just how unwelcome and isolated she was in Rydstrom Hall, she certainly felt it now.

This realization caused a fast, one-blink deluge, to spill hotly down her cheeks. And while brief, it seemed to expand the hollowness that had not only stolen her memories, but now a few beats of her heart as well.

Hating herself for this bout of self-pity, she dragged her fingertips over her cheeks and wiped the dampness on the pleats of pale green muslin.

"Here," he said to Sybil, that hearty gladness still ringing in his tone, "I will show you how to make a proper sailing vessel."

So enthralled by this other side of him, Jacinda took a step forward as if to follow him into the room and see the boat for herself. But when the floor creaked beneath her foot, she lifted it quickly and slipped back into the staircase.

At that precise instant, Mrs. Hemple was coming up the stairs with a tray.

Panicked, Jacinda stared at the housekeeper and lifted a fingertip to her lips. Face white, Mrs. Hemple looked to the open doorway as the sound of the duke's voice and a heavy footfall came near.

"Mrs. Hemple, was that you I heard in the hall?"

Jacinda swallowed, pressing herself against the wall of the stairway, just behind the door. She shook her head, imploring the housekeeper not to reveal her presence.

Mrs. Hemple drew in a deep breath and then let it out slowly. "It was, Your Grace. I had to retrieve a fallen napkin from the tray. But all is well, now." Then, without another glance, she passed Jacinda on the stairs and stepped into the corridor. "Mrs. Limpin prepared a fine feast this morning, sir. Sure to please even Sybil's finicky palate. In fact, I believe I spied a honey-glazed bun underneath the dome."

The announcement was met with the rapid clapping of dainty hands.

"Then the boat will have to wait until after we break our fast, I suppose. No? Very well, I'll make it now, but I doubt I'll find a single place to fold it as there are sketches and papers strewn about," he said with a gentle reproof and teasing chuckle. "See here, when did you become so untidy?"

"She's begun writing a book, sir," Mrs. Hemple said, her tone filled with pride. "Five pages complete already."

"A fine start, and I am curious, indeed. What is the book about?" There was a pause and the sound of a scratching nib over paper. "'An epistolary novel about a quiet young girl who lives in a castle.' Ah. The makings of a fine tale, to be sure. And I imagine that the narrator of such would have a great deal to impart."

It made perfect sense to Jacinda that Sybil, more than anyone, should have enough words trapped inside her to fill dozens of books, if only to have someone finally hear her voice. When Rydstrom did not reply, and the sounds from that room gradually fell silent, Jacinda wondered if he was thinking the same thing.

Oh, how wonderful it would be to ask him such questions, to learn his thoughts, to better understand his temperament. To know why he was so different with Jacinda than he was with everyone else.

The sweet agony of longing caused her breath to stutter out of her. Before she was discovered by Rydstrom, she crept down the stairs.

~

SHORTLY AFTER her descent from the donjon, Jacinda found herself in the music room with Dr. Graham. The sight of the instruments did nothing to cheer her. In fact, she cringed and hoped he wasn't going to ask her to perform again.

Yet, the instant he told her of their agenda for the next hour or more, she decided she would prefer blistered fingertips and wounded ears, instead.

"Dancing?" she asked, the disbelief in her voice causing it to rise to a different octave. "Are you certain that is the best use of our time?"

"I believe that what we need to find are more pleasurable pastimes in order to trigger your memories. While you have surpassed my expectations in your knowledge of languages, and various other studies, I did not detect any passion for them. Our other exercises in embroidery and"—he cleared his throat—"music have made it apparent that your enjoyments lie elsewhere. And since your visit into the village yesterday tells me that you inhabit boundless amounts of energy, I thought you might have a penchant for dancing."

She tilted her head to one side and considered his logic with a measure of doubt. If she were so fond of dancing, then wouldn't she have caught herself swaying or twirling at one point? Then again, what did she have to lose? "Very well."

Jacinda expected the doctor to come closer and demonstrate the dance, but instead he sat down at the pianoforte, puzzling her.

He must have noticed it in her expression because he offered a glance down to his leg, adding, "My skills are better served from here. For the past two dozen years, I have been an excellent audience at assemblies." Then he nudged his spectacles back in place and rolled his fingers over the stained ivory keys from the deeper notes all the way to the highest pings in a lovely, swelling cascade. He offered a fatherly wink, showing off a bit. "Now, for this dance, you will step forward with your right foot, skip lightly—like a hop—then left foot, then turn."

Jacinda followed his directions, speaking them in her mind. "Right foot forward, skip, then—"

She jerked to a sudden stop, hunched over. Somehow the toe of her slipper landed on the hem of her petticoat with an audible tearing sound.

Peering down at the four-inch portion of drooping ruffle, she felt like a graceless idiot. "This method isn't going to work. I cannot picture the dance in my mind the way that I could with the words in different languages, or even when I was reading music, and we both know how that ended."

"Never give up, Miss Bourne," the doctor chided warmly as she knelt down and withdrew a long hatpin tucked into the russet trim border at the hem of her dress. "We have only begun. There are many other steps we could . . . Say, what have you there?"

"A pin," she said absently from her crouched position, repairing the fallen ruffle. It wasn't until she finished weaving the pin through the ruched cotton that she realized what she was doing. She gasped with a start and stood, staring down at the hem of her dress in wonder. Then, she saw the round, silver-beaded head of a second hatpin. "How did I know it was here?"

The question was more to herself, than to the doctor, but he answered. "Perhaps it is a custom for young women to tuck pins into their hems."

"It could very well be, and likely to repair tears such as this when one is away from a mending box," she mused. It was slightly confusing, however, that this was a rather sturdy and lengthy pin for mending.

"I assume that you did not place it there yourself this

morning," he said. And when he received a dumbfounded shake of her head, he continued, his tone clearly pleased. "That is something, indeed. I feel we are getting ever closer. Let us continue with this exercise and see what else we might discover."

Jacinda smiled, not feeling as reluctant as she had been a moment ago. "Indeed."

The doctor stretched his arms before him with his fingers intertwined, folding them backward, and unleashing a series of pops and crackles. "Now then, I have a few more pieces of music in my repertoire. Perhaps, I should play something with more of a slow, flowing cadence. Try closing your eyes for this one, using intuition for the dance without my instruction."

Deciding to trust his method and eager to discover something else, she complied and closed her eyes. As the soft notes filled the chamber, she took it a step further and held her arms up like a marionette, shuffling her feet across the hardwood floors of the paneled room. She waited for a sense of certainty to fill her.

Yet as she turned in a slow circle, she felt something that wasn't related to the music or any particular memory.

A prickling sensation ran along the back of her neck, almost as if someone were watching her. Opening her eyes, she saw that she was right.

A jolt pinned her in place.

Rydstrom stood in the doorway, arms at his side, hands clenched into fists. His countenance, while not quite glowering, was strained with concentration, as if he were mentally trying to will her into the correct steps.

Slowly, she lowered her arms, irked that her failure had gained his notice when her achievements had not.

"Ah, Rydstrom," Dr. Graham said, stilling his fingers on the keys. "We were making an attempt to see if Miss Bourne remembered dancing. It's rather serendipitous that you should stop by the music room."

The duke flicked him a hard glance. "I was merely on the way to my study when I heard music."

"Then we would not wish to keep you any longer," Jacinda said quickly.

Rydstrom's gaze returned to her. His chest expanded on a breath deep enough to furrow the fabric of his cloud gray waistcoat before he let the air out in a strained exhale. "Since I doubt you have ever stood on a ballroom floor alone, your time would be better served with a partner."

"Undoubtedly," she said without a hint of sarcasm.

He arched a brow.

Very well, perhaps her tone held a *taste* of sardonic flavor. "Will you ring for a footman?"

He took an ominous step toward her, his presence filling the room. "No. I believe I am more than qualified to show you the steps of a country dance."

"But Dr. Graham was very insistent that I try to conjure the memory on my own," she said in a rush.

"Rydstrom has a point," Dr. Graham added cheerfully. "Perhaps a partner first, and then we will return to the previous method."

Without delay, he began to play the music again, a leisurely melody. The notes were trying to slow her pulse, but it didn't work. With every purposeful step Rydstrom took in her direction, her heart only beat faster, her breaths quickening, anticipation drawing as tight as a piano wire inside of her.

He stopped within arm's reach. "There are various poses that one learns from a dancing master; however, for the sake of this exercise we will forgo those finer points. The primary object of dancing is to create seamless movements between you and your partner. The best way to accomplish this is to imagine that the pair of you is separated by quadrants. In such, your—" He stopped his explanation to deepen his frown. "Is the subject amusing, Miss Bourne?"

Jacinda pressed her lips together to hide her grin, her high-strung nerves loosening marginally.

The moment he'd mentioned quadrants, she couldn't help but think of how he separated his entire life by them. It shouldn't surprise her that he could do so with a dance, but it did nonetheless. "Not at all. I was merely picturing a ballroom filled with disembodied dancing shoes. Pray, continue."

A grumble rose in his throat. "Perhaps it would be better if I demonstrate. Now, if I take a right step forward, you would slide your left foot backward and so forth, in time with the music. Shall we?"

He held out his hand, long fingers extended. Deep lines in his broad palm formed a triangle in the center, and her fingertips tingled at the thought of settling there. Surreptitiously, she pressed her hand to her muslin to dry any dampness before she lifted it, darting a wary glance up to his face.

He was staring down at her hand, watching every movement, waiting, a muscle ticking along the hard line of his jaw.

She didn't know why she was so anxious. It was only a dance, after all. Yet without having a memory of any other, this would be her first, and—without knowing what awaited her in London—possibly her last. And a foolishly unguarded part of her was glad that it would be with Rydstrom.

Expelling a slow pent-up breath in a thin stream, she laid her hand in his. But far more than tingles met her fingertips. A shock of sensation rifled through her nerves, zinging along her arms and then descending like a bolt of lightning straight through her body to the soles of her feet. Peculiarly, her responses to him seemed to intensify with each interaction, instead of weakening as they ought.

He closed his hand around hers in one quick, reflexive motion. Then he went still as well.

They remained thus, both staring at their hands as if they'd become ensnared in a complex trap that would require a series of carefully orchestrated movements in order to escape unscathed.

Yet Rydstrom managed to recover first. He cleared his throat. "Now then, just as I said."

And when he stepped forward with his right foot, she stepped backward with her left. It was such a relief to complete this single step successfully that she tried to release him.

But he held fast.

"We are not finished, Miss Bourne," he said, though it was clear by the hoarseness of his tone that he wanted to end this lesson as much as she did. "Now step back in place. Good. And toward me. Excellent. And back to the start."

Oddly winded from four simple steps, she breathed in deeply, drawing in the scent of warm cedar through her nostrils and nearly tasting it on her tongue. Still, he did not release her, but prodded her into repeating the same steps with the other foot. And when that was successful, she thought surely that they were finished.

She was drained of energy, drowsy and yet peculiarly perceptive. Her mind was keen to notice every nuance of this moment—how their breaths accelerated in tandem and out of tempo with the music, how the pressure of his fingertips altered as he guided her steps, the errant caress of his thumb over her flesh, the fit of his clothes over his lean body, the shift of his muscular legs with each step . . .

"And again, right foot forward," he said.

Preoccupied, she moved without thinking. And summarily collided full-bodied into him. What made it worse was that they'd both stepped forward, right footed, and with utter confidence.

His hand clasped her waist, gripping her, reminding her of the way he'd held her that night in his study. When he'd kissed her.

His hard, albeit startled, gaze darkened, his pupils eclipsing the green of his eyes and leaving only a rim of soft, russet brown.

She was pressed breasts-to-knees against a wall of warm, solid duke, and wasn't sure what to do next. Likely, she should step back, or in the very least, make an attempt. Yet her body did not agree. Instead, she found herself yielding against him, her limbs feeling pliant and malleable like partially melted candle wax, molding around him.

"You said *right foot forward*," she said, glancing down to the hand she had splayed over his waistcoat before returning to his face.

A breath shuddered out of him. "*My* right foot. Always presume that I am referring to the dominant partner. I lead and you follow. That is the way of things." His hand clenched her waist briefly before he put the barest amount of space between them. But not far enough that he released her.

"Are you suggesting that your quadrants are more important than mine?"

The corner of his mouth twitched, his gaze flitting over her features. For an instant, she thought he might smile at her. Then he glanced down at her hand and its position over his heart, and he glowered once more.

Stepping back fully, he released her. "That is all the time I have for your exercises this morning."

Then he turned on his heel, and left her to stare after him.

CRISPIN GRIPPED the thick handle of the axe with both hands and swung it with hard, unerring precision. The wood splintered with a satisfying crack. Two halves fell from the block and onto the ever-growing pile. Then he set them up again, turning the halves into quarters.

He fell into a rhythm, a series of gestures—legs apart, grip firm, swing, strike. His muscles strained, flexing, tightening. His shirtsleeves clung to each muscle along his shoulders, arms, back, and torso. It felt good to perspire, to breathe so hard his lungs burned.

He never should have gone to the music room. For that matter, he never should have sought out Jacinda in the first place. But he'd been plagued by an unsettling hunger to see her this morning, as if he'd needed to break his fast—those long, sleepless hours in the chamber across from her—by feasting on the sight of her. *Ludicrous!*

He'd ignored the urge at first, going about his morning as usual. But all the while, it was as if he could sense her near, her fragrance in the air whenever he drew a breath, leaving him coiled and tense with expectation.

Even after Fellows had informed him that she was with Graham, and knowing that she was not in the village or causing mischief anywhere else in the castle, it had not been enough to appease him. He'd been compelled to look upon her with his own eyes.

But when he'd found her in the music room with her eyes closed and the light from the window falling on her lashes, turning their tips to a burnished bronze, his hunger had not abated. It only intensified.

He'd never noticed another woman's eyelashes. Certainly not enough to have been captivated by them, or to wonder what they might feel like against his lips. And it was that last thought, that had disturbed him the most. It was entirely too romantic. Lust was perfectly understandable given the circumstances, but he did not know why desire was coupled with tender sentiment.

Clearly, the days of having her here, the evenings in her company in the dining room—and, irritatingly *not* in his study—were starting to wear on him. So, in the doorway to the music room, he'd turned, prepared to leave and end this reprehensible torment. But then her startled turquoise gaze snared him, rooting him in place.

It annoyed him that he'd been caught watching her. In that moment, *he'd* felt like the trespasser. He'd wanted to leave, and could have done so if not for Graham's request to show her the steps of the dance.

Yet, even now as the wood splintered and sweat spilled off his brow, Crispin knew that wasn't the truth. He would have danced with her regardless.

It was the dance that had brought him here to the wooded edge of his estate with the need to expel every last ounce of energy and the incessant desire that hounded him. He frequently chopped wood for the castle—one of the many tiring activities a single man in the prime of health must do in order to keep from going mad.

However, he could still feel her body against his, legs tangled, hips aligned. She'd felt sublime, so soft and fragrant that he'd forgotten himself. He didn't even know how long they'd stood locked together. A few breaths and heartbeats too long, for certain.

Crispin was growing fatigued, but not in the way he required.

He was tired of resisting her and starving for the taste of her lips once more. And if Graham hadn't been in the music room, Crispin might have—no, *would have*—indulged himself. A dangerous realization, indeed.

What he needed was a larger distraction. Something that would draw his constant attention away from Jacinda. He had other matters to attend, after all. Arrangements needed to be made for the festival, such as carrying up the barrels of ale from the buttery, in addition to checking with his cook about the various foods Rydstrom Hall would provide. The servants did not perform their usual household duties on that day, but most assisted with the tables and games.

Thinking back on years past, even Father and Mother had done their part to ensure the enjoyment of all. And the festival had always been ripping good fun.

Reminiscing back to those days of his youth, Crispin felt a grin tug at his lips and, for a startling instant, found himself wanting to share those stories with Jacinda.

He shook himself free of the errant notion. Or, at least, he tried. The idea remained lodged in his mind, resisting his efforts and even compelling him to imagine what it would be like to witness her experiencing the festival for the first time.

The *only* time, he corrected, reminding himself that she would be leaving in little more than a week.

Then for some utterly foolish reason, he wanted to give her a happy memory to take with her. A memory they would always share. And without examining why this was suddenly important to him, Crispin decided to host the Spring Festival at Rydstrom Hall once again.

Chapter 21

"Come, my dear Emma, let us be friends and say no more about it."

JANE AUSTEN, *Emma*

Jacinda heard the news the following day. The Spring Festival would be here, on the grounds of Rydstrom Hall. And tomorrow, no less.

The castle was in a kerfuffle with sweet and savory aromas wafting from the kitchens. Scullery maids and chambermaids alike filled the tables of the Great Hall with preserves, biscuit tins, meat pies, and puddings. Footmen were carrying crates down from one of the garrets and taking them out to the lower bailey.

Jacinda loved the excitement. Everyone rallied together for a day of fun.

Well, everyone except for her.

She wanted to be of use, but each time she asked Fellows or one of the maids, they'd stopped their own tasks in order to direct her to a comfortable chair where she could rest and recuperate. And according to Martha, Rydstrom had left strict instructions for Jacinda not to lift a finger. But what he likely meant was that he didn't want her to touch a thing.

If she needed a reminder that he still saw her as an unwelcome guest, a nuisance, this certainly did the trick.

When she'd first arrived, his obvious dislike had merely annoyed her, much like a splinter beneath her finger. But in these past days, that splinter had shifted positions. It was no longer in her finger, but moving toward her heart, and pinching when she least expected it.

Seeking a remedy for these twinges, she went up the stairs to see Sybil, volume of *Emma* in hand. With Rydstrom occupied out of doors, she didn't have to worry about the floor creaking beneath her feet.

The moment she walked into the cozy room, Mrs. Hemple looked up and smiled. "Oh, Miss Bourne, you are a sight for sore eyes, to be sure. I've been stitching these pennants all afternoon and if I don't look up every whipstitch or so everything starts to blur together. Likely, you saved me from turning my own frock into a pennant."

Jacinda grinned back. At least one person in Rydstrom Hall appreciated her. And when Sybil hopped up from her desk to snake her willowy arms around Jacinda's waist, the number increased to two.

"I'm glad to be of assistance, especially in saving your dress from being mounted from the turrets of Rydstrom Hall."

Mrs. Hemple snickered, pinching the bridge of her nose with her thumb and forefinger. "I'm not certain His Grace expects any adornments at all. But I suppose we've all got ourselves caught up in the thrill of having the festival here again."

"It was nice of Rydstrom to change his mind. He'd seemed quite opposed to the festival when I'd spoken to him about it," Jacinda said absently, peering over Sybil's shoulder to the densely filled page.

Intent on her work, she dipped her quill in the inkpot to resume writing almost before she sat down.

"I'd say someone changed His Grace's mind."

Seeing Mrs. Hemple's sly grin, Jacinda shook her head. "It certainly wasn't me. In fact, Rydstrom has made sure that I'm not even part of the festivities. Each time I try to lend a hand, I'm shooed away like a pesky fly."

Mrs. Hemple blinked, clearly confused. "I was instructed

by His Grace as well, but only to keep you rested. Sir wants you to have the strength to enjoy the festival to the fullest."

That did not sound like the Rydstrom Jacinda knew. "It seems more likely that he would rather lock me in my chamber so that *he* could enjoy the day."

Sybil interjected herself into the conversation with a shake of her head and a knowing grin. Then, lifting one of the drawings from her desk, she handed it to her.

But Jacinda wasn't prepared for what she saw—a pair of figures sketched in the foreground, her and Rydstrom, faces tilted toward each other, and while standing in front of the Whitcrest chapel.

Pretending to misunderstand the inference seemed like the best option. "Very nice, Sybil. Excellent work on the church steeple. Why, there are even gulls flying near the sky."

When Jacinda tried to hand it back, Sybil crossed her arms, refusing to take the page.

Drat. It was no use. Jacinda would have to be direct. "Your sketch is quite romantic and lovely, but I must tell you that Rydstrom and I are never going to marry."

Sybil nodded, but it was in clear disagreement with Jacinda's statement.

"You see," Jacinda began, trying to explain further. "When a man and a woman decide to marry, they hold a certain regard for each other and that is absent between the duke and me."

But as the words left her lips, not even she believed them. There was something between them, and it wasn't the animosity that Rydstrom had claimed. If the feeling were caustic in any way, then she wouldn't spend most of her day anticipating their next encounter, her stomach fluttering at the mere thought of exchanging a few parries, relishing every second his eyes connected with hers, and replaying every episode in her bed each night.

Coming back to her senses, she saw clear doubt in the lift of Sybil's wispy brows, and decided it best to speak even more frankly. "Besides, the Rydstrom title must marry for money and I have no fortune."

Sybil turned sharply toward Mrs. Hemple as if to ask for confirmation.

"I've always thought the practice of marrying for the sake of Rydstrom Hall rather lonely," Mrs. Hemple said easily, whipping several stitches at the edge of the azure blue fabric. "Besides, each one of them have all dropped fortunes into building a grand estate without regard to future generations. But nothing will stop the onslaught of time, and no amount of money will keep this edifice standing forever. I believe that love is a greater legacy to leave behind."

Jacinda grew a bit fonder of the persistent Mrs. Hemple, misguided in her assumptions though she may be. "You and Sybil are a pair of true romantics then."

"I suppose we are." The housekeeper laughed. "What about you?"

Jacinda looked down at the book she'd brought—*her book*—and thought for a moment, mulling over everything that she'd learned of herself these past days. "I think part of me is, but there is also a skeptical side to my nature. If love were to find me, I'd likely frighten it off by wanting to know all of its secrets."

"True love would have no secrets."

"Doubtless, you are right." And Jacinda couldn't help but think of how her entire life was currently a secret. And the biggest part of the mystery was the Duke of Rydstrom. Looking to change the subject, she began, "But at this moment, I'm far more curious about whether or not Sybil is excited about the festival. Are you going to awaken at dawn to greet the springtime sun, too?"

The girl shrugged her shoulders and looked to Mrs. Hemple, but the housekeeper was busy at her task.

Seeing the wariness in her expression, Jacinda asked, "Are you nervous about playing with the other village children?"

After a moment, Sybil pressed her lips together and nodded, shyly tapping her fingertips against her throat.

"Hmm . . . I see what you mean," she said thoughtfully, hiding the fact that her heart was breaking for the girl. "Since I have misplaced my memory, I think that I should stay inside with you, too. We'll let everyone else have the fun, while we complete our lessons."

Sybil vehemently shook her head, pointed to Jacinda and then made a shooing gesture.

"No, I don't think I would enjoy myself at all." She pointed to her own temple.

Sharp as a tack, Sybil narrowed her eyes, apparently understanding what Jacinda was trying to do.

"If you are determined to watch the festival from the window, then don't let anything stop you," Jacinda said flippantly, but then she leaned forward to squeeze Sybil's hand. "But if you are determined to attend the festival and enjoy yourself, then don't let *anything* stop you. And, either way, I'll be right by your side."

Sybil offered a worried smile, but nodded in consideration.

"Oh, *fiddlesticks*, the time!" Mrs. Hemple scrambled to pile several pennants together. In the process, she upset her sewing box and accidentally kicked the pincushion with her toe.

Jacinda hurried to help, holding back a laugh. Sybil snorted, clutching her middle, her dimples aglow.

"You may laugh now, Sybil, my pet, just you wait until you're as old as I am," Mrs. Hemple chided fondly. Then skirting around the table, she pressed a kiss to the girl's head. "I tell you now, I won't have a speck of sympathy for you. Not a one."

Then the housekeeper set off down the corridor. But, something she said lingered in the air, distracting Jacinda with how familiar it sounded. The words *my pet* caused the briefest flash of a girl's face through her mind.

Like Sybil, this girl was pretty and blond, but with blue eyes instead of gray and no dimples.

It must have been a memory. Though, regrettably, like before, it vanished before she could hold on to it.

Now, feeling a bit empty, all she wanted was to sit in a comfortable chair by the fire and read her book. She tapped her hand on the red leather cover. "What say you, Sybil? Shall we be delinquents, skip the French lesson for today and visit Highbury instead?"

Sybil's next grin was full of mischief and Jacinda knew she had found a kindred spirit here.

A WEALTH of pride filled Crispin as the entire household worked feverishly to complete the preparations for the festival. He and a few of the groomsmen constructed tables and booths for wares and games and set them up at each corner of the lower bailey.

Hearing the news, some of the village men also lent a hand. The women even closed their shops and stitched together garlands of greenery, tying them to the old supports left over from the crumbling outer curtain wall. And at a glance, the grounds resembled something of a large, outdoor ballroom.

Crispin drew in a satisfied breath. This would be the grandest festival in Whitcrest's history. He was so pleased with their combined efforts, and preoccupied with anticipation for Jacinda's reaction, he didn't see the dark clouds gathering over the sea until they were almost to the cliffs.

When the first drops hit, he and the others scrambled once again to secure the area beneath large sheets of oil-slicked canvas, and ended with something of a patchwork caravan tent over the entire lower bailey. He wasn't going to let rain or mud ruin his plans.

Yet what he thought was a mere shower, transformed into a fierce storm in the distance. Silver veins of lightning lit the horizon over the water's edge and the low growl of thunder followed. Crispin knew it would be here soon, and a cold chill rushed through him as he thought about Sybil. With Mrs. Hemple busy overseeing the maids, his sister would be alone and frightened.

So the moment the task was complete and the villagers dispersed, Crispin rushed through the gatehouse and dashed up the stairs. First, he went to the long, narrow nursery because sometimes he found her hiding there with the coverlet pulled tightly over her head. But it was empty. Then he went to the private family solar in the donjon.

Carefully, he opened the door, not wanting to startle her more than she undoubtedly was. But he stopped cold at the sight before him. Dread washed through him like a plunge into a January sea.

Jacinda Bourne sat by the fire, and curled beside her in the chair, sound asleep, was his sister.

By all appearances, this was not an infrequent occurrence. Now he had to wonder how often Jacinda visited his sister, and how much she knew.

Even though he was well aware that Jacinda had been here before, he'd assumed she'd been too ill to remember. Not once in the past few days had she asked him about this room or Sybil. Then again, he knew from experience that Jacinda didn't ask questions. When she was curious, she investigated instead.

He should have been aware of this. But clearly, he'd let down his guard. Not only that, but his own sister and staff had not heeded his warnings.

Could they not see the potential risk unfolding once Jacinda returned to London? How a few words spoken about his *supposed* ward—even if only to his aunt—could reveal the truth and sentence Sybil to a life he'd been trying to shield her from all this time?

A roar of thunder filled the keep, lightning slicing through the sky beyond the window. And suddenly his dread turned to anger. What in the bloody hell was she doing in here, invading this private sanctuary?

As if reading his expression, Jacinda lifted a slender finger to her lips. "Shh . . . She fell asleep before the storm," she whispered. "Save your castigations for later."

His low growl blended with the sounds rumbling beyond the window. "Why are you here?"

Jacinda's lips curved, her eyes tilting at the corners with challenge. "I'm her French tutor."

"Have you been sneaking into this room every day?"

"Nearly," she whispered, wholly unrepentant. A person like her never thought about the repercussions of her actions, she only thought about herself.

And yet, that logic did not match the picture before him of Jacinda stroking soothing circles over Sybil's back in a gesture of warmth and caring. Sybil looked so peaceful, too, her cherubic cheeks pink, her head resting against Jacinda's shoulder. And without conscious thought, his panic and fury began to recede, drop by drop, like the rain pattering against the windowpane.

Now the absence of that palpable tension left him sluggish with exhaustion.

"Why is it that you have never once mentioned her to me?"

He did not answer, but stepped further into the room, his legs weighted like cliff barriers.

"I do not suppose she is a secret since the villagers know about her," Jacinda continued, his lack of response meaning little to one who never had enough information to satisfy her. "But I have to wonder, is she your child?"

"No, she is not my child," he said firmly, but saw Sybil's expression frown in her sleep. He didn't want to wake her. But he didn't want to keep her here either. Not like this, peacefully slumbering beside Jacinda. The pure contentment he witnessed added a confusing element to the disorderly emotions roiling through him. "Please, Miss Bourne, ask me no more questions. I have a responsibility to protect her. She has already suffered enough for one lifetime."

Jacinda glanced down and pressed her cheek against the fall of curls on Sybil's drowsing head. "I would not wish to bring her any grief."

Crispin must have lost all sense because, in that moment, he believed her.

Weary, he sank down into the chair opposite her and let his head fall back against the rest.

"Was she born mute?"

He wasn't going to answer at first, believing that the less Jacinda knew the better. Yet, after glimpsing this unexpected, nurturing side of her character, he wondered if telling her just enough might keep her from revealing anything about Sybil when she returned to London.

"No. She came to Rydstrom Hall shortly after her mother died," he said, deciding to take the risk, knowing that this was safer than having Jacinda seek out the answers on her own. "On that very day, a violent storm came, surprising everyone, including my parents. They were standing near the cliffs when the rock face suddenly gave way. Sybil saw it happen through the window. She screamed until she could no longer make a sound."

"Crispin, I'm—"

"Do not call me by my given name, Miss Bourne," he interrupted, a heady jolt lancing through him at the sound, cautioning him to beware of such intimacies. Straightening in the chair, he gripped the armrests, hardening himself against every enticement she represented. "It suggests a sense of familiarity that does not exist between us. I merely shared her story so that you would pry no further."

"You also shared a glimpse of your own tragedy with me." She turned her face toward the smoldering fire.

When he caught sight of the sheen of tears in her turquoise eyes, the harshness gave way to something softer, and infinitely more complex. He swallowed, and his tone was almost tender as he continued. "Let us not speak of it, not with the storm raging beyond these walls."

In the stillness that followed, the anguished regret from that day surfaced, gathering on his tongue. It frightened him how much he wanted to talk to her about it, to tell her the things he kept bottled up inside of him. Yet, somehow, he managed to swallow down the impulse.

"As you wish," she said quietly, surprising him with her easy acquiescence. Then she faced him once more, a ready inquiry posed in the lift of her brow. "But is she not able to speak at all? What I mean is, I've heard her issue sounds, here and there. Surely she should be able to speak."

"She can whisper," he admitted. "But it's not a soft sound as you or I would make. It's more of a rasp, raw and gravelly. Because it frightens her, I do not force her to make the attempt."

"Hmm . . ." Jacinda murmured, but did not make any further comment. Though she did study him intently for a few moments, her mind clearly turning with thoughts or opinions she did not share with him.

He wanted to ask her what they were, to delve inside her mind and learn everything he needed to know. But as the notion came to him, he wondered if *everything* would be enough. He feared, he would always want just a bit more with Jacinda.

"If I may ask one more question, but on another topic?" she asked, breaking the silence.

Though it took effort, he fixed a warning glower in place.

As usual, she chose to ignore it. "Why do you separate everything into quadrants?"

"It is something I've done since I was a child," he said with an absent shrug. "The nursery was arranged in quadrants—bed, wardrobe, washstand, desk. I merely find order and simplicity appealing."

Her mouth quirked as if she did not entirely believe him.

"I happened to notice that your ledger is the same—Oh, do not start to bluster at me again, Rydstrom. The room is already warm enough without your fiery scolding. After all, it is your own fault for leaving your ledger in plain view. At least, you did the evening I moved your bookend. And, through your own actions, you incited my inquisitive nature by writing my name on several of your pages in the bottom right quadrant." Unapologetic to the core of her being, she even wagged a finger at him before she resumed stroking Sybil's back in methodic circles. "Now then, what I cannot decipher is what each section represents."

He stared at her, his blood heating, his pulse running riot in his veins. But it wasn't anger simmering inside of him. Instead, he was nearly awed by her audacity and he had a strange compulsion to laugh.

Sitting in the room with him was the very same woman who'd stolen into his study in London, and robbed him of peace of mind, of order, of sense, of reason. In the place of all she'd taken, she'd let loose a storm of emotions that had gone numb inside of him long ago, buried under years of guilt and self-torment. She made him feel everything at once—anger, joy, fear, lust—and turned him into a bundle of raw nerves under constant siege.

She was what kept him awake at night, prowling through the halls when he should have been in his bedchamber. But his chamber was too close to hers. Too tempting.

So each night he walked to his study, took out his ledger and wrote down her name in the bottom right quadrant. It was supposed to serve as a reminder that it was her fault that he was awake and constantly aware of her. And now she demanded to know why her name was there? Well, he would leave her to surmise that answer on her own.

"In that ledger, the sections are the four parts of the day, beginning with the top left—morning, afternoon, evening and"—he paused—"night."

"Mine was the only name written in that one bottom

quadrant, and yet you have dinner each evening with . . . with both Dr. Graham and . . ." Her words stumbled to a halt. "I'm not sure I understand."

He was fairly certain she might, if she thought about it long enough, and he felt a grin tug on the corner of his mouth to see the bright color staining her cheeks in the glow of the firelight.

Relaxing again into the chair, he closed his eyes. "I am weary of conversation. Perhaps you could read instead from the book on your lap and allow me a moment's peace."

As the storm grew quieter outside, Jacinda began to read about Miss Emma Woodhouse and her luckless efforts at matchmaking. He felt a measure of empathy for what Mr. Knightley must have endured.

Chapter 22

"My dear, I wish you would not make matches and foretell things, for whatever you say always comes to pass. Pray do not make any more matches."

JANE AUSTEN, *Emma*

The day of the festival arrived.

The early spring breeze was cool and crisp and brimming with excitement. The storm had been swift and left nothing behind other than a heavily beaded dew on the grasses and shrubs that glistened like sea glass in the bright morning light.

The courtyard was draped in garlands and colorful pennants, while white linen table covers fluttered like crisp sails. And there wasn't a single cloud in the sky.

"'Tis a grand day for the festival," Martha said, as she, Betsy, Clara, and Lucy came up to Jacinda. "And it is all because of you, Miss Bourne."

The servants were at their leisure now, but a short time ago they'd been scurrying in and out of doors to set up tables for food, wares, and drink. Next to the ale barrels stood a tower of pewter goblets unearthed in the garret, from days long past. And village children ogled the frosted cakes decorated with ribbons and sugared flowers, prizes for those who won the competitions of skill.

"I have done the least of anyone to prepare Rydstrom Hall for this day, and I cannot take credit for the weather either," Jacinda said with a laugh, stopping short as the Olson boys dropped onto the ground in front of her and started wiggling into burlap sacks for the race. She set her hand on Dr. Graham's arm to navigate around them.

Betsy shook her head vehemently. "But you're the reason His Grace is hosting it. Everyone is talking about sir's sudden change of heart."

"And the festival has never been this grand before, not even when the late duke and duchess held it here on the grounds. Why, you can even ask the good doctor," Clara added with a knowing grin.

Jacinda couldn't allow the maids to make such far-fetched assumptions. If Rydstrom heard of this . . . well, he might send her back to her uncle sooner than planned. And Jacinda wasn't ready to leave.

She did not look to Dr. Graham for an answer, but put on her sternest expression and looked at each of the maids in turn. "You mustn't repeat those rumors. They simply aren't true."

The four maids exchanged grins with each other, pausing briefly when Lucy stepped forward and held out a small burlap sack. "Here are your seeds, Miss Bourne."

Jacinda accepted the palm-sized pouch with a measure of confusion. "Seeds?"

"For the sowing ceremony," Betsy said. "It's part of the festival. The old custom declares that all the village women, no matter their age, must spread the seeds in order to bring life, beauty, and prosperity to Whitcrest."

Jacinda nodded, only now recalling that they'd mentioned it before.

"And plenty of healthy, squalling babes during the winter solstice, too," Mr. Trumbledown said from near the ale barrels, lifting one of the pewter goblets in something of a toast.

Believing him to be in his cups, and first thing in the morning, Jacinda paid little mind to his teasing. Even so, her gaze alighted on Crispin.

He stood listening attentively to a group of fishermen, some of them gesturing with arms spread wide as they likely told their harrowing tales. There was plenty of laughter and jesting remarks of disbelief. Then, without warning, Rydstrom's gaze shifted.

He scanned the crowd at a glance but stopped, unerringly, on her. The suddenness caused her breath to catch.

Peculiarly, he no longer wore his glower. It had been absent ever since they'd spent the remainder of yesterday afternoon together, with Sybil asleep at her side and Jacinda reading from *Emma*.

This new expression was not too altered from the glower, however. It was certainly no smile, and held a wary intensity that she did not understand.

But she blushed all the same and tore her gaze away. "Then I will do my part."

"There's a wee pebble in each sack, too," Clara added, "but be sure not to let it fall to the ground with the seeds. That's bad luck."

Jacinda weighed the pouch quizzically. "Why is there a stone mixed with the seeds?"

"It's a wishing stone, o' course." Betsy beamed.

Clara nudged Betsy playfully with her elbow. "How would Miss Bourne know that? Anyway, it's for the fishermen. Cast a wishing stone into the sea to please the merfolk, and in return, they'll put more fish into the nets."

"Most of the maidens wish for husbands," Martha said, surveying the men in attendance. "But I don't suppose you'll be needing yours for that."

The maids all looked over at the duke. Collectively, they giggled, curtsied, and then left to go gossip with the village women. Jacinda was thankful that Rydstrom was too far away to hear.

"I do not know how to convince them of the truth," she said to Dr. Graham as they began to stroll toward the booths on the far side.

"I find that most people tend to believe whatever they choose to see," Graham said in response, his cane sinking into the soft earth. "Never fear, time often reveals the truth to us all."

She sighed. "And time is slipping by quickly. Is it strange that I should feel trepidation whenever I think of returning to my uncle and to my life?" It was almost as if she didn't want to leave at all. But that was a foolish notion. Of course she wanted to return to her family.

"Whitcrest and Rydstrom Hall are currently the sum of your world. It's perfectly natural to fear parting from it."

Her world . . . This place and these people were all she knew, and soon she would leave them, return to London, and lose everything she knew once more.

At the thought, she felt dimmer, the cold breeze slipping through the layers of the same redingote and dress she'd worn when she'd first awoken on the rock below the cliffs. A shiver trampled through her, leaving a path of emptiness in its wake.

"Miss Bourne!" Mrs. Parish called from nearby.

Jacinda turned and waved at Mrs. Parish, who was standing behind the first booth, adorned with ribbons, lace, and bonnets.

In the same moment, Henry Valentine rushed up to Dr. Graham, his eyes bright with excitement, his mouth a blur of movement as he told everything there was to know about the velocipede race. ". . . then straight down the hill to the bottom, and the fastest one wins a cake. A whole cake! You'll come watch, won't you, sir?"

Dr. Graham turned to her, concern etched in lines of his brow. "Miss Bourne, would you forgive my absence for a moment or two? I'm not entirely certain I like the sound of this velocipede contraption."

She patted his arm. "Yes, for the race sounds far more thrilling than your watching me stare at ribbons over the next half hour." And with that, the doctor inclined his head and Jacinda stepped over to the booth. "Mrs. Parish, what a fine display you have."

"Thank you, Miss Bourne." She bent down quickly, rummaging through an open trunk, then stood, grinning as she presented a straw bonnet with a thick gathering of burgundy ribbon. "I happened to notice you are not wearing a bonnet today. Might I interest you in this one?"

Jacinda held it long enough to admire the wide brim that would be perfect to shield her eyes on such a sunny day. Reluctantly, she placed the hat down. "It is lovely, but I have no money for such a fine bonnet."

Mrs. Parish gently pushed the hat in Jacinda's direction. "I'm sure His Grace wouldn't mind, considering . . ."

Jacinda frowned, realizing it wasn't only the maids who were making assumptions. It was one thing to engage in idle gossip, but another for them to presume that Rydstrom would pay her debts, as if they had an understanding. "I'll be returning to London and my uncle next week."

"Many things can happen in a week, like a *betr*—" Mrs. Parish stopped suddenly when Jacinda narrowed her eyes, and quickly amended, "Like a change in the weather. And for that, you'll need a bonnet."

"Good day to you, Miss Bourne. And to you, Mrs. Parish," Rydstrom said as he strode up to the booth.

Jacinda's heart stuttered, and she hoped he hadn't overheard the topic of conversation. "Good morning, Rydstrom. I—I thought you were across the way, listening to fish tales."

He eyed her skeptically as if he sensed she was up to mischief, even though that was the furthest thing from the truth. At least this time. "I was. Though I thought it prudent to visit all the villagers."

"What an honor it is for me, Your Grace," Mrs. Parish said, dipping into a curtsy. "And fortunate that Miss Bourne should be here as well. Why, just now we were discussing bonnets. This one, in particular."

"It is a fine hat, especially for a day as bright as this." Picking it up, he turned it around with his long, adept fingers, and then held it out to her. "Here, Miss Bourne. So you will not have to shield your eyes with your hand any longer."

The knowledge that he'd been watching her and cared enough about her sun-besieged eyes to make this gesture, caused a sudden lift of her stomach, one that made her think of what it must be like to race down the hill in a velocipede. Wondrously exhilarating.

She smiled, ready to thank him . . . until she caught sight of Mrs. Lassater joining Mrs. Parish behind the stand, the pair of them whispering.

Abruptly, Jacinda took a step back and shook her head. "It is not acceptable for a young woman to receive an article of clothing from a gentleman."

The corner of his mouth twitched. "How is it that you know this bit of trivial information, possess an enviable array of scholarly subjects, including mythology from seven different cultures and four languages—"

"Five actually," she interrupted with a grin, solely for the sake of being contradictory. Thus far, she'd only discovered four that she could read and speak fluently.

"Oh yes, *five*. I forgot to include Sanskrit." He took a step forward, still offering the hat. "And yet, you continuously forget the most essential rule of all—whatever a duke says is always right. And this duke, Miss Bourne, says that you are accepting this hat."

Standing perfectly still, she had no idea why she was suddenly out of breath. She felt as if her flesh and bones were made of air, and that she might start to float any second. If she did, she hoped he would take her hand, hold her down to the earth, and keep her at his side for as long as he could.

The sensation of bubbles rising up her rib cage filled her again. And she was beginning to suspect the cause had something to do with . . . with falling in . . .

She swallowed, her throat dry. She couldn't finish her thoughts. And thankfully she didn't, because when Rydstrom next spoke, she was completely cured.

Well, nearly. Perhaps.

"After all, I cannot allow you to return to your uncle with a brown, freckled complexion. He'll think I let you wander atop the turrets."

"When everyone in the castle knows that I only wander the turrets when you aren't looking," she said in an attempt at levity. Which proved impossible now that the bubbles inside of her evaporated and her feet were firmly on the ground. Yet when his glower threatened to return, she quickly amended with, "A mere jest, Rydstrom. I have never ventured that high. Yet. As for the hat . . . Mrs. Parish already offered to lend it to me until I return to London. My uncle will send payment for the purchase."

She gave Mrs. Parish a pointed look and received a slow nod in return. But not without her exchanging a nudge with Mrs. Lassater. It appeared as though the damage had been done and there would be little to convince them otherwise. At least, until Rydstrom married his heiress. Then who would have the last laugh?

Well, it wouldn't be Jacinda. All the same, she fixed the bonnet to her head and tied the ribbon beneath her chin.

Rydstrom nodded. "That should do nicely, Miss Bourne. Now you will be able to enjoy the festival without a headache, blemish, or"—he leaned toward her ever so slightly, his voice dipping lower—"chilled ears."

As if the mention of her ears were part of an ongoing flirtation between them—even though she knew it was only his way of goading her—his gaze raked over them until she felt them grow quite hot.

He hummed a sound of smug approval and turned to leave. But before he went, he withdrew a coin from his pocket and laid it on the booth.

Arrogant, prideful man, Jacinda thought, fighting a grin

as she stared at the breadth of his shoulders and the superb fit of his dark green coat.

"Ah, Miss Bourne. It's a pleasure to see you looking so vibrant today," Mrs. Hemple said, skirting around the row of children hopping with all their might, brown sacks gripped tightly. And beside her, with blue ribbons in her hair and eyes as round as Mrs. Limpin's plum cream tarts, stood Sybil.

Releasing Mrs. Hemple, she rushed over to Jacinda and took her hand, gripping tightly. A palpable shudder coursed through her coltish frame.

"A marvelous day for the festival, is it not?" Jacinda asked, pretending as if this were an everyday occurrence. Intuitively, she felt that making a grand ordeal of this monumental feat of bravery would only make Sybil more uncomfortable. "Of course, I'm simply exhausted from all the work I've done, baking dozens of pies, rolling barrels up the stairs from the buttery, taking a broom to remove every single cloud from the sky . . ."

Sybil tugged on her hand and rolled her eyes heavenward as if she knew what Jacinda was attempting. But then that dimple made an appearance and her grip loosened marginally.

CRISPIN KEPT a watchful eye on Sybil throughout the morning and afternoon, prepared to intervene if a single look of distress crossed her features. He supposed that, sometimes, he still saw her as that six-year-old girl who'd witnessed his parents' deaths, and he wished he could travel back in time to save her from it.

Yet seeing her face light up with Jacinda by her side, and brave enough to join a game or two, those fears subsided.

This was certainly not a development he could have anticipated. Then again, since Jacinda had entered his life there was little he could. She was the embodiment of chaos, a swirling storm bent on upending his life and scattering pieces of it hither and yon. And each time he attempted to put everything back to the way it had been, it proved impossible. He was too altered now. Was it any wonder that everyone she encountered would change as well?

"So yer plannin' to marry, are ya, Yer Grace?" Tom Garner asked, his weathered face spread in a wide grin to reveal gaps where his front teeth used to be.

Crispin knew where this question was leading. All day he'd heard inferences, both of the subtle and blatant varieties, that he was going to marry Jacinda. So, just as he had done the other times, he said succinctly, "Once my guest recuperates and returns to London, I'll begin searching for my bride."

Usually that was all he needed to say. It seemed, however, that it wasn't enough for Tom Garner.

He narrowed one dark eye and looked out across the bailey. "That Miss Barne sure is a pretty thing. Some men might be wantin' to test their mettle to show off a bit. Will ye be testin' yers today?"

Since Tom was one of the older men in the village, who'd been around when Crispin had been a lad, Crispin didn't take offense at his sly insinuation. After all, he remembered being on the cusp of manhood and wanting to prove his worth alongside roughened seamen, with torsos the size of ale barrels and arms the size of oar heads. Older now, Crispin noticed they weren't as colossal as he'd once thought. And there was a part of him that wondered how he'd match up against them in competition.

Yet, as the resident duke, he couldn't very well play their games. He was here to observe and oversee, like his father before him.

"I've seen too many of you pick up barrels full of fish as if they were filled with feathers instead. No, I would hate to humiliate myself in front of all of you."

That earned a laugh and some ribbing from the men who

were in their cups. Today, he was merely one of them. Not a duke in need of an heiress to maintain Rydstrom Hall and Whitcrest for years to come. Just a man enjoying the first crisp day of spring.

His gaze flitted to where Jacinda stood near a table of Mrs. Limpin's golden, buttery pond puddings. Mrs. Hemple and Sybil took one of the crocks of the dense confection before crossing the bailey toward the main door. Before they rounded the final corner, Sybil looked back over her shoulder, spotted him, and gave a merry wave.

Then his gaze traversed the courtyard and met Jacinda's.

She was smiling at him, her cheeks pink from the cold, the breeze catching the ribbons of her bonnet so that the tips fluttered in his direction. And if he were closer to her, he might be inclined to grasp those ends, pull her to him, and warm her lips.

He allowed himself to indulge in the impossible idea until something, or someone rather, blocked his view. Alcott.

Crispin stiffened, watching as Alcott bowed to her and gestured with a sweep of his hand before offering his arm. And Jacinda took it, placing her ivory hand on the sleeve of Alcott's black coat as they walked toward the ale table, where Crispin was standing.

Suppressing a growl, he watched their progress.

Alcott smiled a great deal. Too much, in fact. He seemed to think himself a court jester, too, for how often he made Jacinda laugh. And Crispin didn't like hearing the decidedly mischievous timbre—a laugh that was hers and hers alone—from such a distance away. If she was going to laugh, she should be standing beside him, not Alcott.

And when the pair nearly reached him, Crispin fought the urge to step forward, take her hand and put her by his side. After all, she was his guest, his responsibility, *his* . . .

His *what*? he wondered dimly, not certain what else she was, but only that she was more. More than a meddlesome bit of baggage. More than a young woman with amnesia living beneath his roof. More than . . . anything he could name at the moment because his thoughts were in disorder, his head spinning, his heart pounding hard and fast. And suddenly it seemed simpler just to say that she was his.

His. A breath shuddered out of him as the wayward thought closed around him, filled him, tried to take root. But he could not let it. He had a duty to uphold.

"By the looks o' that snarly vein on His Grace's forehead, I ken sir don't agree a'tall," Tom Garner said with a hearty chuckle.

It wasn't until Crispin noticed that Jacinda's wispy brows were drawn together in what appeared to be concern that he realized he'd missed part of the conversation. He was clenching his jaw and fists, too, his shoulders tight.

Dragging his gaze from Jacinda, he looked to Tom Garner with an inquiring lift of his brow.

"The lad here," Tom said, motioning with a jerk of his head in Alcott's direction, "says he can best anyone in Whitcrest in the wood choppin' contest. What do ye say to that, Yer Grace?"

Just over Crispin's shoulder two massive oak logs waited for the final event of the day. He sized up Alcott. The man was younger by about four years, not as tall, but with a broad, stocky build designed for speed and strength. Crispin knew this was true, because he'd seen him work. The man was tireless.

"Is that so, Alcott?" Crispin asked.

"That's right, Your Grace."

And when Alcott flashed a cocky grin, Crispin decided that he might try his luck among the men after all.

He shrugged out of his coat. "Then let's see, shall we?"

JACINDA COULD hardly breathe. Rydstrom was undressing in front of her. Oh, very well, he was undressing in front of the entire village, but his gaze was on her.

"Miss Bourne, if you would be so kind," he said, folding his coat in half lengthwise and offering it to her.

She wanted to come back with a ready retort about him making presumptions that she was even going to stay long enough to watch the competition. But who was she kidding? She wouldn't miss this for the world.

Accepting the bundle, a sound of acquiescence hummed in her throat, her gaze admiring the cut of his camel waistcoat and how it accentuated the breadth of his shoulders, the expanse of his chest, and leanness of his hips.

Suddenly, all she could think about was the memory of being pressed against his unyielding, solid length, his hand on her hip, his irises darkening from hazel to a rich russet. A rush of heat rolled over her, settling inside her stomach, making it feel heavy and tight.

And the next thing she knew, he was rolling up his sleeves to his elbows, revealing a dusting of dark wheat-colored hair along his thick, corded forearms.

Of course, other things were happening while she was preoccupied. The villagers were crowding closer, chattering and cheering about the event. Some were making wagers on the outcome. Off to the side, Mr. Alcott removed his coat, too, and handed it over to the widow Olson, whose boys, for the first time, were not rambunctious but staring with eager eyes toward the log stands.

Then as Rydstrom walked away, Lucy wedged her petite but determined frame between a pair of fishermen and stood beside her. "How thrilling, Miss Bourne! I don't think anyone anticipated His Grace competing in any event today, let alone this one. Betsy and I were just at the cliffs with our wishing stones when Martha came and told us and—*Oh my*, I think you've spilled your seeds."

Preoccupied, Jacinda glanced down to see a little pile of seeds near the hem of her redingote. She'd completely forgotten she had it in her hand. Turning the pouch right again, she felt the hardness of the pebble still inside and pinched it between her thumb and forefinger. "I didn't lose the pebble."

Then she unfastened the top three buttons of her redingote and tucked the pouch into her bodice. She wasn't even certain if she was the type of person who believed in wishes, but decided that it couldn't hurt to hold on to it for a while. Just in case.

"Are you going to use it to make a wish for His Grace to win?" Lucy asked, letting loose a romantic sigh.

Jacinda stared, wide-eyed at those logs. They were as big around as three men put together. Yet Rydstrom didn't seem to notice. There was no hesitation in his stride, or even when he took his position, resting the long handle of the axe against his shoulder. And when his gaze connected with hers, he looked so fierce and purposeful, that she knew he was going to win. "The duke isn't going to need it."

Chapter 23

"... but I confess that I have seldom seen a face or figure more pleasing to me than hers."

Jane Austen, *Emma*

Dinner that night was a small affair of cold meats, cheeses and tarts leftover from the festival. Dr. Graham had exhausted his knee, and Jacinda had decided on her own to retire after their small meal. Everyone was tired from the full day's events and had turned in straightaway.

But Crispin was too high-strung to sleep and it would not serve him to go up to his chamber when he knew Jacinda was just across the hall.

For the first time in a long while, he dared to pour himself a few fingers of dark amber brandy and sat in his study watching the fire. He expelled a satisfied breath as the heat of the liquor spread like warm fingers down his torso.

Today, he was the victor, beating Mr. Alcott handily, strike for strike. Likely, it wasn't noble of him to set out to prove he was the better axeman, but he had nonetheless. And what made the triumph all the sweeter was the way that Jacinda had cheered for him, laughing and clapping, her cheeks flushed, eyes bright.

He closed his eyes now, savoring the memory, glad that no one would know that he'd done it for her.

"The festival was sublime. Was it not, Rydstrom?" Jacinda asked, her voice weaving seamlessly with his pleasant thoughts and the honeyed brandy on his tongue.

He didn't stir, but kept his eyes closed, content in this moment. "Shouldn't you be in your chamber?"

Ignoring him—*of course*—she stepped into the room, the hem of her skirts whispering over the rug. "It was exhilarating to watch you compete. You wield an axe with great skill, as if you've done it before."

"Flattering your host will not make it any more proper to have you in this room without a chaperone."

She sank down onto the cushion beside his in a *hush* of fabric, and a waft of decadent, bath-oil scented air. "So fussy. You were not so keen on propriety when you bought me that hat. Nevertheless, I've left the door open in full view of the servants."

Yet, he knew that the servants had all gone to bed by now.

Worn out from the events, he'd dismissed them for the remainder of the day. Perhaps he should tell her, warn her that she was completely alone with a man whose thoughts and impulses were not as controlled and orderly as they ought to be. It had been an impulse to buy that hat, knowing that tongues would wag, but he hadn't cared.

Even now, he couldn't explain the reason it had been important to him. He'd simply wanted her to have it.

"Besides, I haven't recounted my memories of the day," she continued, adding a small sigh at the end as she finished fidgeting and arranging her skirts, then finally settled into her seat. "As you know, Dr. Graham said that I should do this each day in order to establish a routine."

He took another sip, swallowing down a wry laugh. "A routine that you only choose to establish when it is convenient for you? I hope you realize that is not how to keep a proper schedule."

"Are you scolding me, Rydstrom?" she asked, her voice lower and curling around the edges the way it did when she smiled.

Crispin could almost taste the sound, sliding down the whorls of his ears, tickling the back of his tongue. "Deservedly so. A thorough punishment for abandoning your daily exercises is in order, beginning with banishment from my study."

"Oh, but I cannot leave now. You are on one side of this sofa and you need me to balance out the other. Without my presence, the room might fall into that disorganized chaos you despise so much, and then where would you be?"

He felt a grin tug at his mouth, but he did not give in to it. "Alone and enjoying my brandy."

When she said nothing in response, he slid a glance to her and found her resting against the back of the sofa and staring at the fire, her cream-colored shawl draped carelessly from one shoulder. He turned his head slightly to watch the flicker of flames reflected in her eyes, and the way the golden light kissed the tips of her burnished eyelashes, nose, and lips. And for a moment, he wanted to be that light, brushing over her features, making her glow.

He turned back to his brandy and took a long swallow. There was only an imaginary line between them that could easily be traversed. Yet, it did feel better to have her here, balancing out the sofa. And as long as she kept to her side, he could handle the temptation.

It was only when she rolled her head against the curved back of the sofa and gave him a sleepy smile that he realized he was watching her again.

She glanced down to his glass. "I've never seen you drink spirits before."

"I'm allowing myself one after a long day." He'd actually been hoping to forget about having been jealous, watching her with Alcott. Even now, he wanted to shoo it aside in favor of a more controllable emotion, but he wasn't fool enough to lie to himself.

"You are quite strict with yourself, aren't you? Everything in its place. No peas straying"—a teasing glint lit her eyes and her grin made them tilt upward at each corner—"no lines crossed. Is there anyone you ever allow into your space?"

Wordless, he offered the glass to her by holding it over the cushion-line between them. "I do believe I know of one impertinent young woman who is always crossing boundaries."

Always tempting him.

"You like me for my impertinence." She reached for the glass, her fingers sliding along his in an accidental caress, stilling briefly as her lips parted, her gaze fixed to where their hands joined. Never one to shy away, she lingered, but too briefly, and took hold of the glass.

Reluctantly, he released it and faced the fire once more. "Never for that."

"But you *are* beginning to like me, nonetheless. Admit it."

He looked at her again—he couldn't seem to help himself. She was far more interesting than the flames. "If I do, will you go to bed and leave me in peace?"

"Hmm . . . perhaps." Lifting the glass, she took a sip of brandy, made a face and then swallowed quickly. She gasped as if she'd just broken through the surface of the sea, her head tilted back, hand touching her bare neck. "It feels like fire sliding down inside of me."

Crispin was unaccountably aroused by her words and the image they evoked. He could not stop a lingering glance down the column of her throat where the firelight bathed her, and to the swells of her breasts cresting above her bodice as she slowly drew her hand away.

When she handed back the drink, he took it and downed the liquor, finding it cooler than the fire burning inside him. Then, closing his eyes again, he willed himself to forget the temptation within arm's reach.

It was one of the most difficult tasks he'd ever assigned himself. He was fully attuned to her, every movement and every sound she made, from the soft sigh of her breath to the silken slide of her skirts over the sofa. And he knew the precise moment she slid closer.

He opened his eyes to see her perched on the edge of

the cushion, poised to leave. It was for the best, and yet he wished she would linger. Apparently, he hadn't had enough torment for the day.

But wishes were dangerous things, especially when answered.

In the next instant, she leaned toward him, her hand curling over the back of the sofa. "Thank you for today," she whispered against his cheek an instant before she pressed her lips there.

Once more, impulse took over. He turned his head to feel her lips on his.

Their gazes locked, hers widening in surprise, his impenitent. And true to Jacinda's nature, she did not withdraw, demure, or ask him questions.

Instead, her lids lowered, her head tilted, and her lips pressed more fully to his. Right this moment, Crispin truly liked her unapologetic curiosity.

His hand found her waist and he drew her closer, blindly placing the crystal glass down on the table. This left him free to curve his other hand around her nape, to angle her lips perfectly off center against his. This was where he wanted her. This was where he'd needed her all day.

As if in agreement, she issued a small sigh, her lips parting sweetly.

Just a taste, he promised himself, remembering what Graham had said about surrendering to small desires to keep from being consumed by larger ones. So, in a sense, Crispin was doing this for his own good. A perfectly rational thought.

And yet, somewhere in the back of his mind, a warning bell rang.

"I shouldn't," he said, more to himself than to her, angling her head and nudging her lips apart to taste that tantalizing vanilla-tinged flavor he'd sampled before. And there it was, waiting for him just behind the irresistible cushion of her lips, lounging on the flesh of her tongue.

She nodded, sliding her hands beneath his coat, over his chest and up to his shoulders, her body soft and pliant, the pillows of her breasts molding against him. Breathless, she said, "You should. Most definitely. After all, you must amend that first *clumsy effort*."

He drew back marginally. "Was it so terrible, then?"

She grinned, mischief glinting in her hooded blue gaze. "Quite honestly, it was the best kiss I ever remember having. But this one shows promise, too."

Damn, but he adored this maddening creature in his arms. Who else could challenge and taunt him in such a way that he was gladder for it?

Having something to prove, he pulled her closer, settling her across his lap, releasing the hold on his control by small degrees. He kissed her again in long, deep, endless pulls like the shore drawing in the sea, again and again, wave after wave until she gasped and sagged against him. He liked her this way, too, breathless and yielding.

Allowing her to catch her breath, he forged a path of heated kisses down her throat, reveling in every tremor, every shiver that swept over her when he found the places to nip and the notches to lave. Her skin tasted like confections, so delicate he imagined her dissolving on his tongue.

When his open mouth sampled the tender flesh at the curve of her throat, she arched her neck, spilling desperate, passion-laden whimpers of *"yes . . . there . . . please"* from her lips.

She shifted in his lap, restless, the curve of her hip grinding against the hardened length of him. And the pleasure she gave him caused that warning bell to clang again. He'd had his taste and now it was time to stop.

Yet his deeply ingrained need for order couldn't allow it. He'd only kissed one side of her throat, after all. And it would be wrong not to kiss the other, to leave both her and him unbalanced. So he drew her closer, angling her so that she straddled him. And it wasn't improper, he told himself, because the fabric of her dress and petticoat was bunched between them, acting as a chaperone, of sorts.

But while his mouth took hers with slow, burning sips, his hands slipped beneath the hems, edging it higher, his fingertips skating over the ribbon garters of her stockings. It wasn't until he grazed the petal-soft flesh above her knee that he realized he should have heeded the warnings. Because with every touch, every taste, he wanted more and forgot the reasons he shouldn't strip her bare and indulge himself for hours, caressing and pleasuring every inch of her.

He'd never been tempted like this. Consumed like this. Not until he'd met Jacinda. Which was all the more reason to stop now.

"Slide over," she murmured, the vibration tingling against his lips, her sweet breath entering his mouth like a siren's call. "My knee is caught on the cushion."

He moved without conscious thought, without heeding his own advice, and slid over, her dress rising beneath his hands.

A pitiable chaperone, indeed. And suddenly, gloriously, she was fully on top of him. The soft yielding cradle of her thighs sent a hot surge of blood to his engorged shaft.

A groan escaped him. He was beyond thought now, deaf to the warning bell. All he could do was revel in the supple weight of her body, the bow of her spine that pressed her stomach and breasts against him. And through the layers of their clothing, he felt the decadent firmness of her nipples, those sea buckthorn berries that he craved.

Just one taste, he thought, his hands coasting over muslin, unerringly finding those four buttons. He made quick work of them and tugged, dragging down her dress and chemise to the gusseted cups of her stays and then further to free her breasts.

With his mouth still fastened to hers, he explored the silken swells with his hands, his thumbs grazing over velvety peaks. She jolted in his arms. Her gasp filled his mouth, even as she arched into his touch and gave him a wanton mewl of acquiescence.

Without hesitation, he dipped his head and discovered perfection in that sweetly distended tip, and in the unabashed woman in his arms who glided her hands to the back of his neck. Fingers twining in his hair, she held him tightly against her. And he suckled her, flicking his tongue over that ripe berry, drawing out more of her soft, broken pleas to *"never stop,"* her hips tilting forward against his.

He groaned again, a spike of sheer pleasure bolting through him, sending another pulsing surge to his cock. Through pleats of muslin, he gripped her slender hips and rocked her against his aching flesh.

"Crispin," she gasped, her back arching.

He released her breast, panting, "You . . . shouldn't . . . call me that."

It was too dangerous. Hearing his name on her lips made him lose all reason. He should tell her, but he couldn't form words. All he could do was fasten his mouth on her other breast and think about how good it would feel to be inside her, enveloped in the tormenting heat of her with nothing between them but a fine sheen of perspiration.

He still thought he could stop, still thought he had control. This was just one prolonged taste. Then she said his name again, taunting him, the sound of it unleashing tumultuous chaos inside him.

He tried to slow them both, but the firm press of their bodies and long, leisurely slide only intensified the pleasure. They were both too greedy, too wanton. And too far gone.

Her hips hitched forward in a telltale sign of her approaching paroxysm. Clutching her, he rolled her heated core against his length in a rhythm that matched the luxurious, unending pulls of his tongue. A choked cry stuttered out of her as her body quaked, her fingers gripping him as if she would never let him go. And he was helpless against the quickening of his own need, the rapid grinds of her hips against his long-denied flesh, and that final surge that caused him to convulse in thick, voluptuous pulses—completely, irrevocably unmanning him. In his trousers.

She collapsed on top of him, her head nestled into the crook of his shoulder and neck. "My heart . . . It's racing. Do you feel it?"

She was out of breath. So was he. Wrapping his arms around her to hold her close, he flopped his head back against the curve of the sofa, entirely undone. "Yes, I do."

"I feel quite sleepy all of a sudden."

He skimmed his hands over her back in an aimless caress that pleased him more than it should. Likely he should feel embarrassed or even the smallest trace of guilt over what he'd done, and how he'd taken more than just one taste.

But he couldn't summon either of those emotions. "Then rest here for just a moment."

"You don't mind that I am not on my cushion?"

He could hear the smile in her voice. "No, imp. We are both in the middle, where we belong."

And in the morning, he would likely regret saying those last words. But for now, he was supremely content to have her sprawled over him.

Chapter 24

> "Your time has been properly and delicately spent, if you have been endeavoring for the last four years to bring about this marriage. A worthy employment for a young lady's mind!"
>
> Jane Austen, *Emma*

Crispin awoke shortly after dawn, slumber still clinging to his brain and making him slow to open his eyes. He didn't truly want to rouse for the day. He'd rather continue the dream he was having, an unbelievably erotic scenario about Jacinda invading his study and making him lose all sense.

The dream had been so real that he could still taste her on his tongue, and smell her scent in the air. A dangerous dream, to be sure, but one he would not mind repeating. Especially because he hadn't slept this soundly in years.

Drowsily, he scrubbed a hand over his face, feeling a growth of whiskers scrape his palm and a grin on his lips. Though, hearing the footsteps of servants, the hushed voices, and the occasional clang of an ash pail, he knew he could not indulge in sleep any longer.

Opening his eyes, he was somewhat disoriented not to find his gray velvet bed curtains around him. He blinked and saw that he was in the study, instead, and lounging on his sofa. That was . . . odd.

Then suddenly, his pulse started to accelerate, sending blood to his brain to clear away any cobwebs. And that was when he sat up with a jolt and saw a cream-colored shawl draped over him.

Damn. It wasn't a dream at all, was it?

He darted a glance around the room, half expecting to find Jacinda still here. But then he remembered the sweet kiss she'd pressed to his lips sometime in the middle of the night and her whispered wish for him to have pleasant dreams.

He might very well still be in one because, at the moment, he felt like laughing. Not in a "Ho, ho, this is terribly amusing" sort of way, but more in a "what in the bloody hell have I done?"

Yet he knew what he had done, and quite honestly, he had thoroughly enjoyed every single heated moment. Worse, he knew that, given the same conditions, he would do it again.

What kind of man did that make him? After four years of abstinence that served as a self-imposed punishment for the life he'd led and the lives he'd failed, he suddenly thought it was acceptable to indulge in an evening of pleasure with the virgin debutante beneath his roof?

He looked down at the shawl, and felt a stab of tenderness for the wearer. Jacinda was not just any young woman living beneath his roof. He was drawn to her in a way that neither sanity nor rational thought could explain. And if he were a man who did not live in a crumbling castle and had ample funds to ensure the happy life his sister deserved, then he might take time to examine his feelings.

Under the circumstances, however, such an undertaking was pointless. Because no matter how he felt about her, duty demanded that he marry an heiress.

Still, he would need to talk to Jacinda and explain how this rash moment changed nothing between them.

In other words, he would have to lie to her.

By the time Crispin washed and donned the fresh clothes his valet pressed for him, he knew precisely what to say to Jacinda. But he wasn't in a rush to do so.

He would wait for the opportunity to present itself. Besides, he didn't expect her to be awake this early and, more important, if he saw her too soon after the dream—that wasn't a dream—he wasn't certain what would happen. She might smile at him and call him by his given name and he might be tempted to scold her fondly and kiss her again. Which was certainly not the best way to begin telling a woman that he wasn't going to marry her.

Therefore, he decided to keep to his usual morning routine, stopping first to speak with Fellows.

Reaching the gatehouse, he instantly noticed dozens of trunks, bags, and hatboxes cluttering the expanse of flagstone. "Fellows, what are these—"

"Good day, nephew."

Crispin lurched to a halt, his gaze darting to the person standing beneath the stone archway. "Aunt Hortense. Wh-what are you doing here?"

She did not answer, but speared him with the same steely gray glare that had always held the power to read every transgression he'd ever committed throughout his life. Or, at least, it seemed to. A willowy woman with the Montague height, she possessed a regal bearing, in addition to a long, angular face, pale complexion, and most especially, marked disapproval in the constant pursing of her lips.

"Your Grace, Lady Hortense has arrived," Fellows said needlessly, rushing forward. Clearly unsettled, he passed a handkerchief over his perspiring pate then lowered his voice to continue. "And her carriage is loaded with a great many trunks. A great many, indeed."

Even now, more of those trunks were being carried in by his footmen.

And while he watched, Crispin still could not move forward. This was like a scene summoned from his nightmare. Quite ironic considering how he'd woken in a lovely dream. Now it felt like someone had thrown a pail of February seawater on him and a shiver coursed through him from nape to knees.

"I assume," Aunt Hortense said in her rounded tone of superiority, "you will need to air my chambers before my maid can unpack?"

Her chambers. He thought of the mural of her younger self, the dust sheet he'd tacked over it, and the likelihood that she would want to remove it. But, of course, she would. His aunt was particular about her apartments, among other things.

He thought of Sybil, who was upstairs and likely waiting to break her fast with him as they always did. Sybil, who was the very image of Aunt Hortense as a child. Sybil, who was wholly innocent but would pay for the sin of their father for the rest of her life if his unforgiving aunt Hortense ever discovered who she was.

He also thought of Jacinda and the host of transgressions he'd committed last night. He still needed time to speak with her, but that commodity was scarce at the moment.

"If you'll permit me, sir," Fellows interjected with a pointed glance upward, "Shall I see to all of the arrangements and ensure that you and your aunt are at leisure to visit for the next . . . hour?"

Crispin nodded curtly, knowing that Fellows would relay the information to Mrs. Hemple.

Now he had an hour to figure out what he was going to do with all this confounding chaos. Stepping into the room, his booted footfalls echoed with dread. "Had I known of your visit, I could have done so ahead of time to better suit you."

His aunt bristled, her shoulders stiff, chin high. "I should hope that I would be welcome in my own apartments. After all, it was my husband's money that built them."

It was true. Crispin's grandfather had added an entire east wing after arranging Hortense's marriage to a wealthy privateer. Then when Father had succeeded to the title, he'd always kept the rooms for Hortense. She'd stayed in the castle for months at a time. And throughout many years of Crispin's childhood, she'd been both his companion and tutor, teaching him about their ancestors. But whatever bond they'd once shared changed four years ago.

Since Crispin had become the reigning Rydstrom, she'd never once lived here. And the reason was because she blamed him for her brother's death.

"This is your home, as it has always been," he said with a convincing amount of feeling. He hoped. Then, like a dutiful nephew, he offered his arm and led her to a small sitting room that hosted a pair of yellow, striped chairs, a briny breeze seeping in through the warped window casing. "Though, just out of curiosity, how long do you plan to stay?"

She slid him another look of disapproval, back straight as a broadsword. "When I received your letter about Miss Bourne's accident, I knew she would need a chaperone. Otherwise, you may well end up being forced to marry her."

There it was again—the same topic that had beleaguered him ever since Jacinda had washed up in Whitcrest. Strangely, the mention didn't irritate him as it had before. Though the likely reason was because he had a host of other things on his mind. "As I mentioned in the letter, Dr. Graham is staying here, in addition to a host of servants."

"All of whom are employed by you. If word got out that you had Miss Bourne alone, under this roof, far away from civilized society, the scandal would be nothing short of monumental."

Hearing that his aunt was only concerned about a potential scandal, he felt prickles of irritation crawl over his skin. "And yet here it is, a week after I sent the letter regarding her condition, but only now do you find it necessary to act as chaperone."

Aunt Hortense sniffed. "The Duchess of Holliford recently brought it to my attention that there may be those among the *ton* who might not believe a country doctor capable of ensuring your good name. Why, Miss Bourne is practically in *service*."

"Oddly enough, I seem to recall how you fully supported the Bourne Agency on the recommendation of the Duchess of Holliford. In fact, your selling point was that Viscount Eggleston and his nieces were all well-bred members of society."

"Well, yes," she hemmed. "They are fine as business associates, but dear heavens I would not wish to be *related* to them. Their father, Lord Cartwright, has a terrible reputation. I do not even know how many illegitimate offspring he has."

"Miss Bourne and her sisters are legitimate," Crispin enunciated, the mention of illegitimacy rubbing a frayed nerve.

"Only by the skin of their teeth, much like your mother had been." She cleared her throat and added an unfeeling, "Rest her poor soul."

Aunt Hortense never liked his mother, believing that Father could have done much better than marrying a woman who came from landed gentry. And yet, Crispin had always suspected there was something deeper that sparked the squabbles and bitterness between them.

"What I cannot fathom is why Miss Bourne came here in the first place. For any well-bred woman to travel such a distance is unthinkable without a compelling reason. One would normally expect such behavior from a person misguided by her affections."

He laughed at the supposition. "Are you suggesting that Miss Bourne traveled to Whitcrest because she is in love with me? That notion is"—a wayward thrill raced through him, catching in his throat—"preposterous."

Hortense cast a shrewd, skeptical glance over him. "Of course, Lord Eggleston explained that it had something to do with his agency but did not have all the details."

"I can hardly enlighten you, nor can the young woman in question, due to her amnesia." Crispin swallowed, the cording along his neck tightening. "It appears we are all at a loss."

JACINDA WAS most certainly, most ardently, in love with the Duke of Rydstrom. *Crispin*, she thought with a sigh, her memory of last night as clear and bright as a bead of dew.

And that kiss . . . Well, it was a good deal more than a kiss, wasn't it? She grinned, feeling every bit the *imp* that he'd called her. Likely, she never should have allowed him to kiss her so . . . thoroughly. Even now a rush of heat consumed her as she reminisced on the wicked things he'd done with his mouth and hands.

"Miss Bourne!" Lucy chirped excitedly from beyond the bed curtains, her shoes rustling hurriedly over the rugs. "Oh, Miss Bourne, how can you still be abed at a time like this, when the entire castle is talking about it!"

Jacinda's eyes sprang open. "The entire castle? But how did they find out?"

She'd been so careful. She was sure no one had seen her leave the study last night.

"It was obvious."

"It was?" Jacinda gulped, wondering if it was because she'd left her shawl behind. But she couldn't have left Crispin there, sleeping so contentedly on the sofa with nothing to cover him. She'd even added a log to the fire before she'd left. But now, it seemed, that everyone knew about what they'd done in the study and—

"When the carriage arrived, yes," Lucy added, interrupting Jacinda's thoughts and confusing her all at once.

Carriage? "What are you talking about?"

The maid threw open the bed curtains with a clatter, her freckles fairly dancing on her lifted cheeks. "Why, His Grace's aunt, of course. And best of all, Lady Hortense has requested to see you straightaway. Everyone is chattering on about how her ladyship must have traveled all the way from London to give her blessing to her nephew. There can be no other explanation. Up, up, Miss Bourne. We must not dally, for I am told her ladyship does not like to be kept waiting."

Jacinda rose, part of her still dazedly content after last night, while skepticism filled the remaining parts. If Lady Hortense lived in London and was traveling last night, then there was no need to give her blessing because she could not have known about the kiss—or kisses, rather—between Jacinda and Crispin. And as for the excitement spreading through the castle, it seemed that it was all due to Lady Hortense's arrival. Which meant that no one knew what happened in the study.

A slow, relieved breath left her lungs. She didn't want anyone to find out about it, because to her it was too wondrous and precious to share with anyone else. And even though her own heart had altered toward him, that did not mean his had altered toward her.

Besides, she still had enough sense to remember that Crispin intended to marry an heiress. Not her.

"There is no cause to be excited. I'm certain it is nothing more than a courtesy," she said, unwilling to be swept up in Lucy's romantic notions any more than she already had done. Thus far, the duke had given her no inclination that his feelings toward her were tender.

And yet, Jacinda couldn't seem to stop her blood from racing in her veins or the frantic, foolishly hopeful flutter of her pulse at her throat.

A quarter hour later, she was sufficiently dressed, coiffed, and was standing at Lady Hortense's door. Unlike Lucy, the dour maid who answered her knock did not appear to have any grand notions, romantic or otherwise, concerning Jacinda. Without a word, she escorted Jacinda through the slightly musty, gold chintz bedroom to the small inner door that lead to the vast dressing room that was as large as the duchess's chamber.

And seated in the corner, within the tufted depths of an enormous, throne-like, golden wingback chair was a silver-haired willowy woman in a pearl-hued morning gown, applying a balm to her elbows.

Receiving a familiar disapproving glower, Jacinda knew this was Rydstrom's aunt, and she curtsied. "Lady Hortense, I hope you are well this morning."

"Do you recognize me, child, or are you just being impertinent by speaking before you are addressed?"

Jacinda rose, bristling. "I do not recall meeting you, no. As for the question regarding my impertinence, I'm not entirely sure, but I have a sense that I might be. Perhaps, like your nephew, you know my character better than I know it myself."

Lowering the lacy sleeves of her dressing gown, Lady Hortense regarded her coldly. "I know of you, child."

"And what you know of me is through my . . . uncle?" Jacinda asked, using the opportunity to gain as much information about herself as possible.

After a moment of consideration, Lady Hortense inclined her head. "In a manner of speaking."

Humph. Jacinda grumbled. "I see that Dr. Graham has spoken to you about my memory."

A pair of thin, silver brows arched. "Are *you* not worried about the delicacy of your condition?"

"Of course I am. I just hate the puzzle of it. Every moment is a riddle and I am standing before the Sphinx with no answers. It's quite trying, your ladyship."

A small grin—but surprising, nonetheless—flitted over Lady Hortense's lips and she gestured to the empty chair across from her. Apparently, Jacinda had earned some shred of approval, or at least piqued her interest. With a subtle tilt of her head, she looked to the maid. "You may pour for Miss Bourne, Gillian."

"Yes, my lady." The chamber maid bobbed a hasty curtsy and then scurried into the next room. The soft click of the outer door closing made it clear that there was not a second cup in the room, and that the extension of this visit was mere happenstance.

"It is interesting that you found yourself here, of all places. Wouldn't you agree?" Lady Hortense took a sip from the teacup waiting on the vanity, scrutinizing Jacinda over the rim.

"Indeed. I have wondered that from the very moment I found myself on the beach. At first, when I found your nephew's card in my book, I suspected that I was here to marry him."

Lady Hortense calmly lowered her cup and issued a low, condescending laugh. "You, marry my nephew?"

"Of course, since then, I have come to a far different conclusion," Jacinda said through her teeth, perturbed by the unfounded amusement. Was the notion that Crispin might want to marry someone who was not an heiress that far-fetched? "Correct me if I'm wrong, your ladyship, but are we not both women of society?"

"We are of a certain society." She subdued her merriment with another sip of tea, her lips pursing over the rim. "That is not to say, however, that we are equals. Why, you could no more marry my nephew than I could have wed a country doctor in my day. Oh, don't get your feathers in a tangle, Miss Bourne. I see you gathering barbs upon your tongue and your eyes glaring icily. And if you continue to fist your hands over your skirt, the pleats will never lie the same. All I am saying is that our family line marries for money. It has always been thus and it will never change. In fact, these rooms in this entire wing are from my husband's fortune."

The possessiveness in her tone when she said *my husband* made it seem as if he'd been something she had acquired in a shop, instead of a man that she had married to satisfy her heart's desire.

"And I do not come from money," Jacinda said pointlessly, almost wishing to be contradicted.

Lady Hortense offered a delicate shrug. “Nothing to speak of, from what I understand.”

It seemed rather unjust that the only information people who knew her—or *of her*—would confirm was the fact that she had no fortune.

“Regardless,” Lady Hortense continued, “while you are at Rydstrom Hall, you must put aside whatever romantic notions you might have for my nephew.”

Jacinda swallowed. “I hold no romantic notions, inclinations, or even general fondness for your nephew.”

“Good. It is best to leave that foolishness to those who can afford it.” Lady Hortense’s gaze flitted to the door. “Never mind the tea, Gillian. Miss Bourne was just leaving.”

Jacinda stood, wondering if she should take the teacup and saucer with her as she walked out, or better yet, drink the steaming liquid in front of Lady Hortense. But after consideration, she did neither. Instead, she held her head up high and walked away.

Chapter 25

"If I know myself, Harriet, mine is an active, busy mind, with a great many independent resources . . ."

JANE AUSTEN, *Emma*

Restless, Jacinda left Lady Hortense's apartments and made her way toward the breakfast room in the hopes of seeing Crispin. Not that anything would come of it, of course. She wasn't foolish enough to believe that he would declare his love for her over a bowl of porridge simply because they'd kissed last night.

While the stolen moment was exceptional for her, it had not made her any richer.

Instead of finding Crispin, however, Dr. Graham was the only one seated at the oval table in the cozy room with the view of the grassy lawn and conical junipers of the upper garden.

"Good morning, Miss Bourne," he said after wiping his mouth with a napkin and laying it beside his now empty plate. "I'm glad I have a chance to see you before I depart."

"You are leaving?"

"I plan to pay a call on one of the village women, who is in her confinement, and with Lady Hortense's arrival"—he paused long enough to shake his head—"you no longer require my chaperonage."

In a terrible flash, Jacinda envisioned long, stuffy dinners sitting across from the imperious Lady Hortense, and the only topic of conversation would be the impending nuptials of Rydstrom and his heiress. "I understand, but I should hate to see you go. After all, if you are not here, who will prod me into my memory exercises?"

Dr. Graham smiled fondly. "I have a sense that someone with your amount of determination might do her own prodding. In addition, having Lady Hortense here will provide a certain type of society of which, I believe, you are more familiar, and perhaps that will boost more accidental memories for you."

"Perhaps," she agreed quickly, trying not to think about how much this felt like a farewell. Everything seemed to be coming to an end, and right at the exact time she felt like it was just beginning. Even her appetite had abandoned her.

"Though I do wish I had a chance to speak with Rydstrom before I left. However, he was called away a short while ago." The doctor removed his spectacles and rubbed the lenses with a corner of the napkin. "Apparently one of the Olson boys backed a horse cart into their mother's home. Thankfully, no one was hurt; however, from what I understand, her entire kitchen lies in rubble."

Oh dear, the trials that poor widow had to endure. The only time Jacinda had seen her boys behaving, and the widow at ease, had been during the log-chopping competition. When Mrs. Olson was holding Mr. Alcott's coat. *Hmm . . .* And during Jacinda's conversation with Mr. Alcott, she had learned that he had come from a large family of strapping boys and hoped to start his own one day soon.

"That's simply awful," Jacinda said absently, feeling that sense of purpose ignite inside her once more. All at once, she knew that she wanted to—no, *needed to*—forge a match between the widow Olson and Mr. Alcott. It's precisely what Miss Emma Woodhouse would have done.

"It is, but at least Rydstrom and a few of the village men are helping to repair what they can."

Her thoughts whipped back to the conversation. "So Rydstrom isn't here to"—*kiss me again and declare his undying love for me*—"see you off?"

"No," he said simply, slipping the curled ends of his spectacles around his ears. "I suppose I must pack my things in order to get a good foot under me."

"Well, then I shall be standing at the front door to bid you farewell."

As soon as the doctor stepped away, Jacinda headed to the kitchens. She knew that with Mrs. Hemple and Mr. Fellows busy with their morning schedules, they wouldn't think of sending the doctor away with all he needed for the call he was paying. Although, since she wasn't familiar with exactly what was needed for such an event, she asked the cook for a basket of food for the expectant family.

While there, Mrs. Limpin bade Jacinda to approve the menu for that evening, and asked if there was anything she would like, in particular. Having no memory of her favorite foods, she was at a loss. However, thinking back to the kiss—because it was never far from her mind—she confessed to liking the flavor of aniseed. There had been a subtle hint of it on Crispin's tongue.

But, of course, Jacinda kept that part to herself.

Mrs. Limpin smiled broadly, her ruddy complexion accentuated by the creases from her smile. "Is that so? As I recall, His Grace was always partial to aniseed biscuits when he was a lad. I'll bake a batch in time for tea, if that pleases you."

"You are a jewel, Mrs. Limpin."

Then, basket in hand, Jacinda headed to the foyer to see off Dr. Graham.

She waved him farewell at the door and watched as his carriage wended its way down the lane. Beside her, Mr. Fellows regaled her with another tale of Rydstrom Hall's history. He was always sharing something with her about the previous generations who'd lived here, the additions they'd made—some better constructed than others—and even some of the battles that had been fought here. She was so enthralled by these glimpses into Crispin's ancestors that she didn't notice Lady Hortense approach.

"Miss Bourne, might I have a word with you?" Though her words were phrased as a question, it was clear from her expression that she would only accept one answer.

"Of course, my lady."

Without saying another word, Lady Hortense turned and strode through the gatehouse toward the arched doorway. Jacinda supposed she was meant to follow.

Lady Hortense continued walking through several corridors and didn't stop until they'd reached the Great Hall. Framed in front of the massive stone hearth, she turned her pinched glower on Jacinda. "Gillian informs me that you had the kitchens prepare a basket for one of my nephew's tenants."

"Yes, my lady. With the duke away, I wanted to lend a hand."

"The task should have fallen to me. After all, I am a member of this house, and you are not," she said crisply.

Jacinda offered a clenched smile. "I never thought otherwise."

"Good. Then we have an understanding."

"If I may, my lady, but what are your plans for Mrs. Olson?" When Jacinda was met with the inquiring arch of silver brows, she decided to enlighten her. "She is one of your nephew's tenants as well. In fact, it is her house that he is helping to repair."

Lady Hortense sniffed. "*He*, Miss Bourne? I believe you meant to say *His Grace*. And as for his tenant, it is common practice to leave the villagers to settle village matters."

Apparently, not too common. According to nearly everyone in Whitcrest, Rydstrom was always ready and able to assist them. And when Lady Hortense walked away as if the matter were settled, Jacinda knew with an equal amount of certainty that it wasn't.

At least, not yet.

WEARY AFTER a long, arduous day, Crispin dragged his feet through the front door of Rydstrom Hall and gave Fellows an abbreviated recounting of events before inquiring about the state of things here.

"Nothing out of the ordinary, sir, just a standard day in Rydstrom Hall." Fellows glanced away and began tugging on the cuffs of his livery coat.

Crispin eyed the butler, taking note of the uncharacteristic fidgeting. "Has something happened?"

Fellows released a nervous, gusty exhale. "Of course not, sir. Whyever would you"—he broke off, his gaze darting toward the corridor where one of the village women was meandering slowly, gazing up at the tapestries as if she were on a museum tour—"imagine anything was amiss?"

"Who is that?"

Fellows cleared his throat. "I believe that is Mrs. Parish, sir."

Before Crispin could ask what she was doing in Rydstrom Hall, he saw Aunt Hortense storm past the woman and head directly to him. Without even knowing what had transpired, he knew Jacinda was at the center of it.

Crispin walked heavy-footed toward his aunt, already seeing the marked disapproval in the lines around her pursed lips. "Good evening, Aunt."

"Miss Bourne," she began without a word of greeting and confirming his suspicions, "needs to remember her place. She has begun to assert herself in matters that a guest should not, and now this."

She gestured with a sweeping arm down the corridor to Mrs. Parish. And further down, he could see other village women milling about as well.

"And what is *this* precisely?"

"She has turned Rydstrom Hall into a circus. Commoners are roaming at will, lining up in the Great Hall, and all because you have allowed her to be treated and regarded by your servants as your equal. Perhaps if you hadn't allowed her to remain in the duchess's chamber, this would not have happened."

Crispin frowned. He'd wondered how long it would take before word reached her. "It was merely a matter of necessity. Rydstrom Hall has many rooms in need of serious repair, as I explained earlier when I showed you the paneling placed in front of the mural in your private sitting room."

The tall accordion screen, from one of the rooms he'd closed off years ago, was the only thing he'd had time to set in place this morning. He'd known that his aunt wouldn't have stood for having a dust sheet hanging from her wall. So he'd concealed it, anchoring the dark mahogany to the wall, then explained that he would pay an artist to refurbish the painting once he was married. Thankfully, that had appeased her.

At least, until this event—whatever it was—happened.

"I spoke with your housekeeper on the matter and she said the same thing," she said. "Then I took a tour myself and found none of the reported issues. There are many guest chambers that are more suited to accommodate Miss Bourne, that are a more respectable distance from your own. Quite honestly, I'm appalled by the fact that you did not see to this matter yourself."

"She was quite ill."

"Perhaps, but no longer. She was the picture of health this morning when I summoned her to my dressing chamber."

"You *summoned* her to your . . . rooms?" Crispin cleared his throat. While part of him was relieved that he'd hidden the mural, another part dreaded the coming days when his aunt would surely ask about the collection of miniatures that had once been on display.

"Certainly. After all, one of us needed to ensure that the girl knew her place and did not entertain any romantic notions, but clearly it will take a much firmer hand."

"I will see to the matter." Regrettably, Crispin knew that his aunt was correct. Allowing Jacinda to stay in the duchess's chamber had weakened him and likely contributed to his actions yesterday and the growing sense of familiarity.

Leaving his aunt to fume in the corridor, Crispin strode to the Great Hall.

When he reached the room, he stopped at the threshold, astounded by the mess before him. There were dishes and silverware strewn over the surfaces of the tables. Jars and crockery filled with mysterious foodstuffs. Sacks of grain and lentils piled haphazardly. Groups of village women were standing about and chatting as if they were attending another festival.

And in the center of it all, Jacinda was bent over the table, scribbling on a page.

"Your Grace," Mrs. Hemple said in a rush, worrying the center of her apron. "I hope that all went well in the village today."

"It appears that Rydstrom Hall has been rather busy in my absence."

"Indeed, sir. And Miss Bourne has been ever so kind. Were you aware that she ensured the good doctor had a basket of food to take to the Matthews' residence before he left? And also a bundle of fresh linens. I'm sure no other young woman would have thought of such generosity. It sheds a most favorable light on Rydstrom Hall and all who reside here."

The clenching of his jaw gradually receded as he learned what Jacinda had done. He never would have suspected that the young woman he'd met in London had such a warm and giving heart. Then again, a great deal had altered since then. More than he cared to admit.

He shifted uncomfortably. Looking around, he gained a

fresh understanding of his aunt's concerns. For Jacinda to act on his behalf, indicated that there was an understanding between them.

He should have set matters straight first thing this morning.

"Mrs. Hemple, please see that these women are removed from my home with the utmost haste. And bring the maids to clear all this away."

The housekeeper looked at him with a pleading gaze and then her shoulders slumped. "Yes, sir."

Crispin crossed the expanse of the hall, his boots hitting hard on the stone floor. Jacinda straightened, paper in her grasp, and watched his approach with wary eyes.

She glanced around to the women leaving in murmuring swells and then back to him. "I had to do it, Rydstrom. You weren't here and your aunt thought it beneath her."

Weary, covered in chalk, his boots caked in mud and who knew what else, the last thing Crispin wanted to deal with was the complete wreck of the Great Hall. But he had to admit, he was curious about Jacinda's motives. "You're blaming my aunt for your sudden whimsy to turn Rydstrom Hall into Bedlam?"

"Well"—she pressed her lips together briefly—"yes."

"Explain yourself, then."

"I spoke with your aunt and she said, in her imperious tone, that the *villagers saw to the village*, and I'd heard that you were busy—"

"Now you're using *me* as an excuse for your complete annihilation of the Great Hall?"

"*Annihilation?* You're being a bit dramatic, Rydstrom."

Losing his grip on both his patience and sanity, he growled. "Before I stepped into this room, Miss Bourne, I was perfectly content with my life but now you've robbed me of that."

And in so many ways, he couldn't even fathom them all.

"I think, perhaps, that you have had a trying day and

are not open to being reasonable." Then turning toward the table, she picked up a small basket with a bit of cloth folded inside and held it up in offering. "Mrs. Limpin said these were once your favorites."

"I don't want whatever is in that"—he watched distractedly as Jacinda flicked open the folds and a deliciously familiar scent wafted up to his nostrils—"basket. Are those aniseed biscuits?"

His mouth was already watering, his breath short. And something inside of him stirred, shifting like a foundation stone falling into place.

"They are, indeed. And if you stop grousing long enough, you might find they taste quite delicious."

"You asked Mrs. Limpin to bake these for me?" His gaze met hers and he was caught by the softness he found there as she nodded hesitantly.

A week ago, this entire episode would have made him send her back to her uncle, regardless of Graham's warnings. But suddenly, the only thing he wanted to do was kiss her. Soundly.

"Thank you," he said instead, his voice lower. "And also for sending the basket with Dr. Graham. That was something I wouldn't have thought of."

"I must disagree."

Jacinda *disagree*? He nearly laughed, feeling no ounce of censure, only fondness. "I should expect nothing less from you."

Smears of watercolor red tinged her cheeks. "I saw you among the villagers yesterday and it is clear that you look after their best interests. And it was with that thought in mind that I asked the village women to help put the widow Olson's kitchen and pantry back in order. I even made a list of the most essential things, but . . . I did not separate it into quadrants."

He glanced down at the paper and around the Great Hall, only now understanding what the chaos meant, and he was mystified by the fact that Jacinda Bourne had surprised him yet again.

Though, as much as her gesture pleased him, it did not alter the reality. Jacinda Bourne had overstepped. "I'm sure Mrs. Olson will be grateful to you; however—"

"Of course, I told everyone that this was your idea and I was merely following your orders." She smiled at him, her gaze a tender, brushed turquoise. "I'm not a nitwit, Rydstrom. I know what they'd think otherwise—that there was something between us. And you and I know that isn't true."

"Not a single thing between us," he said in agreement, his breath coming up short, his heart racing. He felt himself listing toward her as if he were pulled by the force of the tides and it took a monumental amount of willpower not to take her in his arms.

But thoughts like that had gotten him into this situation, and it was best to stay clear of wayward impulses.

After a glance about the hall to ensure all the villagers had gone, he set the basket down, adopting a more serious expression before he addressed her. "There is another matter which I should like to discuss with you, Miss Bourne. A somewhat delicate topic."

"Concerning a certain . . . incident in your study?" She drew in a deep breath that gained his brief, but appreciative, attention to the rounded swells of her breasts.

He nodded and tried not to think about how her flesh felt against his lips, the flavor of her still lingering on his tongue. And far sweeter than a basket of aniseed biscuits.

He cleared his throat, regaining his objective. "As you know, I am not one to apologize, nor will I now blame the events that transpired last night on the spirits I consumed. Nevertheless, those very events have made it clear that you should no longer inhabit the bedchamber across from mine."

After a moment, her lips curled in an unexpected grin. "I understand."

Confused by her reaction, he asked, "Is that *all* you have to say? You're just going to stand there and agree with me?"

"Indeed. Did you expect to hear something else? A mournful lamentation, perhaps? A vow to cry into my pillow every night until I leave?"

"Don't be ridiculous." And yet, he had expected something of the sort. "I was merely noting how you've managed to disagree with everything I've said until now. I should think I was speaking to a stranger."

She continued to grin, those eyes of hers full of mischief, tilting up at the corners. "How can I disagree with this? After all, you've essentially stated that you must have me moved to another chamber because you find me irresistible."

She sauntered away, leaving him to watch the tempting sway of her hips in lavender muslin, and he realized that she was absolutely right.

Damn.

Chapter 26

"You are very fond of bending little minds . . ."

JANE AUSTEN, *Emma*

The following morning, Jacinda entered the humid hothouse, summoned once more by Lady Hortense. "You requested to see me, my lady."

The summons had come as a surprise to Jacinda. After all, last night at dinner, she'd only received stony silence from Lady Hortense. At least, directly.

Indirectly, however, she'd had plenty to say. To Crispin. *I'm certain the Montague family could have done more for your tenant if not for the unforgivable breach of etiquette that caused pandemonium to overshadow the unfortunate occurrence.*

In fact, *the unforgivable breach of etiquette* had become a mainstay in most of Lady Hortense's comments.

Now, standing at a narrow plank table, Lady Hortense didn't even look up from the flower arrangement in front of her. "While you are a guest at Rydstrom Hall, Miss Bourne, it is important that you find a proper occupation. After yesterday's incident, it is clear that you need guidance in this area."

Doubtless, anything other than a cordial response would become the topic of this evening's dinner conversation. Therefore, Jacinda stepped forward without uttering a word. Assuming the *proper occupation* had something to do with flower arranging, she began to pinch off the dead leaves.

They worked in a semblance of cooperation for a few moments before Lady Hortense said, "You are very good at noticing details and finding what is hidden, are you not?"

"I suppose I am." Even now, Jacinda noticed that Lady Hortense had a particular way of choosing the blossoms that were nearly identical in shape, color and size, situating them at precise distances apart. Perhaps requiring a sense of order and balance was a family trait.

And it was this small thing that loosened some of the tightly wound annoyance Jacinda felt toward Crispin's aunt.

At least, until the odious woman spoke again.

"Good, for that will aid you in the task I have for you. If you will turn around and pick up the paper waiting on the bench, you'll find a list of names."

"And what am I to do with this list?" Jacinda asked, curiosity compelling her to cross the room and pick it up.

"Find a wife for my nephew."

Jacinda blanched, her hand automatically opening to release the page as if it had spontaneously burst into flames. Subtlety was certainly not Lady Hortense's strongest trait.

"Arrange it as you see fit," Lady Hortense said offhandedly. "If any name sparks your memory or stands out, make a note of it. A brief description accompanies each, listing matters of importance—class, wealth, landholdings, etcetera."

She picked up the page once more with numb fingers. Scanning the names, Jacinda saw that the *etcetera* portion listed all the things that she valued as more important in finding a matrimonial candidate—interests, hobbies, and beliefs.

And even though Jacinda had not recognized any of these heiresses, she felt a distinct dislike for each of them, their families, fortunes, and property.

Expelling a tense breath, she straightened her shoulders. "I feel certain that any man thinking of marriage would want to know the character of his potential wife, someone he could respect, and perhaps one who earned the respect of his servants and tenants as well. I cannot know that by looking at this list."

"My nephew is not like other men," Lady Hortense added, not in a prideful way, but as an unalterable truth she had come to endure over time. "In fact, he does not intend to have his wife live here at all. Ah, but this brings up an important point—you must find a debutante with a great deal of property. She can live in her own estate, and those tenants can help support Rydstrom Hall into the future."

"Separate residences? How could that make for a happy marriage?"

"Marrying for the sake of happiness is an infantile notion." Lady Hortense issued a patronizing, dusty laugh. "Such an undertaking must be met with maturity. Miss Bourne, I am trying to make allowances for your injuries, but explaining the obvious is quite tiresome."

Jacinda bristled. "I'm not certain I am up to this task, my lady."

"Why not? Surely you have nothing else to occupy your time now that my nephew has been clearer with your actual duties as a guest of this house."

Oooh! This woman drove her mad! Jacinda refrained from growling. "Clearly I have little understanding of what a marriage for the sake of duty entails."

"Then I shall enlighten you." Lady Hortense began the systematic demise of several blossoms with each snip of her clippers. "After all, I should like to avoid the unfortunate circumstances my very own brother suffered. He was set to marry an heiress from a fine family, but was lured away by my nephew's mother"—she pursed her lips, then added absently—"rest her poor soul."

This sparked Jacinda's interest. "His Grace's father married for love instead of money?"

Her own foolish heart fluttered at the thought. If Crispin's parents had done so, then perhaps—

"She had a small fortune of ten thousand pounds, but only

two small properties," Lady Hortense said before Jacinda could finish the thought, and her hope suffered the same fate as the snipped buds, falling like colored hailstones onto the table and rolling to the floor.

Lady Hortense continued. "Her wealth was only enough to add to a portion of the north wing, in addition to the library. Oh, and I believe they rebuilt the chapel in the village, among other things. But as you must have seen from my most excellent apartments, that my own very profitable marriage contributed much more. My nephew will want to leave his own mark as well."

Jacinda had never heard Crispin mention anything other than wanting to repair Rydstrom Hall. As far as she knew, he loved his home as it was and only required a bride's dowry to maintain it.

She wondered if Crispin had been so focused on the longevity of Rydstrom Hall, that he never considered his own happiness. Distracted, she stared down at the list. "And that is what you are asking me to do—find your nephew a bride that will help him leave his mark on Rydstrom Hall."

Plucking out an overblown rose, Lady Hortense gestured to the page with it, the petals rustling. "Quite so. My nephew and I have little time for these things. It is enough work for me to interview the candidates you choose in order to weed out those who are too weak and feebleminded to understand their duty."

Did Crispin know that his aunt was asking for assistance in finding a bride? It didn't seem likely. In the week that she'd been here, each time she'd mentioned his need for an heiress, he'd gruffly diverted the topic. Therefore, this seemed more like a lesson from Lady Hortense, to ensure that Jacinda knew her place.

"If you put forth a modicum of effort, Miss Bourne, I'm sure you'll be able to give yourself over to the process and perhaps even find it enjoyable." Lady Hortense lifted her face, her mouth creasing on either side with a semblance of a smile. "Sort through the list for the most qualified candidates, and be sure to tell me if a name sparks your memory at all. I'll expect your findings tomorrow morning. The Rydstrom line must move on into the future, and the sooner the better. Good day."

At the abrupt dismissal, Jacinda didn't hesitate to leave the room. But strolling down the corridors with the list in her hand, she wished that Dr. Graham was here to force her into some mundane task. She would even be willing to attempt the viola again, if only to serve as a distraction.

She had no intention of doing anything about the list. How could she, after all? There was nothing in the description that told her about the characters of these debutantes. For all she knew, the entire lot belonged to a secret club of kitten pinchers and puppy kickers. For that matter, they might be weak little ninnies who would never challenge Rydstrom when he was being overbearing.

Or worse, they might be raving beauties who would make Rydstrom forget the woman with amnesia who'd somehow found herself in love with him.

Jacinda looked down at the list with a desire to accidentally drop it in the nearest hearth.

"Miss Bourne," Crispin called out in greeting, surprising her with his sudden appearance in the minstrel's gallery.

From the opposite end, he strode toward her with hard, purposeful steps that pulled his gray breeches taut over well-muscled thighs, his toned limbs flexing. Her attention drifted upward from there, to the cut and fullness of his fallfront, and she felt her cheeks grow hot, discovering that there were moments when her curiosity made her blush.

Then she lifted her gaze higher, beyond the crisp lines of his dark blue waistcoat beneath a charcoal gray coat, over those barely contained shoulders, and finally to the angular features she saw each night when she closed her eyes, and each morning before she opened them. And just as it was when she last dreamed of him, there was a ghost smirk toying with the corner of his mouth.

"Have I done something to amuse you, Rydstrom?"

"Not at all," he said, stopping in front of her, his expression unchanged aside from a warmth emanating from his russet-rimmed gaze. "I was just wondering if you were finished admiring the view . . . of the gallery, or if you intended to continue."

Not realizing that her brazen observations had been so obvious, this time her blush spread to her ears. But she did not look away from the challenge in his gaze and the lift of his brow. "It is a grand sight, indeed, and ought to be admired as often as possible."

A low, hungry sound rumbled in his throat. He crowded closer, his gaze dropping down to her lips. Her pulse fluttered, her breath coming up short, and she wondered if he was going to kiss her. Yet, as if she'd spoken the question aloud, he shook his head in answer.

She felt compelled to contradict him with a nod.

His heated gaze lifted to hers. "No. We cannot repeat what occurred in the study."

"Of course not," she said, boldly stepping closer, laying her hand over his waistcoat. "We are in the minstrel's gallery."

He growled again, took her by the waist, and lowered his mouth.

But in that same instant, a door closed around the corner with a great booming sound that filled the corridor. They sprang apart.

Soon after, they heard the quick clatter of servant's steps, receding down one of the winding corridors. Even though they weren't about to be discovered, the moment was lost.

Crispin blew out a breath and looked over his shoulder. After waiting a second or more, he turned back to her and withdrew a pouch from his inner coat pocket. "This was the reason I sought you out. I was in the village this morning, and Mrs. Olson bade me to give this to you, along with her gratitude."

"Then I cannot accept," she said, disappointment turning her tone sullen, "because it should be known that you were the one who arranged to have her kitchen put back in order. And besides, you and the village men did the hard labor."

Without arguing, Crispin moved closer once more, reached down to take her hand, and dropped the pouch in her palm before closing her fingers around it. He remained thus, with his large callused hand cupped around hers for a moment, his voice lower when he said, "Even though your intentions were honorable, I believe everyone knows the truth—that you are kind, generous, and selfless. Now, accept this gift."

"Very well." Pleasure swarmed through her in a flurry of warm pulses that she could feel even after he released her. The gift he'd just given her was more precious than anything she could think of, and she wasn't speaking of the pouch. All the same, she was curious . . . "What is it?"

"Bluebell seeds."

Her breath caught and her head spun as a flash of blue petals floating through the air entered her mind. *"Bluebells."*

Crispin took her elbow and tilted up her chin, his brow drawn together in a frown. "Are you unwell?"

She shook her head and just as quickly the image vanished. "I think it was a memory, but I'm not certain."

"Do you have these spells often?"

"Not very." She studied his expression, wishing she knew how his words could express concern while his gaze, intense and seeking, held no tenderness. This time, she was the one to step back, her heart splinter aching again. "I still don't feel any closer to remembering who I am."

"For your sake, I hope that alters soon. I can send for Dr. Graham," he said with a surprising amount of sincerity, making her wonder if she was hoping for more from him than he could give. After all, there was affection in his sentiment, even if not in his countenance.

Fondly, she shook her head. "Dr. Graham is needed elsewhere, and I was just heading up to continue Sybil's French lessons."

"A prepared lesson?" He glanced down to the paper in her other hand, eyebrows arched in teasing disbelief. They both knew her impulsive nature would not permit her to plan too far ahead.

"No. This is . . ." She stopped, not wanting to cast a dark shadow over their encounter. Tonight, when she closed her eyes, she only wanted to think about what it might have been like to kiss him in the minstrel's gallery. ". . . nothing important."

And then, as they left in opposite directions, she crumpled the list in her hand and felt a satisfied grin tug at her lips.

CRISPIN'S PREOCCUPIED gaze drifted out beyond the window in his aunt's solar, the wavy glass distorting the view of the park beyond. With his thoughts on his brief encounter with Jacinda a few moments ago, he only listened with half an ear as his aunt droned on about marriage. She was saying something about the importance of finding a woman who would have a firm grasp of her duties and rise above any romantic inclinations.

Even though, a week ago, he'd wanted the same thing, it now left a sour taste on the back of his tongue. He imagined consummating his marriage with a woman such as that, who simply laid beneath him stoically as she performed her *duty* as a wife. Likely she would never ogle him hungrily as he walked toward her.

". . . and that was why I decided to give Miss Bourne the list," his aunt said, drawing his attention with the mention of Jacinda's name.

"What list?"

Aunt Hortense stared at him quizzically, likely because she'd been talking to him for an inordinate amount of time and he should have been hanging on every word. "I brought the list of potential matches from Viscount Eggleston with me."

Crispin's temper suddenly ignited. "And you gave it to Miss Bourne? Without even consulting me?"

"I have already paid her uncle."

"Is money all that matters to you? Have you not once thought about her injuries?" Crispin couldn't help but think about how pale she'd grown when that spell overtook her. He hadn't seen her face that white since the day he first found her on the beach. A day that seemed to have happened years ago.

So much had altered since he'd first stepped into the Bourne Agency. The traits she possessed that had once incensed him, he found that he admired. In fact, her sharp wit, courage, and doggedness appealed to him a great deal. "It isn't right to use her."

"Use her." Hortense scoffed, then narrowed her eyes at him. "You are sounding suspiciously soft. Do I have need to worry?"

What, worry that he would forget that he needed money to repair the walls that surrounded him each day? Not likely. Or worry that Sybil would have the funds to live away from society's scorn for the rest of her life? Never. And yet, for the first time in years, Rydstrom Hall felt like a prison to him once more.

"Of course not. I know my duty."

Chapter 27

"There is one thing, Emma, which a man can always do, if he chuses, and that is, his duty . . ."

JANE AUSTEN, *Emma*

The following morning, Jacinda stood at the threshold of Lady Hortense's gilded rooms, a sense of firm resolve straightening her backbone. "I cannot find a match for your nephew."

She'd thought about it all night and decided that she couldn't endure the torment. Just seeing the names on the list that one time was enough to fill her with burning jealousy.

Sitting at an ornate writing desk, Lady Hortense did not bother to lift her gaze up from the letter beneath her long-fingered hand and scratching quill. "Of course you can, Miss Bourne."

"The list you provided gives me no means of determining which woman would best complement your nephew's character. Therefore—"

"As I said before, such sentiment does not concern my nephew," she interrupted, pausing long enough to dip her pen into the inkwell. "And since I have come to believe that this answer will likely not satisfy you to an acceptable degree, I will enlighten you further and tell you that my nephew learned that happiness in marriage is as fleeting as it is fruitless."

Jacinda wanted to disagree, knowing in her heart that

happiness in marriage was the ideal state between husband and wife, but Lady Hortense continued.

"While I stayed here, I saw my brother's marriage failing each day. He and his wife argued incessantly about one topic or another. And it was no wonder. My brother's wife was always preoccupied and melancholic, neglecting her duty as a mother, letting my nephew run wild enough to charge up a list of debts from clubs, shops, and gambling houses. In fact, from what I understand, they were arguing about this very thing out on the bluffs just before my brother . . . died."

Jacinda went still, her heart breaking for Crispin. She could not imagine the amount of guilt he must carry over this. Though, it seemed to explain so much about his nature, and how obsessed he was about keeping those beneath this roof safe. "How awful."

"Indeed," Lady Hortense responded after a lengthy pause, her voice quiet and detached. Then, looking down at the ink pooling on the paper, she shook her head and the usual hauteur in her tone returned. "The financial strains were a constant source of my brother and his wife's discontent, among other things. I, of course, assisted my brother with his own debts from time to time, purchasing some of the Montague landholdings to ensure they did not end up in a stranger's hands, but I refused to pay my nephew's arrears."

Jacinda frowned. Was Crispin a man who'd gambled so much that his father had been forced into poverty?

This did not sound at all like the man she had come to know, who valued his home and the people who lived here. He would never have put them in jeopardy. "And His Grace's debts were so extensive that your brother was willing to sell off part of his estate?"

"In truth, those instances occurred before my nephew grew into an age to follow in his father's footsteps." Lady Hortense sniffed, a slight uncomfortable shift in her stiff posture. "However, my nephew caused his share of damage later on, and it is because his mother was too soft on him. He needed a firm hand to guide him, to live up to his duty, as every Montague ought. If I had been his mother—"

"But you were not." Jacinda's temper flared. This cold woman wanted to cast the blame onto Crispin's mother, when it was clear that the father had far more to do with the financial strains on the Rydstrom estate and providing an example for his son.

"I am fully aware of that fact, Miss Bourne, as my own children did not survive infancy." A taut, pained sigh escaped her. "That was the one thing I had in common with my brother's wife. After my nephew, all the others were stillborn. For that, I did pity her. But she was weak, allowing those losses to make her lose sight of the healthy, bright child she had—the boy who needed firm guidance in order to become the man he is today.

"And I am glad to say," Lady Hortense continued, her voice warming, "that after four years under a stern hand of isolation, my nephew has run this estate without any assistance. He has proven himself worthy of the title he holds."

A slight shift in Lady Hortense's demeanor caught Jacinda's attention. Each time she mentioned her nephew, the light in her gray gaze softened, and her lips curved ever so slightly.

"You care for him," Jacinda said, working through the puzzle that Lady Hortense presented. And, perhaps, she'd even been jealous of Crispin's mother.

Without so much as a blink in Jacinda's direction, the lady in question rose from the desk and walked through a white glazed archway that led to her sitting room. "Affection has little to do with it. We are family and that bond is unbreakable."

The woman was a contradiction of rigid censure and a guarded demeanor that, quite possibly, hid a wealth of tenderness for her nephew. And if the latter was true, Jacinda hoped it would aid Crispin in the future.

Lady Hortense arranged herself on the edge of a gold chintz cushion and waved her hand in the general direction of the bellpull. "Ring for tea, if you please. I find that I am quite willing to tolerate your company for a short while longer."

High praise, indeed. Jacinda felt nearly dizzy from the whirlwind that was Lady Hortense as she crossed the room to pull the tasseled cord.

Spotting a collection of miniatures on the wall, she paused to study them, and seeing one that looked very much like a younger version of Crispin, and with a decidedly rakish gleam in his eyes, she smiled. There was another one beside it that struck her with familiarity, a girl with ringlets and gray eyes that looked like Sybil, but only with a narrower face.

But why would Lady Hortense possess a likeness of Crispin's ward?

Then slowly, those familiar prickles skittered down her spine as the kernel of a notion started to grow. "My lady, who is the girl in this portrait?"

"The small one there? Why, that is of me, when I was a girl of thirteen. Even then, I had impeccable posture—the artist said as much. Thankfully, I'd packed a few of my own miniatures and brought them here, for it seems the ones that were in this room have gone missing."

Jacinda's breath stalled in her throat. There was no reason why Sybil should look nearly identical to Lady Hortense, not unless . . . unless they were related somehow.

Yet the lady herself stated only moments ago that her children had not survived.

Suddenly, she recalled that Sybil had arrived four years ago, on the very day that Crispin's parents died while they'd been, presumably, arguing about money on the cliffs.

But what if it hadn't been about money, after all?

What if . . . Sybil was not Crispin's ward? But his sister, instead.

I have a responsibility to protect her, he'd said. *She has already suffered enough for one lifetime.*

And all at once, Jacinda knew the truth.

"Is Sybil your father's child?"

Crispin looked up from his desk to see Jacinda striding into his study, and went numb from the top of his head all the way down to the soles of his feet. He couldn't even feel the quill in his hand.

"What . . . did you say?" he managed through the panic choking him. Then he shook his head because he had heard her. He didn't need her to repeat it. His gaze searched the empty doorway behind her, a swift pins and needles sensation sweeping through him as he forced himself to stand and he walked, wooden, to check for anyone lingering in the corridor. *Empty.*

Closing the door, he pressed his forehead against it before facing her again. "Who have you told?"

"I came to you first, of course." A quick defensive frown drew her slender brows together. "Since I was just with your aunt, I did not want to reveal my suspicions that her brother had another child."

"Will you stop saying that! You cannot rush around the castle flinging accusations of this magnitude."

"But it's true, isn't it?"

Breathing through his gritted teeth made it hard to catch his breath. Yet even when he relaxed his jaw, he still couldn't. Reaching up, he pulled on his cravat, but it didn't help either. It was happening—his worst fear coming to fruition.

"You have overstepped again, Miss Bourne," he rasped. Raking a hand through his hair, he glanced at his desk searching for order, rightness. Yet his ledger was off center, angled, a spill of ink staining the surface near the red discoloration from the smear of sealing wax that Jacinda had touched little more than a week ago. He had to look away, but then the pillows on the sofa drew his attention and only made him think of Jacinda and that night they'd spent in here. He couldn't even look to the shelves without thinking of the way she'd moved his bookends.

She'd disturbed every single part of his life, from the very beginning. He'd been a fool to forget the damage she could inflict. He'd let down his guard, instead of seeing to his duty.

Heedless of the tenuous control he had over himself, she continued. "Sybil's illegitimacy must surely be the reason you've been hiding the truth about her. Why? Because it would sully your father's memory?"

"Because society scorns children born on the wrong side of the blanket. Unless illegitimates possess great wealth, they are outcasts, living half lives and skirting scandal wherever they go. And Sybil deserves better."

"Is that also the reason you do not want your wife to live here?" She stepped toward him, crowding him with her questions.

Over the past days, he'd forgotten how dangerous it was to have Jacinda here. His own blissful amnesia had allowed him to feel things that he'd never felt before. And he didn't want her as the enemy. Or to only think of her in regard to the secret she discovered.

Now he had so much more to lose than ever before. "Whispers travel great distances. I do not want Sybil to suffer any more than she already has done."

Jacinda reached out and curled her hand over his sleeve. "I do not think that shielding her, masquerading her as your ward, is the answer. Surely you saw the way she blossomed at the festival. In time, she will build on her own strength if you give her the chance."

"You have known her for only a few days," he chided,

shrugging free of her and pointing to a place beyond the wall, where his most painful memory still lingered. "I have known her since the day she first walked through the door and asked to see her father—*our* father. Therefore, I believe I know her better than you do. In addition, I am a far superior judge of seeing after her welfare than a young woman who carelessly traveled here from London and put her own life in danger just to expose a secret!"

Jacinda went still. "Is that the . . . reason I came to Rydstrom Hall?"

He gave her a curt nod.

She winced, her skin fading to that frightening white, her colorless lips parting on a shallow breath. "And all this time . . . you've been protecting Sybil . . . from *me*?"

"Yes, Miss Bourne." The instant the words left him, he wanted to haul them back. He shouldn't have spoken with such vehemence. The fury he'd once felt for her was no longer inside of him. This was only panic, not anger or even blame.

She staggered back, her brow furrowed, her gaze shooting to the door. "What kind of person am I for you to feel that I am capable of—" She shook her head. "No. Please do not answer that. I believe I already know."

Without another word, she flung open the door and rushed out of the room.

But her absence brought Crispin no peace. He paced the study, feeling caged. The knot of tension that usually resided at the back of his neck now settled coldly in the pit of his stomach.

Regret. He knew the feeling of it all too well.

He wanted to call her back, explain his worries, share his every thought, the same way he'd been tempted to do when they'd sat together during the storm, and every moment they'd spent together since.

Yet those ideas brought a new wave of panic as that unnamed emotion that had been with him for days suddenly came forth.

Damn it all.

He cared for Jacinda. *Hell*, it was more than that and he knew it.

Was this love? No. Surely not. Crispin raked a hand through his hair again. Clearly, he'd been spending too much time in her company, his thoughts constantly distracted by when he would see her again, hear her laugh, and talk to her. His arms felt empty without her. The air stale without her fragrance. He couldn't even eat his dinner without wanting to catch her impish smirk as she looked at his plate. This was madness, not love.

But it *was* love.

How had she done this to him? How had she infiltrated his life so completely that he could no longer imagine it without her?

Tenacity. Her sheer, unrepentant tenacity was the answer. And it filled every drop of blood and every breath in her body.

Before he knew what he was doing, he strode out of the room. First, he went up to her bedchamber, but found she wasn't there. Then thinking he would find her in the library, he descended the stairs. But she wasn't there either. *Sybil*, he thought. Jacinda was likely with her in the donjon.

"Your Grace," Fellows called, catching Crispin at a near run down the corridor, heading toward the stairs once more.

He slowed only enough to call over his shoulder, "Unless it is a crisis, I have an urgent errand."

It was vital for him to find Jacinda and tell her that he'd fallen in love with her. A shout of laughter escaped him. Yes, this *was* madness!

"Of course, sir. I was only concerned about the storm that's arrived, you see. Mrs. Hemple is with Sybil, but Miss Bourne went out of doors a short while ago and has not returned yet."

Crispin stopped. In that exact instant, a growl of thunder vibrated the floor at his feet. The eerie sound flooded him with the memory of four years ago. He'd been in this exact spot when the cliff face had sheared off and dropped into the sea.

A terror, stronger than he'd ever known, sent his feet flying back down the corridor, through the gatehouse and out into the storm.

Chapter 28

"... if a woman *doubts* as to whether she should accept a man or not, she certainly ought to refuse him."

JANE AUSTEN, *Emma*

Jacinda ran out the door, wishing to escape what she now knew. She was a horrible person. The type of person that a man like Rydstrom wanted to keep far away from the people he cared for.

How could she have been so blind that she hadn't seen it? Crispin had never wanted her here. And suddenly she was glad she didn't have a memory of who she was. She never wanted to remember that person either.

The rain came down in hard, icy needles, pelting her cheeks and soaking her dress as she dashed through the gardens of the upper bailey. She took a set of stone stairs without knowing where they led, but when she saw the cliffs, she veered toward them.

Pointlessly, she wiped away the tears that stung her eyes as she stopped to look out at the dark, roiling sea. Tucked in her bodice, she felt the scratch of the leather knot that tied the pouch of her wishing stone. She'd kept it with her ever since the Spring Festival for an idiotic reason—a wish that Rydstrom would no longer need an heiress.

Drawing it out, she poured the pebble into the cup of her hand. It was only an ordinary pebble. One of millions on the beach below. And yet, if she could have one wish, she would ask that she might never remember who she was. She wanted to be this new version of herself and start her life today, this moment.

Clutching her wishing stone, she squeezed her eyes shut, repeated her wish and reared back her arm, ready to fling it far away into the churning waves below.

"Jacinda!"

She looked over her shoulder to see Crispin running fast toward her, the wind parting his coat. For an instant, she had a hope that he'd come to make amends. Then she saw his glower, fiercer than ever.

"Come away from the edge!"

She turned back toward the sea, and by her estimations, she wasn't even close to the edge. Clutching the stone, she said her wish once more, reeled back, and then let it loose.

But with the driving rain saturating the ground, and the wind pushing her off balance, she slipped. The soles of her slippers were no match for the thin wet grass and clay beneath her feet. She fell hard on her backside, knocking into the large white slab beside her.

"Noooo!" The anguished cry tore through the roar of the storm.

Jacinda barely recognized Crispin's voice. It was too feral and raw to be his.

Lying on the ground as she was, she could not see him. Was he hurt? "Crispin!"

She tried to right herself, but the rain was relentless. She slipped again, down to her knees this time. Then finally, she set her hand on the large rock and stood, only to find Crispin already upon her, his face bleached white, his hands outstretched like claws.

He took hold of her roughly, hauling her against him, dragging her away from the edge. Breathing hard through his open mouth, he stared at her in disbelief and gave her a slight shake, that vein pulsing at his forehead. "Why didn't you stop, you fool? I thought I'd lost you."

Then, without warning, he crushed his mouth to hers. His arms wrapped around her like manacles, stealing her breath. And he was shaking, the tremors wracking from him into her.

There was no way for her to answer. He was a force stronger than the storm breaking over them, and so she clung to him, yielding to the unapologetic reprimand his mouth was giving hers. His hands raked over her back, gripping the layers of muslin and cambric until they were soaked and plastered to her. But she didn't care. All that mattered was that she was in his arms.

Then a roar of thunder shook the ground and lightning split the sky. They began to move, the power of his legs driving them across the hill with her dangling from him like a stringless marionette. She would need to breathe at some point, but she couldn't bring herself to pull away just yet.

After a minute or more, she became aware of the fact that the rain no longer doused her in drowning swells. She could hear the harsh, ceaseless rush close by, but only a few trickles fell on her face. Drawing back marginally, she swallowed down a few needed gulps of air and saw that they were beneath a thick canopy of pine boughs.

Crispin slid his hand to her nape and tucked her against him as he bent down. "Watch your head, darling."

Too stunned by the endearment, it took her a moment to notice their altered surroundings. In the dim light, she saw rocks mortared in a low, shrinking dome around them.

"We are in a grotto—a cave of sorts," he said, answering her unasked question. He sank to his knees, holding her legs against his hip to move them deeper inside. "It was built centuries ago by the first inhabitants, to protect the natural spring. We'll be safe enough here to wait out the storm."

A bed of lush, green moss covered most of the ground and climbed partway up the walls. Beside them lay a narrow trail of moon white rocks, glistening beneath a quiet trickle of water that had smoothed away a blade-thin channel over time. And as he lowered her gently, Jacinda wondered if she had fallen into a dream or off the cliff's edge, because this was all too magical to be real.

Cupping her face, he brushed the dripping locks of hair away from her forehead, his fingertips tracing down her cheek, over her lips. "Are you hurt?"

Hurt? She could feel nothing but joy. "Did you call me *darling*?"

His response was a featherlight kiss. He shrugged out of his coat and laid it down on the bed of moss behind her. Then his hands roamed along her neck, down her shoulders and arms, squeezing gently as if to verify that she still had tissue, sinew, and bones. Each touch elicited a series of warm tingles throughout her body, rousing her from one state of exhilaration to another.

He continued without pause, prodding gently through the drenched garments plastered to her skin, against the outside of her ribs, her hips. Methodically, his hands skimmed down her legs, but stopped when he reached her feet and freed her of her sodden slippers as he rotated her ankles.

She was breathless by the time he finished. "Are you satisfied that I am in perfect health?"

"No." His hard gaze fixed on hers before he took her face in his hands and pressed his lips to her forehead, her eyelids, nose, cheeks, and mouth. "I thought I'd lost you, Jacinda, and I"—his breath hitched, raspy and tight—"I couldn't bear it."

Gazing up at his glower, she wondered if she was wrong about what emotion lay at the root of this expression. Perhaps it wasn't anger at all, but something far more tender. Could it be that he cared for her?

She lifted her arm to trace that vein with her fingertip. Then she set her hands over his waistcoat, over the pounding in the center of his chest. "Crispin, you are my entire world. I'll always find my way to you."

The hardness over his brow relaxed, his features shifting, softening. Then a sudden smile broke free.

Unreserved, he unleashed the full potency of his handsome face in a flash of straight white teeth, broad lips that canted slightly to one side, and a vertical row of shallow creases that promised to deepen over time. "You would, would you?"

Awed, her heart thrummed, lungs tight. She couldn't respond with anything more than a nod. Besides, there weren't any words to describe the love she felt in this moment. All she could do was take his face in her hands, and press her lips to his.

"You're shivering." He yanked his cravat free. Folding it by half, and half again, he patted the warm side over her forehead, drying her face, nose, cheek . . . And all the while, Jacinda's gaze dipped to this new exposed part of him. Even when he'd wielded an axe, he hadn't removed his cravat. And now it was here, before her, and in easy reach of her fingertips.

She stroked the corded flesh, interrupted by the knobbed protrusion of his Adam's apple. Then further down, she drifted to the crisp golden-brown hairs rising up from the opening of his shirt.

Pausing in his ablutions, his gaze fixed on hers. He must have seen something in her expression because the fine points of his pupils expanded in a spread of scorching, inky black. Covering her hand, he slowly dragged it up his neck to his lips and closed his eyes as he kissed the center of her palm.

This time a shiver rushed over *him*.

Jacinda leaned toward him, seeking his warmth. She huddled closer, pressing her face into the nook between the length of his neck and the rise of his shoulder muscle, breathing in his wet cedar scent. Yet she could not get close enough to him.

He seemed to know this and wrapped his arms tightly around her. His hands floated along her back, over the layers of damp fabric at first, then beneath, peeling them away. Every inch he touched heated her skin, his rough calluses causing delicious ripples of pleasure.

Wanting more, she inched between his widespread knees, burrowing closer.

"Let me warm you, darling," he said, his voice raw and shaky.

He tugged on her skirts, drawing them out from under her knees, high enough to reveal the ribbons of her stockings. Then gathering the dripping fabric, he pulled upward with such assuredness that she didn't hesitate to lift her arms. She didn't even know when he'd unfastened her buttons. But it mattered little, because in the next instant, she was clad only in her chemise, stays, and stockings.

Every garment was transparent from rain. Shyly, she lifted her gaze and saw that he'd gone still, his arm still holding her dress and petticoat aloft as rivulets of water sluiced down his arm, saturating his sleeve. Yet the ardent hunger she saw as he stared at her emboldened her to rise up and straighten her shoulders. "I'm not warm yet."

Her dress fell, unheeded, in a soggy heap on the ground. Then his hands were on her, drawing her up against him, his mouth slanting down on hers. The kiss was ravenous and needy. She yielded her body eagerly, her back arching, her lips parting, welcoming the sinewy slide of his tongue.

The storm came on harder. Flashes of lightning penetrated the sheets of water pouring outside the grotto. Every clap of thunder amplified the urgent demands of their hands and mouths. She felt a sharp tug, heard an unmistakable tearing sound, and her stays and chemise went slack. He peeled them down her flesh, the vellum-thin cotton dissolving beneath his hands. And then she was fully bared to him.

His growled sound of approval made her brazen. So she gripped his shirtsleeves by the fistfuls, and drew out the tails from his trousers. Crispin released her long enough to rip at the opening of his waistcoat, sending black buttons soundlessly to the moss. Then in one motion, he whisked away his shirtsleeves.

Dear heavens, he was magnificent! A broad wall of thick muscle, accentuated by a mat of springy brown hair tapered down the ridges of his abdomen.

"So this is what you've been hiding beneath your coat all this time," she said, hardly recognizing the throaty sound of her own voice. Reaching out, she splayed her fingertips over his chest, feeling a primitive desire to claim him and to explore every inch.

He grinned and moved over her, nudging her back onto his coat. "And this is what you've been hiding beneath muslin, hmm?"

"Yes," she said on a gasp as his mouth rasped the underside of her chin. "Though mine is not nearly as impressive."

He began sipping away the droplets of water down the length of her throat, over the subtle rise of her breasts, murmuring hungry sounds of approval that vibrated against her, through her, pulsing low in her body. He paused over a berry-stained peak and met her gaze. "I beg to differ."

Then slowly, reverently, he rasped his lips over the distended tip, teasing until a helpless, strangled whimper escaped her. Part of her wanted to close her eyes and just feel everything, but she couldn't look away.

He grinned rakishly, then closed his mouth over her nipple. Gasping, she grasped him, her fingers sliding through his sleek, wet locks, her spine bent into an arch of supplication. She would do anything he asked in this moment. At least, as long as he promised not to stop.

And yet he did stop, but only to move to her other breast. She forgave him on a breathy *"Yes. There."*

An insistent visceral pulse throbbed between her thighs in low, heady surges that matched the satiny flicks of his tongue. Reflexively, she pressed her knees together to appease the ache. As if sensing her discomfort, Crispin's hand slid down the shallow rise of her stomach and skimmed over the thatch of dark auburn curls that cloaked her sex. Shamelessly, her hips rose to meet him and he cupped her, fully. The breadth of his hand urged her legs apart. Even trusting him completely, she still couldn't keep from trembling when she opened for him, exposing her vulnerable core, and feeling him slip further down to graze one fingertip along the swollen seam.

At that first touch, he issued a jagged growl. Leaving the wet tip of her breast to pucker in the cool air, he lifted his head to watch his ministrations. Brazenly inquisitive, she watched, too.

Silver beams from the lightning outside caught the glistening dampness on his fingers as he parted her slick, sensitive folds. Unhurried, he explored her in unending, voluptuous strokes, the pulse in her body growing more insistent and heavy. But when he dipped a long adept finger inside her sheath, she could no longer watch. Her neck arched back, lips parting on a gasp, her hips tilted against him, seeking.

Now *his* breath fractured. Her name spilled forth on broken syllables like a new language that took on a multitude of tender, erotic meanings. He shifted then. Hovering over her, he nudged his thigh between hers.

Exhilarated with unspent pleasure, she watched him once more, her gaze roving over his body as he unfastened the fall of his trousers. The placard gave way to his thick, jutting column of flesh and her breath stalled in her throat. Rising up from a thatch of dark fur, the solid length of his shaft and rounded dusky head seemed to rear at her, feral and ravenous.

Unaware of her stirrings of trepidation, Crispin bent down low, his focus on the dewy curls of her sex. Parting her thighs, he nuzzled her, breathing in deeply. "I've dreamed of tasting you and licking away every sweet, dewy drop. Then I would wake up, prowl past your chamber and into my study, to write your name down in my ledger."

The lower right-hand quadrant, the one she'd questioned him about. And now she knew why her name was there.

His words, and the raw desire in his voice, sent a helpless, frantic quiver arcing through her. It centered there, where he parted her. She sucked in a breath, embarrassed to have him look so closely at her most intimate flesh.

At the sound, he looked up, his eyes hooded and somewhat wicked. "Not curious enough yet? Very well. Later, then."

Grinning, he rolled his tongue over her in one long, lazy lick that made her forget whatever nonsense she'd been worried about a moment ago. Then he moved over her. Skimming his mouth along her stomach, he paused to suckle each breast until she clung to him, her hands clutching his shoulders.

He continued his torment, pausing to nip at her earlobe. His hot breath and the brush of his lips against the sensitive flesh made her tremble. "I love it when you blush, even your ears color."

She wanted to say something in return, but she couldn't think of anything at the moment. Couldn't think at all. Her breasts tingled from the crisp hairs on his chest as the hard length of him settled with purpose at the cradle of her thighs. Edging forward, he only penetrated her flesh the barest degree, and yet she felt the sting of being stretched, the faint burn of forewarning.

Kissing her again, hungry, coaxing, he slowly pushed that rearing flesh deeper into the slick, confining grip of her body. He looked down at her, his gaze fiercely tender, his breathing labored with restraint. Then he withdrew marginally and suddenly pitched forward, breaking into the shrinking channel.

Jacinda cried out, gripping the shoulder muscles that flexed beneath her hands as hot tears slipped out from the corners of her eyes. It had been so beautiful and thrilling . . . until she was impaled. Her body tried to stretch to accommodate his flesh, but she didn't think it was possible. Now she was beginning to wonder why she'd been so eager.

Making no apologies, he brushed her lips in a tender caress. "There'll be no more pain now, darling."

She didn't believe him. Even *his* expression revealed the strain of agony. Yet because of those lines of tension etched over his brow and cording his neck, she forgave him, taking comfort in the lock of his embrace, but not in his certainty.

However, he took his time to prove that there would only be pleasure from that point forward.

As the storm rumbled past and all that was left was the quiet music of the rain hitting rocks and branches, he roused her in slow, unfolding kisses. The gentle cambering of his hips increased by degree into leisurely thrusts.

Her breath began to quicken once more, and she was surprised to find herself anticipating each deep push and slow, thick withdrawal. Gradually, the tight cinch of her flesh welcomed his intrusion, the pleasurable friction, the unhurried rhythm. She held on, gripping his shoulders, his nape, his back, anywhere her hands could reach.

His kisses deepened, the rock of his hips more intense, focused, bringing her throbbing pulse to life again. He drove inside her, insistent, unleashing a frantic sort of restlessness, her body clenching tight without giving way. The maddening sensation robbed her of speech and stole her breath. Desperate to assuage this terrible constriction, she wrapped her arms tighter around him, her legs winding around his hips. Still, there was no release, only this tireless, rigid throbbing.

She broke from his kiss, her lips skimming along his cheek, tasting the salt of his sweat on the tip of her tongue. When he shifted, lurching out of rhythm, he set off a torrent of tingles cascading beneath her skin. And suddenly she fractured, her body pitching upward, quaking in unending pulses, the ecstasy wringing needy mewls from her throat.

Crispin issued a choked grunt. Jolting back, he spent himself in long, scorching strokes against her inner thigh.

Then he came down on her, his labored breath hot in her ear as he gathered her close and pulled her with him as he rolled to his side. Her legs tangled with his, her head resting against his shoulder.

Curled naturally into his embrace, she caught her breath after a moment. "Very well, you no longer owe me an apology."

He kissed her temple, lingering as he skimmed a hand down her back and her arms, touching and caressing. "You may say that now, but you have not seen the state of your undergarments. I may well owe you another restitution. But later, when you are snug and warm in your bed. For now, as much as I would love to remain just as we are, I do not want you to catch a chill."

"If you keep me in your arms, I will not," she said, nuzzling him and pressing kisses against his neck, licking more of his tantalizing sweat. Never before this moment, would she have imagined doing such a thing and enjoying it so thoroughly. She wanted to taste him everywhere and gained a new understanding about the bottom right-hand corner of Crispin's ledger. Even so, the reason behind having her name there still made her blush.

"But, darling, with the worst of the storm gone, the servants are likely searching for us."

Imagining how embarrassing it would be to have Mr. Fellows stumble upon them helped her make the decision. She did not want this moment to be part of Mr. Fellows's *History of Rydstrom Hall.*

Sitting up quicker than she ought to have done, she felt a twinge of soreness between her thighs, along with the thick dampness of his seed. But Crispin seemed to read her mind, and in a dreamlike daze, she watched him reach down with a handkerchief to wipe away the residue that melded with the pink-tinged traces of her virginity. He brushed his lips over her temple and cheek.

Then she saw the evidence of her destroyed undergarments and reality intruded. There was no way to wipe away this evidence. "What am I going to tell Lucy? Surely, she will guess what happened while you and I were waiting out the storm."

"Tell her whatever you like." He tilted her chin up to meet his gaze and kissed her. "We will be man and wife soon enough, and rumors will not matter."

"Man and wife? But, Crispin, there are so many—"

He kissed her again, long and deep, causing sensual tremors to roll through her, clenching sweetly and leaving her breathless. "Later, darling. With your tendency to disagree with me, I would rather be in a better position to persuade you . . . for hours on end."

Chapter 29

> "And have you never known the pleasure and triumph of a lucky guess?—I pity you.—I thought you cleverer—for, depend upon it a lucky guess is never merely luck. There is always some talent in it."
>
> JANE AUSTEN, *Emma*

When Crispin and Jacinda returned to the castle, Mr. Fellows greeted them with his usual bow, his expression impassive as if the pair of them weren't drenched from head to toe, and the lord of the manor wasn't missing all of his waistcoat buttons. Even so, Jacinda fought the urge to blush and burrow deeper into the coat Crispin had draped around her shoulders.

"Your Grace, I am ever so grateful that you and Miss Bourne are safe. I've taken the liberty of ordering hot water from the kitchens."

"Very good," Crispin said, keeping Jacinda at his side, her arm tucked within his. "Have a bathing tub assembled in Miss Bourne's chamber, and send a tea tray as well. And Fellows . . . is the entire castle aware of Miss Bourne's absence during the storm?"

Jacinda lost her battle against the blush as she watched Mr. Fellows carefully not look in her direction.

Clearing his throat and keeping his shoulders straight, the butler simply said, "No, sir. I had every confidence in Your Grace's abilities to keep her safe."

Crispin reached out and laid a hand on Mr. Fellows's shoulder without saying a word.

After this brief exchange, Crispin led Jacinda down the hall, not slowing his stride until they reached the arch of the library. Then he pulled her inside the room and kissed her soundly, turning her knees into wobbly jelly. "I'm going to inform my aunt that we—"

"Not yet," she interrupted, out of breath and clinging to him. "I haven't given my answer and marriage requires careful consideration."

"Rather the horse before the cart at this point, darling." He chuckled, nuzzling the underside of her jaw, eroding her resolve. "But do not fear, I was only going to tell my aunt that I would be taking dinner in my rooms this evening. After venturing into the storm, I should think that you might have caught a chill and will be in your rooms as well?"

"You never allowed me to catch a chill," she teased, but he made a liar of her when his mouth grazed the sensitive place just behind her ear and a shiver tumbled through her.

Grinning again, he pressed his lips to hers. "Perhaps I should ensure that you don't by escorting you to your chamber this instant."

Loving this new intimacy between them, she was tempted to give in. And she found herself wondering if this was what marriage to Rydstrom would be like, verbal parries interlaced with a constant hum of desire, the sweet ache rolling over her skin and through her limbs, that yearning to be close to him, flesh to flesh.

In such a moment, it was difficult to recall any of her reservations. But she did, nonetheless.

With gentle pressure against his shoulders, she stepped back. "We have much to discuss."

He growled his disapproval but conceded with another promise of "later."

Yet when *later* came, Jacinda realized that Crispin intended to make it impossible to resist him.

The instant her bedchamber door closed, he took her in his arms and kissed her. Through his shirtwaist and green-and-gold silk banyan, hungry murmurs rumbled in his chest as if the hours apart had been weeks or months. And clearly it was a mistake to have donned only her night rail. The ruffles and thin cotton were no barrier beneath the heat of his ardent, capable hands, and the gentle scratch of the fabric over her skin only heightened her own appetite.

She'd missed him, too. And when his fingers splayed over her back, sliding down to the curve of her derriere, hitching her against the hard length of him, her determination to sort out matters nearly gave way to the need to assuage the tender, aching pulse, deep inside her body.

"I've been thinking," she said, breaking away from the enticing pull of his lips and panting. But he stayed the course, his mouth blazing a wicked, tantalizing trail down her neck. "Considering the circumstances . . . it is possible that our actions were a bit . . . rash. *Oh*—that's nice. Right there—But no. What was I saying? Oh yes. *Yessss.*" He found a new place near the curve of her shoulder that tingled all the way to her toes, making them curl and the rest of her argument spilled forth in one slow breath. "Right now, you might be feeling some regret and it would be perfectly understandable if you wish to rescind your offer."

He lifted his head, his lips glistening in the candlelight, his brow furrowed. "Do you regret what happened?"

"Not for a single instant." Impulsive, though she may be, she wasn't an idiot.

"Good. Neither do I." He grinned and began walking her back toward the bed. "Now, with that settled, I believe it's time to demonstrate those dreams I've been having . . ."

Face flushed, her heart sputtered into a lopsided rhythm, unsure of whether to be nervous or intrigued. In the end, she couldn't decide. Her womb shifted, clenching in aroused curiosity, and her palms grew damp in maidenly discomfiture.

"But surely you never anticipated this occurrence," she

persisted, hands splaying over his parted shirtwaist, her fingertips weaving into the crisp brown hair on his chest. "How could you want to marry the very woman who—as you said—carelessly put her own life in danger in order to expose your secret?"

Once again, he lifted his head and nodded on an exhale of apparent compliance. "You are right, Jacinda. I need to clear up the matter that I thoughtlessly put between us."

Instead of continuing toward the narrow tester bed in the smaller chamber she now inhabited, he took her hand and led her to the tufted rose chair, angled near the hearth. Turning, he folded his broad frame into the seat and pulled her onto his lap, situating her against the undeterred hardness at her hip.

He kissed the tip of her nose and skimmed his fingers through the locks of her unbound tresses, brushing them away from her cheek. "Darling, I was never afraid that you would do something deliberate to hurt Sybil if you discovered the truth. What frightened me was your tendency to act on impulse and not think about the repercussions until later."

Her cheeks grew hot. "Under the circumstances, it seems I have not changed much from the person you knew in London."

A slow, wicked grin lifted one corner of his mouth, his hand gripping the curve of her hip and drawing her closer until her breasts were flush against his chest. "I've come to believe that impulsiveness is one of your many fine qualities."

"Of course you would say that now."

He waggled his brows and kissed her, but all too briefly before he drew back and revealed the sudden serious set of his features. "Teasing aside, I am in earnest, and I also am in awe of your tenacity and courage. Though, as for the latter, I should rather keep you safe by my side."

Her heart fluttered at the sincerity of his words, speaking more than truth as they tunneled into her. So much had altered between them that it seemed they were different people. And yet, they were not.

"I still do not understand the reason you have kept Sybil's illegitimacy such a well-guarded secret," she continued, "and one that you haven't even shared with your aunt."

"Because I could not bear it if Sybil suffered the life that so many illegitimate daughters of noble blood do. I can see doubt in your expression—your eyes reveal you, darling—but it is the truth. There is a great unfairness, and I know this because I was once part of it."

"The set of your jaw tells me that you would rather not go on, but if we are to be married—"

"*When*, Jacinda."

"If," she said firmly. After all, wouldn't such an impulsive creature be doing them both a disservice by leaping into a marriage that he had wanted no part of just a day ago? "I should like to know everything about you."

"Even if it involves another woman?"

Oh. She had not expected that response. After hearing in the village that she'd been his only visitor in four years, she'd hoped that he hadn't had any other women in his life. But that was foolish, she supposed. He was a virile man with—from what she gathered earlier—a healthy appetite for pleasure. But did she truly want to learn about how another woman affected his life?

Still, the answer was yes. Hesitant, she nodded.

He drew in a deep breath and released it slowly before pressing his lips to hers in a soft kiss, lingering as if he thought it might be the last. "The day my parents died, I'd come home to request additional income from one of the properties I was set to inherit. I'd learned that the land was making a tidy profit and had a mind to take a mistress."

He paused, allowing her to absorb this, and she felt an acidic rise of unmistakable jealousy, burning in her stomach. Instantly, Jacinda wanted to know the name of this harlot, to hunt her down and . . . Well, she wasn't sure what next, but she felt she had to do something to make sure this *woman* knew that Crispin was Jacinda's, and hers alone.

"And did you?"

"No," he said gently, a sadness in his eyes as he cupped her face, his thumb coasting over her bottom lip. "What I did was even worse. Are you certain you want to hear the rest?"

Nervous now, she drew in a shaky, but resolved, breath. "I am."

He swallowed and dropped his hand. "I was proud, boasting over the noble thing I was doing by becoming the protector of a marquess's bastard daughter, and giving her the best life she could hope to have. And I was thoroughly surprised by my father's reaction. He became incensed, railing that I'd become selfish and reckless, acting as though I was entitled to behave without morals. And at the age of four and twenty, full of my own self-righteousness, I was not about to let him shine such a sanctimonious light on me. So, I responded in kind.

"We argued for hours. When he threatened to cut me off altogether, I stormed through the corridors of Rydstrom Hall, vowing never to return. Yet, at the door, I met Sybil for the first time, and she asked to see her father. *Our* father, I quickly surmised." He paused, his mink brown lashes drawing together as if pained, his gaze turning distant.

"Brewing my own outrage, I found him in the morning room and began ranting about his hypocrisy, not realizing that my mother was nearby. And at the time, I loathe to say, I did not care. I only thought of myself. Then, leaving a path of destruction in my wake, I prepared to leave once more, but then the storm came." He exhaled brokenly and fixed his sorrowful gaze on hers. "The rest, you know."

She took his face in her hands. "Oh, my dearest Crispin. You've carried this burden with you all this time, but you cannot blame yourself for what happened."

Carefully, he encircled her wrists and drew her hands

down. "They wouldn't have been arguing on the cliffs, if not for me."

"I don't agree." She shook her head with absolute certainty. "They had much to discuss that day, and I'm sure they'd wanted privacy to do so. As for that, they could have just as easily been in a section of Rydstrom Hall that collapsed around them. Just because they were near the cliffs is not your fault." But she could see that he did not agree with her. "If I would have fallen today, would you have blamed yourself as well?"

"Of course. I am the one who sent you running out in the storm."

"No, you didn't. I chose to run out into the storm like a ninny. I chose to stand too close to the edge. But in my own defense, it hadn't *seemed* that close at the time. Nevertheless, I stood there, knowing how dangerous it was. If anything should have happened, it would have been my own fault. Not yours. Therefore, you must let go of your guilt and be at peace."

He slid his hand to the nape of her neck and drew her forehead against his, closing his eyes. "I shall take the matter under consideration."

"Mmm . . ." she murmured, doubtful, but pressed her lips to his. "And so, for the past four years, you've nobly protected Sybil from a scornful society until a rather curious young woman found herself on your beach without a memory."

His focus returned to her, his mouth giving way to a tender grin. "And I am all the better for it."

And there it was again, that happy rise of bubbles in her lungs and the glad, eager beat of her heart. Oh, how she loved this man.

Her fingertips wandered aimlessly over his shoulders, down the lapels of his banyan, and found a loose golden thread. Absently, she plucked at it. "Whatever happened to your mistress? Did she ever come to . . . visit you here?"

"She found another protector, and no. In the past four

years, there has been no one but you. And that is the way it will always be."

Pleased by his answer, she grinned, sliding out of his lap to stand in the space between his parted thighs. "No mistress at all?"

"Only the mistress of Rydstrom Hall. My wife. At least, when she finally consents." He reached out as if to pull her back, and likely to convince her.

But Jacinda had other plans. She evaded his capture, skirting out of his grasp, and walked backward toward the bed. "And she, I imagine, wouldn't ever have a need to find a lover."

Crispin grinned darkly, rakishly, and rose from the chair in a sinuous, predatory motion. "I will keep her well satisfied."

A thrill pulsed through her, hot and startling in its intensity. She could already feel herself grow damp and he wasn't even touching her. Yet. "And when you awaken, aroused in the middle of the night, will you write her name in your ledger?"

"No," he said when he reached her in four prowling strides. Taking her by the waist, he hauled her into his arms, settling her hips against the fall of his trousers and the unashamedly hard length of male flesh. Then he lifted her, sipping the startled gasp from her lips, his purposeful steps guiding her to the edge of the mattress and peeling away her nightdress, inch by inch. "I'll turn to her in our bed, slide my hands, my mouth over her body, until she is equally feverish. Until her neck arches back in the pillow and my name spills from her lips like a prayer. Until she trembles and cries out, with my flesh buried deep inside her." A blur of white cotton sailed overhead and he nudged her backward onto the coverlet, his gaze darkening at the sight of her sprawled naked before him. "And she'll never forget that she's mine."

Chapter 30

"It was a melancholy change; and Emma could not but sigh over it, and wish for impossible things."

JANE AUSTEN, *Emma*

For a brief, decadent few hours, it had been easy to imagine herself as Crispin's bride.

Had she been able to form a coherent thought, then perhaps before he'd left her chamber at dawn, she might have forced him to have the conversation that they'd been avoiding—his need for a wealthy bride in order to repair Rydstrom Hall.

Instead, she'd given over to his kisses and allowed him to fulfill his promise of feasting on her body. When she was sated—and frankly, quite awed by all the shameful, delicious things he'd done to her—he tucked her drowsy, pliant body against his and settled the coverlet and his banyan over her. And while all of that was like living in a wondrous dream, afterward he surprised her once again.

She could not help but smile wistfully at the memory as she stared down at her hand.

"What are you doing?" she'd asked, watching in the low flicker of candlelight as he tugged that gold silk thread from his banyan and began to wind it around her finger.

"I should think it obvious. I'm tying a string around your finger, so that you cannot forget that you are mine." He'd pressed a firm kiss to the top of her head. "And I'm tying it to this finger to leave room for the gold band you'll have on the other when we marry."

And that time, she did not correct him by arguing with an *if.*

Now, however, in the excruciatingly bright light of morning, Jacinda was all too aware of how a moment of passion could lead to lifelong regret. Not on her part but, she feared, on his.

After all, knowing how deeply rooted his sense of duty was to his feelings of guilt, how could she not feel this way? If she had done *her* duty as a sensible maiden by guarding her chastity instead of practically flinging it at him, he never would have proposed. Sensibly, she knew this to be true.

So where did that leave them today?

With a need to have a brutally honest conversation.

Even so, she did not leap out of bed in a rush to speak to Crispin. Instead, she lingered, mindful of the tender, intimate places on her body, and decided to decipher the puzzle box waiting on the bedside table. With her thoughts elsewhere, however, it was impossible to concentrate. She only pushed and prodded absently, lounging against the bolster pillow as Lucy quietly swept around, preparing tea and laying out clothes.

"That's a pretty melody, miss," Lucy said, bringing over a cup of tea. "I didn't know that was a music box all this time."

Absently listening to the notes, Jacinda hummed along. "It was my mother's. I imagine that Ainsley must have—"

Jacinda bolted upright and stared wide-eyed at the box as a kaleidoscope of images flooded her mind.

Suddenly, she remembered how her mother would wind it up and let it play while she brushed her long blond hair, sitting on the vanity stool in their little cottage. "My mother's hair smelled like lemons and she always hiccupped when she laughed. And Briar, my younger sister, does the same thing, and she looks just like our mother. And Ainsley . . . Oh, Ainsley will be so disappointed about what I have done. There will be no living with her after this."

Tears were streaming down Jacinda's face and she couldn't tell if the sound bubbling out of her throat was laughter or sobs. Uncle Ernest would understand, she imagined, thinking of the dear man who knew every emotion inside the human heart.

"Miss Bourne, you have your memory back!" Lucy shouted with joy while black tea sloshed over the rim, into the saucer and onto the rug. "Do you remember meeting me as well?"

Jacinda nodded, that last day in London coming back to her in detail, starting with her encounter with Crispin in his study. *Oh dear.* "I remember seeing you crying as you put your advertisement in the window of the servant's registry. I thought it was fate that we should have met right then and there."

"Yes, that's just what you said, miss!" She set the teacup down on the table and bent to blot the rug with a serviette. "Now you can write to your sisters and invite them here for the wedding."

Jacinda had never said she'd intended to marry Rydstrom. But when Lucy had discovered the remains of the underclothes, she'd leapt to conclusions, all the while vowing to keep their secret from the other maids until *after* the wedding. And Jacinda, too immersed in a dreamlike afterglow, hadn't corrected her.

Now she had more problems to face than ever before.

His wedding. Her sisters.

The agency.

Oh dear. Oh dear. Oh dear.

She'd made a terrible mistake by coming to Whitcrest. She was Crispin's matchmaker, not his potential bride!

But she already knew that, at least the latter part. He needed to marry an heiress, and someone good and kind, too. Not someone who would badger his solicitor or steal into his study. Not someone reckless enough to hire a maid, travel to Whitcrest, and nearly drown in the sea for the sole purpose of ferreting out a secret to see if he was the *wrong sort.* Not a woman who acted without thought to consequence or the repercussions of her actions.

A woman like that did not deserve him.

In that moment, sitting there with his gold thread tied around her finger, Jacinda realized something heartbreaking. *She* was the wrong sort. Not him. He was perfect, and would make the best husband. And he deserved far better than her.

The deluge continued to roll down her cheeks as she anticipated the conversation she must have with him. Crispin, of course, would state that because he took her virginity he must marry her. It was a matter of duty and honor. Knowing him, she imagined that he'd already spent the morning thinking of ways to keep Rydstrom Hall standing since he now planned to marry a woman with no dowry.

Now, because of her, the home he loved would fall into further ruin, and Sybil's chances of marrying well in the future would all but disappear.

Jacinda couldn't let that happen.

Wiping her tears on the sleeve of her nightdress, she said, "I'm afraid we'll have to leave for London today, Lucy."

Standing up from the rug, Lucy's features listed downward into a puzzled frown. "Whyever would we do that?"

Because it was the only thing Jacinda could do. She had to find him an heiress and complete the assignment she was given. Though, not wanting to list all the reasons, she kept her response simple and vague. "With my memory intact, I want to see my sisters. And my uncle as well."

But her heart shattered into a thousand pieces at the thought of finding Crispin a bride. She didn't want to at all and would much rather continue onward, regardless of the consequences. This, she knew, was further proof that she was the wrong sort. The right sort would be selfless at a time like this.

And yet, Jacinda still wished she knew of a way to keep him *and* give him all that he needed.

Oh, if only she had a small fortune! Or, at least, was very good friends with someone staring into the chasm of death who might bequeath one to her in the near future. But that was a self-serving, greedy thought for which she should be ashamed. And she would be, later, when she wasn't so preoccupied.

It was absolutely abominable that Crispin was being forced to marry for money at all when his aunt could just as easily . . .

Jacinda's thoughts veered suddenly to Lady Hortense.

She had every means available to save Rydstrom Hall from ruin. And quite possibly, allow Crispin the freedom to marry for love instead of duty. At least, when he found a woman worthy of him.

"It will be a busy morning for us, miss," Lucy said. "Would you like me to ring for your breakfast tray or would you rather dress?"

"I will dress straightaway," she said, flinging back the coverlet. Jacinda needed all of her armor in place before she faced Lady Hortense.

"CONGRATULATIONS, MISS Bourne. Now that your memory has returned, you will make fine progress on the list," Lady Hortense said from the throne in her dressing room. Dipping her fingertips in an open jar of balm, she generously applied it to the column of her throat. "Perhaps, even by the end of this morning."

Jacinda stood stiffly in the gilded room, wishing that she'd come here with a prepared speech, rather than only a general idea of what she might say. "I'm afraid, my lady, that I will be returning to London posthaste. However, I should like to speak with you briefly before I leave."

"London? Why should you need to return when all the information your uncle's agency possesses is on the paper I gave you?"

"As I have stated before, the list was incomplete." Not only that, but it had been crumpled and turned into ash days ago.

Lady Hortense expelled an impatient breath. Continuing her beauty regimen, she patted the skin beneath her jaw, her chin jutting upward. "Please, Miss Bourne, I cannot bear to hear any more of your misguided, romantic notions. The children of high-ranking nobility have an obligation to uphold, to marry for money and property, and that is that."

The words came forth by rote, as if they were rehearsed from some tragic play. It was still just as irritating to hear them now as it had been the first time. Even more so, with so much at stake. "Didn't you ever long for happiness?"

"I am quite content," she said sharply, her teeth clenching as if the subject flicked a raw nerve. Lowering her hands, she fixed her attention on Jacinda. "Do you truly believe that Rydstrom Hall could remain standing simply because its occupants were happy? There is not enough land to allow the estate to support itself, not without a profitable marriage."

There it was again, the reminder that Jacinda was trying to escape. But it was futile. Crispin needed an heiress, and only an heiress would do.

An icy, harried sort of desperation filled Jacinda. She went cold all over, her fingers numb, her thoughts turning to every possibility that might alter the inevitable outcome of this hopeless conversation. "Perhaps you could provide aid to your nephew. After all, you said that you'd done so for your brother."

Lady Hortense frowned, gripping the carved claw arms

of her chair. "Miss Bourne, you forget yourself. I will not be spoken to with such familiarity. And while it may be true that I assisted my brother, he never borrowed a farthing. A true gentleman would never stoop to such behavior. My brother sold the deeds of several properties to me. As for my nephew, he has nothing to sell."

There has to be a way, she kept thinking over and over again. Yet each path her mind took only led her to a wall of impossibility. Well . . . not every path. There was one, and only one—leave Whitcrest and find Crispin an heiress.

"You have taken quite an interest in my nephew's affairs," Lady Hortense added, eyes narrowed with suspicion. "So much so, that I wonder if I should contact your uncle regarding an inappropriate degree of fondness."

Jacinda swallowed. "That is not necessary, I assure you. As a representative of the Bourne Matrimonial Agency, I am merely conveying our collective wish that all of our clients have the freedom to choose whichever candidate best suits him or her."

"Then, I should think, finishing the list should be your sole occupation."

Chapter 31

"You think I ought to refuse him then . . ."
JANE AUSTEN, *Emma*

"We cannot marry," Jacinda said, walking into the study.

Crispin looked up from his desk and felt a grin curve his lips, along with a contented thrumming in his heart.

"Darling, you have an unfortunate habit of saying unsettling things every time you walk into this room." Placing his quill in the stand, he rose from the chair and stepped around to greet her with a kiss. But only then did he notice her pale, troubled expression. Taking her hand, he felt a chill emanate from her soft skin. "Are you unwell?"

"We cannot marry," she repeated, slipping free of his grasp and stepping apart from him as if she were in earnest. "I remember everything."

He frowned. "What do you mean?"

"This morning, it was as if I'd never forgotten at all. I can recall each memory from my childhood and all the ones"—she blushed, her ears turning pink as her gaze held his—"since."

"Good. I am glad that your memories have returned and, most especially, that you have not forgotten the most recent ones that are causing your cheeks to color. Because of what happened between us, we *will* marry." His tone was indisputably final, his jaw clenched as he crossed the room and closed the door for privacy. "A gentleman does not take a woman's virginity and leave her to face the repercussions alone. Now, I do not know if you are having second thoughts, but I am not."

"Then you are not thinking clearly, just as you weren't yesterday when you found me by the cliffs," she stated, her gaze imploring.

Ah. Now he understood. This morning's meeting was her way to seek his reassurance.

His shoulders relaxed. Returning to her, he took her hands and settled them over his heart, where they belonged. He took comfort in the fact that she stayed, allowing him to smooth his hands over her shoulders and down her back in an ambling caress. "As I thought I'd made clear last night, I do not regret what happened between us. Far from it."

"This isn't about regret." She looked down at her hands and, disconcertingly, covered the one bearing the finger with the golden thread. "You require an heiress. My paltry dowry would not even buy the linens for Rydstrom Hall, let alone afford the repairs it requires."

Leave it to Jacinda never to say what a deflowered virgin was expected to say. She should be wailing, demanding that he marry her out of honor. Telling him that she loved him and would do anything to be with him. Not saying all the things that had passed through his mind over the course of the past hours.

He already knew that he'd neglected to think of the longevity of Rydstrom Hall and even Sybil when he'd asked Jacinda to be his wife. He'd only been thinking of satisfying the demands of his heart. It hadn't once felt wrong, but now she was making him question whether or not they'd both been swept away in the moment.

"I've thought this through. Using materials from the rooms I've sealed off, I can make the most essential repairs on my own. I may not have the skills of a mason or master carpenter, but I've done a fair job of it so far."

She expelled a breath and shook her head. "While it is

admirable, it is not a true solution. If you will not think of yourself or your home, you must think of Sybil and her future."

"Circumstances have altered since then."

"You know that I am right. I can see it in your eyes, and that twig vein on your forehead is glaring at me." She traced that vein with her fingertip, her palm cupping his cheek, briefly, before she slipped away again, leaving his arms empty and useless without her to hold.

He remedied that quickly enough. Closing the distance, he took her face in his hands and kissed her. Not tenderly, but with an urgency she needed to understand. She was his, damn it all! And when her lips parted on a gasp, he used that to his advantage, laying claim to her mouth, his hands drifting down her body and feeling her rise against him in a glorious wave of surrender.

Yes. This is where you should be, he thought, destroying any doubts. He never should have left her bed, and she should never leave his side. As if in full agreement, she clung to him, each breath drawing them closer. And he swallowed down her soft, almost frantic, whimpers, reassuring her with the heat of his hands.

But, in truth, it was more of a comfort to him. He wanted to lose himself for hours in the taste of her kiss and the perfectly off-center alignment of their mouths. And she wanted this, too. He knew it. He could feel it in the way their hearts beat in the same frenzied rhythm.

Believing that he'd proven his point, he drew back marginally, ready to lock the door and make a better use of the sofa if she required further proof. She sagged against him, lips damp, cheeks flushed.

"There now," he crooned, feeling triumphant as he skimmed his lips over her brow. "Let's have no more of that talk."

He shouldn't have been surprised when she didn't listen.

"If I'd never had amnesia, none of this would have happened. You would have continued to despise me, just as you did when we were in London."

"Jacinda," he warned, but she continued, her hands leaving their perch on his shoulders and drifting down to his wrists, extricating herself.

"Yet because you have such a strong will when it comes to your duty, you took me in and for that, and so much more, I will always"—her breath hitched—"be grateful." Then, lifting her chin, she brushed his favorite lock away from her forehead and moved to the door. "I have your list of requirements for a wife on my desk at the agency, or at least what you gave me at the time. Nowhere on it does it state that you desire a woman with less than two hundred pounds to her name and I . . . I will return to London and endeavor to send you a bridal candidate who will be all that you could desire. I was hired to find the right sort of bride for you, and that is what I shall do."

He swallowed, his fist clenched. "You're planning to leave today?"

Hand on the door, her head jerked in a nod. "If you would allow me the use of your carriage. And please . . . if you would tell Sybil that I will not be able to see her today for her lessons."

He refused to believe this was happening. Surely, she would come to her senses. Perhaps, if she thought more about what she was leaving behind, she would understand her mistake. "You are more than a tutor to her."

"And she is more to me"—she looked away and drew in a stuttered breath—"both of you are."

"Then stay." He hated the strained tremor in his own voice, the feeble coldness rushing through him. Her tenacious, impulsive nature was supposed to keep her here, not drive her back to London.

"There is no other way, Crispin. I'm sorry," she said, tears glistening in her eyes as she gave him the apology he never wanted, and then she swept from the room.

"IT LOOKS like a fine day for a journey, Mr. Fellows," Jacinda said as he helped her on with her coat later that morning. Her voice was high, tight, and she was doing her best to hold back tears.

"Aye, miss." He sniffed, but tucked his handkerchief out of sight as she turned to face him. "Soon, Rydstrom Hall will have flowers in bloom. Every year in the spring it's quite a sight to behold."

But she would not be here to see it, not even the seeds she had dropped during the sowing ceremony, or those of the bluebells still tucked in the pouch at the bottom of her satchel beside her volume of *Emma*. "I imagine it is. I hope you put a button rose in your lapel and think of me."

"I will, miss, most assuredly." His cloudy eyes misted over as he cleared his throat and moved to the door.

It was time to leave, but Crispin was not here to say farewell. Then again, she imagined he'd said as much in the study, sending her off with a kiss that was now branded into her soul. If she hadn't been certain of his determination to uphold his word of honor, to marry the woman who'd given her virginity to him, that kiss had convinced her of his sincerity.

This only furthered her good opinion of him. Yet, in time, she knew he would have come to regret his decision as the home he loved fell to waste around him. *This was for the best*, she reminded herself, just as she had done for every second in the last hour.

Still, she wished he was here. She needed just one last, lingering look to keep inside her heart and take with her.

Turning to go, she stopped when she heard the rapid clatter of hard-soled shoes on the stone. Her breath stalled when she saw Sybil rushing up to her, eyes round with worry. She flung her arms around Jacinda's waist, clasping her tightly.

Jacinda squeezed her eyes shut, her heart ripping open. She did not want to leave and every moment she lingered, made it all the harder to go.

Bending down, she brushed the golden locks away from Sybil's unusually pale face. "I shall write to you twice each week, and we will continue your French lessons. And I'll want to know how your book is progressing."

Sybil shook her head wordlessly, tears streaming down her cheeks.

"Dearest, I remembered today that I have a very important occupation. You see, I am a matchmaker. My family was hired to find Rydstrom a bride, and I cannot stay in Whitcrest when they are all in London, waiting to meet him."

And suddenly Crispin strode in, glowering fiercely, the muscle along his jaw ticking when he swallowed.

She continued to speak to Sybil, but she kept her gaze on him. "Just think of our dear friend Miss Emma Woodhouse. Making matches was very important because she wanted the people dearest to her to be happy. Yet, for all the days of her life, she would continue to love them with all her heart, even if she couldn't be near them."

Sybil offered a small, sniffling nod, though it did little to console either of them, Jacinda supposed. They'd grown too attached to each other, and thinking about leaving left her in misery. Why, oh why, did her memory have to return now, reminding her that her whole world was in London, not Whitcrest?

Her heart did not seem to understand this and lurched inside her, causing a wealth of tears to clog her throat. She pressed her fingers to her lips, hoping to stem the flow. But his name came forth, broken and desperate. *"Crispin."*

He moved a step forward, his hands clenched at his side. But Jacinda, like an awful coward, slipped away and dashed through the door.

CRISPIN COULDN'T breathe. His chest felt tight, raw, as if it had been split open and hollowed out, the contents ripped to pieces and scattered into a state of permanent disorder.

He couldn't live like this, not without her here. He needed to stop her before she left, but all of her sensible arguments weighted him down, rooting him to the floor.

A wheezing sob left Sybil as she rushed up to him. Kneeling down, he held her and let her bury her face against his coat and cry for as long as she needed.

"Nephew, who is this servant girl and why, pray tell, is she blubbering in your arms?" Aunt Hortense said from behind him.

His back stiffened but he was past the point of caring about secrets any longer. They had not served him well. "Aunt Hortense, I should like to introduce you to Sybil Montague, your niece."

Part 3

Chapter 32

". . . and she had then only to sit and think of what she had lost."

JANE AUSTEN, *Emma*

London
Two weeks later

In the days that followed, Jacinda spent the majority of the time focused on her place at the Bourne Matrimonial Agency, diligently working through the tasks that had gone neglected in her absence. There were many people waiting for their perfect match. And she needed to stay occupied or else she would think about everything she'd lost—her purpose, her heart, her soul, her reason for . . .

"What happened to your desk?" Briar asked as she walked into the sitting room they'd turned into an office.

Jacinda quickly blinked away those pesky, ever-present tears and looked down at the polished grain of the rosewood. Her inkstand was to the right, a neat stack of applications sat in a basket to her left, and *Emma* was tucked safely out of sight. "I see nothing out of place."

"Precisely. I should hardly know that I am in your office at all without a mountain of papers strewn on every surface. But perhaps that part of your memory didn't return. Ainsley will surely be glad of that, as it will save her from grousing twenty-three times each day." Briar's teasing expression abruptly transformed to one of worry. She'd worn those tight furrows over the bridge of her nose often since Jacinda's return, and came forward with a quick embrace. "Oh, that was thoughtless of me. I did not mean to bring up all that unpleasantness."

Jacinda shook her head and leaned in to kiss Briar's cheek. "Fear not. I have no unpleasant memories of Whitcrest. The people were all quite amiable and welcoming. I just have many matches to investigate and they occupy my mind."

For the most part, she worked by rote, numbly sorting the pertinent information on the application, waiting for those curiosity sensors to prickle with the alarm that told her she needed to investigate. But that never came. Every application in front of her was simply a name on paper, seemingly honest people who were willing to put their fate in her hands. And she could not help but feel they were all fools to rely on her—the woman who thoughtlessly fell in love with a man she could never marry.

"As I have said before, and *many* times," Briar stressed, "I am ready to add to my list of responsibilities. I think I could be quite a good investigator, if given the chance. I have my own set of skills to bring to the agency, and they do not all revolve around bringing someone tea."

"Of course not, *p*—" Jacinda stopped. She was about to call her *pet*, as she'd always done, but lately she'd started seeing her younger sister in a new light. While she might resemble their frail, brokenhearted mother, Briar was strong in her own way.

Looking at her sister now, Jacinda would hate for anyone to underestimate her. So instead of calling her *pet*, she lifted the basket from her desk. "Thank you, Briar. I would appreciate any assistance you can offer."

"Truly?" She beamed, so hopeful it was nearly heartbreaking. At Jacinda's nod, Briar embraced her again, her affectionate nature never denied. "I am so glad you are safe and back with us."

"You've said that before." Their reunion had been tearful and solemn, each of them reminded of what might have been lost.

After a day of weeping over each other, gorging themselves on Mrs. Darden's orange scones with fig preserves, retelling stories of their past, and asking Jacinda questions that she answered as briefly as possible, they'd fallen back into their routine. It was a comfort, of sorts.

Briar grinned cheekily, her blue eyes dancing. "Oh, but I *mean* it this time. You are, after all, my favorite sister."

Jacinda laughed, the sound quiet and somewhat brittle from disuse. She hadn't had much of a reason to laugh of late.

"Come now, what's this I hear?" Ainsley asked as she stepped through the adjoining door at the back of the Pomona green room. "A few hours ago when I was admiring the pink-striped trim you pinned to your bonnet, matching your dress, you said that I was your favorite. Your affections are rather fickle."

Briar sniffed. "I prefer to refer to them as *persuadable*."

"If only you and the Duke of Rydstrom had that in common," Ainsley said, holding up an opened letter. "He dismissed all of the candidates again."

Jacinda frowned, taking the page and feeling a pinch in the center of her heart at the sight of his precise handwriting. She folded it, hoping she would not give in and tuck this one under her pillow like she had with the other two. Though, she likely would. "Did he bother to give cause?"

"As before, he did not. It seems to me that he should amend his application and cite the specific criteria he wants in a wife. Did he mention having a change of heart before you left?"

"No," she said, the word choking her. He had not mentioned his heart at all. He'd only glowered at her, and it came as a great surprise that she missed that expression terribly. "I am certain that these debutantes meet his requirements of wealth, property, and an interest in travel. Certainly, there are a few with smaller dowries than others, but there simply are not that many heiresses among our client list."

Ainsley pursed her lips, nodding thoughtfully. "Perhaps it is time to acquire invitations to a few more balls and parties, in order to recruit more clients. I was dearly hoping that, once we found a bride for the duke, clients would come crawling through the door like that swarm of ants we once battled at the cottage. Mother and Mrs. Darden tried everything to get rid of them."

"Everything but finding those comfits that Briar was hiding in the cupboard," Jacinda said.

Briar gasped. "You knew about them?"

"Of course," Ainsley interjected, answering for Jacinda. "Nothing was safe from Jacinda the Great Snoop."

"I'm not certain I believe that," Briar said, crossing her arms. "After all, if you knew about my favorite spot to hide sweets, then why didn't you eat them?"

Jacinda shrugged. "I'm not partial to sweets."

"Yes, Jacinda prefers to feast on secrets," Ainsley said with a cool, but teasing stare.

Jacinda grinned, feeling a spark of her old self ignite. She was ready with a rejoinder about how she'd spied Ainsley yesterday, peering out the upstairs window to ogle Reed Sterling as he escorted, not one, but two unwieldy clients from his gambling establishment by the scruff of their necks, and how Ainsley's breath had fogged up the glass and her cheeks were flushed pink. For a woman who claimed to despise him, she certainly didn't mind the look of him.

But instead of bringing it up, Jacinda bit her tongue, and allowed her sister this secret.

"Then why did you not find whatever His Grace was hiding?" Briar asked.

"He has every quality one would expect in a duke—noble, kind, self-sacrificing. And other than the fact that he requires the assistance of a stone mason and carpenter, I found that he had nothing concealed." Thinking of an idea, Jacinda dipped her quill into the ink and jotted a quick note. It just so happened that they had two men, trained in those occupations, among their client list. Distractedly, she began to wonder if perhaps she might make a match for one or two of the women in Whitcrest.

"Aside from Uncle Ernest, this is the first time I've heard you speak so well of a man," Ainsley said, scrutinizing her. "I hope you did not form an attachment."

Briar clutched her hands to her breasts. "Oh, wouldn't it be romantic if Jacinda married the duke!"

"No, it would not." Ainsley was frowning, her hands on her hips and giving Jacinda that accusatory *I know you read my diary* look. "The Bourne Matrimonial Agency would become a laughingstock. Society would believe that we use our business to trap clients into marrying us."

"I wouldn't be too sure," Briar added. "I'm certain there would be quite a few clients encouraged by our determination to make a match, no matter the risk."

Jacinda drew in a shallow breath, wishing they could change the subject.

Now Ainsley was pinching the bridge of her nose, her eyes squeezed shut. "Regardless, we need to marry off our most prestigious client, posthaste."

"Then I will try my hand at it. Jacinda said I could help." Briar reached forward for the letter, but Jacinda stopped her, holding firm.

"I know I did, but not with this one," Jacinda said carefully, absently smoothing out the creases. "You may choose any of the others, you like. But I believe that I have already found the perfect bride for Rydstrom."

Ainsley lowered her hand. "Oh?"

Truthfully, Jacinda had seen this application on her desk the very first day she'd returned, but she had been avoiding sending the name to Crispin because there was no way he could resist this one. And part of her had been glad that he'd rejected all the other candidates. But Ainsley was right. Jacinda had to stop being selfish and let him go.

"Miss Throckmeyer of Hampshire," Jacinda said, finding the application too easily, as if it were taunting her. "She is one of four children and the only girl, her dowry is forty thousand pounds, and her father is willing to gift her husband with one of four properties. There is no way Rydstrom can resist her."

Chapter 33

"Prejudiced! I am not prejudiced."

Jane Austen, *Emma*

Whitcrest

"I'm sorry, Your Grace, but Sybil is taking breakfast in Lady Hortense's apartments this morning," Mrs. Hemple informed Crispin when he entered the family solar.

Annoyance building within him, he descended the stairs. He'd had enough.

For the past fortnight, he'd been keeping to his and Sybil's morning routine, but each time, his sister had sat across from him, sullen, angry, and refusing to acknowledge his presence.

He'd tried to talk to her about her lessons, tease her about her handwriting, do whatever he could to bring her out of her belligerent shell, but nothing worked. The little termagant was punishing him for allowing Jacinda to leave.

He didn't blame her. He'd spent every second of every day hating himself for letting her go, and feeling empty.

Though, of late, that hollowness was gradually filled with irritation and anger, fueled by the letters from the Bourne Matrimonial Agency—nothing more than coldly professional, unfeeling scraps of paper. As promised, Jacinda was doing her utmost to ensure he found a bride. But it felt like an assault on his heart instead.

More and more, as each day passed, he'd begun to wonder if—when Jacinda's memory returned—she'd realized that she'd been swept away in a moment of passion and her heart had not been involved.

Soon, he would have to end this torment, this constant plague that besieged him, and choose a bride. But he wondered if he would ever be able to forgive himself for it.

"Ah, there you are, nephew," Aunt Hortense said, her tone a little too cheerful to suit his current mood. "My niece and I have just finished breakfasting. I'm afraid there isn't much left of our small feast, though you are welcome to it."

As soon as Sybil saw him, her brow flattened into an unmistakable Montague glower. She lifted the napkin to her lips and set it down on the table as she stood. Then, after offering a nod to Aunt Hortense, she summarily left the room, walking past Crispin, head high, shoes slapping smartly over the stone floor.

He closed his eyes and squeezed his hand over the knot of tension at the back of his neck.

"It will pass, in time," Aunt Hortense said, her nose twitching in amusement.

Testy, he grumbled an inarticulate response and walked toward the window where a view of the gardens of the upper bailey awaited. And in the distance, he saw the round, rocky dome of the grotto.

Shortly after Jacinda had gone, he'd gone there to see if there was anything else left behind, other than the shredded remains of his soul. He'd found the lost buttons of his waistcoat, all but one, and after collecting them, threw them over the edge of the cliffs like wishing stones, one after the other. But it altered nothing, for on that very same day one of the old chimneys collapsed, reminding him of his duty.

"Sybil will come to forgive you, just as I did."

He looked over his shoulder, brows lifted. "This is news, indeed. When did you give up blaming me for what happened to your beloved brother?"

"No, nephew, I was speaking of forgiving you for keeping

Sybil a secret from me all this time," she said flippantly as if there was not still a wedge lodged firmly between them. "I shouldn't have pardoned you so quickly, but I find my spirits much cheered whenever I spend time with my niece. She is quite handsome, and accomplished. Why, I even believe she would make the perfect candidate for the Royal Academy."

"You are not taking her to London and exposing her to all manner of cruelties." He scowled, an edge of warning in every syllable.

Aunt Hortense, usually the one doling out the threats, arched her haughty brows, her lips pursed. "Then, we shall say that this is a matter to discuss at a later time."

"My answer will still be the same."

"Hmm . . . perhaps not," she said, but then changed the subject by lifting up a neat stack of correspondences. "Miss Bourne did a thorough job. I must say I am impressed. A complete list of accomplishments, income, property, lineage, and she even provided an accounting of temperament. She discovered details about these debutantes that I doubt even their mothers know about them."

He turned back to the window, gritting his teeth, fighting the urge to press his fist over the welling emptiness inside his chest where his heart used to reside. "Yes, Jacinda—*Miss Bourne*, rather—has a knack for discovering secrets."

"From what I see, each one meets your list of requirements. All you need to do is arrange a meeting with the one who most appeals to you."

"I find the list lacking."

"Come now"—she tsked—"not one of these women appeals to you? Why, any one of them could suit your needs."

Another surge of irritation swept through him like icy spindrifts. Oh yes, Jacinda had certainly been thorough. She even listed their best qualities. Yet he would have been happier to see a bit of spiteful slander instead. At least then, he would have known that she—

He broke off with a growl. Those thoughts were only an

exercise in futility. "No, there isn't a single name on that list that appeals to me."

"I am almost ready to believe that you intend to reject all of the names that the Bourne Agency supplies, and while Rydstrom Hall crumbles down around you."

He grunted a response, neither confirming nor denying. But it was true, nonetheless. If he must, he would close off room after room as they fell into disrepair. He knew that, in the end, he would not have it in him to marry anyone other than Jacinda.

Turning to leave, he saw Hortense standing in front of the door, hands clasped, and a foreign tenderness softening her gray eyes.

"I was wrong to have treated you so coldly, to have blamed you for my brother's death," she said solemnly. "I see now that your parents had far greater reasons for discord than I was aware."

"No," he said, his voice raised as he pointed his finger at her. "Do not think for a moment that Sybil is at fault. Neither her birth, nor her arrival that fateful day had anything to do with their deaths. My parents argued by the cliffs, and a terrible accident happened that no one could have prevented."

But as his own words echoed down to him from the vaulted ceiling, he went still. *An accident.*

This was the first time in four years that he'd said that. And in this moment, he could hear Jacinda's sweet, earnest whisper. "*. . . you must let go of your guilt and be at peace.*"

He shuddered out an exhale and drew in a breath, deep enough to pull his waistcoat taut over his chest.

"I could not," Hortense said, her voice frayed with emotion. "Seeing Sybil, knowing what she has suffered, one cannot help but feel fondness for her. I only wish I'd been as understanding to you. I think, perhaps, sometime during these four years I confused my grief and loneliness for anger and bitterness."

He held her gaze, seeing once more, the aunt who'd first

kindled his love for this land and the history of Rydstrom Hall, by sharing stories with him about her father, and her father's father. The bond they shared was flawed and disorderly, but they were family nonetheless. "I hold no spite toward you."

She sniffed, blinking away the moisture collecting in her eyes as she turned. This glimpse of her softer demeanor surprised him. But then, with her back to him, he saw her spine turn rigid, her shoulders straighten in a small shake as if she needed to slough off this brief episode of tenderness and don a cloak of pragmatism that was more comfortable.

Crispin could not help but smile wryly.

"Regardless, I should like to make amends," she said, moving toward her desk. "I have decided that Sybil should have lessons in decorum. After all, she is the daughter of a duke and carries fine, noble blood in her veins. Therefore, she must have all the advantages to ensure a bright future. In so doing, I have decided to provide a dowry of five—no, *ten*—thousand pounds, with the added stipulation that, should she not marry before she reaches her majority, the money would be hers to do with as she pleases."

Stunned, Crispin felt his jaw drop, amusement melting from his expression like a molded jelly left too near the hearth. He could only stare at her for a full minute.

Had he heard her correctly? Sybil would have her own fortune? If that were the case, then it was possible that she could decide her own fate, marry a respectable man, and live a life that was far greater than that of so many other illegitimate young women.

He felt his first shred of hope since the instant Jacinda had left Rydstrom Hall.

"Aunt Hortense, that is very generous. Thank you." He crossed the room and embraced her, kissing her cheek. "You have no idea what a relief it is to know that she has a future to which she can look forward with gladness."

She patted his shoulder awkwardly. "Yes, well, we needn't

make a fuss. Young women do not often have the same advantages as men." Taking a step apart from him, she smoothed her hands over her gray frock. "This is something I've thought about since my last conversation with Miss Bourne. She mentioned that her uncle's agency strives to provide their clients the freedom to choose whom they wish to marry. *Freedom to choose . . .* Those are three compelling words and they have lingered with me."

And he went still all over again. The mere mention of Jacinda caused a profound ache to roll through him like rip currents threatening to drag him under.

"She has a forthright manner, that one."

He nodded succinctly. "She does indeed."

"At first, I thought she was rather impertinent and interfering. I even assumed she was trying to rise above her station by purposely placing herself in your path." She held up a hand to stay his comment and eyed him shrewdly. "Yet a young woman with that goal in mind would hardly have spurned a duke's offer of marriage."

Crispin shifted, but did not answer, refusing to reveal anything that might damage Jacinda's reputation.

"It shows a surprising amount of good sense—putting another's interests ahead of one's own. An admirable quality, to be sure," she said, turning back to her desk and sitting down on the slender fiddleback chair.

"She has a great number of admirable qualities."

"Well, of course you say that because you're in love with her. And that is the true reason why none of the women on the list appeals to you." She picked up the stack of letters and shook them at him. "Does Miss Bourne share your regard?"

Crispin, you are my entire world. I'll always find my way to you.

Yes, she does, he wanted to say with absolute certainty, but he could not. The tender words she had spoken while in his arms were different than those she'd said in his study after her memory returned. She had not professed her love, but continuously pushed him away by citing all the reasons they could not be together. And it made him question if she'd felt profound regret and nothing more. "We did not exchange such sentiments."

"Piffle." Aunt Hortense scoffed and shook those letters at him. "You know very well that she loves you. Why else would she willingly sacrifice her own happiness in order to give you everything for which you asked?"

As much as he wanted to believe it, the Jacinda Bourne he knew did not shy away from taking what she wanted. And he loved that about her.

"It is possible, now that Sybil's future is in hand," his aunt continued without waiting for his answer, "that a man who has four thousand pounds per annum might be able to accomplish great things with such a fortune, and without the need of an heiress. If he were so inclined."

Crispin shook himself away from his thoughts. "I do not have four thousand pounds per annum. The rents alone barely keep Rydstrom Hall upright. As per our bargain, upon my marriage—to a woman of whom you approve—I shall receive a gift of four thousand pounds."

"Indeed. However, you are neglecting to factor in the monies from your other properties which will, in fact, bring you four thousand pounds per annum."

"No. There are no other properties, and you made it quite clear that it was only—"

"You dare correct me? I have had all I can take of your sullen behavior and impudence." Aunt Hortense straightened, her words sharply edged like a chisel through stone. "I am speaking of your two additional properties to the north. These were part of your inheritance from your mother, but were mistakenly entrusted to me when my brother required the sale of such in order to settle a few of his own accounts. Therefore, I should know very well how much they earn per annum. If you misunderstood our original bargain, then let that be on your own head." She flicked her wrist in a dismissive gesture. "Regardless, I have no use for them since I intend to live here year-round."

Astonished by this turn of events, Crispin quickly calculated that four thousand pounds per annum would not only afford the repairs on Rydstrom Hall, but keep it well into the future.

"However, when it concerns my wedding gift to you, I am still quite firm in my stipulations," she said, penning a letter at the same time as if this conversation were a mere triviality instead of a life-altering occurrence. "You must marry a young woman with admirable qualities. No. Strike that, for I am making an amendment just now. I hereby state that your chosen bride must also have a fondness for my niece, have earned the respect of your servants, and make you . . . inordinately happy."

Chapter 34

> ". . . she had always wished and promoted the match; but it was a black morning's work for her."
>
> JANE AUSTEN, *Emma*

"This just arrived, dear," Uncle Ernest said to Jacinda as he walked into the room and laid a missive on her desk.

"Thank you, uncle. It's awfully early for the post."

It was still too early for her sisters to be at their desks. Lately, she'd taken to using their client's applications as a means of dealing with her heartbreak and insomnia.

Looking up from the stack, she noticed that Uncle Ernest didn't quite look awake either. His handsome face possessed that soft, sleepy grin he usually only wore after he'd stayed awake all night writing poetry to the latest in his long list of true loves. More than anyone she knew, he loved the idea of love. It never broke him.

Then, looking at the red seal, she recognized it instantly.

All the blood drained out of her and surely puddled on the floor beneath the chair.

"Hand delivered from St. James's Square, I believe," he said with that same smile and then whistled a cheerful melody as he walked out of the room and left her to stare at Crispin's letter.

Was he back in London, then? And had he returned because she had found him the perfect match at last?

Her hand trembled violently as she touched the seal beneath her fingertips. Did she truly wish to open this letter?

The answer was simple. No, she didn't. She would sooner cast the thing into the fire. By accident, of course. Yet at the moment, she didn't have the strength to rise from the chair.

"Come now, Jacinda, where is your determination?" she whispered to herself. It would be better to finish this once and for all so that she needn't think about him any longer.

And in twenty years, or so, she might actually forget him.

Bother. Drawing in a deep breath for courage, and ignoring the terrible buzzing in her ears, she broke the seal.

Inside was the letter she'd sent to him, extolling all of Miss Throckmeyer's perfection. In addition, there was a short note penned by him, that read:

Dearest Miss Jacinda Bourne,

Thank you, no.

Yours,

Crispin Montague

"What?" She read the missive again, turning it over to see if she'd missed something on the back. Once she realized that "Thank you, no" was all the response she'd received, her temper started to flare.

Gradually, the blood on the floor seeped back into her veins in a fury. "'Thank you, no'? That's it? After all I've been through!"

She rose from the chair prepared to storm into Rydstrom's town house and demand an answer.

"And what have you been through, Miss Bourne?"

Jacinda's gaze jerked to the door. There, standing beneath the arch of white glazed molding, the shoulders of a green coat nearly touching either side, was Crispin, hat in hand.

All the bluster fueling her suddenly turned her bones to jelly and she wobbled a bit, needing to hold on to the desk for support.

"How could you have rejected Miss Throckmeyer?" Jacinda huffed, ignoring his question. "She was perfect."

He stepped into the room, his expression impassive. "Did you meet her?"

"I did, and—"

"And she was about as bright as a low-wicked candle." He stopped at the other side of her desk, which seemed suddenly to have shrunk to half its size.

If she wanted to, she could reach out and touch him. And, of course, she wanted to, that's why she curled her hand into a fist instead. "You never put intelligence on your list."

"I mean to amend that presently," he said with a glance down to her orderly desk, and he frowned. "That is why I am here. Do you still have my application? It looks as though you've recently thrown every scrap of paper in the bin."

"I have *organized* my desk. Why is everyone making such a fuss about it?" she muttered.

She didn't need to search for his application in the stack, because it had taken up a permanent residence on the top. Placing it before her, she focused on the list, not wanting to look directly at him. Seeing him and standing so close—close enough to touch him, she needlessly reminded herself—made her too short of breath, and that itchy hives sensation was starting to cover her skin. But when he didn't begin speaking, she gestured with an impatient whisking motion to hurry him along. "Very well, what are your amendments?"

"If you are in a rush, I can return at a more convenient time."

She expelled a breath that caused an auburn lock to droop over her forehead, but she hastily swept it back in place. "I have no other business to attend at the moment. We do not open our doors for business"—she glanced at the clock—"for an hour and a quarter yet."

"Ah. Then it is simply that you are uncomfortable in my presence," he said, his voice gruff. "I feel the same."

She swallowed. Likely this wasn't easy for either of them. After all, little more than two weeks ago, they were lying completely naked in each other's arms. It seemed rather foolish for her to be so tense and cross with him, considering their intimate history, no matter how brief.

She could adopt a professional demeanor and put her hurt feelings aside for a few minutes, couldn't she?

Of course, she thought. All she had to do was stand up straight and look him directly in the . . . eye. *Oh dear.* She stared longingly into those early-autumn eyes, her poised quill forgotten. "And your amendments?"

He seemed to lean closer without moving at all, almost as if he meant to kiss her. Which made it all the more difficult to concentrate.

"I want my wife to live in Rydstrom Hall with me. So it is not necessary that she have property."

Jacinda gave herself a shake. Surely, she hadn't heard him correctly, she'd been too busy staring at his mouth and remembering how talented it was. "What do you mean? I thought you wanted separate residences."

He slid his hat to the corner of her desk, disturbing the stack of applications she'd been working on before he came in, turning them at odd angles. "I have changed my mind on that. It was enjoyable to have someone to dine with, to see at random moments in the hall, to exchange meaningful conversation. You helped me discover that."

"I'm so glad I have been of service," she groused under her breath. "Is there anything else?"

"I would prefer someone with a sharp wit. Someone who speaks several languages." He pointed to the list with an expectant nod, as if asking her to jot that down. "After all, I would want only the best qualities passed down to my future heirs."

The tip of her quill slid off the page. "You're going to have children with her as well?"

Of course he would. It only made sense that he would have children with the woman who lived beneath the same roof. Yet, hearing him say the words filled her with such agonizing jealousy that it would surely consume her from the inside out.

"I've come to believe that when a man finds the right

match, the idea of spending his life with her consumes his every thought." He looked down at her desk again, his hands searching through the pages. Making a mess of things, really. Then, apparently not finding what he was looking for, he withdrew a letter from inside his coat, unfolded the page, and laid it over his application, heedless of the wet ink below it. "If it helps, I do have a name in mind. It is on the list you sent. There. At the bottom of the page."

Jacinda tried hard not to shake as she put the quill back in the stand. Her heart was cracking open, thudding in painfully draining gushes and leaving her cold. She did not think she could survive past this moment.

He'd chosen a bride. She'd thought it would feel better once it was over, that some measure of relief would take over, but this was worse than anything she could imagine.

Her breath came in tight, raw gulps as she held back her sobs. "Miss Bassett?"

"No. The name below hers."

With the page shaking in her grasp, she turned and tapped her fingertip against the name. "Hers *is* at the bottom."

Crispin covered her hand, eclipsing her flesh in a hot sting that was so pleasurable that it was agonizing. He slid her index finger—the one that still bore his golden thread—down the paper. "This one here, signed *With Warmest Regards, Miss Jacinda Bourne*."

She couldn't catch her breath or slow her heart. He was determined to destroy her, wasn't he? Why else would he say such a thing when she was so weak and empty without him?

"I should never have let you leave," he admitted, his low tone tight with restraint. "I should have locked us both in the tower and tossed the key out the window."

Had anyone ever made imprisonment sound so appealing? Likely not. She found herself listing toward him, tempted to ignore the reason he'd come to the agency in the first place. But she couldn't.

"We've been over this, Crispin—I mean, *Rydstrom*. You require an heiress. Your home needs repairs, and there's Sybil's future to consider, and"—here, she realized that she was starting to ramble, but was unable to stop herself—"your aunt despises everything about me, and—"

In the midst of her torrent, he stepped around the desk, and set his finger over her lips. He smiled tenderly. "Actually, my aunt is rather fond of you. But as for Rydstrom Hall, I told you before that it didn't matter to me. I wanted to marry you no matter what. And I was determined to send back every name you sent until I wore you down."

She closed her eyes on a sweet, sharp twinge in her heart. Those words were so beautiful, and yet they would torment her forever. "But it matters to me. I would not have our marriage be burdened with financial strain that would cause any discord between us."

"Darling, since you and I will always find something to disagree about, that isn't a valid argument." He reached up to brush a lock of her hair—not to sweep it away from her forehead, but to draw it down, over her brow. "There. That is better. Everything in its place."

"Why are you making this so difficult?" Her breath stuttered into her lungs as she tried to hold back her tears.

"But it's simple. All you have to do is tell me that you'll marry me. Or in the very least, tell me that you love me."

"Of course I love you, but that doesn't—"

He kissed her, hard, then soft and searching, then hard again, pulling her against him. And he was relentless, too, refusing to let her think for a moment about how foolish it was to cling to him and return his kiss, revealing all the love she'd had bottled inside. Because then, he only dragged more out of her, wanting every last drop she could offer. And she would have given it all to him, just to be rid of it for good, but she knew there would always be more, like an endless spring that just wouldn't let up.

She would love him completely until there was nothing left of her.

He broke away, breath hot against her lips, his hands on her face. "If a man came to the Bourne Matrimonial Agency looking to find a wife, but then fell irrevocably in love with the tenacious, sharp-witted woman taking down his application—and she with him—would she consent to be his wife?"

"Yes," Jacinda said without hesitation. And oh, how she wished . . .

He smiled and kissed her again, holding her closer. "Then that settles it. We are going to be married. Do you want the ceremony in Whitcrest or here, in London?"

"But what about—"

"Rydstrom Hall is no longer a concern."

"But you have to think of—"

He shook his head. "Aunt Hortense has settled a fine dowry on Sybil, the money to be hers upon her majority. I would share with you all the details, but I would prefer your unequivocal answer first. Will you marry me?"

"You are a relentless plague on my senses and my poor heart," she ranted, helpless. He was impossible to resist. Rising up on her toes, she brushed her lips across his, giving herself over to whatever fate held in store for her. "I want to live inside your quadrants for the rest of my life. After all this, did you think I could let you leave this room without going with you?"

Before he could kiss her again, the sound of clapping greeted them from the doorway. Standing there, crowded together were Uncle Ernest, a rumple-browed Ainsley, a dreamy-eyed Briar, and a wet-cheeked Mrs. Darden.

"That was so romantic," Briar said. "But I didn't understand the bit about the quadrants."

Jacinda laughed and slipped out of Crispin's embrace, walking over to the door. "It would take too long to explain."

Uncle Ernest grinned and patted her cheek. "It feels as if your mother is here with us right now. I'm proud of you for listening to your heart."

Mrs. Darden broke in with a happy, watery sob. "Would you like me to bake some scones for you and your betrothed? The lemon-aniseed ones that were always your favorites?"

"That would be lovely," Jacinda said before she closed the door. After all, she had a duke to kiss.

But Ainsley wasn't finished yet. From the other side of the door, she issued a dramatic sigh. "Jacinda, the agency has only one rule—*never fall in love with the client.*"

"Well, if it makes you feel any better," she said with a grin as she slipped her arms around Crispin's neck and fit her body blissfully against his, "he isn't a client any longer. The Duke of Rydstrom is officially off the list."

Epilogue

"He had made his fortune, bought his house, and obtained his wife; and was beginning a new period of existence, with every probability of greater happiness than in any yet passed through."

JANE AUSTEN, *Emma*

Whitcrest
Five years later

Crispin let his head fall back against the top of the sofa, completely spent as Jacinda sagged against him, her panting breaths rushing over his neck. "I enjoy this way of settling our disputes."

"I agree. Especially . . . since I was the victor," she purred, her fingertips coasting aimlessly over the swath of bare skin exposed beneath his open shirtfront and parted waistcoat.

"I beg to differ, darling. You cried out first—*and second and third*—if I recall." He grinned when she gave the hair on his chest a playful, scolding tug, the warmth of her blushing cheek nestled into the curve of his shoulder. Aside from the absence of his cravat, they were both fully dressed, though their clothes were in a sublime state of disorder.

"Yes, but I was on top. Everyone knows that the person on top wins the dispute."

"Is that so?" Beneath her skirts, he gripped the decadent fullness of her hips and rolled her against him, earning a breathy gasp and a responding clench around his flesh. *Sweet heaven*, but he loved this woman to distraction. "We can continue our . . . discussion in a few more minutes. However, I will tell you once and for all that we are not naming our son Knightley."

She sat up, bearing her weight more fully onto him, her face flushed, lips swollen from his kiss, and an impish glimmer in her bright blue gaze. "I'm not afraid of a challenge, you know."

"Indeed. You are even more tenacious than when we first met." And she used every advantage over him, much to his constant delight. Even now, she taunted him with the lush swells of her breasts spilling over the edge of her bodice, their heavy ripeness and taut, velvety buds making his mouth water and his blood quicken in a thick, fervent rush.

Apparently, he wouldn't need a few minutes after all.

"Mummy, why are you on Daddy's lap?"

Jacinda went still as a statue—well, a pink statue, considering the color of her cheeks and ears—and peered past his shoulder, toward the door of the study. "Emma, dearest, what are you doing out of bed?"

Suppressing a laugh, Crispin worked in stealth. Under the cover of Jacinda's skirts, he lifted her away, blotted the residual fluids with his handkerchief and set all matters down below to rights, while Jacinda arranged her sleeves and bodice.

"I couldn't sleep without hearing one of Auntie Sybil's stories," their four-year-old answered, her voice growing closer as she padded into the room on tiny bare feet. "Daddy's stories are too loud. I like whisper stories."

Sybil had begun to speak shortly after Emma's birth, deciding that communicating with pictures was something that a child would do.

"Daddy's stories are too loud, hmm?" Jacinda's brows arched in teasing reproach as she pressed a quick kiss to his lips before she stood and smoothed her skirts. "We'll have to work on his softer voice until we follow Auntie Sybil and Great-Aunt Hortense to London. The Season is about to begin and we have many happy matches to make."

"I want to make a match for E.E.," Emma proclaimed with a sleepy yawn.

"Dearest, I asked you not to call your brother E.E. Every time you do it sounds as if you've spotted a spider," Jacinda said earning a giggle as she gathered Emma into her arms. "Besides, at two years old, Edward Ernest is a bit young to be married."

The bow of Emma's bottom lip pulled into a frown and she looked close to tears. "Then I don't know how else we'll manage."

Worried, Crispin reached out and brushed his hand over her wispy auburn hair. "What do you mean, sweetkin?"

"Well, the nursery is lopsided. There are four beds, but only two of us."

Jacinda slid him a look, biting her bottom lip to keep from grinning. "It seems that someone takes after her father."

Crispin felt a resplendent fullness inside his chest as he fought his own grin and then drew their daughter's petite frame into his arms. "But if you marry off your brother, that will only be three places taken in the nursery, not four."

"Not when I marry Henry Valentine."

"Ah. I see," he said with mock gravity. "Well, that leaves us with something of a problem, then. What will we do with the new baby your mother will have in autumn?"

Emma's hazel eyes sparkled with drowsy delight, her cheek resting against his shoulder. "Oh, that's much better. I didn't think I could find anyone to marry E.E. anyway. He's always sneaking out of the nursery and getting into mischief."

This time, it was Crispin's turn to lift his brows at Jacinda, who smiled back at him sheepishly. "It seems that someone takes after his mother."

And he wouldn't have it any other way.

Next month, don't miss these exciting new love stories only from Avon Books

Cajun Persuasion by Sandra Hill

Alaskan pilot Aaron LeDeux came to Louisiana with his brother to discover his Cajun roots. But any hopes he had of returning home are extinguished when he agrees to help a crew of street monks and nuns rescue sex-trafficked girls. Plus, he's in love with a gorgeous almost-nun named Fleur . . .

Moonlight Seduction by Jennifer L. Armentrout

Nicolette Besson never thought she'd return to the de Vincents' bayou compound. It's where her parents work, where she grew up . . . and where she got her heart broken by Gabriel de Vincent himself. Avoiding Gabe should be easy, but escaping memories of him, much less his smoking-hot presence, is harder than expected—especially since Gabe seems determined to be in Nikki's space as much as possible.

Dark Challenge by Christine Feehan

Julian Savage was golden. Powerful. But tormented. For the brooding hunter walked alone. Always alone, far from his Carpathian kind, alien to even his twin. Like his name, his existence was savage. Until he met the woman he was sworn to protect. When Julian heard Desari sing, emotions bombarded his hardened heart. And a dark hunger to possess her overwhelmed him . . . blinding him to the danger stalking him.